ALSO BY PAUL J. BARTUSIAK

SOURCE*FORGED ARMOR

COOL
JAZZ
SPY

COOL
JAZZ
SPY

A NOVEL

FRËGE.....001

ØRSTED

PAUL J. BARTUSIAK

This is a work of fiction. All characters, companies, organizations, agencies, and situations in this novel are either fictitious and the product of the author's imagination or, if real, used fictitiously without any intent to describe actual conduct or situations. Any resemblance to real persons, living or dead, is purely coincidental.

Quote from *Mushashi* used with permission from Kodansha USA, Inc.

for my family

thanks for letting me close the door for a while.

CONTENTS

PART ONE

PART TWO

PART THREE

Executive Order 12333 (Dec. 4, 1981, as amended)

1.1 *Goals.* The United States intelligence effort shall provide the President and the National Security Council with the necessary information on which to base decisions concerning the conduct and development of foreign, defense and economic policy, and the protection of United States national interests from foreign security threats. All departments and agencies shall cooperate fully to fulfill this goal.

...

(c) Special emphasis should be given to detecting and countering espionage and other threats and activities directed by foreign intelligence services against the United States Government, or United States corporations, establishments, or persons.

(d) To the greatest extent possible consistent with applicable United States law and this Order, and with full consideration of the rights of United States persons, all agencies and departments should seek to ensure full and free exchange of information in order to derive maximum benefit from the United States intelligence effort.

1.5 *Director of Central Intelligence.* In order to discharge the duties and responsibilities prescribed by law, the Director of Central Intelligence shall be responsible directly to the President and the NSC and shall:

...

(d) Ensure implementation of special activities;

(46 FR 59941, 3 CFR, 1981 Comp., p. 200)

SELECT CONSTITUENTS
OF THE
INTELLIGENCE COMMUNITY

Director of National Intelligence, Head of the Intelligence Community
JAMES F. FREEDMAN

Defense Secretary
CHARLES BRADLEY

Director of the CIA
SAM NELES

Deputy Director of the CIA
ERNEST MCCOY

Deputy Director of the National Clandestine Services, CIA
ADAM WRIGHT

Division Head of Counter Intelligence Center, CIA
FRED BANKS

Director of the NSA, Commander of U.S. Cyber Command
GENERAL WILLIAM POWERS

Deputy Chief of U.S. Cyber Command, NSA
LIEUTENANT GENERAL HAROLD MANMOTH

Director of the Department of Homeland Security
MIKE HOLDMAN

Director of the FBI
ADLAI CORVER

001000110

000110011

PART ONE

110110001

101011100

011010111

001101011

1

A Reach Forward into the Past

Friday, June 5

IT WAS STRANGE THAT THE BARBERSHOP WAS OPEN SO LATE on a Friday night, but Arthur Spence just took it as another one of those odd idiosyncrasies of life in a small town. He didn't even believe it when the waitress at the local diner told him it'd be open. It was around 8 P.M. and he still had time to kill. He was in McAdoo, Texas, right off Highway 82. An unexpected stop. He'd be spending the night there so a service station could repair his car the next day. Broken fan belt, the attendant told him; should have a new one delivered tomorrow morning. McAdoo was the last place he had in mind for an overnight. Spence kicked himself for not having the car checked out before the trip.

He was in his mid-seventies and in pretty good shape for his age. He was also tired, anxious to get to Dallas to see his daughter and granddaughter. The whole time he was driving he couldn't stop thinking about them; it had been a long time since he last saw them. He couldn't get over the fact that his granddaughter— "Little Chelsie" as he used to call her—was getting married. Life flew by.

As he stepped out of the restaurant, he considered calling his daughter to let her know what had happened and where he was. Not yet, he decided, opting instead to wait until he got back to the motel. There was still enough time to get to Dallas and make it to the rehearsal dinner; he had to keep telling himself that or he'd go crazy. After close to three hours on the road, he was nearly halfway there. He couldn't miss that rehearsal dinner tomorrow evening.

A walk would make him feel better. He went in the direction where the waitress said the barbershop was located, curious to see the place.

There were hardly any people out that evening; it was quiet. He supposed that most of the residents stayed home on weeknights—sitting out on porches, watching television, whatever people did in small towns. As he walked along the sidewalk and passed the storefronts, it seemed like he had gone back in time; all of the buildings looked so old. The town had a quaint feel to it. It reminded him of Mayberry: Sheriff Andy Taylor would be right around the corner.

Everything was closed. All the lights were off and it was dark outside, save for the streetlamps and some signage on a few of the storefronts. The sound of crickets permeated the air, or were those cicadas? He couldn't tell the difference.

It was certainly an inconvenience, this layover because of his car breaking down. He should've just flown to Dallas, his first inclination, but he thought it would've been a fun road trip. No, he'd still have time to get there, he again reassured himself; as long as that auto mechanic was good at his job, it shouldn't be a problem. Spence knew, however, that it wasn't every day a mechanic had to replace the fan belt on an Audi A6. It wasn't a straightforward job. Spence started to get apprehensive the more he thought about it. He decided that when he got back to the motel he'd call a car rental agency—the closest one to town—and have a car delivered just in case. To hell with cost.

As he continued to walk he eventually came upon the

barbershop.

"Hello...you still open?" he said as he peaked through the screen door and gave a short rap on the door's wooden frame.

A man inside was slumped in one of the barber chairs, his back to the door. As if Spence's inquiry woke the man from a slumber, he slowly lifted his head, looked over his shoulder, and with a passive expression on his face, rose from the chair.

"Come in," he said as he turned the chair around and extended his hand toward it.

Spence paused for a moment, still peering through the screen door. Something he detected in the man's voice caught his attention; it struck him as peculiar for some reason. Only two words, yet they didn't sound right. Might as well go in, he finally said to himself; better than being alone and watching television at the motel.

As Spence sat down he said, "I'm glad you're open. I'm sort of stuck here tonight until my car gets fixed, and when I was told your shop was still open, I figured, why not get spruced up? I'm on my way to Dallas. My granddaughter's getting married."

"Hmph," was all the man said in response. He sported a traditional barber's shirt, un-tucked, with clippers protruding from his shirt pocket. He was tall, in his mid-thirties, and had slightly unkempt, dirty-blond hair, which itself could have used a trimming. Spence subconsciously noted the disheveled appearance but ignored it.

The man draped a black apron around Spence, snapped it in place around his neck, and carefully tucked a portion of it under his shirt collar; Spence could feel the skin of the man's fingers rub against his neck.

Then, for the briefest moment, the man's hands, both of them, went around Spence's neck; pressure was gently applied, as if estimating a size and firmness. The hands remained a bit longer than would have seemed normal. It unnerved Spence, especially because of how quiet it was in the shop and how little the man said.

The man turned the chair so that Spence faced the mirror.

Spence could see the man's reflection, and it was the first opportunity he had to study the man's visage. It was a tired one; not tired from a long day's work, a different kind of tired. Maybe tired wasn't it: distant, detached, weary.

Their eyes met in the mirror. The man said nothing and remained expressionless, not even a slight smile. Spence began to feel uncomfortable, sorry he had ever entered the place. He should've just gone to the motel.

Before he knew it, scissors were clipping his hair. It jarred him from his thoughts. He suddenly raised his hand from under the apron and said, "Hey, um, just a trim, okay? Not too much; the same style and a trim."

The man said nothing and kept clipping.

Eventually, Spence relaxed. Getting a haircut always relaxed him. He looked at himself in the mirror as the scissors moved and made a snipping sound. How old he seemed. His face had become fleshy, the crevices on his forehead seemed deeper than ever. His thin hair was snowy white. Bags were under his eyes; he wondered if they were there because of how tired he was or whether they were always there. He didn't want to look at himself anymore, so he closed his eyes. Exhausted. Comfortable.

Sleep.

It was some time later when he was stirred awake. Spence opened his eyes, and as he looked up, he didn't see the man's reflection in the mirror anymore.

He turned in his chair to look around, and an uncomfortable feeling came over him. The only sound that could be heard was that of a low buzzing noise from the fluorescent lights. They emitted a dull glow which, combined with the buzzing sound, gave the place an eerie feeling, dreamlike.

On one side of the room Spence saw the customary items of a barbershop: empty chairs, magazines, stacks of old newspapers, a lot of pennants hanging on the wall. He turned to look in the other direction. The first thing he saw startled him: it was the man sitting by himself on a short stool in an empty corner of the room. He looked at Spence with that same blank expression on his face, a look devoid of any emotion. The wall behind him was unadorned and painted a pale green, adding to the weird, almost creepy feeling he now got from the place.

Spence became nervous, hesitant to speak. How long had the man been sitting there? What in the world was he doing? Spence's eyes moved sideways and followed the bare, pale green wall, as if his head were being nudged to look in a different direction. There was a door, presumably a closet door, and when he looked down, there was a pool of blood at the bottom of it.

Alarmed, he turned back to look at the man. The two stared at each other. Who was this man, some maniac? A serial killer? Thoughts raced through Spence's mind.

Then the man mumbled something; it was almost imperceptible. Spence could barely hear it and got that same feeling as before, like there was something familiar about the way the words were spoken, the sound of them. All of a sudden it dawned on him: the man had a slight accent.

He looked deeper into the man's eyes. Time passed with neither of them moving or saying anything. A slight smile appeared on the man's face, and then, there was an understanding.

A chill ran up Spence's spine. He involuntarily shuddered. How could the man have known Spence would be there? How did he even find him? Then a feeling of disappointment came over him. He had been careless, sloppy after so many years of retirement. He had let his guard down.

He knew that physically he wasn't even close to the man he once was; there was no question of that. The other man, who initially appeared disheveled and weak, now appeared strong and aggressive. How could he have not noticed that before? He had the physical advantage over Spence by far.

The man slowly rose from the stool and stood there. Spence was frozen with fear. Maybe he should scream or grab something to throw at him. What could he use? He looked at the utensils on the counter next to him, but nothing struck him as useful. It seemed futile.

An image of his granddaughter flashed in his mind, then a vision of her walking down the church aisle. He knew at that moment that he was never going to see her again.

"How'd you make the connection?" he suddenly said to the man. Talking was good, he thought to himself. Keep talking. Start a conversation. His voice quivered, but he continued, "Who told you about me?"

The man didn't answer. As if prompted by the questions, he cautiously approached Spence; he was respectful of his prey, ready to take action.

"Was it someone out of Germany? The German contingency?" No answer. "I...you have to tell me. After all these years, I need to know. Please, just let me have that."

The man continued his slow approach. He was almost to Spence.

At that moment, a burst of courage rose up in Arthur Spence. Maybe it was the talking that did it. He was too proud to sit back without a fight.

But the other man was too strong and too quick. Too young. He slammed his fist into the side of Spence's face.

"Wait, please!" Spence pleaded.

A blow to the stomach. Spence buckled in the chair. The man took the opportunity to go over to the door and close it. Then he turned off the lights.

"What do you want? I don't understand," Spence feebly said in the darkness, struggling to regain his breath.

Unbearable pain was inflicted. Arthur Spence held out for as long as he could. His body was old and couldn't take much more punishment. Then the questions came.

When the man was done and had what he needed, he took the scissors out of his shirt pocket and jammed them into the side of Spence's neck. Blood spurted everywhere. Afterwards, there was a contorting of Spence's dead body; bones were snapped—twice.

He carefully made his way in the dark over to one of the sinks and washed the blood off of himself. Then he quickly changed his clothes and put the soiled ones in a bag he carried with him. After that he stepped outside and closed the store. No one was around.

He needed to get the GPS beacon off Spence's car. It was a simple task for him to break into the service station without setting off the rudimentary alarm. Spence's Audi was sitting in one of the repair docks, the hood still open. The man walked over to the car, lay on his back to edge underneath it, and grabbed the beacon magnetically attached to the underside. The corresponding compact receiver was already in his possession.

When he went back outside, he looked around for a car; the one he used to follow Spence was probably reported stolen by then. The thought occurred to him that any of the vehicles parked on the station's lot likely needed a repair; he couldn't take a chance with any of them, so he went back through the town looking for something else. He went down a side street and eventually came to a small apartment complex; several cars were in the parking lot. He spotted a non-descript Buick LeSabre that looked to be about fifteen years old; easy to hot-wire, he thought to himself. The door was unlocked. What luck. He got in and reached under the dash for the ignition wiring. It started right away, and the gauge indicated almost a full tank of gas.

Then he left, with no intention of ever returning. He still had about four hours to drive in the dead of night in order to get to Dallas for his flight the next morning. He'd dump the bag of bloodied clothes somewhere along the way.

The stolen car was parked in long term parking at Dallas/Fort Worth International Airport. He slept in it for about three hours before the alarm on his wristwatch told him it was time to get up. It was 5 A.M., not much sleep.

A professionally forged identification allowed him to easily pass through security. Soon he was at the departure gate for his flight. He sat in one of the gray leather seats and looked out of the large windows as planes taxied along the tarmac. The departure monitor indicated that his flight was still on time.

He did his best to look like any ordinary traveler, full well knowing he wasn't. A Starbucks kiosk was open, so he purchased a cup of coffee and a newspaper and went back to his seat, sipping the coffee while using it as an opportunity to look around. He put the coffee down and raised the newspaper in front of him, pretending to read it while continuing to survey the area.

The airport became very busy—terminal A was filled with business travelers anxious to get home for the weekend. CNN aired on a flat screen television hanging overhead. He checked his watch and saw it was 7 A.M. With his trained eye, he spotted a couple of plain-clothed security men milling about in the area.

Then something happened. At first it was subtle. Out of the corner of his eye, he noticed a flickering. When he looked up, he saw that almost in unison all of the airport monitors flickered. When he looked directly above him he noticed that the CNN broadcast was flickering as well. For the briefest moment he thought he saw an unusual, whitish blur appear across the newswoman's face on the telecast. A casual observer wouldn't have noticed it, especially among all of the other flickering monitors, but he did. He was sure he saw it, trained as he was to notice the smallest anomalies, even amid general turmoil.

A stir grew among the people in the terminal. Many rose from their seats, unsure of what was happening.

Suddenly a loud buzzing noise sounded throughout the area over the PA system—a four-second blast that jarred everyone and unsettled them. Then an even bigger malfunction occurred: the information on DEPARTURE/ARRIVAL monitors began to de-pixelize; it looked as if the words and numbers were melting away from the screens. It all seemed to dissolve into a slow, floating mass of pixels.

The man didn't know what was happening, and although he was concerned, he tried to remain calm. He continued to look around and studied everything, searching for some clue as to the cause of the problem. He noticed that not only were the DEPARTURE/ARRIVAL monitors malfunctioning, but the large LCDs behind all of the gate counters were as well. They were displaying gibberish. People began approaching the gate counters and asking airline personnel what was happening. He moved closer to one himself to listen to what was said. The airline employees had no answers. They were just as puzzled, franticly typing away at their computer terminals.

He forced his way through the people and leaned over the counter to look at one of the computer screens under the countertop.

"Sir, please step back," a woman said without looking up or stopping her pecking at the keyboard. He could tell that her computer wasn't functioning.

Seeing that she'd be of no help, he stepped away and tried to think about what he should do. He saw the woman behind the counter pick up a phone and wave off another employee that was trying to say something to her. He went back to the counter.

"Hello? Hello? Is anyone there?" the woman said. No one answered. She shook her head with an exasperated look and hung up the phone.

The man stepped away again and stood by a column along the main aisle. By that time, no one was sitting. What's more, no one's cell phone seemed to be working. They couldn't connect to the network. He noticed a couple of policemen who had moved into the area. They looked just as perplexed as everyone else, but they were clearly on guard. A crowd formed around them, so the man went closer.

"What's going on?" a nearby woman asked one of the officers.

"We're not sure, ma'am. Please remain calm. Everyone needs to step back and give us some room." The policemen put their hands over their guns to prevent anyone from grabbing them.

The ceiling lights suddenly turned off, causing the overall level of noise from everyone to increase significantly; there were even a few shrieks. Questions were shouted at no one in particular.

Soon more security appeared.

Airline personnel at gate counters continued to try and get help by telephone, to no avail. Everyone was helpless. Pandemonium ensued. Some began to leave the area, then more joined. There was an exodus toward the terminal exit.

The man wasn't sure what to do. He couldn't stay there by himself. He had to follow the crowd.

Just then a security officer with a bullhorn stood on a chair and addressed the crowd:

> LADIES AND GENTLEMEN, WE ARE EXPERIENCING A TECHNICAL MALFUNCTION IN OUR SYSTEMS. AIR TRAFFIC CONTROL HAS TEMPORARILY GROUNDED ALL FLIGHTS. FOR YOUR OWN SAFETY, EVERYONE WILL NEED TO STAY WHERE THEY ARE—NO ONE IS ALLOWED TO ENTER OR EXIT THE TERMINAL. THE ENTIRE AIRPORT IS BEING LOCKED DOWN.

There were yells of alarm, hands raised to ask questions.

> PLEASE REMAIN CALM. THESE ARE ONLY PRECAUTIONARY MEASURES — THERE IS NO INDICATION OF ANY DANGER.

No indication of any danger, the man repeated to himself. He was glad that no attention was being directed at himself—he was sensitive in that regard—yet there was a lot of security in the area. Not a positive development. If they found his stolen car in the parking lot...all the way from McAdoo... He had no idea what was going on, yet he knew one thing was certain: he needed to get out of that airport, out of Texas, and as far away from that barbershop as possible. He needed to get on a flight. Yet he was helpless. He kept telling himself not to panic and to remain calm.

The situation stayed like this for about an hour when all of a sudden there was a loud "THWOOM" sound heard throughout the terminal, like there was a sudden burst of activity from a giant power generator. Computer monitors throughout the area became active; systems seemed to be resetting themselves. DEPARTURE/ARRIVAL monitors had alphanumeric information vertically scroll across them like they were going through some kind of a reboot sequence. After about ten minutes, the displays seemed to be functioning again; they weren't displaying the correct information, but ordered fields were forming, like they were getting ready to be populated with data. After another twenty minutes, flight data began to appear, although there were only dashes in the "STATUS" column next to each flight.

The man wondered whether it was airport personnel that had rectified the systems or whether something else had happened. It didn't seem like the workers were responsible; they were all talking on phones from behind the counters, feverishly trying to get information—the phone system was clearly working again—but everyone still looked bewildered.

A PA announcement went out that all of the flights scheduled to depart that morning were cancelled. At that point it was all he could do to remain in control of his emotions.

Hours passed without any additional information. Everyone was in the same predicament, scrambling to find a flight out of there. At about 4 P.M. he was finally told that the first flight they could get him on was at 6:05 A.M. the next day, a newly added flight to help with the backup from canceled flights. He eagerly accepted, thinking it a miracle they even got him on a flight given how many were delayed or canceled.

He had a lot of time to kill between now and then. He was reluctant to leave the airport because he didn't want to go through security again. At around 6 P.M. planes finally started to move on the tarmac. A good sign, he thought. The first one took off a half-hour later.

He decided to sleep at the airport overnight. They gave him a blanket and a pillow, assuring him he would be on the flight the next morning. It had been a long day, and now it was going to be a long night. His dirty-blond hair looked messier than ever.

After all the precise planning and execution, he couldn't get caught at that damn airport, he thought to himself. Computer glitch due to a power surge: that was the official explanation—it seemed like it was a lot more than that. He lay on the floor next to a large window. After a while he turned on his side to look out of it and watched the jets take off into the night.

2

Fresh Snow

Jay, Vermont
Saturday, June 6

SHE HAD PROVEN HERSELF AN EXCELLENT SKIER. That had become readily apparent over the past week. Now John Angstrom could hardly keep up with her; she wasn't holding anything back. They were on Jay Peak, and at her insistence they were "glade" skiing for the first time. They'd been out so long that the sun was setting; part of the trail, if it could be called that, was in the shade. Evergreen trees were everywhere; branches from fir trees whizzed by as they raced down the slope. He marveled at her speed. They passed fallen trees, stray logs, and only partially visible tree wells along the way; any of the obstacles could've easily taken him out if they weren't spotted in time. Although markings from ski patrol gave him some comfort that hazards were identified, he was certain that not all of them were; they were skiing on a remote trail. What's more, she was skiing with confidence, and it was clear that she was keen to take chances.

The experience was both exquisite and exhilarating: indescribable natural beauty, the quiet solitude of the forest, clean, fresh air, and just the two of them skiing on the pristine snow. The added danger of glade skiing heightened the adrenaline rush. What was most significant, though, was that Angstrom was with *her*: Anna Czolski. So much was learned of her during the debriefings, yet he was just beginning to learn what *he* cared about: her thoughts, what she felt, and what *moved* her. Even though Angstrom had been in near-constant association with her for the past seven months, he was still in awe of her beauty and the mysterious aura that surrounded her. This woman, a defector from Russia, had suddenly come into his life and turned it upside down. She was beautiful. Her hair was a deep black now, returned to its natural color as opposed to the harsh, bleached blond when he first saw her. It only enhanced her beauty in his eyes. Her physique was perfect. Athletic. Yet it was her face, and her eyes, that initially captured his attention and still enchanted him. There was a coldness to her countenance, an impersonal nature that seemed to indicate she was unobtainable. Yet she wasn't; she was with him. His personal life had been over in so many ways before he met her—divorce, his two girls grown up, away at college and independent, his career spiraling downward—but now, here he was, with Anna; and she wanted to be with him just as much as he with her.

The last several months had flown by; she hadn't even assumed a new name yet. That was a discussion they promised to have later that evening.

Anna's speed had created some distance between them. He could hardly hear the sound of her skis against the snow anymore; it was mostly his own—that and his breathing. At forty-seven, he was eight years older than her, and though he was in excellent shape, it was all he could do to keep up with her on the slope.

It became lighter; they had reached a clearing. That was it, he realized, they had made it out! He was so glad; that was one of the most challenging runs he'd ever been on, and they finished just in time. Soon the orange sky would turn dark…too dark to be skiing downhill through a forest. While it was thrilling to have made it through—there was a tremendous sense of accomplishment—he was also greatly relieved. He wondered if she felt the same way.

She was about fifty yards in front of him with another fifty yards to go before she reached the bottom. He saw a small berm of around two feet high and fifteen feet wide at the bottom of the run. The trail that kept on giving, he thought.

He watched as Anna skied toward it, took it, flew through the air for around twenty feet, and skidded sideways to come to a stop. Then she watched to see if he would do the same. There was no choice, he thought; he'd made it that far, might as well go all the way. He was going faster than he expected by the time he hit the berm and was launched higher and further than he anticipated, but he maintained control.

She'd pushed him to his limits.

Her goggles were already up and her face was a glowing smile as he neared.

"That was awesome," Angstrom said as he reached her. He was catching his breath as he removed his goggles. "That had to be one of the most incredible experiences of my life!"

"Yes, for me as well." Steam came from her mouth and nostrils, her cheeks a bright red.

He loved her Russian accent; it was heavy, yet the soft tone of her voice balanced it and made it sensuous, captivating. He could listen to her voice all day.

"John, you're an excellent skier…I'm so grateful that you took me to this wonderful place."

She looked across the country at the impressive Green Mountains and took in the beauty. The mountains were everywhere, surrounding the two of them and reaching up to the sky. The last remnants of an orange sky lit up each of the mountain peaks, with big crags of rock showing through the blankets of snow, a green forest spread over the mountainsides. She could hardly believe it was real.

It was hard for her to comprehend that she was there; there with a man she had met only a relatively short time ago; a man with whom she could tell she was already falling in love. Being at the mountain range with him was like a dream, far removed from the difficult life she had led in Russia. The painful memories. It was a life deserving of no woman, her least of all. There wasn't an evil bone in her body, yet she had been forced into service, forced to train to become a specialized FSB[1] agent, one that would specialize in *killing*. The FSB, or more specifically, a half-crazed, rogue agent in it, forced her into service as a means of leverage against her father: a brilliant military scientist who refused to continue in the development of military technology. Not only did her father refuse to continue engaging in such research, he even went so far as to speak out against the government, leading rallies and giving speeches that any sane man knew would only lead to trouble. Now he was dead, killed while he and Anna tried to defect to the United States. Fortunately she never had to act in her new role as an FSB assassin. She got out of the country before that could happen. When Angstrom first learned of her background during the CIA interviews, he couldn't believe it.

John Angstrom watched her as she admired the countryside; he could tell what she was thinking. He was sad and happy for her at the same time: sad that her father was dead, sad that she had to leave her country just to be free, but happy that she was with him...after all that had happened. It was bittersweet and made Angstrom care for her even more.

"Anna, let's go back to the lodge and get cleaned up. We'll order room service tonight. I hope that's okay. I don't feel like going out or being around other people."

His speaking had interrupted her thoughts.

"Yes, I agree. I like that. You read my mind."

They looked at the expanse one last time to burn a lasting image of it into their memories. Then, after briefly glancing at each other in acknowledgement, they bent down to remove their

---

[1] The FSB is the state security organization in Russia, the successor to the KGB.

skis. When they were done, they exchanged a warm smile and began their journey back to the lodge. It would be a long hike to get there, and Angstrom was already feeling the pain in his legs from the skiing.

From outward appearances the lodge was of a rustic, log cabin architecture. Inside, however, their two-bedroom unit was sleek with many modern accoutrements.

While Anna took a shower, Angstrom ordered dinner from room service and opened a 2012 bottle of Acrobat, a Pinot Gris out of Oregon that was one of his recent favorites—he was thrilled upon learning it was available.

He had an extensive music collection stored on his iPhone, and he connected it to the Harman Kardon sound system in the room. As he scrolled through his phone's display, he searched through different artists and albums for music and created a play list.

Anna's parents had fostered in her an appreciation for classical music, but now she had become fond of the jazz music that Angstrom had introduced to her. She especially liked the relaxed tempos and classical undertones of the style that was Angstrom's favorite, the style known as "Cool Jazz." For some reason she couldn't quite articulate, it resonated with her. Maybe it was because of a sensed connection with Angstrom; the mood it evoked reminded her of him: there was a subtle power to it, one that seemed to grow the more she listened to it. There was also a sort of complexity, one that otherwise belied the simple, straightforward manner on the surface. In Angstrom it was a complexity she didn't yet understand, but she was trying, and it fascinated her.

Angstrom finished entering his music selection and went over to the fireplace to start a fire as the first song began to play. There was plenty of wood in the pile, and he spotted a few pieces of aged cherry. The aroma was heavenly after the first piece took to flame. He stood in front of the fire warming himself, staring into the lively flames, lost in his thoughts.

Anna eventually emerged from her bedroom wearing flannel

pajamas. She approached him unnoticed as he stood in front of the fire. She stood next to him and gently rubbed his shoulder.

"Hi," he said softly.

Anna smiled, and they each turned to admire the fire. Angstrom put his arm around her waist; she put her head on his shoulder. Their relationship had been platonic; neither of them acknowledged it expressly, but each wanted it to be so. They viewed their relationship much more than a sexual attraction or infatuation, and neither wanted to rush what was happening. They hadn't even kissed yet. This purposefully slow progression of their relationship heightened their attraction to each other, even their awareness; nothing one did, no matter how small, went unnoticed by the other. Every little movement of her lips, every inflection in her voice, he noticed it all, and for her it was the same.

"This music is beautiful," she said. "Who is it?"

"It's by Oliver Nelson; something called *Stolen Moments*."

A trumpet played the melody, a saxophone answered, and then the trumpet began a powerful solo.

"It reminds me of being in a big city," she said. "Maybe a nightclub, dark, cool."

"That's it, exactly. That's what I get." He paused, then with hesitation asked: "Should we talk about it now?" He was anxious about her new name...and her new future.

"No, not yet, John. Let me sit by the fire for a while...while you go shower. Do you mind?"

A flute interceded. It soared in its sweet pitch and carried flowing notes as drums lightly carried the rhythm.

"Not at all. Please, enjoy." He motioned toward a chair off to the side, but Anna declined, electing instead to sit on the carpet in front of the fire. Angstrom brought over a glass of wine and a small plate of cheese for her, along with a throw pillow, and then he left the room.

Their plan was that she would live with him in the small home he purchased in Georgetown. The CIA had suggested otherwise: an "integration" program with a new identity, a home somewhere in a small, remote town, anonymous, never to be heard from again. Angstrom wouldn't hear of it and threatened to quit if they insisted. He fought vigorously for her cause—as if he was struggling for his own life.

Surprisingly the CIA eventually conceded, allowing Angstrom to live with her. He didn't really understand why the approval was given. Why would the CIA agree to a union so incongruent with rules and policies?

Needless to say, a lot of careful deliberation occurred at very senior levels. In the end, one of the reasons was the thought that perhaps something might come of it, something that could be learned. And while that may have been true, there was an even bigger reason: Angstrom himself. He was a prized asset in the organization: a field operative who performed the most dangerous missions under the deepest cover, one who was without equal in what he did. He was that rare individual around whom entire teams could be built, whole departments. So many times, on so many missions, he was the one that turned the tide and pulled the proverbial rabbit out of the hat. There was no doubt as to the advantageous positions he obtained for the CIA in many critical situations over the years. For that reason as well, perhaps above everything else, they tolerated his "union" with Anna Czolski.

Later, while they were at the table eating dinner, Angstrom raised his glass in a toast: "Anna, to a wonderful day!"

"Yes, wonderful. More special than any other in my life."

Their eyes met, silently adding more to the toast beyond the words that were spoken.

"So, Miss Anna Czolski, what would you like to be called from now on?"

"John, you can't wait for me to settle on my new identity, can you? It's hard, you know, for one to pick a new name for oneself. I'll bet you have something in mind, don't you? Come on, what is it?"

"I don't know...maybe...maybe a *Mary*. Mary Weathers?"

Anna let out a laugh. "Where did that come from?"

They each took a bite of their food and pondered the subject, still smiling to themselves.

"I want to keep my first name, John. I don't want to lose that. Anna Czolski can't be completely obliterated from existence, as if she was never...."

"That's just it. She has to be. It's for your own safety."

Anna knew he was right; she'd been thinking about it for months.

"My first name will be Anne. That's as far away from Anna as I'll go."

She watched Angstrom as he considered the notion.

Though it seemed too close to "Anna" he didn't immediately rule it out. He didn't want to discourage her.

"Okay...Anne what? You've clearly thought this through, so what do you have in mind for your *last* name?"

They both stopped eating as Angstrom eagerly awaited what she'd say next.

"Well, at first I thought *Coltrane*. Anne Coltrane, in honor of John Coltrane, the first jazz music I ever listened to with you. You remember that?"

"Of course I do. How could I forget? I'll never forget."

"Mm. But then I thought, 'too obvious'... maybe even too different, or distinctive...somewhat ridiculous."

"Yes...okay...maybe so. Go on. I'm listening."

"So, my new name: Anne Davis."

He let out a laugh. "*Davis*? Really? Well, there's certainly a concern about being too distinctive, but *Davis*? That's going way over in the opposite direction. Did you know that Davis is a very common last name in the United States?"

"Yes, I know."

There was a pause, and then Angstrom continued, "Let me guess: Anne Davis, in honor of Miles Davis."

"Of course."

They looked at each other, cherishing the moment.

By this time much progression had been made through Angstrom's play list. It was just then that a new song began to play: Chic Corea's *Windows*. It was music bliss. They toasted to the new name and clanked their glasses. For some time afterward they ate in silence, listening to the music and enjoying each other's presence. It was a momentous occasion: a new life was beginning...for *Anne*.

When they were almost finished eating, Angstrom's phone rang. He saw via caller ID who it was and took the call in another room. She wished he didn't have to take the call out of her presence but understood why he did.

When he returned he said, "Well, that's it. We have to go back. That was my office. Something's come up."

There was disappointment evident in his voice.

Silence for a moment—dismay in both of them; their time away was coming to an end.

"At least we had the week," said Angstrom.

"...and I have my new name."

"Yes. Yes indeed. Here's to...*Davis*," Angstrom said, wine glass once again raised.

"No, it's *Anne* to you."

"Huh? First name basis? Sure, sure...we'll see."

Angstrom tried to remain composed and lighthearted, but Davis could tell that there was a change in his mood. The call must have been about something serious, she thought. Or maybe he was as disappointed as she was that their time in Vermont was coming to an end sooner than they had expected.

He was a CIA agent called back into service. It was a part of him, a big part of him, she would never be able to know about. Something he could never share with her. She was being reminded of that fact by the mysterious phone call and the resultant change in his mood.

"What about our flight? Do we need to call the airport to change it?" she said.

"It's already been taken care of. We're on the 9 A.M. flight tomorrow morning."

"Oh, that's too bad. I was really looking forward to another

Sunday brunch at the lodge. I can't get over how wonderful that spread was."

There was obvious disappointment in her voice. She wasn't eating and looked right at him. She knew it couldn't be helped, but it was a disappointment just the same.

"I know. I'm sorry. What can I say? Hey, look, at least they didn't put us on the 6 A.M. flight. And we'll have all day tomorrow to spend together when we get back home."

"You mean you don't have to be in the office until Monday?"

"That's right," he said, a rejuvenated smile on his face.

"Hmm, I really wish they could've given us a later flight then." She wished she hadn't said that, noticing the slight change in Angstrom's smile. "Well, let's do something fun when we get back. Something outside. I just can't get enough of the fresh air," she said. There was warmth in her voice, levity.

Angstrom appreciated it.

3

Intangible Assault

National Security Agency Headquarters
Fort George G. Meade, Maryland
Monday, June 8

ANGSTROM DROVE STRAIGHT TO THE NSA EARLY MONDAY MORNING. The meeting was set for 7 A.M. and he didn't want to be late; it wasn't often he was called to NSA Headquarters.

As his car approached the large campus, he leaned forward over the steering wheel to look upward at the OPS-2A Building, one of the two main buildings on the campus. It always impressed him, even fascinated him. It was completely covered with one-way glass, preventing inside light from escaping it. The windows were also fabricated with an embedded, copper-mesh film that prevented electronic signal leakage or penetration. The building was like a black hole in the shape of a giant cube, electrically impervious.

When he checked in at the front lobby of OPS-2A, he was directed to the VENOMA auditorium. Angstrom took the elevator to the seventh floor, and as soon as he stepped out, he came into a hallway that was packed with men. The auditorium must have been right off the elevator, he figured, and for some reason everyone was standing outside.

He quickly estimated at least thirty people, with more arriving by the minute. He was glad he wore a jacket and tie because he could tell there were a lot of senior people present, both from the NSA and the CIA, as well as other agencies. Many he didn't recognize. Not the type of meeting he was used to.

He worked his way through the crowd toward a less dense area, and when he found a spot, he saw the Division Head from CIA Counter Intelligence, Fred Banks, who happened to be the person who called him in Vermont. He was Angstrom's new supervisor. His old one, Garrett, who himself used to report to Banks, recently retired. Garrett's position was split in half; Angstrom was promoted into one of the slots, and a man named Tom Franklin the other. By the time Garrett had retired, the group had greatly diminished in number; some claimed it lost its effectiveness. Garrett used to complain that he couldn't find the right people anymore. The speculation, however, was that he was just burned out. Fred Banks intended to rebuild the group around John Angstrom. He would be the new foundation. That was Garrett's last recommendation before he left.

"John. Welcome back," Banks said as Angstrom approached.

"Fred, good to see you."

They shook hands.

"Yeah, well, sorry I had to cut things short. You still had a few days left, didn't you?"

"I did. Just a few, but it's okay...not a problem."

"Right."

Banks looked at Angstrom for a moment, like he was delving into his mind. Angstrom couldn't help but notice. They had barely spoken to each other over the years; Garrett kept it that way, forming an artificial barrier between Banks and the agents under him. Banks and Angstrom had still only spoken briefly since Angstrom's recent promotion. Banks mainly knew about him from what Garrett used to tell him in reports. Now he would get to know him first hand.

They stood in silence for a while, waiting for the doors of VENOMA to open. Banks was in his late sixties, hair completely white, and stood at five-feet, ten inches. Angstrom, at six-feet, four inches looked like a giant next to him.

"We'll catch up later," Banks suddenly said while looking at the other people.

"Of course. What's going on here, though? Do you know?"

"Information Assurance called it. It's big. Look." He nodded toward someone standing several feet away; it was the Director of the CIA, Sam Neles. He was talking with NSA Director General William Powers. "It's not too often you'll be at a meeting where those two are present." CIA Deputy Director Ernest McCoy was also standing in the group, as well as Deputy Director of the CIA's National Clandestine Services, Adam Wright.

Angstrom acknowledged to Banks that he saw them.

Banks leaned over and whispered, "It's been a long time since a meeting like this. Last time was right after nine-eleven. Not a good sign."

Angstrom's brain started working. There wasn't any catastrophe like nine-eleven that just happened—at least none he knew of. He had been out of pocket while in Vermont and wasn't completely up to date on the latest news. He wanted to say something but wasn't sure how much he should talk. He didn't have a good read on Banks yet and didn't know how much the man liked to say. He was just about to lean over and say something when a loud voice was heard from among the group.

"Can someone please unlock the door? What're we standing around for?" It was CIA Deputy Director Ernest McCoy.

As if on cue, the auditorium doors opened and everyone went inside. It took about ten minutes for everyone to get situated. All of the senior representatives of the Intelligence Community sat in the first two rows. Angstrom sat next to Banks, four rows back. The auditorium seated about fifty people, and the place was filled.

A man from the front row went onto the stage and stood at the podium.

"Good morning. Thank you for attending, especially on such short notice. I know you are all very busy. Many of you don't know me. I'm from the Cyber Threat Intelligence Integration Center, and for security purposes, you may refer to me as Q-Directorate during this meeting. For the record, senior leadership is here from most branches of the Intelligence Community, including Sam Neles, Ernest McCoy, and Adam Wright from the CIA, General William Powers and Lieutenant General Harold Manmoth from the NSA, Mike Holdman from DHS, and Adlai Corver from the FBI. James Freedman, Director of National Intelligence, has authorized the following disclosure under Executive Order 12333.

"Now, we're here this morning because of a significant cyber attack that occurred this last Saturday, June 6th, starting at around 7 A.M. The biggest part of it, or rather, the one that was most visible to the general public, occurred at Dallas/Fort Worth International Airport."

Angstrom hadn't watched any television over the weekend— he hadn't watched any all week—nor had he read any newspapers, so this was news to him.

"Publicly, the DFW incident was blamed on an extraordinary power surge. The press, as well as lay experts in the field, are already challenging this notion. Point of fact, the situation at DFW was the result of a highly sophisticated intangible assault involving multiple, simultaneous components."

The speaker paused for a moment to gauge any reaction from the audience. Then he signaled to someone in the back to start the presentation. An overhead system began to project onto a large screen at the back of the stage. Q-Directorate remained at the podium.

"We've been preparing for such an attack for some time now.

In fact, prior to the DFW attack, DHS, in cooperation with the FAA and USCYBERCOM, was already working with major airports around the country to assess cyber attack vulnerability. These assessments were performed with a statistical combination of different attack scenarios, along with the most up-to-date, sophisticated probability analysis available—state of the art.

"DFW was one of the airports participating in the assessment, including several of the airlines serviced by it. Needless to say, this was highly confidential."

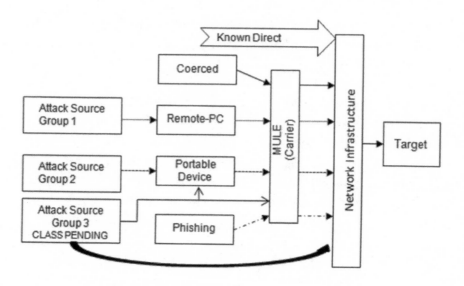

Note: Cyber attack risk analysis model. Individuals responsible for manually delivering or installing computer malware are normatively referred to as "mules."

"As you can see from the figure I'm now showing, Big Machine modeled a multitude of both "direct" and "indirect" attack scenarios. This partial block diagram depicts a subset of the analysis for a single target within the IT network, using a modified simulation technique developed out of City University London. Attacks were organized into 'Source Groups.' You'll note that three of them are shown. The first two comprise just about everything we know in terms of the most lethal types of

28

attack vectors. I'll discuss Source Group 3 in a moment.

"The arrows represent the different paths a particular attack may take to get to an intended target. Some take a direct route, going from a Source Group directly to the target network. This set of attacks is generally denoted by the large arrow at the top labeled 'Known Direct.' It's not shown, but they can originate at any of the Source Groups. Other attacks take an indirect route through various means, usually relying upon what are referred to as 'mule' carriers. A mule can be thought of as some manual action that transfers malware to the intended target. In some cases, the mule is fully aware of the transfer—let's say, euphemistically, as a type of corporate espionage—and in other cases, the mule is unaware. As depicted in the figure, a mule is not required in every case in order to infect infrastructure with malware. In addition, be aware of the fact that while the Known Direct path may only be represented by a single arrow at the top, it nonetheless represents a significant number of attack threads.

"Now, Source Group 1 involves network computer attack scenarios, such as remote code execution, sinister email, phishing, rogue websites, and instant messaging Trojans. By way of example, a peer-to-peer software-sharing website, considered one of the most lethal contamination sources in Source Group 1, was modeled utilizing the BitTorrent protocol with a worm propagation chosen to provide the required input data for a botnet growth simulation. Source Group 2 involves personalized target penetration, such as via sub-prime number generation for private key replication."

"Wait a minute," a man interrupted. Heads turned to look at the speaker, Lieutenant General Manmoth, Deputy Chief of U.S. Cyber Command. "You should explain to everyone why you're presenting the results of a risk assessment of DFW Airport after-the-fact. This is all very interesting, Q-Directorate, but you've got to provide some context."

"Good point, sir. Sorry. You're right," Q-Directorate responded.

Manmoth knew everything that Q-Directorate was about to

present, and therefore he could follow everything that was being said. But that wasn't the case for everyone else. It was complex material, and they were hearing it all for the first time, at least at such a detailed level.

"By way of further background," Q-Directorate continued, "we're trying to figure out just what happened at DFW on June 6th — the exact nature of the attack. Because of how extensive and complex it was, this is easier said than done. You see, many attacks of different kinds occurred simultaneously, all in unison and on many different levels. We've been able to attribute certain effects with certain types of attacks, but all aspects of an attack this sophisticated can't be immediately detected and characterized. Therefore, if we go back to what we've modeled before, we can start to peel away the onion, so to speak. In essence, we can look at the data through a broader lens and at the same time with increased precision. This is important because each attack thread not immediately accounted for represents vital evidence that could ultimately lead to the perpetrators."

Q-Directorate stopped and looked down into the audience. Manmoth nodded in confirmation, but before the speaker could continue, there was a question from the audience.

"Your figure is showing an additional, unidentified source group. You mentioned it before...Source Group 3." It was FBI Director Adlai Corver.

"Yes, that's right. The additional source representation was not part of the original simulation; it represents unknown aspects of the DFW attack. As I've said, we detected some of the effects from it, but not its actual nature. Therefore, it's a 'yet-to-be identified' derivative in the model; we believe it has the components of both a direct attack as well as indirect via mules. Big Machine is still parsing, for example, the massive number of IP packet headers to distinguish between normal and deviant. To be clear, however, the additional source group didn't form a part of the *a priori* risk assessment. Sorry if that caused any confusion."

Corver raised an eyebrow, a look of exasperation evident on his face.

Q-Directorate realized that he was already losing key members of the audience; he was getting into the weeds too soon and too deep. He noticed CIA Director Sam Neles lean over and say something to General Powers of the NSA.

"Perhaps I should skip the risk analysis and proceed to our current analysis of the attack," suggested Q-Directorate.

No one objected, so he moved to the next part of the presentation.

"Right. Big Machine is running various algorithms for cyber attack detection and classification. The principal algorithm involves remote-to-local and user-to-root classification; for this analysis we're utilizing a Fisher Linear Discriminant (FLD) Analysis. This approach was previously validated via correlation under the features of a modified 1999 KDD Cup Set. The attack can be described as follows.

"At approximately 7 A.M. on Saturday, June 6th a series of Denial of Service (DoS) attacks began at DFW: fake reservation and flight change requests flooded the computing resources of all the airlines serviced at the airport. This was in fact a 'Distributed' Denial of Service attack, or DDoS, resulting in an almost immediate over-consumption of network bandwidth, as well as the memory and processing power of computer systems. The DDoS was multi-faceted: simultaneous ping flood, SYN flood, and modernized teardrop transmission of corrupted IP fragments with overlapping, over-sized payloads.

"This next figure, a Time-Integrity plot, shows the progression of a particular DDoS attack on a travel reservation system of one of the airlines. Interviews with airline personnel revealed that the first noticeable symptom was a general slowdown in computer performance—files took longer to open, response times were degraded. The FLD Analysis showed that an inordinate amount of live-chat sessions were requested in a very short time frame, and the 'Help Request' service was bombarded with email requests."

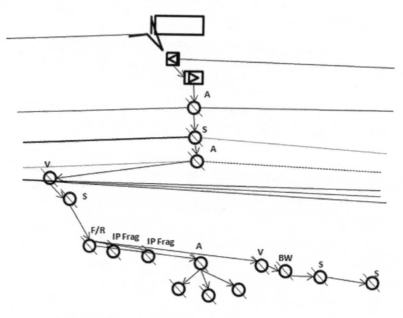

Time-Integrity plot showing progression of a particular DDoS.

A=attack action
V=vulnerability exploit
S=Ping/Syn flood
F/R=Fail, retry, repeat
BW=Router/switch bandwidth contraction

An unidentified speaker from the audience asked a question: "Why wasn't auto-ping response disabled? That would have solved that problem right away."

"Good question. It *should* have been disabled," responded Q-Directorate. "I think it was a careless oversight. In the grand scheme of things, however, it wouldn't have mattered. The DDoS was just too powerful and multi-faceted. For example, the number of user ID entry/failure/retry sequences greatly exceeded safe thresholds, and further login attempts were disabled. Blackholing was also invoked. But ultimately this had little effect against such a massive assault: bandwidth was filled with excessive, uncontrollable instances of outbound traffic. The outbound IP packets were returned as undeliverable, or were redirected with rogue responses—IT scans have shown that routing information was corrupted and TCP sessions were randomly reset. It was just too much.

"At the peak of this DDoS attack, previously undetected malware was then invoked. What you're now seeing is a replay of an actual sensor recording, one of the few we have: the computer screen of an arrival/departure monitor appears to melt away into a mass of random pixels. Many other strange things happened on computer systems. It's remarkable that reservation system computers hadn't crashed from the DDoS, but it was some time shortly thereafter when they did.

"And then, about an hour after the attack commenced and the crashes occurred, the computer systems, along with network equipment, somehow performed a system restore without any human intervention. We believe this started with the power being cycled throughout the building—there were reports of a loud sound just before things began rebooting.

"Fortunately, some of these attack signatures were manually captured, and Big Machine compared them to our stored profiles. This was in part how we identified the characteristics represented by Source Group 3, although the signatures don't correlate well. Quite frankly, it almost seems like we were *allowed* to capture some of this trace data."

The speaker turned to look behind him and stared at the screen for a moment, letting the implications of that last statement take its full significance.

"That seems rather absurd," said FBI Director Adlai Corver. He was always the most vocal person in the room, but no one resented him for it. Far from it. His questions and criticisms sparked some of the best debates and sometimes even led to breakthroughs. His "input" was almost always appreciated.

"I know. It's a preposterous notion," responded Q-Directorate. "But look, we're just sharing information at this point. In a matter of only one day..." He caught himself mid-sentence and looked down at Manmoth, who shook his head "no" like he was trying to say, "Ignore the comment, keep going." Q-Directorate complied.

"Of course, the DDoS was just the opening salvo. Not only were external-facing systems affected, but airport infrastructure itself was compromised...lighting, HVAC.

"I know I'm moving fast here, but as far as potential mules are concerned, we've been working with each of the airlines, as well as DFW airport administration, to obtain records of all employees. Big Machine is processing the data to assess bribery risk, psychological trauma profiles, geopolitical tendencies, et cetera to identify high-probability mule candidates. Needless to say, the process is slow. Not because of Big Machine, but because of the electronic personnel records we've gotten. In some cases we don't have everything we need; the airlines and DFW administration aren't giving us everything, citing privacy concerns. However, we've already developed some theories on mule source points-of-entry, and just as with the DDoS attack, it's quite extensive; we foresee a whole host of malware instantiations, with high probability vectors at the logic level, the control plane level..."

The speaker stopped mid-sentence, both because he knew he was giving the audience a lot of detail at a very fast pace, and also because he was somewhat exasperated himself at the enormity of what he was disclosing.

Taking advantage of the pause, Mike Holdman, newly appointed Director of the Department of Homeland Security, asked, "Was the airport infrastructure disassociated with external networks?"

"No, not completely, and that's part of the problem. There are a number of high-probability tunneling paths. We're working with DFW to correct this."

Holdman's question, along with the speaker's answer, gave rise to a momentary pause in the room. It gave Angstrom a chance to catch up. He was stunned by the severity of the attack. It wasn't like the feeling he had when he first saw footage of the nine-eleven attack on the World Trade Center, but it was unnerving to say the least. It gave him a queer feeling, the notion of a cyber attack of such scale and sophistication directed at an entire airport terminal.

Q-Directorate continued for another forty minutes on the attacks against the airport network infrastructure. "Total time elapsed from T_0 until completion and system restoration was only one hour, twenty minutes."

Angstrom thought the presentation was ending, but Q-Directorate had more.

"Next we'll discuss tangential attacks that occurred in parallel with the one at DFW. As has been publicly reported, there was a cell-phone outage at the airport. That's what caused some people to question the power surge theory. Cell phones themselves obviously operate with their own power source, so a power surge wouldn't directly affect them. And cell towers are not technically part of the airport infrastructure. Thus the skepticism.

"Telecom operator data shows that only subscribers registered on cells substantially covering airport geography were affected, and all of those cells were sectorized, such that only those sectors providing direct airport coverage were compromised. Some type of malware took control of the network—we're *postulating* that text messaging could have been the entry point. We scanned effected mobile units but found nothing of consequence. The Short Message Service Center within the network has been scanned as well, but so far nothing; it's peculiar, because Big Machine keeps indicating the tendency of origin there."

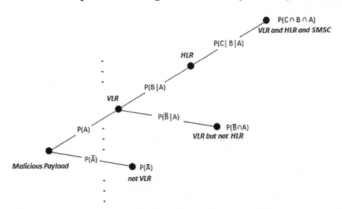

Partial tree illustrating the probability algorithm used by Big Machine to predict highest probability trajectories for malicious payload instantiation through the SMSC.

"This separate attack on the telephone network is very concerning: separate system analysis, separate mules—if in fact there were any involved—separate technology, yet effectuated simultaneously with the airport attacks.

"And if this level of complexity isn't sufficiently alarming, Big Machine has detected an additional, unreported sub-attack with relevance to DFW. What you're seeing on the screen now is a replay of the CNN broadcast that was being transmitted between T_0 and T_0+delta. If you watch closely, you'll notice a white blur that momentarily and ever-so-slightly overlays the telecast."

Q-Directorate instructed computer control to repeat the transmission at 45 frames per second.

"Note how the blurred line across the woman's face becomes more noticeable. Repeat at 20 FPS...freeze."

The television frame paused, the image of the news anchor froze, half-smiling, mouth open. Superimposed over her image was the following in white, computerized font:

угроза: одномерный массив единица- одновременный.

Translation: "threat: vector unity-synchronous."

"In case anyone is wondering, it's Cyrillic—Russian Cyrillic."

There was a stir in the room. Individuals leaned over to speak to one another.

CIA Deputy Director Ernest McCoy spoke out: "A CNN telecast would have been broadcast all over the country. What makes you think it has anything to do with the DFW attacks?"

"There are several thoughts on this, but part of the reason is the contents of the message itself."

"I see. And has meaning been ascertained?"

"No. Not yet. Our current theory is that it's some sort of classification, such as a type of attack...along with, perhaps, a flag—'synchronous'—to indicate it's supposed to be synchronous with something else, perhaps other attacks. But this is conjecture. Big Machine hasn't found a high correlation match yet, but it's working on it. We're sure there is one."

"What about the cable operator?" said DHS Director Mike

Holdman. "Did you contact them to see what they knew?"

"We did," said Q-Directorate. "Believe it or not, they were unaware of the whole thing until we brought it to their attention. At least, that's what they claim."

Another stir in the room.

"Q-Directorate," Adlai Corver said, "with regard to the attacks in general, has Big Machine identified geography...or at least geographic routes for the attack? For any of the attacks?"

"No, not yet. Of course we have this Russian message in the CNN spam, with the obvious implications, but that's it. Server jumping, IP address encapsulation, ISP masking, ISP rerouting, MAC address scrambling...the source cloaking is the most sophisticated we've ever encountered. Big Machine is working on it, but we're nowhere close to determining point of origin."

"Why Russia? I don't get it. And for what?" Corver interjected. He was asking his characteristically provocative questions. "Quite frankly, this sounds more like China. Are we sure the tag, or this spam as you call it, isn't just a trick? A false trail?"

"Of course that's possible; we just don't know...yet."

"And why were systems restored? There was no permanent damage to systems," Corver continued. "What's the point?"

"We're not sure. We think it may have served as a type of warning, maybe a harbinger of more to come. Or else, it could have been a test—a type of dry run."

There was a general rumbling of voices. Speculation resumed. Manmoth half stood and signaled for Q-Directorate to move to the end of the meeting.

"For those of you invited here for the first time," Q-Directorate said, raising his voice to speak over the din that had developed, "it's not by accident. You've been chosen to be part of a new operation." The room got quiet. "Defense Secretary Charles Bradley has authorized Operation Cyberknife. We'll be meeting regularly like this as a group, sometimes on short notice, to provide updates and share late-breaking developments and theories. Teams will be assigned. In addition, there will be a new, remote IAD outpost created as soon as we're closer to determining the geographic location for the source of the attacks. Discussions with potential countries in the Eurasia region have already commenced. End goal of Cyberknife: threat termination. We have no idea when the next strike will occur; our guess is that this is leading up to something big. Needless to say, our best minds are working on this, twenty-four-seven. We'll meet again as soon as we have more concrete information."

Everyone in the room began to rise. Adlai Corver remained seated and said, "Q-Directorate, I have a question."

Those in the room didn't hear him over the noise, so he stood up, turned to the audience for a second, and said even louder, "Hold on a minute, people."

Everyone turned to look at Corver.

"Thank you." He turned back to Q-Directorate and said, "You mentioned at the beginning that the attack on DFW was the *most* visible intangible assault that occurred over the last few days."

All eyes turned to Q-Directorate.

"Yes, that's right."

A pause.

"Were there more simultaneous attacks? More than what you disclosed this morning?"

Before responding, Q-Directorate looked down into the audience at General Manmoth, Deputy Chief of USCYBERCOM.

Corver turned to Manmoth as well.

"Yes, there were more simultaneous attacks," Manmoth said.

"And where were *those*?" Corver said, alarmed.

Another pause.

Manmoth responded, "We have incomplete information at this time. We'll have more information tomorrow." His eyebrows furrowed as he looked sternly at Corver.

Corver was a little miffed by the response. It made him feel like he was being left out of something. But he didn't challenge Manmoth. He knew how far to push things and when to stop.

4

Cool in a Blackness

ANGSTROM, LIKE MANY OTHERS IN THE AUDITORIUM, was amazed at what he had heard. At the same time, he was a bit puzzled as to why so many high-ranking members of the Intelligence Community would have been called to a meeting at such a preliminary stage, before more information was available. As everyone in the auditorium began to leave, he leaned over and said as much to Banks.

Banks stopped where he was, standing in between two rows of seats, and responded, "They have more information than that. They wouldn't have invited all of these people if they didn't. What they don't have is answers."

Banks knew he was going to have to work closely with Angstrom, spend more time with him and mentor him, so he took the time to say more. "That was a difficult presentation Q-Directorate gave. He talked to people at a lot of different levels. He did an excellent job; got the important points across and sensitized everyone to the severity of the situation. It was important for those in the front row to be there." He nodded in their direction. "It demonstrated how important Cyberknife is."

When they made it to the front of the auditorium, Banks joined the group of directors who gathered at the base of the stage. Angstrom stayed back and watched as Banks shook hands with many of them. As they talked, Angstrom noticed that Adam Wright, Deputy Director of National Clandestine Services, who Banks had pointed out to him before, left the group, nodding to Angstrom as he passed by.

Angstrom observed other members of the audience as they filed out of the auditorium. The mood was reserved. When the group discussion was over, Banks rejoined him and they left the auditorium together. Banks put his hand on Angstrom's elbow and said, "Let's talk. We have a conference room reserved down the hall."

Angstrom wasn't sure who the "we" was that Banks referred to, but he followed. When they reached the small conference room, Adam Wright was already there, sitting at the table and studying a paper file.

"John, this is Adam Wright. Adam, John Angstrom."

"John, nice to finally meet you," Wright said as they shook hands. "I've heard a lot about you." He looked intently into Angstrom's eyes. "Garrett always spoke highly of you. Anyone he approves of is good in my book."

"Thank you. It's an honor to meet you."

"I've read your file, John, what little there is of it. The honor's all mine."

They all sat, Banks and Wright on one side of the table, Angstrom the other.

"So, once again, welcome back, John," Banks said.

A vague opening for sure, thought Angstrom. There was an ambiguity in it. Did he mean welcome back to the CIA after returning from his temporary two-year stint at DARPA, or did he mean welcome back from his vacation in Vermont?

Angstrom decided to go with the latter.

"Thanks. I wasn't expecting to be back so soon. I'm guessing I was called because of what Q-Directorate presented."

"Indeed," said Wright. "It's only the beginning. I don't think it's clear to everyone how big this is."

Banks watched Angstrom closely. He was reflecting on the slight hesitation he detected before Angstrom responded to his opening comment. He could tell Angstrom had already begun going through some type of thought process. Banks waited before saying anything, chancing to see if Angstrom might say more, but there was nothing. Not surprising; he knew from what Garrett used to tell him that Angstrom was a man of few words, especially when the motivation behind something was vague, like in the present case.

Angstrom's mind also continued to race, wondering what merited a meeting with the Deputy Director of Clandestine Services. His training instinctively kicked in, quickly assimilating recent threads of information: the DFW briefing, Operation Cyberknife, hasty recall, vacation with female Russian defector, woman part of FSB, CIA agent living with woman. The last three were the outliers.

He'd gone through a lot already because of his continued association with Anne Davis. It caused a lot of headaches within the organization. He had received all kinds of pressure to change his mind, but he resisted, even threatening to quit and walk away from it all. The Vermont trip had been a new point of contention, a reopening of the wounds. He knew the pressure would continue, and the scrutiny. He was in the organization too deep and her background was too suspect for the CIA to just let the issue slide. No doubt pressure was mounting from a number of different factions: Counterintelligence, Counter Proliferation, HUMINT...and now, perhaps, Clandestine Services.

As for the present situation, without anything else being said, Angstrom knew he was in for a questioning. Again. He'd been through it so many times already, including more than once with Banks, and with HUMINT—so much pressure, but never with a Deputy Director present. Banks was going to probe and Wright was going to watch. That was it, Angstrom decided. This was for the benefit of Wright: for him to see for himself what Angstrom was like, and how he responded to Banks' careful prodding.

Banks, as if he could read Angstrom's mind, said, "Where'd you go again?"

"Vermont."

"And you took the woman, Anna Czolski, right?"

Banks was going right for the jugular, thought Angstrom. Direct and quick, no wasting time on circuitous lines of questioning.

And as for Banks, he knew who he was dealing with; Angstrom was an expert in the techniques of interrogation. It wasn't going to be easy to get anything out of him, and if Angstrom was going to work for him, he didn't want to antagonize the man. It was a delicate line to balance.

Angstrom said, "Yes. I took...*the woman*."

Banks caught the intonation immediately. Angstrom didn't like Bank's referring to her as "the woman." She was more than that to Angstrom, and he wouldn't stand for it. He had developed a protective attitude toward her, something Banks had already noticed during previous interviews. So Angstrom threw it right back at him, no holds barred, right in front of the Deputy Director. The tone was set. Banks turned momentarily to Wright, who continued to look directly at Angstrom. He thought for a moment and considered the different approaches he could take. He needed to be careful and pay particular attention to every word Angstrom spoke, every inflexion in his voice.

"Of course we noted previously, John, how unorthodox the situation is: a CIA field operative living with an FSB spy—one that supposedly just *defected* to the United States—and even going on a skiing trip with her."

There was a lot of information packed into that one statement, thought Angstrom. Part of it was self-serving; a way for Banks to get it on record, with Wright present, that Banks objected to Angstrom's situation. Angstrom didn't mind. It was understandable. Everyone had to cover his ass, no matter how high up he was in the organization. The other points in Banks' statement were more subtle, and Angstrom would not let them go ignored.

"Look, as I've said before, she *has* defected. She's not going back and isn't part of the FSB anymore, never really was. As she told you herself, she was forced into that training. Hauled off in the middle of the night, blindfolded, dragged to some bootcamp-for-killers in the middle of nowhere. And another thing, she wasn't an FSB *spy*. She wasn't out creating a network, gathering intelligence, or stealing secrets. They trained her to be an assassin, a killer...a hit woman. That's different. And what's more, she never completed an assignment. She got out before they could give her one. She never completed a single hit."

"So she says."

"Yes, that's right, that's what she says. And there's no information that contradicts that."

Banks looked directly into Angstrom's eyes. His message was unmistakable: he wasn't going to back down just yet.

"We warned, check that, we *discussed* with you, John, how your being with her could seriously affect your future in the organization. You're risking a lot."

There was no question asked, so Angstrom provided no response.

"...especially after you were getting back on track after your...after what happened in Syria."

Both Banks and Wright studied Angstrom, but there was still no reaction. Angstrom remained stoic.

Banks looked sideways again at Wright, looking for any indication as to whether he should continue this line of probing or not. Banks seemed to be saying to Wright: *See, he's not going to give on this.*

Wright, however, provided no acknowledgement, no indication of what to do. He was almost as stoic as Angstrom.

Banks turned back and thought for a moment. This was the most firm he'd seen Angstrom yet. It was like Angstrom was making a point for the benefit of Wright: *I'm done discussing this. Either fire me or move on.*

Realizing that the decision was being left to him as to how far to take the interview, Banks made the call. He reached into his briefcase and pulled out a paper file, opening it on the table. It contained a list of candidates Banks had previously suggested, along with a set of written responses by Angstrom as to why he rejected them. It was fascinating reading for Banks, providing unique insight into the man now sitting across the table from him. After studying it for a moment, he looked up at Angstrom.

"How's the assembly of your new team coming?"

That was it, Angstrom thought, Banks was changing the subject. He must've passed the test. Just the same, be careful, he reminded himself.

"Slow," he responded. "So far I have Gordon—he's the only senior field operative—and then I have two mid-level transferees. One from within, one from without. It's a start."

"I haven't seen the paperwork yet. How do you feel about them? Are they compromises? I mean, I know you're trying to move as fast as you can to replenish what Garrett left behind."

Banks knew Angstrom held great respect for Garrett, as everyone did. But it went without saying that Garrett had gotten old and the CIA had let him stay on for too long.

After some hesitation, Angstrom said, "Garrett was highly selective in picking the members of his team, and I'm going to be the same. So no, the transferees are not compromises. Admittedly I'll need more, but they're a start. The rest will come with time. I've got other candidates I'm considering."

"Yes, well, things are moving fast. There's not a lot of time given what's going on. You heard the briefing. You're going to be part of Cyberknife."

"We need you on that, John," Wright suddenly interjected. "We need your talent and what you bring to the table. What you were able to do on that DARPA project makes that abundantly clear. You're more than just a field operative now; not because of your new title and position, but because of what you demonstrated at DARPA; the way you saw what no one else did. *You're viewed differently now.*"

Angstrom parsed through everything Wright said. It was

significant, to say the least. Not to mention the person delivering the message. He just wasn't sure what was coming next. They were building up to something. Was it going to be an ultimatum about Davis? Were they not going to let him have his own team?

"The window for assembling your team has collapsed," Banks continued. "We can't wait. Therefore, you're going to have to take what you've got and partner with Franklin's group for the rest."

Banks wasn't sure how Angstrom was going to react to that. Nor was Wright, based upon what was told to him beforehand. There was known friction between Angstrom and Franklin.

"John, you were a far superior field operative than Franklin. Everyone knows that. Franklin just happened to be promoted before you were, and as a result, he inherited a large team. Essentially, he has the organizational bulk we need for Cyberknife, but not the intangibles that you bring. Granted, this is going to be a bit cumbersome. There'll be no mistake, however, about one thing: You have the lead. While Franklin will directly manage his team, you'll make all the strategic decisions."

"Understood," Angstrom said. "We'll make it work."

Banks and Wright were a little surprised at how quickly Angstrom accepted the proposal, no questions asked.

"Good," Wright said. "Our estimation is that when we eventually identify the source of this threat, it's going to be significant. The Navy SEALS are going to help us with transport, but we run the show. You'll be in the center of it, John, the center of the blackness."

Banks let out a small cough and closed the file resting in front of him. He was hoping to ask Angstrom about some of his written assessments but decided against it—maybe later. He said, "How soon before you're ready to submit the paperwork on the transfers?"

"I'll submit it today."

"Good. Let's you and I talk about them later. They're going to be dropping right into it. No time for any trial runs, no room for screw-ups. Cyberknife is too important."

"Got it." An impulse came to Angstrom. "There's probably one more thing you should be aware of.

"What's that?" Banks said, slightly nervous about what might be coming.

"I just want to make you aware of the fact that one of the transfers is going to be from Franklin's group."

"Really?" Banks said, leaning back in his chair. "Well that's certainly going to rub salt in the wound, isn't it? Who is it?"

"Reed."

"Mm. Good choice. And Reed's interested in the move?"

"Without question."

"You sure know how to pick 'em, I'll give you that," said Banks. "He's cream of the crop. Well, I did give you free rein in your search, so that's fine. Put in the paperwork. We'll deal with the backlash later."

"Right," Angstrom responded. He looked at them both, waiting. There still seemed to be more. "Well, is there anything I should do between now and the next NSA meeting to prepare for Cyberknife?"

"For now, let's just get your team solidified."

"Of course."

Banks looked at Wright and then back at Angstrom. "Um, listen John," Banks said. "Did you know Arthur Spence?"

Angstrom thought about the question, searching his memory.

"I can't recall the name. Why?"

"He was in the CIA—one of us. Spent most of his time in Germany running a small network. Retired about twenty years ago."

"Hmm. That's just about when I started. Still don't recall the name, though. I don't think we ever crossed paths. Why, what's up?"

"He's dead," Wright said, studying Angstrom carefully.

Angstrom hesitated. "I'm sorry to hear that." He watched Banks and Wright closely, waiting for more, but nothing came. Clearly the conversation was headed somewhere—some new direction—but he couldn't see where. "I'm not sure where this is going. Do you want me to attend a closed funeral? You need some people to fill the seats? Is that what you're asking?"

He knew it wasn't.

"John, he was murdered," said Banks. "He was on his way to his granddaughter's wedding in Dallas, and his car broke down off Highway 82 in McAdoo, Texas."

"Sabotaged," Wright added. "Fan belt was tampered with. Guy who did it got it perfect. Real professional."

Angstrom said nothing, waiting for more.

"He was followed," Banks continued. "A stolen car was found in McAdoo; it was left in the parking lot of some podunk restaurant."

Angstrom listened carefully; he wasn't getting a good feeling as to where this was heading.

"Arthur was found in the town's barbershop the next morning, body sprawled in a chair, puncture wound to the neck. The proprietor of the barbershop was also murdered—stuffed into a closet before Spence got there."

"That's awful," said Angstrom.

"Some of his limbs were broken, too."

"A struggle?"

"No...not really. Arthur was too old. Forensics indicated he had two bones broken. Snapped, really, supposedly after death."

Angstrom alternatively looked at Banks and Wright.

"His right forearm was snapped backwards off of its elbow socket, and his left foot was broken at the ankle. Again, all done after he was dead."

There was a long period of silence in the room while Angstrom comprehended the ramifications of what was just revealed.

"The infliction..." Angstrom said, "the bone fractures at those two joints...they mirror the two places where Gordon shot the FSB agent in St. Petersburg."

Banks and Wright knew this already. They were letting Angstrom get to the same point.

Angstrom continued, "When Gordon was in Russia to help with Anna's...er...I mean with Davis' defection, he had to incapacitate a Russian agent, and rather than kill him, he shot him twice: once in the elbow, and once in the opposite ankle."

Banks and Wright said nothing.

"Do you think it was retribution? Retribution for Gordon's shooting the Russian agent...and on their own soil?" Angstrom asked.

"John, I need to say this again," Banks said. "She may be in danger. *You* may be in danger by being with her. The CIA has strong objection to your remaining with her. She needs to be put into an official protection program."

Angstrom remained firm. His mind was racing, but he remained steady. "What's that going to do? My being close to her will allow me to keep an eye on her. In any event, you said it yourself: The CIA still isn't convinced she's disavowed her status as a Russian agent. This way I'll be able to watch her, to verify that she really has."

Banks knew that Angstrom was settled on the issue, so he let it be.

But an impulse came to Angstrom. Another idea he'd been mulling around in his head came to the forefront because of what he'd just heard.

"One last thing," Angstrom said. "There's one other person I want to bring in...even given the time crunch." It was a spur of the moment move, but he figured he should grab the opportunity while it was there.

"Another?" Banks said, curiously. "Who? There's not a lot of time, John."

"I know. I know. This guy is key, though. I want him in my group."

"Okay, so who is he?"

"Magdos. Gino Magdos"

Banks leaned back in his chair. "*Really*? You've got to be kidding. You've seen his file, haven't you? He's been taken 'off track.' "

Angstrom didn't know that. He *hadn't* looked at his file. Not yet, anyway. He remembered him from several years ago at a training session Angstrom led, and he was impressed by what he saw in him. The only thing he knew about Magdos since then was that he was still in the CIA, albeit for some reason in Global Services of all places. So now Angstrom knew why: he was being pushed out.

"Does he know yet? Have you interviewed him?" Banks said.

"No. Not yet."

"You should think this through carefully, John. It'll be a reflection on you if something goes wrong."

"What's wrong with him...in your opinion?" Angstrom asked. "Why did he get taken off track?"

"He was uncontrollable; undisciplined. Stellar physical ability, great intelligence, but he held himself in too high a regard. He thought he was superior to everyone. He's not cut out for it, John."

"I don't know...I met him once," said Angstrom. "Saw something in him...reminded me a little of myself."

"John, he's nothing like you. I'm afraid you won't be able to control him."

"I will. I'll bring him along carefully. He just sounds like someone who hasn't had the benefit of good leadership. I did see in the HUMINT system that the last two managers before his current one aren't even in the CIA anymore."

There was silence after that. Angstrom didn't want to say anything further until he'd had a chance to study Magdos' file and interview him.

"Well, he's gonna be pretty damned pleased if you bring him in, that's for sure. He's *your* project, just remember that. And make your decision quick. If you can't get him on board ASAP, put him on the backburner."

"Got it."

Angstrom had the feeling that the meeting was over and he began to rise.

"John," Banks said. "I'm going to just come out and say it point blank: I think you're making a big mistake by allowing Czolski to live with you. No good's going to come from it."

"Her name's Davis now...Anne Davis. Look, is the waiver going to be signed off or not? I submitted it over a month ago."

Banks and Wright momentarily looked at each other.

"Mm, fine. We'll approve it," Banks answered. "Only...be careful. Be careful with what you say to her. You don't want to embarrass yourself. You never know."

Banks and Angstrom exchanged glances. The meaning was clear: he was being monitored. His own organization was spying on him. He figured as much, and now he knew for sure.

After Angstrom left, Banks and Wright remained behind to talk.

"What's the issue with Magdos?" Wright said.

"It's just like I said: he's a person unto himself. We couldn't convince ourselves that we could control him. He got pegged with the insubordinate tag, but quite honestly, I never had the time or inclination to check into it myself. I relied upon the reports of others."

"Hmm. Others who are no longer with us, apparently."

"Yes, exactly. It may have been an oversight on my part."

"And Angstrom...you're sure he's stable?"

"Like I said, the doctors said so. The woman and her effect on him is a wild-card, but all indications are that he's fine now. No aftereffects from the nervous breakdown. "

"And you believe we can count on him."

"Of course. I wouldn't have recommended him for Cyberknife if I didn't. The guy's just like his file says: the real deal. Garrett always said he was his number one guy, far above anyone else. Gordon was the closest after him, and then Franklin. Gordon is just a few too many years shy or he would've been handed Franklin's team."

Wright thought for a moment. "You're sure we're not pushing things too fast? I mean, he's really moving slow in building his team."

"It's *really* slow. He's following Garrett's footsteps: too selective, criteria too high. It's a wonder he even found two new recruits, not counting Magdos."

"So the long term solution is to have Angstrom take over Franklin's group."

"It has to be. We can't let what happened with Garrett occur all over again. We're eventually going to have to put the two groups back together, all under Angstrom."

"And you think it'll be okay with Angstrom and Franklin working together on Cyberknife in the short term?"

"We'll make it clear to Franklin that there's no choice."

"What's the friction between them, by the way? Do you know?"

"I think so. Angstrom is all about loyalty, operating on the up-and-up, letting his actions do the talking. He's almost a throwback to a different time, where honor, respect, and patience were all tenets of conduct. Franklin, maybe not so much. Don't get me wrong, he's still an excellent agent. Let's just say that he's good at managing up. If he can say or do something he believes would make himself look better than his peers, he wouldn't hesitate. My guess is that Franklin probably crossed Angstrom at some point, stabbed him in the back or something, and Angstrom's the type who never forgets. At least, that's my guess. That, and Franklin probably just feels threatened by Angstrom. Angstrom fell into his role because Garrett retired. He never asked for it. Franklin, on the other hand, campaigned for it, spent years positioning himself for it. He's probably afraid Angstrom will show him up. And he'd be right."

"Hmm. Well, watch the situation closely."

"It goes without saying."

There was a pause in their conversation.

Wright said, "You're going to leverage Redblood, right?"

Banks was surprised by the sudden transition. "I think we're going to have to, given the short time frame involved. I mean, the detailed plans are still being developed, but I would think he figures prominently under the circumstances. Do you see any problems with that?"

Wright said, "Of course not. That's what he's there for."

Wright paused again and then said, "And this thing with

Spence, what's the consensus? Retribution?"

"It has to be. There's no question there's a connection. The broken bones were too odd to be a coincidence. It wasn't random."

"So what are we doing about it?"

"We're watching it. Like I said, we offered the woman anonymity and protection. She declined. Wants to stay with Angstrom, and as you just heard, the feeling's mutual."

"In the meantime, a killer tied to the FSB is still out there, right in our own backyard, perhaps tracking this woman down as we speak," Wright said.

"Who knows, maybe Angstrom and Davis will help flush him out," replied Banks.

Wright winced.

"Anyway," Banks said, "it's not clear how the killer would ultimately find her, if he is in fact after her, unless maybe...."

"Unless Spence gave up some names. That's what you were about to say, wasn't it?"

"Yes. But we have no indication of that," Banks answered.

"Correct. But then, how did they know about Spence in the first place? After all these years?"

"Good question. Who would've thought that Arthur Spence could get caught up in something like this after being out of it for so long? I mean, that came out of nowhere. I'm not sure how it happened. I suppose it could have been someone with connections in Germany—someone from a long time ago who decided to give him up, cashing in on some old information. Hard to say."

"So what do *you* think? You think Spence talked? Gave up names?"

"I'd like to think not," said Banks. "Our records indicate he was solid when he was with us, but that was a long time ago. It's possible, given the pain he went through. His face was beaten to a pulp, and there were severe blows to the body, heavy internal bleeding. And yet, there were no sounds, no cries for help reported by anyone from the town."

"You didn't tell John about any of that part, the disfigurement, the punishment Spence experienced."

"No."

Wright thought for a moment. "Strange, it was so overt. But if it's not over, if there's going to be more on U.S. soil…"

"Yes, well, that's the Kremlin now: there's no restraint in it; they're out of control. We've gone backwards in the whole thing."

"I think at some point we ought to tell John the complete picture. If there's going to be more, I don't like the idea of him being blind about any of it."

"John knows. He's already run it through in his head. I could see it in his eyes when we were explaining it all to him."

5

Silhouette of a Shadow

CIA Headquarters
Langley, Virginia

ANGSTROM DROVE STRAIGHT TO HIS OFFICE AT LANGLEY AFTER the meeting with Banks and Wright. There was a lot he needed to do; most of it related to Magdos.

It was too much of an impulse, he realized, even borderline reckless, to have proposed Magdos as a candidate without having even interviewed the man first or studied his file. Banks' reaction caught him off guard; Angstrom hoped it wasn't warranted.

Although it had been several years since they last met, Angstrom still remembered Magdos to the day. Like Angstrom, Magdos struck an imposing presence. He was six-foot four, dense bone structure, all muscle. He was twenty years younger than Angstrom. His eyes were penetrating narrow slits, and he had black, closely cropped hair, high cheekbones, and tan-colored skin. He seemed to tower next to others, statuesque, a god-like centurion of ancient Rome.

The question for Angstrom was: What happened to him? As far as he knew, the last time he met the man Magdos' whole career was ahead of him. He really did remind him of himself, which was why he was considering him after all these years.

Angstrom used the password HUMINT had given him to gain access to Magdos' electronic file:

EMPLOYMENT SUMMARY

Name: Magdos, Gino   Education: B.S., Forensic Science, 2008
Birthdate: June 1, 1986   Syracuse University
Place of Birth: Brooklyn, NY   Service Date: 08/14/08

CHRONOLOGICAL WORK HISTORY:

1. Aug 2008 - Sep 2009: CIA: Science & Tech. Division
   - Rotation program. Rating: Satisfactory.

2. Oct 2009 - Nov 2010: CIA: NCSD- Counterintelligence
   - Rotation program. Rating: Satisfactory.

3. Dec 2010 - Mar 2012: CIA: Intelligence Division- Weapons Intel.
   - Manager: Jim McManus.
   - Feb. 15, 2012: Disciplinary Action. Reason: Insubordination-Level 1.
   - See Incident Report: 021512-48234.
   - Transfer by request.

4. Mar 2012 - Nov 2012: CIA: Intelligence Division- Terrorism Analysis
   - Manager: Shawn Alston.
   - Sep. 10, 2012: Disciplinary Action. Reason: Insubordination-Level 2.
   - See Incident Report: 091012-48234.
   - Evidentiary video file included at employee request [edited]:
     090912_Magdos_combat.tvl.
   - Directed transfer per Policy 672.

5. Nov 2012 - Present: CIA: Intelligence Division- Global Services
   - Manager: Steve Shaw.
   - Employee on "Probation."

Angstrom saw that Magdos had been in the CIA for about five years. It must have been during his second rotation, Counterintelligence, when he met Magdos at the training session.

Everything looked fine in his employment history all the way through his first two assignments of the rotation program. It wasn't until his first official assignment when something negative surfaced in the record. McManus was his supervisor, one of the two Angstrom knew was no longer with the CIA. Angstrom kept staring at the summary: Level-1 Insubordination. Magdos must've really irked the guy for it to have escalated to an incident report. Then Magdos requested a transfer. Who wouldn't?

New division, new supervisor. Alston was the other manager that Angstrom knew was no longer with the CIA. It was all downhill from there.

He turned to the incident reports, hoping he'd be able to read between the lines and figure out what went wrong. Such a promising career ahead of Magdos, derailed.

INCIDENT REPORT 021512-48234 *[excerpt]*

Employee Name: Magdos, Gino
Submitter: McManus, Jim
Position: Manager
HUMINT Rep: Tammi Epp
Recommendation: Transfer
Disposition: Employee denies; no appeal

Incident Level: __1__
Classification: Insubordination
Incident Date: Nov. 17, 2011 (start)
Report Date: Feb. 15, 2012

Incident Summary:

1. Repeated failure, then absolute refusal, to submit regular progress reports (starting ~11/17/11).

2. Repeated periods of absence during normal working hours. Colleagues report frequent sightings at CIA library and gym (starting ~11/17/11).

3. Frequently arrived late to work and left early.

4. Growing failure to cooperate with colleagues; refusal to share information or his work product with others after direct orders to do so (email attachments enclosed).

5. Disrespectful attitude and non-participation at team meetings.

6. Co-worker reported intimidating, abusive behavior during multiple phone communications. Witness report for at least one occurrence. Conduct unbecoming, disrespectful, rising to harassment.

7. Employee became confrontational with supervisor at team meeting; near physical altercation; witnesses present (02/14/12).

HUMINT notes: Cumulative nature of insubordination over time, rising to final confrontation with supervisor, meets criteria of Insubordination-Level 1.

From the first incident report, things started to go bad after Magdos was in Weapons Intelligence for about a year. From November onward, the pattern of behavior seemed so incongruent with what Angstrom saw in him. The report made it sound like he had mentally "checked out." Angstrom wondered what could have caused that. Even his colleagues seemed to turn on him. Maybe that was part of it.

A quick check into the HUMINT file of Jim McManus, Magdos' manager when the first incident report was filed, didn't reveal too much: he resigned after nine years in the organization, just shy of qualifying for a minimum pension. Nothing in the file to indicate why. Something finally caught up with him, Angstrom guessed. It was enough to give Magdos the benefit of the doubt. Angstrom referred to the second incident report.

INCIDENT REPORT 091012-48234 *[excerpt]*

Employee Name: Magdos, Gino
Submitter: Shawn Alston
Position: Direct Supervisor
HUMINT Rep: Tammi Epp
Recommendation: Transfer; Probation
Disposition: Affirmed after appeal

Incident Level: _2_
Classification: Violence to employee
Incident Date: Sep. 9, 2012
Report Date: Sep. 10, 2012

Incident Summary:

1. Employee participated in mandatory combat instruction.

2. Nine other students present, all male. Instructor: Ben Weathers.

3. Instructor reported verbal exchange with employee during session.

4. Employee reported being taunting and belittled.

5. Instructor said employee was belligerent, refusing to heed instructions. Expressed disagreement with instructions, ridiculing them.

6. Employee claimed instructor physically provoked him and was belittling others during demonstrations.

7. Employee sparred with instructor; broke instructor's jaw with heel-of-palm jab to face; employee alleges it was a counterattack to instructor's move. Prior to incident, instructor repeatedly told employee not to use technique.

8. Incident captured; see *090912_Magdos_combat.tvl* file, abbreviated.

HUMINT notes: Upon review, including video recording, interviews of instructor and employee, as well as other witnesses, determined there was possibility that employee's strike was premeditated. Even if it wasn't, use of physical force in context of fact pattern gives rise to Level-2 Insubordination.

The second incident report was curious. None of the witnesses would corroborate any of Magdos' allegations, almost like they were intimidated not to. Then to file an incident report based upon an injury incurred during a hand-to-hand combat exercise, that was quite extraordinary in Angstrom's mind.

Angstrom reflected upon how this file on Magdos, short and succinct as it was, encapsulated the complete collapse of a man's career. How easy it seemed for that to happen, all with just a little bad luck...and the wrong people above him.

The file on Alston, Magdos' manager during the second incident report, didn't reveal anything remarkable either. The HUMINT rep in both cases was a woman named Tammi Epp. Curious how the same rep was involved in both cases. A certain amount of bias could have played into the second incident report decision. He supposed he could talk to her if he really wanted to.

He closed his office door and went back to his computer to open the video file associated with the second incident report. The footage started playing, and the scene began innocently enough. There was a gym with agents dressed in white Keikogis sitting around the edge of a training matt. An instructor, a black belt, stood in the center. The file was edited such that the footage started with the instructor already in the middle of a lesson. A student rose and stood opposite the instructor, and an attack-defend sequence ensued. The instructor posed as the attacker. Another student rose and the process repeated itself. Over time, Angstrom could see that the collection of moves was the same, but the sequence in which they occurred changed depending upon the attack the instructor initiated. Therefore, it wasn't a completely rote exercise.

After a sudden skip in the video, Magdos was seen standing across from the instructor. He was a foot taller and much greater in frame. There was no sound, but it was clear that the instructor said something to Magdos. He kept talking, and as he did so, he mimicked a strike to Magdos' chest with his fist. An attack-defend sequence did not commence. Next, the instructor crouched and mimicked a low kick to Magdos' knee. Magdos remained motionless. The instructor stood back up and continued to lecture, pacing the matt and addressing the sitting students. Then he turned, faced Magdos, and said something. Magdos shook his head in the negative and could be seen saying something. The instructor appeared to get aggravated and reached for Magdos' arm; it looked like he was trying to urge Magdos to go through the physical motions of a particular defend sequence, but Magdos only half-heartedly responded. Finally, the instructor waved his hand and told him to sit back down.

The video was edited to skip to another point, and Magdos again stood at the center of the mat across from the instructor. Magdos appeared calm. He must have been ordered to mimic an attack, because he slowly threw a punch at the instructor, who then countered it in slow motion. Magdos kept his arm extended outward while the instructor held his forearm against it and spoke to the other students.

Angstrom felt uneasy as he watched the video. Even without sound he began to feel the tension exuded from Magdos.

The instructor turned back to face Magdos and then all of a sudden became angry. Something must have ticked the instructor off. Angstrom replayed that section of the video and focused on Magdos' face; he thought he saw a slight grin, but it was subtle, hard to tell for sure. Perhaps the instructor thought Magdos was laughing at him.

The instructor again turned to the sitting students and said something, then back to Magdos, with more talking. After Magdos responded, the instructor became more agitated, his facial expression tense. His right hand rose upward like he was going to use it in a karate-chop fashion to strike Magdos, and he held it in the air. Magdos remained poised, arms to the sides. Then the instructor moved his hand swiftly downward, and just before he was about to strike Magdos in the side of the neck, he stopped. Magdos didn't flinch. Furious, the instructor began tapping his index finger into the middle of Magdos' chest.

Angstrom couldn't understand why Magdos didn't just do what the instructor asked and be done with it, but he also didn't understand what the instructor was doing. He seemed to be taunting Magdos, antagonizing him. If he was unhappy with Magdos' failure to respond, he should've just asked him to leave. He could have written him up later, talked to him privately, or something. Instead, he seemed to continue to escalate the issue, inflaming the situation.

Then there was a pause. The instructor said or did nothing, alternately looking at Magdos and then at the other students. Angstrom leaned closer to the monitor to try and see the other students' faces, but the video was slightly grainy from the digital compression and the students were too far in the background.

Something was again said between Magdos and the instructor; both took their positions to spar. As if heeding Angstrom's thoughts, Magdos appeared like he was going to do as the instructor had asked. Magdos was first to strike, and the move was easily blocked. Angstrom knew the strike was not in concert with Magdos' obvious physical ability: it wasn't a powerful thrust at all, nor was it with great speed. The instructor must have thought the same thing, because he dropped his arms to his side and shouted something at Magdos. Then he even shoved him, saying something else.

They resumed their positions, and this time the instructor lunged with an attack, full force. It was easily deflected, but not to the instructor's satisfaction. The sparring was momentarily halted so a point could be made. He grabbed Magdos' right arm firmly and positioned it in the air, and then, in slow motion, moved his own arm against it to indicate what the instructor wanted the students to do to counter such an attack.

Magdos jerked his arm away, visibly aggravated at having his arm forced into the air. Yet another verbal exchange, the instructor yelling at him, getting close to Magdos' face. Magdos was not intimidated; he remained calm and said nothing, but a smirk appeared on his face. This time it was clearly visible. The instructor paused, staring at him, and then became furious, vehemently spewing words at Magdos. Spittle came from his mouth. Angstrom could see it. Magdos wiped his face and took a step back. There was no smile on his face now. Angstrom had a bad feeling about what was coming. Neither instructor nor student would bend. Angstrom wondered whether the instructor thought he was a drill sergeant at basic training it had gotten so bad.

The instructor barked an order or asked some sort of question—it wasn't clear from the footage—and was beside himself with anger. Veins were visible on his temples and the sides of his neck as he began yelling at Magdos.

Angstrom again strained to see the reaction of the students; all he could tell was that they sat erect, no backs hunched over. They didn't appear to be talking to each other, either. What was unfolding in front of them held their complete attention.

All of a sudden the instructor became calm. He turned to the students and said something, then back at Magdos. He entered a fighting stance and said something to Magdos. It must have been an indication that he was going to come at him for real.

Angstrom didn't need to watch what happened next. It was obvious. He did anyway. He wanted to see the full, unrestrained power and speed of Magdos, the man who would be working for him.

He wasn't disappointed. The action was clean and swift. Angstrom thought there was almost a graceful beauty to it. With one powerful blow, the instructor was on the ground, his jaw clearly broken. The video abruptly ended after that.

At least now Angstrom could understand the surprise Banks expressed at the mention of Magdos' name: on paper the man looked uncontrollable, lost. Looking deeper, however, Angstrom saw otherwise. Maybe it wasn't himself twenty years ago—Banks was right about that—but it was a man of great potential and value, nonetheless.

He turned his attention back to what was left in Magdos' electronic file. Nothing jumped out at him as out-of-the-ordinary: born in Brooklyn, both parents college educated, father a high school teacher, mother a nurse, no siblings, prominent athlete in high school. He was single, no legal record, not much travel, very little activity over the internet from his home, respectable savings account for someone in his position, no debt. Angstrom guessed he was still a gym rat. Phone records showed less than normal activity. CIA Security background checks went through without issue.

The only aspect that statistically appeared as an outlier seemed odd to Angstrom when he uncovered it. Magdos frequented local libraries and checked out a lot of books. Angstrom clicked down into the data and saw that Magdos was a voracious reader with broad interests. In the fiction genre there was a propensity for spy and crime novels, but he read a lot of non-fiction as well, especially U.S. and world history. The subject Magdos appeared to read the most was philosophy—philosophy of all kinds: Chinese, Indian, Japanese, Greek. It even looked like at some point he tapped out his local library's holdings, because records showed that requests were made to pull books from other branches.

This made Magdos even more intriguing. Angstrom was anxious to meet him. No one was perfect—everyone had his warts. The key was whether one could rise above them. Could they be controlled and mitigated? Angstrom wasn't even sure what those warts were with Magdos. He questioned the incident reports. It almost appeared as if Magdos had just crossed paths with one or two of the wrong people in the system. Maybe it was as simple as a green recruit being politically "lacking" when it came to navigating through the morass of the CIA. It wouldn't be the first time.

Angstrom read the entire file; he wanted to make sure he didn't miss anything. He went to the recruitment section, the part dealing with when Magdos was originally brought into the CIA out of college. That yielded a big surprise. One of the people that interviewed Magdos was Garrett; his only comment in the file was a belief that Magdos was likely a high-performance candidate.

Garrett liked him. That sealed it for Angstrom. Magdos would be on the team, pending the informal, unscheduled interview he intended to conduct.

It was way past lunchtime; it took longer to review Magdos' file than he thought it would. He was pleased that he identified at least this one additional candidate before his window of time was closed.

In no mood to see anyone at the moment, he decided to eat lunch alone at his desk. Opening the cloth bag he brought from home, he took out plastic containers of the meal he had prepared the night before: leftover salmon, whole-grain rice, and blades of asparagus. Then he clicked on his computer to play a music file of a live recording of Dizzy Gillepsie's *Kush*. A flute began, slow, pensive, mysterious. Angstrom heard shouts from the audience, and clapping. He tried to imagine what it would've been like to have been there: dark, smoky, drinks flowing, probably very late in the evening, people of all kinds mixing together, excited to see the great bebop master. The saxophone rang, and then Dizzy himself. Jazz always seemed to make the meal better, Angstrom thought. He sat back and listened for a while.

6

Rescue

LATER THAT AFTERNOON, ANGSTROM WENT TO SEE MAGDOS. His intention was to make an unannounced visit so that he would catch the man off guard in his everyday environment. That way there'd be the least chance of Magdos putting up some kind of a front. If he kept a messy desk, dressed sloppily on a normal day, Angstrom would see it.

As Angstrom made his way through the building, the walk provided an opportunity to reflect upon a few things. They were positive thoughts, healthy, as opposed to the disturbing ones he used to have while he was recovering from a nervous breakdown during his stint at DARPA. The breakdown had occurred about two years ago after a failed mission in Syria. When it happened, the CIA didn't want to give up on him, so they put him on temporary assignment in DARPA to give him time to recover. It was during that period when his mind used to travel in all different directions, wandering without control from one bad memory to another. That was no longer the case. He was better now. The overt proof was the mission he recently oversaw involving the defection of Anne Davis. The administration took a chance by putting him in charge of it, and he passed the test, running the small operation cleanly and maintaining a strong focus the whole time.

Utmost on his mind now was the urgency of Cyberknife. It interrupted his efforts to assemble the new group he was tasked to build. So far he had only four people: himself, his old friend Gordon, and the two others. He was glad he at least had Gordon, a seasoned operative he knew he could trust. He was loyal, reliable, and good at what he did. The other two were solid as well. They performed well during multiple interviews, and he was satisfied with the gunmanship and physical ability tests. He was fortunate to have found them, especially the one from the "outside," because after being on an extended, temporary assignment outside of the CIA for the last two years, his knowledge of the people in the "pool" was dated.

If Magdos joined, that would make five—not even close to his goal of fifteen, but he knew that was ambitious. The types of people he needed didn't grow on trees. They needed to have a rare combination of physical ability, intelligence, and mental toughness. Without that last requirement an agent would wither under the pressure experienced during long, deep-cover operations. Better to build slowly, Garrett used to say. Hiring the wrong person will come back to bite you.

Cyberknife. It seemed like a different kind of mission. He was used to deep cover operations. That's not the impression he was getting about Cyberknife. So far nothing had been disclosed as to expectations, other than the implicit notion that the people perpetrating the cyber attacks needed to be stopped, and fast. It almost sounded like it was going to be a "move-in-and-strike" type of initiative: storming the warehouse, pulling the plugs, and shooting out monitors, so to speak.

It had to be more than that. Otherwise why not just have the SEALS handle it? They were proving superb in those types of situations. He hoped it wasn't politics. The CIA had been under a lot of pressure over the years. The pendulum swung back and forth between accusing the CIA of being too aggressive and secretive to being too timid and risk averse. It was the age-old problem for the organization: successful missions couldn't be publicly disclosed and remained secret, while failures always seemed to get leaked and make the headlines. In between, there was a lot of fear, suspicion, and questioning of tactics. For him, he knew the things he worked on, his missions, were necessary. He could see the dangers that were otherwise posed and the good that resulted. How does an organization explain to the general public that the unorthodox methods and actions, so far removed from the normalcy of everyday lives, were ethical and necessary in the face of the challenges and dangers the country faced? He hoped Cyberknife was not an overcompensation—a response to the pendulum swinging too far in one direction.

If it *was* the Russian government perpetrating the cyber attacks, what could Angstrom's team do? If they stormed onto Russian soil and took some kind of action, Russia would claim it was a kinetic attack that verged on an actual declaration of war. Angstrom wished he had more visibility into what the top brass was thinking.

As he neared his destination, his thoughts returned to the immediate. He hoped he wouldn't be disappointed by what he saw in Magdos. The more he thought about Cyberknife and the disclosure about Spence, the more he realized the urgency of getting at least one more person on his team. He was beginning to see the need for someone with a special set of skills.

When Angstrom arrived at the post location, he found himself in a rather large sea of cubicles. The one with Magdos' nameplate was found easily enough. It was located along the main hallway. Angstrom approached it and saw that Magdos wasn't there.

In fact, looking around for a moment, Angstrom noticed that there wasn't much activity in the whole area; many of the cubicles were empty. The whole area was as quiet as a ghost town.

Angstrom returned his attention back to Magdos' cubicle and entered to look around. Other than a computer, not much was there. So this was what it looked like to be "off-track," he said to himself.

He continued to look around the cubicle and noticed a black, soft-covered Bible sitting on the desktop. Stubs stuck out of the pages as markers. It felt strange for him to see the Bible out in the open, right there in the office environment. Religion was not something that was often thought about for someone in his line of work; it was incongruent with what he did. Angstrom had come to that conclusion a long time ago. Memories flooded his subconscious, harkening back to a different time, a different period in his life. The Bible looked like the one he used to have when he was in Catholic high school. A memory from a different life, a memory long suppressed.

Looking to his left, there were a few policy and procedure manuals resting on a shelf; otherwise, the office was empty—no pictures stuck to the peg board, no papers lying around, no personal effects. Angstrom noticed a small, rather well-worn black book nestled among the manuals. It had Japanese Hiragana printed in faded gold leaf along its thin spine. Under the Hiragana there was an image of an open hand with the thumb folded inward. He started to reach for it when he sensed a presence. Turning around, Magdos stood behind him at the entryway.

Their eyes met but no words were immediately spoken. He was just as Angstrom remembered him, still a formidable presence.

Searching for something to say, and slightly embarrassed at being caught snooping in the man's office, Angstrom finally motioned to the Bible resting on the desk: "I see you're a reader."

Magdos looked at him with no change in expression, no physical reaction to the statement. "It's more than that, John," he finally said.

Angstrom was startled at being referred to by name, but he was pleased that Magdos remembered him after all those years. It was an important point Angstrom noted: Magdos not only remembered faces, but the names that went with them. A good sign.

"Gino, it's good to see you again after all these years."

"Likewise."

A firm handshake.

"You want to borrow it?" Magdos said.

"Huh, what's that?"

"The book. The one on the shelf."

"Ah, right, what is it?"

"I picked it up at a used book store out in Portland. It was printed over forty years ago. It's a translation of an ancient Japanese manuscript from one of their fighting schools. Loosely translated, it's called *Book of Scream*."

"Really?" Angstrom turned to glance at the small book but didn't reach for it. "Interesting."

"It's on the art of using the voice as a weapon...ways to train and develop the voice as a weapon. Part of the overall arsenal, if you will. Most people don't understand how powerful the voice can truly be."

"Hmm, I see."

"So, you want to borrow it?" Magdos said with a smile.

"No, that's all right, but thanks. I'm pretty satisfied with my arsenal."

"Yeah, well, I guess I can understand that."

"Eh, and why's that?" Angstrom said.

"Come on. Your reputation precedes you."

"Hmph."

"By the way, why don't you ever teach one of those hand combat training classes anymore? It would've been a great opportunity to learn from someone of your reputation."

"Ha, that's a laugh." Angstrom thought for a moment and then said, "Hopefully it would've turned out better than the one I saw of you." He looked deeply into Magdos' eyes.

"So you know about that. Well, I guess I shouldn't be surprised."

Angstrom said nothing, still holding his gaze.

"You want to hear my side of it?"

"No, I don't. I could read between the lines. Let's just say, I don't hold it against you."

Magdos shook his head slowly. Then, in a more lighthearted mood, he said, "What brings you to *this* fine area?" He looked over the walls of his cubicle, out to the empty area. Both men were taller than the cubicle walls and could easily see over them.

"I was hoping to have a talk with you, Gino. I'm sorry for catching you off guard like this, but do you have time?"

"Heh, yeah, I have the time."

Angstrom noticed a slight grin, like Magdos was saying: *What the hell else am I going to do?*

"Great. Well..." Angstrom looked around the cubicle and how small it was. They couldn't talk there. There wasn't even a second chair for him to use. "Is there a conference room we can go to?"

"You bet. Follow me."

Magdos led Angstrom down the hall past a lot of empty cubicles. A few faces looked up here and there in surprise. As Angstrom followed him he noticed the strength in Magdos' arms and shoulders. They were huge. Magdos' career may have atrophied, but his physical strength certainly hadn't. That was good; now the question was: Where was his mind?

"So, you remembered me after all these years, eh?" Angstrom began as they both sat down in the room.

"Sure. I remember you from that seminar. Back then I wanted to follow your footsteps."

"Back then. What about now? Not so much anymore?"

"You've read my file. You know where I'm at."

Angstrom suddenly had a strange sensation. The conversation he was having with Magdos was like the ones he used to have with Garrett, almost cryptic in nature, anticipatory, where every notion didn't need to be expressed in order for it to be conveyed.

"Tell me, what are you doing now?" Angstrom said.

"What for? What's the use?" Magdos hesitated, but then relented. "I'm not doing much of anything...logistics. I make sure equipment gets where it needs to be, field offices get what they need, and so forth."

Angstrom listened, studying Magdos and processing everything he said. Magdos sensed this, but it didn't change his demeanor or what he said.

"Basically, I'm in at six and out at three."

Angstrom looked at his wristwatch. "It's almost three now. I'm sorry to be keeping you."

Magdos smiled. "Are you kidding? This is the most excitement I've had all year."

"Are you ready for something else?"

"I was."

"What do you mean *was*?"

"I thought maybe you knew...that maybe your being here was somehow even related to it, as farfetched as that might be."

A puzzled expression appeared on Angstrom's face. "Sorry, I don't follow."

"I turned my notice in two days ago."

That stunned Angstrom, but he refrained from showing it.

"What're you going to do? Do you have something lined up?"

"No. But if you saw how I lived...my *humble* abode...let's just say that I saved a little by living a lean lifestyle. Enough to ride it out for a while. I'm not sure what I'm going to do next. It can't be anything like this."

Angstrom drew in a deep breath and exhaled. "How'd you like to come work for me?" he said.

Magdos looked at him for a moment and then looked away to think.

"I'm done here, John. Mentally checked out a long time ago. You don't want me...and I don't want to be here."

"You're right. You don't want to be here," said Angstrom, looking around to emphasize the point. "But what my team does is different than this; it's nothing like it. And I *do* want you. You'd be a valuable addition. I'm reassembling an old group that's been dying on the vine. In the meantime, I've got some

70

important issues that are already at hand, including a new operation. I need to move fast. Things need to move fast."

Magdos said nothing at first. As he said before, he had already mentally checked out of the place. Now he was being asked to stay. It was a surprising development. He looked at Angstrom, looked into his eyes. Finally, with a slight grin he said, "Alright, sure. I'll cancel my travel plans."

Angstrom smiled at how easily Magdos changed his mind. Then he motioned to the Bible resting on the desk and said, "And there's no conflict with that, right? You know I get into some pretty deep shit."

"No. Not as long as it's legitimate, you know, for the real cause. And I'm sure it is."

"And you don't need to know any more to change your mind about quitting? That's it? No more details on what's coming?"

"Knowing what you're about, that's good enough for me. I'm in. Only..."

"Only what?"

"You saw my file..."

"To hell with the file. I make my own judgments. So, are we set?"

"All right then, John. Yes, we are."

"Good. Then I'll have your notice revoked. Hang around here. Someone will call this afternoon to make arrangements so we can get you out of here and over to my area. Welcome aboard, Gino. I'm looking forward to it."

"Me too. Thanks, John, I really appreciate it."

Gino stood up after Angstrom did and shook hands with him—a firm grip. Angstrom noticed the strength in it.

"You're not rusty at all, are you," said Angstrom with a grin.

"Do I look rusty?"

"No, you don't." Angstrom was about to leave when he stopped himself and said, "By the way, I've got a special assignment for you, immediately. You're not going to be able to tell anyone about it...*no one*. Got it?"

"Sounds good."

71

They looked at each other for another moment, Angstrom a slight smile on his face, Magdos more serious.

As Angstrom walked out, Magdos remained standing and watched him leave the conference room.

Magdos couldn't believe it. It was like something fell out of the sky for him. He went back to his cubicle and sat down. Then he picked up the Bible and began to read one of the marked passages.

7

Epistrophe with Synchopation

NSA Headquarters
OPS2A Building-VENOMA
Friday, June 12

NO MAJOR CYBERKNIFE BRIEFING WAS CALLED AGAIN for several days. Teams of cyber experts worked around the clock. Incremental progress was reported to CIA Deputy Director Ernest McCoy and USCYBERCOM Deputy Chief Lieutenant General Harold Manmoth. The next major briefing was set for Friday at 11:30 A.M. Angstrom and Banks drove to it together from CIA headquarters. The audience was the same as before with one notable exception: Director of National Intelligence James F. Freedman was in attendance. In four days Cyberknife had risen to the utmost level of importance. Senior members of the Intelligence Community once again filled the first two rows.

Q-Directorate took the stage. The presentation began with no introduction.

"Big Machine signature recognition, supplemented by manual review of signature attack patterns, has uncovered seventeen separate attack vectors on the DFW systems. The ten with highest prevalence are shown:

Network Attack Designation	Prevalence
DoS.Extended.SYNFlood	89.4%
Intrusion.Win.NETAPI.buffer-influx	73.8%
Scan.Append.UDP	68.9%
Scan.Modify.TCP	67.6%
Intrusion.Win.DECOM.exploit	53.4%
Search.decrypt.on-verify	33.2%
Memstem.replace.geobase	32.2%
Deciph.IPnet.filt.instan	31.8%
Ping.selective.trigger	11.8%
Handshake.SMTP.RCPT	9.8%

"There are some important points to take from this.

"First, note that attack patterns *not* listed were deemed nominal. They're known, encountered in the normal course, and under normal circumstances would've been repelled.

"Second, we initially questioned whether the last one listed should have been included—its prevalence was relatively low. However, as we continued to analyze the overall profile of the network attacks, we realized that the 'handshake' strain worked in concert with some of the other threads, likely performing a critical function. The other threads, in a sense, masked the presence of the handshakes, sort of like decoy 'flares.' The importance of the handshake strain is thus reflected by its inclusion.

"Third, you won't recognize any of the designations for these threads. They're all new. Needless to say, enterprise-grade software didn't stop any of it.

"Finally, and this is most important, what we're learning is that this whole set of network attacks was intermingled. They depended and fed off of each other. Think of it as a coordinated kinetic attack—ground, air, sea—only in cyberspace. The SYNFlood was the initial carpet bombing, disrupting systems, tying up defense mechanisms, and overwhelming network sensors. Other attack threads served specific purposes, acting in concert, timed, synchronized, complementing and aiding each other, and in some cases, triggering previously instantiated malware."

The speaker paused for a moment. The whole room was quiet, listening intently.

"The three designations you see in the thirty-percent range served as the core of the network attack; they did the heavy lifting and caused the most damage, severely bogging down resources. Note the string ending in 'geobase,' and the other with 'IPnet' in its designation. These represent attack threads that relied upon a number of mechanisms—geography, IP network designations, and so forth—in order to focus their attacks on very specific targets. As a result, unintended proliferation was essentially eliminated. You'll see this 'targeting' in spades when we get to the malware discussion.

"It should be noted that so far Big Machine has uncovered two zero-day exploits utilized in the network attacks. In other words, weaknesses that even the software vendors didn't know about. One was O/S-based, the other in a major app. By way of comparison, there were four zero-day exploits in Stuxnet. I'm not going to get into them here, but to some extent their nature may be gleaned by virtue of the specific attack thread names that worked in concert with them."

Lieutenant General Manmoth, who was sitting in the front row next to Freedman, held up a hand to stop the presentation. He turned in his seat to address the audience: "We've already notified O/S and software vendors regarding the exploits. For one of them, a patch has already been created; for the other, we're still working on it." He turned back around and signaled for the presentation to continue.

"Excuse me," someone from the audience interrupted, "but why would the perpetrators give up two zero-days? Given how nothing was ultimately gained by this attack, at least as far as we can tell, why use them at all? Zero-days aren't something found every day; they're rare and valuable. It seems odd...or at least a little sloppy and careless."

"Good question," responded Q-Directorate. "We wondered the same thing. We don't think it's because of sloppiness or carelessness; we're pretty confident of that. At minimum, it's a serious indication of how powerful the hackers are; it demonstrates that they don't even care about the loss. They must have more...or rather...they're capabilities must be so great that ultimately it doesn't really matter that they gave them up."

For those in the room who truly understood how valuable zero-days are, how rare it was to find even one, Q-Directorate's answer got their minds buzzing with concern.

"So the network attacks were the beginning of the DFW attack, the beginning of the chaos," Q-Directorate continued.

"Just a minute," FBI Director Corver interjected. "Have you determined the source of the network portion of the attack yet? What were the origin IP addresses?"

"Good question. Thus far Big Machine has extracted over two-hundred-fifty thousand unique addresses. We traced most to U.S. locations. Obviously this suggests botnets are being used on a massive, coordinated scale. We don't know the manner of control yet."

"We should expedite warrants to find out," Corver responded.

Q-Directorate looked down into the audience at Manmoth and then back to Corver. "The process has already been started for a subset."

Corver, surprised to hear that, leaned over and said to Manmoth in a low voice, "I didn't hear anything about that. Why wasn't I consulted? That's domestic."

"You are now," Manmoth whispered back. Corver frowned, prompting Manmoth to add, "C'mon, Adlai."

Corver turned around and whispered something to a person that reported to him who was sitting in the row behind him.

When Q-Directorate was sure that the side conversation in the front row was finished, he continued, "Now, as I was about to say, the most lethal part of the overall DFW attack, the one that caused the glitches in the systems, came from malware.

"This is where it gets difficult. In fact, the malware in question forms a part of what we referred to in our risk analysis model yesterday as the yet-to-be-determined 'Attack Source Group 3.' We continue to represent it as a combination of multiple strains, supplemented by real-time interaction with the network attacks. In an effort to isolate it, Big Machine compared end-state software conditions with known, good profiles. From all of the analysis to date, there are two major problems we're now focusing on.

"The first one relates to finding the actual malware itself—the type of malware that would have caused what happened at DFW, such as flight arrival/departure monitor de-pixelization. Quite frankly, it hasn't been found."

"What's that supposed to mean," someone said.

"Please, be patient," Manmoth quickly responded, standing up and looking at no one in particular in the audience as he did so. His sudden interjection was almost as if he were on the edge of his seat, prepared to intercede at any moment in order to control the presentation and defend Q-Directorate. "This is a fluid situation. We are working non-stop around the clock, and quite frankly, it's perplexing. You're getting what we know real time, and we just don't have it all yet. We've got the best teams working this, and then some. We've already made some excellent progress in an extremely short time. Let's keep this in mind." He turned back and motioned for Q-Directorate to continue.

"Thanks," said Q-Directorate. "What I meant to say before was that the malware seems to have an ability to...to disaggregate itself...to somehow fracture its lines and syntax according to predetermined, hidden...or encrypted...we're just not sure how yet. The current thinking is that the malware is still in the systems, potentially waiting to be reconstituted for another strike. It's a type of cognitive software with the ability to monitor, sense, and detect the conditions of its operating environment, and then dynamically reconfigure itself in response."

"I'm not aware of anyone outside of our labs having anything close to that," said a man sitting toward the back of the room. It was a mid-level head from DARPA. "And our stuff is top secret."

Q-Directorate responded, "Make no mistake about it: this malware, this whole attack, it's state of the art."

He paused for a moment, wondering if he wanted to say something further to emphasize the point. He decided he did.

"Not all of you in the room are aware of it, but the CIA was recently involved in an attempted defection of a Russian scientist from St. Petersburg."

Angstrom's ears perked up. He listened closely. The sudden reference to the Russian scientist was something he was intimately familiar with. It was Anne Davis' father, Professor Romanov Czolski, that Q-Directorate was referring to.

"He was part of a special group of scientists," Q-Directorate continued, "one that specialized in the development of military technology. I bring it up because the steganographic means utilized to communicate with us and provide us information was highly sophisticated. It involved using steganography to embed hidden microcode inside of other code. As a result of all that, we now know that Russia is far more advanced in steganographic technology and covert communications than we previously assumed. It looks like that will have to be extended to cyber warfare technology as well."

He paused for a moment, looking into the audience to gauge the immediate reaction, and then returned to the presentation.

"So, referring again to this cognitive malware, except for a few trace fragments in memory we've been able to find, shrapnel from the battle, if you will, it's essentially gone. It must be that after system repair the malware essentially wipes itself, hides in files, or somehow, as I said, disaggregates and camouflages itself."

Someone from the audience: "Do you think it may be completely wiped, only to be reconstituted in the next attack through the complex network handshaking process you described?"

"Possible, but it's not our strongest theory. That's probably not very feasible. You see, computer and network resources are too bogged down during a DDoS attack to be able to download the sizeable malware likely responsible for what happened at DFW and elsewhere. Therefore, portions of the malware had to have been installed prior to the network attacks for this whole scenario to have worked like it did. That's why we're placing so much emphasis on the mules that may have been utilized. Unfortunately, that's turning out to be a slow, laborious process. Anyway, we don't think the malware has been completely removed. Especially if there's an intention to invoke it again, which we think there is."

The speaker turned his attention to the screen behind him and stared at it; there was a hard drive profile displayed for one of the airline computers; fragmented sectors were identified with red arrows pointing to them, delineating portions of the drive where the malware was believed to have resided. Q-Directorate continued to look at the display like he was puzzling over it, contemplating the memory frags. The silence seemed interminable to some in the room.

Someone from the audience asked: "Did you trace back system restore points to see if you could tell where malware changes occurred?"

Q-Directorate turned back to the audience, realizing how long he had been studying the screen. "All system restore points were deleted. The malware was surely responsible for that."

"Even in server backups?"

"Yes."

There was a momentary rumble of noise from the audience with the realization that the attacks reached all the way into backup storage systems.

Again from the audience: "What about the trace fragments? Is there anything to glean from *them* at this point?"

"Not so far. We continue to try."

Another pause. Q-Directorate waited to see if there were more questions. He wasn't being completely forthcoming about the fragments, but he was following instructions.

"Q-Directorate, you said there were two malware problems being tackled. The first was that you can't *find* the malware. What's the other?" FBI Director Corver finally asked.

"Yes," Q-Directorate responded, "the second problem. It's one of encryption. To explain that, I'm going to expand the scope of the presentation beyond DFW.

"Recall that yesterday we mentioned that the DFW attack was one of the most notable attacks that occurred on June 6th. By now many of you know that there were other significant attacks across the country that same day. They all involved assaults on systems in the private sector. We enjoy a slight benefit from that, if you will, because those companies are loath to publicize such events. However, rumors of them are already starting to leak to the press. Anyway, for those who are not aware of those other attacks, you're now looking at a pictorial representation of where they occurred."

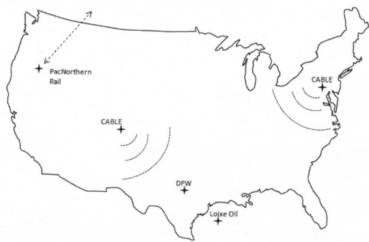

Four major cyber attacks mapped across the United States.

"As you can see, there were four other major attacks across the country. Not separately accounted for here is the localized intrusion in the Dallas-Fort Worth area that temporarily affected cell phone coverage at the airport. Although it's technically another discrete attack, the situation appears to be under control: the malware causing the disruption has been identified and allegedly resolved."

Corver interrupted, "What do you mean allegedly?"

"Well, the telecom operator insisted upon tackling that situation themselves—they said they have a highly sophisticated cyber prevention unit—and they claim they've identified the malware and removed it."

Corver offered, "We can easily get you access to their systems if you need it."

"Not necessary," said Q-Directorate. "We've got more than enough to deal with from these other attacks right now, and it's not worth the legal fight or the publicity to get it. We do know, however, from what they've disclosed to us that the cellular network malware didn't have the same overall profile as what we're tackling in the other systems, and it was also not a new one. A USB exploit was the entry point. Telecom operator records revealed that there was a particular period of time a while back where a lot of USB sticks were reported as being found around the operations hub, including in the parking garage. Employees picked them up, and some were placed into computer systems, thereby infecting them. Their own employees using the infected sticks served as the so-called mule. The company is expanding its employee training to avoid such situations in the future. It should be mentioned, however, that even though the malware itself in that case was not new, nor the manner of infection, we do believe the malware was related to the overall attack."

"Why's that," someone asked.

"Because it was synchronized with everything else; it was set to trigger at the exact same time. I'm not going to say anything further about it at this point except to say that we think it's a big mistake their not allowing us to get more involved."

Adlai Corver took a note for himself. He could hear the aggravation in Q-Directorate's voice, and he decided that he was going to have someone on his team look further into the situation, despite hearing otherwise.

"Anyway," Q-Directorate said, "back to the other main attacks. As shown on the map, the other four involved the following: a Loixe Oil rig off the coast of Houston, a PacNorthern Rail depot, and two cable hubs, one in Colorado, one in New York.

"No major damage was experienced at the cable hubs. In fact, the only noticeable trace was the ghost image previously reported as appearing across the cable transmission. There wasn't even the barrage of network-based bombings at the two installations. We believe it was all malware instantiation through mules. This was more than a nuisance event, however, because of the timing involved, as well as the content of the resultant message, and that's why it's included in the set."

An interruption from the audience: "Did you find the malware this time?" It was Corver.

"No, not quite, but I'll get to that in a minute. Before I do, I want to discuss how the cable system attacks are significant for another important reason. We don't believe it was a coincidence that the malware executed synchronously with the other attacks shown on the map. In fact, for all of these attacks, their main trigger points occurred at roughly the same time. This reflects incredible coordination. Think of the different complex systems involved that were the subject of these attacks, even the different time zones. This level of sophistication approaches our own cyber capabilities: coordinated, multi-geographic, multi-institutional injection and activation, with synchronous precision. It's another one of the most disturbing aspects in all of this.

"Now, referring back to the map, for PacNorthern Rail..."

"Wait a minute," Corver interjected. "I'm sorry I'm the one doing all the interrupting," he turned to Freedman for a moment, who held his hand up to indicate it wasn't an issue, "but why would anyone go through such trouble to launch an attack and risk discovery, just to temporarily flash a cryptic Russian message across a television screen?"

"Mm, excellent question," said Q-Directorate. He was about to answer when there was another interruption.

"Let's hold off on that topic for the moment," Manmoth stood up and said. "Stay focused on the presentation of the facts right now—the technical nature of the attack. We can discuss hypothetical motives later."

"Yes, sir," Q-Directorate said. "For PacNorthern Rail, the supervisory control and data acquisition (SCADA) system was overtaken. For those of you unfamiliar with SCADA, it's a computer-based control system used to monitor and control industrial processes. Its use is prevalent throughout industry: manufacturing, power generation, water treatment and distribution, oil and gas pipelines, electrical power transmission and distribution, civil defense systems...you name it. Anyway, the manner of attack at PacNorthern was similar to DFW, starting with the initial carpet bombing through a barrage of network attacks. What was extremely fortunate—and this may have been dumb luck—was that no trains were in transit at the time. If there *had* been, at a minimum train derailment would have occurred. At worst, there could have been collisions, or even a train running beyond barricade into the station itself, full speed. Tracks were switched incorrectly, indicators were scrambled. Other than that, there's nothing more to observe from this particular attack.

"Wait, stop!" This time it was the Director of the Department of Homeland Security, Mike Holdman. "You just skimmed over the whole cable network attack, and now the rail attack. Are these major attacks or not? Because if they are, you're giving 'em pretty short shrift." He was sitting in the second row, directly behind his colleagues in the front. He leaned forward and put his arm on Manmoth's shoulder. "C'mon Harold, what gives?"

Tension was starting to build. People were feeling like they were being left out, excluded from something that fell within their purview, or that they might get blamed for.

Manmoth said nothing, frustration evident as he turned around to look directly at Holdman. He was about to say something when NSA Director General William Powers grabbed his arm.

Q-Directorate saw this from his position on the stage. Big pockets of power were beginning to collide with each other.

Q-Directorate continued after a nod from Powers.

"Regarding the Loixe Oil drilling platform in the Gulf of Mexico, the profile of the attack was once again similar to DFW. The result, SCADA systems controlling rig operation were overtaken. The effect was not quite as benign as at DFW, the potential damage orders of magnitude greater than what would have occurred at the rail depot. Yes, displays were corrupted, yes, network connectivity was impacted. But in addition, control of hydraulic systems was temporarily lost. Pressure readings were temporarily sabotaged, overhauling started to occur. It could have been a catastrophic disaster in the Gulf."

Q-Directorate was looking at the screen behind him, which showed graphical readouts of system pressure at various nodes on the rig, along with pipeline runs with various nodes highlighted in red to demonstrate the danger. He turned to the audience.

"Fortunately it wasn't a disaster. Before safety thresholds were exceeded, the activity was suspended. This mirrors the type of attack suspension and autonomous system reboot experienced at DFW. Whoever the perpetrators were, it's clear no damage was intended. At least, not yet."

"Bingham, get to the malware," Manmoth interjected. It was an accidental reference to Q-Directorate by his last name. He was startled by the break in protocol.

"Yes, sir. The malware. The story's the same at all the locations. It's missing. However, something happened at the Loixe Oil rig. We believe something went wrong. Wrong for the perpetrators, that is. As a result, Big Machine found an encrypted payload. An undetonated warhead, if you will. As with all the attacks, we still only have trace fragments of the malware itself, but we do have a copy of this payload. We've designated the yet-to-be-found malware as 'Ørsted' after the Danish physicist Hans

Christian Ørsted. He discovered that magnetic fields are created by invisible, electric currents. Figuratively speaking, the invisible fields and current corresponds to our invisible malware. We've named the payload 'Frëge' after the German mathematician of the same name. This is because of the encryption involved.

"Our theory is that Ørsted is a next generation version of the Gauss and Flame malware—similar architecture, but with much more sophisticated modularization, and the already-mentioned disaggregation ability making it an even greater threat.

"We believe Ørsted installed the Frëge payload on specific machines at the oil rig using unique identifiers. In fact, Frëge was likely installed in a multi-step process. When a computer was initially infected with Ørsted, Frëge wasn't included. Only a smaller payload was. Later, the network gathered identifier information for particular computer systems on the rig, which was then forwarded to a remote Command and Control server. Finally, the identifier information for a particular computer was used to compress, encrypt, and infect the computer with the full Frëge payload."

"Why were you able to find this payload...this *Frëge*...at Loixe Oil and not the others?" came from the audience.

"Not sure. As was already stated, something went wrong. Something was not accounted for by the perpetrators, maybe because the Loixe system was more advanced in its security protocols. When the network attacks began, the system's sensors didn't get overloaded as quickly. We're talking seconds here. That was enough time for the Loixe system to decouple certain systems from network connectivity. We believe the interruption did not prevent disaggregation of Ørsted to occur, but it did allow our finding an instance of Frëge in transit. To which system in the network was it traveling? We're not sure. It is, however, the first major breakthrough."

Q-Directorate took a drink from the bottled water that rested on the podium, then continued. "Assuming we're correct in classifying Ørsted as a more potent, advanced derivative of Gauss and Flame, then what would happen next after Frëge is delivered to an infected computer is that Ørsted would attempt to decrypt it using several strings from the infected computer's hardware information, like maybe the Organizationally Unique Identifier, or OUI; when the information finally matched, we believe Frëge would be decrypted for its intended purpose. A sort of electronic bomb waiting to go off."

"So you think Frëge was the same payload at each location, but only the appropriate part of it in each case was invoked?" came from the audience.

Q-Directorate hesitated before responding. "That's possible. That would mean Frëge, together with Ørsted, constitutes the most powerful, sophisticated malware known to man; a giant leap forward in complexity: a master, universal payload, adaptable to the specific nature and functionality of each target it infects, perhaps coded with a comprehensive laundry list of targets, system specs, and corresponding execution modules. This giant payload would then be sub-divided in actual application; otherwise the file size would be too large. This is just a theory, though. It's not clear to us yet if that's what's actually happening."

"What's the alternative?"

"Well, we don't have any alternatives."

Q-Directorate waited to see if there were any additional comments.

"One thing's for sure," he eventually said, "at least part of Frëge must contain the module that caused the digital tearing in the airport displays. And then another module would need to have taken control of the signaling and switches at PacNorthern, and another the control systems at Loixe Oil. In each case, the specifications for each infected system would need to be polled, ascertained in advance...or something, and then Ørsted performed its decrypting function, and the corresponding execution module would be invoked from Frëge. It's incredible to contemplate."

"You think Frëge is responsible for all of that?"

"Yes," came the answer from Q-Directorate. "In a sense, we refer to a particular payload as Frëge not because of the payload content itself, but because of the manner in which it is delivered, decrypted, and invoked. What's most troubling of all, what we're spending a lot of resources on, is that we don't think we've seen the full capacity of Frëge yet. A large part of it hasn't been exercised. The ultimate functionality and operation of it is still a mystery. Put simply, Big Machine has been unable to crack Frëge's encryption."

These new revelations caused a somber mood in the room. Those in the audience were already alarmed at the potential damage Ørsted could cause. Learning that the full power of its payload hadn't yet been unleashed was incredibly disturbing.

Angstrom was fascinated. He had been to briefings about hacking networks in the past, and he kept up on the technology as best he could by reading the internal tech bulletins, but what he was hearing went way beyond that.

"From what we can tell," Q-Directorate continued, "Frëge has three encrypted sections: one code and two data—note again the similarity to Gauss. As already stated, dynamic generation of the decryption key is involved, in each case utilizing information that would be specific to the infected computer system. Herein is part of the problem. The decryption key depends upon specific parameters from the target computer system, thereby preventing any other means from extracting the contents. That's one of the reasons why we haven't been able to decrypt the payload we intercepted. This process, by the way, also allowed for high-precision targeting, thus the near-zero spurious proliferation.

"Anyway, the three sections of Frëge are as follows:

Section	Size (KB)	Contents
.extsdat	512	Code
.exrtedat	128	Data
.exvndat	64	Data

"Now, brace yourselves, because this next part will really throw you for a loop. We believe Ørsted creates the encryption key using a derivative of the SHA-3 cryptographic hash function; we've designated it 'SHA-3-xtent.' As you know, SHA-3 exhibits high collision resistance. The xtent resistance is even higher. Again, the hash function is complicated by the fact that salted versions of executable files of the infected machines are utilized.

"Big Machine is processing 2^{20} permutations per cycle, with up to a 128-bit salt, running through all language and numeric symbology to try to decrypt Frëge. It's a mammoth exercise, and it's not clear we're even close. In order to increase our chances, we've sent an Ørsted/Frëge package to mathematicians and cryptologists across the country—those that have the proper clearances."

There was a short pause, and then Q-Directorate abruptly said, "That's it. That's the present status."

No one initially said anything. They were processing it all. There was a natural desire for more information. The picture was still very incomplete. Some felt that more should have been known by then with all the resources available, including Big Machine.

The other sentiment in the room was that it didn't add up. The whole coordinated attack was so complex, so intricate, yet without apparent purpose. What's more, with all the precision and complexity involved, why the overt Russian message that streamed across television screens? It didn't make sense.

Angstrom ventured a question.

"Q-Directorate, what's the current thinking, or what more do we know, about the Russian message that was transmitted through the cable television network? And also, what's the current assessment as to the purpose of this coordinated attack— the motive. There's been no serious damage that occurred. Why risk discovery of all of this cyber technology with nothing to show for it?"

Direct questions. Broad questions. Some in the room leaned over to ask their neighbors who the person was that asked them.

No one knew (except for Banks, and perhaps a few people in the front row). But the questions were appropriate and were what everyone in the room was wondering.

Q-Directorate hesitated at first, slightly taken aback at such direct questions ventured by someone so unknown, a mid-level at that.

"We don't know the motive. It was most definitely a concerted attack, yet there was no severe, permanent damage. Your questions are certainly appropriate. Why reveal the source of the attacks, or least hint at it via the Russian message inserted onto the cable transmission? It was a potential showing of one's hand, if you will. If we were to extrapolate and draw the corollary to traditional, armed engagement, this could be viewed as a military exercise, perhaps a demonstration of strength. Yet that doesn't make sense: such exercises are normally done to demarcate an area of geographic sovereignty, whereas these cyber attacks happened on our own soil. What's to demarcate?"

No one responded. There were more questions, obvious ones, but no one asked them. None of the senior people in the front row volunteered anything further, and others took their cue by remaining silent.

Banks leaned over to Angstrom and said, "It sort of feels like a test run for a modern day Pearl Harbor."

Angstrom nodded. He realized that he had been thinking the same thing, which means they probably weren't the only ones.

The meeting was over. Eventually everyone was gone except for the directors and deputy directors who were sitting in the first two rows.

Freedman, the Director of National Intelligence, stood leaning against the edge of the stage. Holdman, Manmoth, Corver, Powers, and McCoy huddled around him. Q-Directorate remained as well, even though he was not at their level. A rare privilege.

"I'm briefing the President tonight, along with Defense Secretary Bradley," said Freedman. "I wish we had more to go on. We're not really sure if it's Russia or not, are we?"

"That's correct," Manmoth responded. "But there aren't too many other options—not with this kind of capability. Maybe China, North Korea, or Iran...maybe a rogue group in another part of the middle-east, though that seems unlikely. Possibly some hostile pockets in Africa. Considering the complexity involved, I doubt it. It's one thing to have the ability to wage a single, powerful attack. What we're seeing here—the broad scope, the advanced, deep infection, the mule coordination, the synchronous nature—it's shocking."

"What about the criminal element?" offered Freedman.

Everyone turned to Q-Directorate to see what he had to say to that.

"Uh, we're pursuing that as well. It's not out of the question, but we have no tying evidence. As Lieutenant General Manmoth said, with the breadth of this attack, it would need to be a large sophisticated group to perpetrate it. We're talking coordination among different criminal factions over a long period of time, years. That's what it would take to develop something like this. Recruitment of the necessary computer and network scientists would be pretty difficult. Even if they got some takers, it would be hard for us to not know about it: developing something of this magnitude would be hard to keep a secret for very long, especially given how the criminal element invariably likes to talk. And it would cost a lot of money and development activity for a long period of time without anything to show for it. That's a difficult proposition for organized crime."

"Even for the Russian mafia?"

"Well, admittedly we have less intelligence on that, and less visibility to any corresponding 'recruitment' activity, but it wouldn't be a simple matter. It would need to be a massive, incredibly sophisticated and patient criminal enterprise. That's not to say that the criminal aspect couldn't serve as part of the mule activity. I can see that happening, especially of course here in the United States."

"Could it be the beginning of a real attack? I mean, a true *military* attack?" said CIA Deputy Director Ernest McCoy.

Everyone turned to look at him.

"This could be retaliation for Stuxnet," he continued. "We know Iran's cyber capabilities are sophisticated; this could be a response to the Stuxnet worm that destroyed their Natanz uranium enrichment complex."

NSA Director General William Powers then said something for the first time during the meeting: "That, of course, would be a huge escalation under the *Manual on International Law Applicable to Cyber Warfare*. Iran was in breach of its nuclear restraints when Stuxnet hit. That was the justification. An escalated response on their part would likely be construed severely under the manual. I can't see Iran risking us declaring it an act of war."

"Yes, but we all know the manual is a nonbinding restatement, and still in the draft stages at that," Freedman said, testing the theory.

"Anyway," Q-Directorate ventured, "we may never be able to identify the cyber attacker with definitive proof; not unless another one comes to give us more information. I don't mean to sound like a defeatist, because we're working hard on this, but from what I'm seeing, it's going to be very difficult."

There was silence.

"Look, the bottom line is, we don't need to," Powers finally responded. "If we gather a lot of circumstantial evidence, enough to create a 'theater' of responsibility that points to Russia, that should be sufficient for us to declare this as an act of military aggression against the United States." He turned to Q-Directorate and said, "Keep the information coming. Call the next meeting when there's a sufficiently concrete update. Any major developments, I want to know ASAP."

8

The Wisdom

ANGSTROM WAS MENTALLY EXHAUSTED BY THE END of the day. The more he drove on his way home, the more tired he got. It had been a full day with many important developments, and now that it was over, his mind had a chance to decompress. He only then realized how busy he'd been.

It started to rain. The drizzle appeared in the beams of his headlights, the drops audible as they hit the roof of his car. He turned on the windshield wipers. If the weather forecast was right, it was going to be the first big storm since he moved into his house in Georgetown. He was looking forward to the rain because he wanted to see how well the small, hundred-year-old wood frame home withstood the elements. He still felt fortunate to have found something in his price range and in the neighborhood he did. It was pretty small, much smaller than the house he used to live in with his ex-wife and two daughters, but he didn't need that kind of space anymore. What he had now was perfect, and he loved the location.

He also looked forward to the rain for another reason—the bigger reason: he wanted to experience the rainfall in his home with Davis, who had moved in with him. *Davis*, he repeated to himself. At first he thought it would be kind of fun calling her by her new last name, but it didn't sound right; it didn't do her justice. He was going home to see *Anne*. She would be there waiting for him. Her image came into his mind: her eyes, her hair, her skin...her beauty. When he thought of her, and the prospect of being with her, all of his other concerns faded away.

There was no music playing in the car; he didn't want any. He wanted to hear the rain as it fell. By the time he pulled in front of his house it was coming down hard. He sat in his car at the curb for a moment, listening to the rain. With the darkness of night enveloping his house, light flowed from the front window.

She was in there, moving about, living in his home. It was as if he could sense her. He thought about how he was everything she had in the world.

Then, for just a moment, he saw her through the window. She was in the kitchen. It reminded him that there was going to be another one of her attempts at cooking dinner. He laughed. After all the time that had passed, they were both still getting a kick out of her failed attempts at cooking, but she never stopped trying. It was a challenge for her to master it, like an art.

Before he stepped out of the car, he looked around through the windows, scanning the neighborhood for anything suspicious. It was force of habit, now even more necessary after learning what happened to Arthur Spence.

He didn't see anything, so he readied himself to make a run for it. He opened the car door and quickly dashed to the front of the house. A veranda overhung the front door, but he still got pretty wet even over that short of a distance because the rain was coming down so hard.

The door was locked. Good, he thought, she was being careful.

When he went in, the aroma hit him immediately; whatever she was cooking, it smelled delectable. Maybe she finally got it, he thought.

As small as the house was, he could never tell whether she heard him coming in or not. She never came to greet him, yet as part of her specialized training she surely would have been taught to always be aware of what was going on around her. Was she subconsciously re-programming herself so that she *wasn't* aware, thereby forcing herself to be "normal?" Or was she just pretending it to be so, ignoring what she heard so that it would at least *seem* normal?

"No peeking," she said with a big smile when he poked his head into the small kitchen.

"At what—you or what's cooking?"

"Both."

"Sorry, can't comply."

All of a sudden, on impulse, he entered and walked toward her, ignoring her admonition. He felt compelled, and the urge surprised him. It also caught her by surprise; her smile dissipated slightly. She turned completely from the stove to face him as he approached. The food was cooking; something in one of the pots made a bubbling noise. The rain pelted the outside of the house. Otherwise, there was silence. He was directly in front of her. All smiles were gone. Even since their ski trip they still hadn't kissed each other. This seemed like an important moment, mysterious. He slowly reached and caressed her cheek, and she continued to look into his eyes. He leaned closer and slowly, ever so delicately, they kissed. It was just long enough, and then he pulled away to look at her; he watched as her eyes slowly opened, a warm smile on her face. She seemed so pure just then, vulnerable.

"Hello, Anne," he said softly.

She said nothing and continued to look at him. He had called her "Anne" instead of "Davis," and that pleased her.

A short moment longer, and then a big smile appeared on Angstrom's face. "So, I see it's dinner again."

It was a transition, and she agreed with it.

"Yes, John, it's dinner. And you're going to like it."

"What, you nailed the recipe?"

"No. I mean you're going to like it, *regardless.*"

94

With a playful smirk, she tapped her index finger into his chest.

"Okay, okay. How about I set the table while you finish?" He tried to peek around her to see what was cooking.

"It's already set," she said as she leaned in his way. "You go change. I'll put some music on and open the wine."

"Wow. Okay, I'll be right back."

When they sat down to eat and Davis served the first part of the meal, Angstrom said with surprise, "What *is* this, Caviar?"

"It sure is. I made the blinis myself, as well as the crème fraiche, and the caviar is sturgeon."

"My, you *are* getting better," he said with a big smile.

"On special occasions, my mother would serve this, only she'd use *beluga* sturgeon from the Caspian Sea.

After that she served lobster bisque she made herself.

"Mm, this is delectable," Angstrom said. "I can taste the ocean. Not too creamy, either. It's perfect."

Their dinner that evening *was* delicious; Davis was getting the hang of it. No doubt their first kiss also contributed to the food tasting better. Chic Corea's album *Return to Forever* played in the background. Flora Purim's spiritual vocals accompanied the sound of an electric keyboard, along with a jazzy melody carried by a flute. Heavenly music, perfect for the occasion.

There were moments during dinner when neither of them spoke; they ate in silence and enjoyed the music, as well as each other's company.

It was funny when he thought about it, but he didn't have any desire to talk about work. There was no urge to "unload" like he used to have with Breann. There was no way he could have anyway, given the sensitive nature of his job, but he was able to put it aside when he was with her, to compartmentalize it.

That was a revelation. It's said a man changes and eventually becomes a reflection of his wife. That may not have been happening per se with Angstrom, but she was having an influence on him nonetheless. Her coming into his life helped continue an evolution that was occurring inside of him, moving him to a different "place" in his life.

Angstrom looked up from his food and chanced a look at Davis. He loved to watch her. He marveled at the fact that he was still enchanted by her. There was no diminishment in her beauty the more he came to know her. How could that be? Nothing she said or did detracted from what he saw in her. How could any sane man *not* want to spend every waking moment with her, never letting her out of his sight?

"Good music selection," he finally said.

"Yes, I love this. I found it in your album collection and have been playing it all day."

"I haven't listened to it in a long time, but it's perfect. So many different layers to it. I'm glad you chose it."

More quiet.

"Speaking of music," she finally said, "I thought of what I'd like to do."

Angstrom looked up from his bowl of bisque and stopped eating. "Huh? What do you mean?"

"As a profession. Something I can do as a job."

"Anne, you know there's no hurry. Don't rush it; you're making a big adjustment in life already."

"I know, John, but it's time. You've given me a lot of time to make this transition, this adjustment to your country."

"*Our* country!"

"Yes, *our* country. I'm grateful for it, but I want to start doing something, something meaningful. I think I've found it."

He kept looking at her, waiting. "Well, okay, what is it?"

"I want to give music lessons."

"*Music lessons?*"

"Yes. I want to teach children how to play the cello."

"Where'd that come from? You never told me you know how to play the cello."

"There's a lot you don't know about me yet, John. We have so much to learn about each other. I've played the cello ever since I was a child. My mother dreamed of it as a career for me."

"What happened? Did you ever pursue it?"

"No, I didn't. My father wanted something else for me. He wanted me to be in, don't laugh, politics. I was to facilitate change, to be a new voice. I think that's how one would say it."

"Yes, I understand. So your father won out?"

"Yes…but…I don't want to talk about that. What I *do* want to say is that I will teach cello to children. I already went to the music store on 38th street and applied. The owner liked my playing and agreed to hire me on a trial basis."

"What did you tell him?"

"I did not tell him anything. I explained my knowledge of music. The man was impressed, so I got the job."

Angstrom sat in silence. He couldn't believe she had done that without telling him. He was almost at a loss for words.

"How…when will you start? What will your hours be?"

"At first I will start slow. I may even give some lessons for free so that children and parents get to know me. Then I will give more lessons at the store."

"You used your new name, right?"

"Of course. And the other information you gave me."

"And how will you get there? Walk?"

"It's only a few blocks away; it's a pleasant walk."

Davis watched as Angstrom pondered the issue. "John, I can't stay locked up here forever."

"Anne, it's great. I'm happy for you." After a slight pause, "You're sure this is what you want? You know that the kids around here are…privileged. They're going to be pretty challenging."

"I can be challenging too," she said, flexing her arm up as if to flaunt great muscles.

The matter seemed settled.

"Well, be careful, Anne. You know how we talked. Just keep your eyes open, okay? If you notice anything that seems strange, anything, let me know immediately. Don't take anything for granted."

"I will. And someday soon, I will play for you."

He didn't respond to that immediately. He was still thinking about how she needed to be careful.

"I'd like that," he finally said, stirring himself from his thoughts.

Davis noticed the pause and could tell he was thinking about something. She could guess what it was but didn't pursue it.

"Hey, wait a minute, that's a good point. You don't have a cello," he said.

"The store will let me borrow one during the lessons, and I can practice there. The owner, a man named Mr. Shulman, likes my playing."

"Maybe we'll need to think about getting you your own. It sounds like you're going to need one. I'd love to hear the sound of a cello playing in this house."

"Yes, maybe that *would* be good. We shall talk about it. Let me see how this goes first."

They each took a few sips of their bisque.

"John, how is work going?"

He was surprised by the question. "It's going well. Good." He looked at her strangely. "You know I can't talk about it."

"No, I know. I just want to make sure my being with you is not hurting your career."

"That isn't the case at all, Anne. In fact, they've been quite tolerant of the situation ever since I made my position clear."

"Good. I'm glad." She looked down at her bowl for a moment, composing her thoughts. "I know it's a part of your life that you'll never be able to share with me, and I don't *want* you to. I just want you to be okay."

"Yes, I understand what you're saying." He was touched by what she said and by how simple yet eloquent it seemed. "It's not a problem...but thank you. It's very thoughtful of you to consider it."

"Technical Glitch Halts Stock Trading"
IP Newswire
[Excerpt: June 17]

Trading was temporarily halted at the New York exchange due to a technical glitch that occurred in computer systems. Because of the transition some years ago to electronic trading, not enough floor traders were available to handle the resultant trading volume. As a result, trading was closed.

Fran Heidel, President of Milleniux Capital, LLC, said that as soon as her firm noticed erratic behavior on the network, her traders literally ran down Wall Street to try to have some important trades made manually. By the time they reached the floor, however, all trading had been suspended. Others that were on the floor reported chaos as traders scrambled to get orders fulfilled via traditional means.

The exchange declined to comment. Some Wall Street firms were not surprised that this happened and wouldn't be surprised if it happened again. "The systems are getting too complex...too many different platforms that have to be interfaced, too many systems running at different speeds, racing for the fastest trades...there's just too many areas where things can go wrong," one executive indicated, who wished to remain anonymous. Others speculated that perhaps something more clandestine was involved, like the system was hacked. The financial gain someone might reap from it if that were the case is already being theorized.

9

'Round the Potomac

Potomac, Maryland
Thursday, June 25

IT WAS LATE AT NIGHT. THE MOON WAS OUT, FULL AND BRILLIANT, not a cloud in the sky to block its reflected light. The illumination cast a fine glow over the large homes along Bit and Spur Lane. There were no streetlights in the area. Their absence was not by accident; it was what the residents of the exclusive community wanted — seclusion and privacy.

Each of the large lots, at least an acre in size, had a large brick home on it. Most of them easily exceeded the 4500 square foot minimum established by the neighborhood covenants. The landscaping was lavish, heavily planted, including many different varieties of evergreen trees. Evergreens were clearly the tree of choice, desirable for their year-round beauty as well as the privacy they afforded. In some cases, the trees were planted all along the property line between homes, thereby forming a natural barrier between them. A few of the houses even had lush foliage planted along the front, making it difficult, if not impossible, to see the houses from the street. In the extreme, wrought iron fencing encircled the property, even cordoning off the driveway with automatic gates to prevent general access.

The people that lived in these homes were stories of success, an enclave of the Washington elite. When they were at home, they wanted to leave their work behind them and to be left alone—a sanctuary from the political skirmishes and struggles they constantly faced at work.

Tennis courts, heated swimming pools, all the symbols of luxury were there. It was enough to elicit a significant amount of resentment from those who otherwise had no chance of attainment. The opulence certainly didn't help the cause of one particular resident that evening.

Bit and Spur Lane terminated into a cul-de-sac that abutted a small forest. All of the lots at the end of it except for one were vacant and undeveloped, prime real-estate held in trust by people who always intended to build there, but for whatever reason never got around to it. Thus, it was an especially dark and secluded part of the street. At around 10:30 P.M. a car arrived and parked near the cul-de-sac. It turned around so that its front pointed into the neighborhood rather than the forest, facilitating a quick exit when the time came. The car didn't belong to any of the residents in the neighborhood, and the two men inside of it weren't friends of anyone that lived there.

If the moon hadn't been out, it would have been difficult to see the car in the darkness, but the black finish on the Chevy Malibu reflected the moonlight perfectly. The two men exited the car, careful to close their doors quietly.

"It's too bright outside, Mitslov," whispered Treshenko, the man who came from the driver's seat. "Someone from one of those houses might see the car if they came outside."

Mitslov didn't answer. Instead he looked around the area, making sure no one *was* outside. He listened quietly for a moment. Treshenko watched him. The first few houses were several hundred feet away; they had dense plantings along their property lines, including their front yards. The houses could barely be seen from where the two men stood.

Mitslov ran his fingers through his dirty-blond hair, pulling it out of his eyes and to the side. He looked at his partner impassively for a moment, and then, without saying anything, went to the trunk and quietly opened it. He pulled out several black blankets and tossed a couple of them to Treshenko, who stood in silence, unsure of what they were for. He watched as Mitslov began to drape them over the most reflective surfaces of the car. Treshenko understood and followed suit.

It was still a risk to leave the car parked where it was; if it was happened upon, say by someone taking a leisurely walk late in the evening, the car, with the dark blankets haphazardly thrown over it, would've certainly raised suspicion. Mitslov knew this. He also knew from having previously staked the area out that no one tended to be outside after 10 P.M.—certainly no one from the nearby houses that Treshenko was so concerned about. Some of the most nearby houses didn't even seem to have people living in them—they were probably in another country, an extended break in Europe or something, Mitslov figured. More good luck; it seemed to follow him. He also knew that he and Treshenko could easily dash into the forest and make a run for it if in fact the car was discovered and drew police.

So there was only the one house located at the cul-de-sac of Bit and Spur Lane: the target house. The situation couldn't have been any better as far as Mitslov was concerned. The seclusion was perfect. Mitslov had performed the necessary surveillance over the course of the last week. It was tedious. Every night Treshenko would drop him off, and Mitslov would make his way to the forest edge with binoculars in hand. There he would stay, late into the night, taking note of neighborhood patterns and making a mental log of the activity of the residents living in the target home. Mitslov was pleased to learn that there was only one person living there. It was just as Arthur Spence had said at the barbershop: Ralph Bensley lived there alone.

He was a widow, his wife dead from cancer some years ago. It was unfortunate timing for Bensley, because in just another week he had planned to put the house up for sale. It didn't make sense his living in that large house all alone—it was too much for one person. There were no children to speak of, their having graduated from college and already moved out a long time ago. A small townhome was all the CIA Head of Resource Management needed at that point in his life.

Putting the house up for sale, and the resultant foot traffic, would surely have been enough to scare away Mitslov and Treshenko, or at least discourage them in their efforts. Mitslov couldn't believe his luck when Spence had originally given Bensley up: a man who would have access to everything in the human resources database for his division, carte blanche as far as names were concerned. It was too good to be true.

But it *was* true. A double agent within the CIA had helped confirm it, right at the time—right in the middle of Mitslov's interrogation of Spence.

First recruited over a decade ago, the FSB took advantage of an intricate confluence of psychological, socio-economic, and physical conditions associated with the double agent at the time. The FSB then slowly and carefully nurtured its relationship with him as the double agent gradually solidified his standing within the CIA. Only on rare occasion did the FSB actually call upon him to do something, and it was never too extreme; usually it was something as simple as delivering a trace amount of intelligence. The Russians purposefully overpaid him for these services, thereby helping keep him in the fold. Secret payments into shell accounts were the salve against any latent guilt he might otherwise experience, and they also helped keep his attention and fuel his stamina over the years. Finally, a more important need for his help arose. It would come from an unidentified man who would call him within a certain timeframe and request verification of a certain name or two. The double agent had already laid the groundwork. He had taken advantage of the circumstances surrounding a certain woman in HUMINT, a woman who had fallen for him. The double agent made sure to let the FSB know of this woman when he first snared her, all in the hopes of elevating his status in their eyes, maybe even garnering bigger payments.

And when she was called upon for a one-time favor—the double agent insisted it would only be that once—she begrudgingly complied. It was *she* that verified the name of Ralph Bensley in the database. She knew it was wrong, but the double agent was too good at coaxing her. Just this once, he insisted, hopefully never again. Don't worry about what it's about; it's an "internal" thing, just something to help get a long-overdue promotion. But why at such a strange time? she pushed back. Why did it have to be just then? Never mind about that, he responded, it had to be; it's complicated. *Please*, just this once, he would say to her as his hand fondled her breast over her shirt while she sat in the dark room in front of the computer terminal. She was too lonely, too smitten for a man half her age to refuse, too weak to question it like she should have. The sexual favors she received afterward almost made her forget what she had done.

The double agent was the key, there was no doubt about it, Mitslov thought to himself. He was the one who made it all possible. When Mitslov was dealing the punishment to Spence, pulverizing his face and pumping him for information, there would've been no way to trust what Spence said under such duress, full well knowing that he was probably trained not to betray his brethren, even under such severe conditions. That's where the double agent's lover came in: Mitslov would have the double agent contact her real-time, have her check the data base, and verify the veracity of the name Spence provided. When it all went down at the barbershop and Arthur Spence saw that the first name he gave was quickly debunked by someone on the other end of a cell phone, he relented from the torture and provided a name in truth: Ralph Bensley.

It was the jackpot!

So much so that Mitslov couldn't believe it at first when the order was given for him to stay on track with his original directive and maintain his quest for the woman. Mitslov considered the potential, the names this man Bensley, a Head of Resource Management, could give up. In the end, however, he understood the restraint; he understood why the limited directive was maintained: such overt action against a high-ranking official within the CIA would certainly trigger conflict and tension of a scale not seen since the cold war, which was to be avoided at all cost.

So that would be the tricky part: getting the information he needed from Bensley without killing the man—to let him live and thereby demonstrate to the CIA that the pursuit of information was contained, the scope of the pursuit limited. Limited to only the information necessary to find the woman. If Mitslov did it right the assault on Bensley would be perceived as merely the relentless pursuit of the woman, a Russian traitor, and nothing more. Although such pursuit on American soil was still an extreme action on Russia's part, it was not out of the realm of plausible reactions to the vagaries a CIA operative committed on Russian soil while trying to "steal away" a prized Russian scientist along with the woman. Equally important, keeping the scope limited to the pursuit of the woman and not allowing it to spill into anything broader would hopefully prevent the double agent from being discovered. Too much time and too many resources had been invested in him for his cover to be blown by this side mission. No, Mitslov understood. He got it. And he would remain focused on the singular task assigned to him and his partner Treshenko: the woman known as Anna Czolski.

He had developed his plan for Ralph Bensley as he staked the place out over the past week. Penetrating the house directly was out of the question; the security system was too sophisticated. Mitslov knew it couldn't be disabled from the outside. Even if he got in, he couldn't take the chance of being caught interrogating Bensley.

He would have to be patient, to lie in wait for the opportunity to present itself. Friday morning was trash pickup, and Mitslov noticed the previous week that Bensley put his out at about 10:30 P.M. the evening before. He was hoping the same thing would happen that Thursday evening.

Mitslov lay in wait in the back yard, just at the edge of the darkness.

It wasn't long before Bensley came out in his pajamas. The light over the garage door automatically turned on when the sensor detected Bensley's movement in the driveway.

"Who is that," Bensley said, the plastic garbage can pulled behind him on its wheels. "Who's there?"

Mitslov didn't hesitate when he was spotted. His appearance had the effect he had intended, startling Bensley and freezing him. He dashed into the light and slammed his fist into the side of Bensley's face, knocking him to the ground and unconscious.

Security camera footage later showed that Bensley was jumped by a man dressed all in black, a dark ski mask over his head and completely covering his face. The last thing seen was Bensley being slung over the man's shoulder, and then the two of them disappeared from view. Needless to say, that footage would be studied *ad nauseam* for clues.

Bensley awoke and found himself in the back seat of the Chevy, his hands tied, his eyes blindfolded. He could tell the car was moving, taking him somewhere.

Bensley offered, "Whoever you are, you don't know what you're doing." No response. "You have no idea who I am." Still nothing. "Let me out, you son of a bitch! Let me out and you can be on your way…no ramifications. I promise."

Mitslov, who was sitting next to him as Treshenko drove, rammed an elbow into the side of Bensley's face, then another, the second more powerful than the first. It was enough to shut Bensley up and almost knock him unconscious again. Mitslov put a gag over his mouth just in case.

Eventually the car arrived at a junk yard. Treshenko turned the car's lights off as he drove it further into the area, being cautious in case someone was there.

When the car stopped, Bensley felt himself being pulled out of the car. Treshenko reached under Bensley's arms and dragged him into a small area surrounded by a wall of scrap metal. Bensley was seated on the hood of a car that had been chopped off and was lying on the ground. His blindfold and gag were still in place. Then he heard a voice. It was in English but with a heavy Russian accent.

"I'm going to take the gag off. We're going to talk."

Bensley felt fingers against his face as the gag was removed. The blindfold remained, but the minute the gag was removed Bensley started to scream.

Treshenko immediately punched him in the mouth, knocking Bensley sideways and to the ground, his hands unable to stop his falling over as they were still tied behind his back.

"I don't want to hurt you, I just need a little information," Mitslov said to him as Treshenko helped him sit back up on the hood.

"You can go to hell," Bensley said.

There was stillness after that. Bensley sat silent, waiting for whatever might come next, but there was nothing.

"I need a name," Mitslov finally said. "You're going to give me a name. That's all it takes, and then we leave you alone. Make it easy on yourself. Not like your old friend. What was his name...Spence? Arthur Spence?"

Bensley's head tilted upward, like he was trying to look at something even though he was blindfolded.

"Ah, yes, you know about him, eh? You don't want to suffer like he did, do you? Just give me a name and we'll leave you alone."

Again Bensley mustered his energy. He took a deep breath and screamed at the top of his lungs.

Treshenko punched him in the mouth again. This time two teeth were dislodged as Bensley fell over. Treshenko sat him back up and then punched him in the stomach. Bensley buckled in pain. Treshenko sat him up yet again.

Mitslov said, "You're not going to tell me anything, are you, Bensley? You're too strong. Is that what it is? Well, we are prepared for that."

Fear came over Bensley. He braced himself for the worst, but nothing immediately came. There was only silence. He thought he heard footsteps, someone walking away, leaving. It didn't make sense. Then he heard running; someone was running toward him. A powerful body suddenly slammed into him and knocked him over, forcing the wind out of him. The full weight of Treshenko's large body remained on top of Bensley. A hand went over Bensley's mouth, and another pinched his nostrils shut. With the wind knocked out of him, Bensley struggled to breathe— muffled sounds, the fear of suffocating.

With his mouth and nose still covered, Bensley was punched in the stomach. He still couldn't breathe; they were killing him.

Just before he was about to pass out he felt a needle being stuck into his arm. In all the struggle and gasping for breath, he felt it. Without knowing what it was, he relented, relaxing his muscles. The heavy body remained on top of him, but the hand pinching his nostrils was removed, allowing him to breathe furiously through his nose. Then Treshenko took his hand off of Bensley's mouth.

Bensley became even more relaxed. He lost the urge to scream and began to feel light-headed.

"It's taking its effect," Bensley heard someone say.

His cheek was slapped a few times as if trying to revive him. Really, however, it was a verification that the drug was working.

Once again the double agent was waiting with his lover in a dark office at Langley; she reluctantly sat at the computer screen, ready to access the database. He had coaxed her to cooperate one last time. This was it, he promised, she wouldn't have to do it again after this. He even persuaded her with sexual favors ahead of time; more would follow, he promised, just check the names he gave her; after this they would be together forever. She almost cried as she complied, knowing that what she was doing was wrong, but too weak to resist. He fondled and caressed her as she typed into the computer, kissing her face and neck, reassuring her that it was alright. He spoke on a disposable cell phone with Mitslov as he did so.

Bensley awoke early the next morning with no physical harm to his body, save for the two missing teeth and a swollen mouth from the punches to his face. His blindfold had been removed.

It was cold outside, a fog was in the air, and he found himself in the middle of a junkyard, lying in the dirt on the ground, still bound at the arms. He was curled up in the fetal position and shivering.

The smell of the Potomac River was in the air. He knew the smell, knew he was close to it. His head hurt and he had dry mouth: the tell-tale signs of Sodium Pentothal. He tried to think back to what happened, what he might have said, but he couldn't remember. His recollection was as blank as the air around him.

It was a brazen assault, Mitslov thought to himself as he lay in his bed and reflected on what he and his partner had done to Bensley the previous night. They were getting into it deeper and deeper. The more they did, the more they risked being caught. For the first time, he truly questioned what they were doing. The long investment of time, the potential exposure of the double agent so painstakingly developed, the sacrifices he and Treshenko had made, and for what? Who was this woman? She hardly seemed worth it. He and Treshenko had been living in the United States on expired visas for over two years. Two years of lying low, living in the dumpy apartment, nothing to do, and then *this* was the mission they were given?

Anger welled up in him. It was an effort for him to suppress it, yet he knew he had to. Otherwise he would drive himself crazy. There was no place for doubt—that would be the end of him. Doubt would have prevented him from being able to kill like he had to, and from killing again like he knew he would need to.

He had to stay the course, follow orders to the end. Blind obedience. He'd go insane if he didn't. The life he led would mentally crush him. As if to confirm this, he looked around at the small, squalid room in which he and Treshenko lived—it all seemed to look back upon him and mock him.

He shook it off. He had what he needed now, he told himself. Czolski was within reach. Now all he wanted to do was get it over with. Then this crazy mission would be over. He refused to think about what might come next. He hoped home, a return to Russia. That would only be possible, he realized, if he could get to that woman without being caught in the process. With all the luck he had experienced up until then, he still wasn't sure he could. Not after what they did to Bensley.

It was time to drink. To drink to oblivion. To once again sterilize his brain and cauterize the bloody memories of his actions.

"Let's drink, Mitslov," Treshenko said all of a sudden, as if he were having the same thoughts as Mitslov.

"Eh? Ah, yes, let's."

"We drink to home. To Russia. It's getting closer, eh?"

"Mm."

As Mitslov reached for the bottle of vodka and poured them each a glass, Treshenko said, "By the way, I meant to ask you before..."

Mitslov was already drinking. "Yes, what is it?"

"I don't get it with the Sodium Pentothal."

"Eh? What do you mean?"

"Well, we took great pains to keep our questioning of the man limited to only the woman. We did that so that the CIA wouldn't...so that they would take it as a sign—a signal that our search was narrow in scope, right?"

"Yes, that's right."

"But how will the CIA know what we even asked about? The Sodium Pentothal will make the man forget everything."

Mitslov pondered this question for a moment and slowly drank from his glass. He looked at Treshenko. "They'll find out about our questions. They'll use their own techniques to do so. The Sodium Pentothal may make Bensley forget, but it won't wipe his memory; our questions are still there, lingering within his subconscious."

"ATMs Experience Large-Scale Attacks"
IP Newswire
[Excerpt: June 26]

In the latest of a string of hacks against the nation's financial infrastructure, the Federal Government has sent notices to banking institutions around the country to warn of a new type of attack. Withdrawal limits in ATM machines were circumvented. In an odd twist, the manipulation allowed more money to be withdrawn from individual accounts than was actually in those accounts. The ATM machine was, in essence, instantaneously drained of all its currency in a single transaction.

By the time the matter was discovered, over $70 million dollars had been taken from ATMs in several states across the northeast. Regulators are enforcing quick upgrades to ATM software, requiring that the vulnerability be patched before any particular ATM machine is reactivated for service.

Regulators have also generally warned that there has been a significant, dramatic rise in the number of cyber attacks on banking institutions. The ATM hack is only one example of the large number and breadth of attacks involved. The U.S. Senate Committee on Banking has called a special session to address this alarming trend.

10

Loss Leads to a Lament

NSA Headquarters
OPS2A Building-VENOMA
Saturday, June 27

THE PRESSURE ON THE U.S. INTELLIGENCE COMMUNITY grew as the cyber attacks increased. The latest string of attacks was different than those of the June 6th variety. While more isolated and unrelated to each other as compared to what happened at DFW, they nonetheless inflicted significant financial damage. The newer attacks seemed to be focused exclusively on financial institutions, or at least on financial gain. Nothing was safe or off limits. The net effect was that a lot of money was siphoned out of the U.S. economy.

It was certainly an inconvenience for the individuals personally affected, but in the end, Federal deposit insurance, banking laws, and other types of commercial guarantees served as the salve against any real long term pain. For financial institutions and the Federal Government, however, that was another story. They were left holding the bag and footing the bill. The U.S. Department of the Treasury couldn't print money fast enough to replace what was stolen. Cyber crime was growing at an exceptional rate—one that could not be absorbed much longer without grave effect on the national economy.

Also alarming was that every time the newest defense mechanisms were installed to safeguard assets, every time a gaping security hole in a piece of software was patched, another vulnerability seemed to be discovered. It was as if some great criminal mastermind constantly raised the bar and found newer, ever more creative exploits. Criminal enterprises had seemingly become IT powerhouses in their own right, growing richer by the day. And yet, it was all "clean"—not a shot fired, not a drop of blood spilled.

While the Intelligence Community dealt with this new wave of financial cyber attacks, Big Machine worked on Ørsted and Frëge. Bandwidth was consumed at a phenomenal rate, terabyte after terabyte of information scanned from the internet seeking information that might aid in the analysis—some relationship between all of the malware, a trail that would lead to what was postulated as the "super-entity" behind it all. Every make, model, serial number, and system configuration of every pc, server, router, hub, switch, and programmable logic device that was subject to the June 6th attacks was fed to and processed by Big Machine. Hashing permutations, salted paths and executable name pairs, semi-prime number calculations, it was all simulated a million times over in all possible combinations. Still, however, there was no solution to Frëge's encryption and no clue as to the entity behind the attack.

While Big Machine toiled away, the financial cyber attacks continued. Large sums of money disappeared. Answers were needed. It was imperative that a solution to the problem be found. Freedman himself felt the heat from the President. "This cannot continue, this operating in the dark, twiddling one's thumbs waiting for a machine to spit out an answer," the President was overheard lamenting. "Meanwhile, the country is bleeding money. And to where? To whom? We don't even know."

At just about the time when morale reached its lowest, when it began to feel like the only solution would be to shut everything down, rip out all the electronic infrastructure, and start all over again, there was an important development.

The manner in which this took place was quite extraordinary in its own right. The Ørsted/Frëge malware pair was the first big assignment for the government's newly procured, massively parallel supercomputer. In fact, it was the first supercomputer of its kind, and no one, not even its creators, completely understood its full capabilities.

Big Machine had been parsing the millions of computational threads as it sought to crack Frëge's encryption, continually pulling massive amounts of data from the internet, and as it did so it zeroed in on an important data point associated with some of the most recent financial attacks. From this most minute thread of information—a faint relationship between data from opposite sides of the world—Big Machine autonomously formed new inquiries, and then new paths of investigation, working back and forth between the present and the past. Pre-programmed correlation thresholds were automatically modified and adjusted, new ones created, all without those overseeing the operation of Big Machine ever knowing the difference. It was what the creators of Big Machine had envisioned all along: figuratively large gaps in the instruction set, dangling, unutilized strings of code, and extra stores of undefined, unused subroutine variables made available, all for the purpose of accommodating autonomous expansion of processing algorithms—Big Machine would learn and reprogram itself as it grew older. Highly complex artificial intelligence was the engine that fueled such "intellectual" growth.

And so it was that Big Machine discovered something. It was the occurrence of an event that, to the supercomputer itself, was nothing more than a simple, straightforward occurrence of a mathematical relationship, a collection of ones and zeros characterized by certain combinatorial traits. In human terms, however, it was known as something much more significant and wonderful: a lead!

It was Saturday, 2 A.M. when Q-Directorate got the call. He wasn't upset in the least when he had to reach from his bed to grab the phone. He was waiting for such a call, dreaming of it, that Cyberknife would call him out of the night, a breakthrough ready to be announced.

"We have something...can I talk?" said the caller.

"Hell no!" Q-Directorate responded, half smiling at the news. "I'm assuming this is big enough that I should come in, based upon your calling me in the middle of the night?"

"I think so...it's kind of..."

"Don't say anything. I'll be there in thirty...forty-five minutes. Keep at it. I'll be there."

"Of course."

Later that day at 7 P.M., after a full day of people canceling plans and rearranging schedules, those in the D.C. area that were available gathered at VENOMA for another briefing. It was envisioned that the room might only be half full, not only because it was Saturday night, but also because fatigue had set in and morale wasn't great. In fact the room was packed, with even more people standing at the back. All of the heavyweights were there and sat in the front rows. A formal briefing had not occurred for some time, and everyone was hungry for information and anxious for progress.

"We've got a lot of new information to report," Q-Directorate eagerly began as he stood behind the podium on the stage. He could hardly contain his enthusiasm, even as exhausted as he was from lack of sleep.

All of a sudden someone yelled from the back of the room: *"What happened, did Big Machine find its ass?"*

The whole room burst out laughing, as if a pressure valve had been released.

"Shh, quiet, it's listening—you'll hurt its feelings," someone else added. More laughter. The momentum was gaining.

"No, don't tell us: Big Machine was infected with Ørsted."

"Oooh."

Even Q-Directorate laughed, as did the high-ranking officials sitting in the front. A good laugh was just what they needed. Finally, Q-Directorate held up both hands and said, "All right, all right, point of order, gentlemen...and ladies...point of order."

The room settled down—a few coughs, clearing of throats as it were, and the mood grew serious.

"Right. As I was about to say, a lot has happened since our last meeting."

"Please tell us you've cracked Frëge," said someone from the front row.

"No, we can't report that. What I can report is that we've found something significant. The kind of break we've been looking for. The kind that will allow us to act."

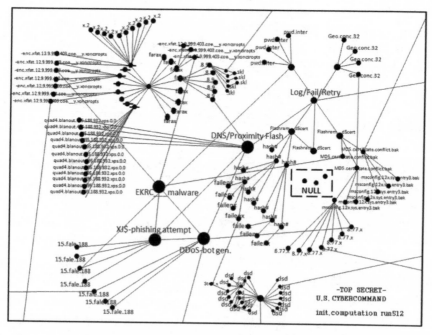

Figure: Partial view of cluster histogram showing correlation between attack threads.

"Referring to the figure, this cluster histogram depicts the results of an analysis related to the June 6th attacks. Notice the high correlations among the subcomponents. Some of the linkage, if you will, is surprisingly rudimentary: packet header redundancy, substantially similar but non-standard IP routing..."

"What would be considered non-standard?" someone from the audience immediately asked, a technologist from the middle of the room.

"An inefficient path—one so indirect that the route was clearly for purposes other than speed or efficiency. In other words, one used to mask the source. Look at it this way: even though we can't trace particular attack threads all the way back to their points of origin, we can make assumptions about them along the way by virtue of header extension changes. When that's done, one can see, for lack of a better term, an exaggerated zig-zag route that's clearly inefficient...grossly so," Q-Directorate answered. "Anyway, through a combination of IP geolocation, net interrogations, 'tracert' command analysis, and ping-length triangulation, we also found geographic interdependencies in almost every malicious event recorded. Everything, that is, except for the three events shown in the box labeled 'Null.' "

All heads moved in unison to look at that portion of the figure.

"These three events represent an anomaly—isolated occurrences in the DFW, Loixe Oil, and PacNorthern Rail attack threads. Route tracing and correlation analysis were uneventful. There's, uh...there's even speculation that these three items represent a type of temporary portal for each of the attacked networks, thereby allowing the delivery of Frëge, and enabling the most serious phase of the attacks."

"Wait," Q-Directorate stopped himself and said, "I'm getting ahead of myself. Let me back up. Sorry." He scratched his head out of nervousness. "This information was gathered real-time, right up to the beginning of this meeting, so bear with me." Q-Directorate looked at his handwritten notes resting on the podium to further collect his thoughts.

"As I was saying, when Big Machine initially identified the three anomalous events, there was no correlation found between them and any of the other attack threads. In fact, it was remarkable that Big Machine even classified the sparse code as separate events, given how little of it there was. Remember the memory fragmentation we showed at an earlier meeting, and how we believed large portions of Ørsted were disaggregated after the attacks? We now believe that's not necessarily the case, at least not for all of it. It may have been just plain deleted. Large portions of Ørsted deleted until needed again, in which case it would be delivered when called upon.

"Big Machine flagged the three code fragments and found an ever-so-slight correlation, not with any of the other attack threads, but with each other. The correlation was extremely low because all it comprised was a unique character string present in a 'comment' portion of a header in each fragment."

Q-Directorate advanced the slide presentation and displayed a code fragment with an embedded programming comment:

```
Section Table
  01 T3RROR
    VirtSize:          0001A674  VirtAddr:         00001000
    raw data offs:     00000400  raw data size:    0001A800
    relocation offs:   00000000  relocations:      00000000
    line # offs:       00000000  line #'s:         00000000
    characteristics:   60000020
    CODE  EXECUTE  READ  ALIGN_DEFAULT(16)
```

Q-Directorate continued, "Compilers use specific names for each section of an executable. It appears that this header fragment is associated with an instruction to call the section 'T-3-R-R-0-R,' or as I'll occasionally pronounce it, 'Terror.' "

There was a small stir in the room.

"Obviously this term caught our attention, what with the number '3' replacing the letter 'E' and the number '0' replacing the 'O,' as well as the connotation of the word itself. Who is it? *What* is it? The answer to that is the key.

"At first, Big Machine didn't seem to know what to make of the term, but it created a new processing thread, a big one by all accounts, and continued to investigate it. Then Big Machine kept referring back to the thread, considering it again and again, including it in the context of other extraneous data, such as data associated with the more recent financial cyber attacks occurring across the country.

"It turns out that there's extremely high occurrence of this term in the internet with the unique spelling. For example, the first instance we found was as a gamer-tag for someone registered for a particular online first-person-shooter videogame. Big Machine checked the game's server log database, traced registration of the name to a credit card, and then we got an expedited search warrant for the address corresponding to the card. It turned out to be a fourteen year old boy in Hauppauge, New York. There was no suspicious internet activity associated with the household, so that case was ruled out, the unique spelling of 'Terror' deemed a coincidence. Big Machine parsed through a multitude of other use cases like this, each one unfortunately leading to a dead end."

Ernest McCoy, CIA Deputy Director, interrupted to ask a question. "I'm gonna go on a tangent for a second, but any chance Big Machine did a search like this on the Russian phrase that was streamed across CNN during the DFW attack? Was there anything found with that?"

"No. I mean, yes, Big Machine did perform such a search, but no, no other instances of it were found," Q-Directorate responded. He waited to see if there were any follow-up questions. Looking into the audience, he saw McCoy urge him to continue.

"Now, as I was saying, Big Machine was running into dead ends—we watched real-time as Big Machine spit out result after result for each investigative thread. But then Big Machine zeroed in on something…a particular instance of the term on the internet: it was on VKontakte, a type of Russian Facebook. What you're seeing now is a private page on VKontakte of a person named Sergei Strenzke. Actually, the page is technically not available anymore; it was posted over four years ago and then taken down a day and a half later; PRISM has been mirroring everything on the site for years, and Big Machine found it in the archive. Notice the photo in the lower right-hand corner as I scroll down the page."

Q-Directorate scrolled down and then clicked to enlarge the photo. It was the man referred to as Strenzke sitting alongside someone else on a picnic bench, with his arm around the person. A tree partially overhung them, casting a dark shadow on the man sitting next to Strenzke. It was also clear that the photo was doctored so that the shadow on the man's face was darkened even further.

"The caption translates to: 'Me and T3RR0R.' As you can see, the image of the man referred to as Strenzke is relatively clear. Unfortunately the image associated with the person referred to as Terror is obscured. We tried post-capture processing, but the image was flattened; there's nothing we could do to reveal the man's face. Other than this one additional reference, Big Machine could find no other *relevant* instance of T-3-R-R-0-R in the internet, no other clues or information about the man referred to by that name. Nothing. He's a mystery."

Q-Directorate paused for a moment and stared at the photo. He couldn't help from studying it every time he saw it.

"Our belief is that we've uncovered the correct association between the computer program section called 'Terror' and the man with the same name, but we haven't found anything else on him."

The room was extremely quiet. No one stirred.

"It's a different story, however, with Sergei Strenzke. We were able to get some information on him through Interpol; they didn't have anything on him on hand, but they reached out to their contacts in the local Russian police precinct and were able to get some information. Needless to say, Interpol didn't tell the Russians the information was being requested for the benefit of the United States.

"Strenzke was arrested twice, so there was a fairly detailed record on him. Frankly, from what we learned, I'm surprised the whole record wasn't expunged a long time ago. That oversight was a huge break for us. There's even an old transcript of a police interview from his first arrest."

Adlai Corver had something to say. He hadn't had his first interruption yet and he was long overdue. "Why couldn't the so-called *tentacles* of PRISM or Big Machine have found this information instead of having to go to Interpol?" he said, waving his hand in the air to emphasize the point.

"Ah, well, none of the police info was stored electronically. The local precinct hadn't yet electronically scanned all of its old documents into electronic form; it's all paper."

Q-Directorate waited to see if Corver was satisfied with the answer. Corver nodded, and Q-Directorate continued.

"Sergei Strenzke. He's a lifetime hacker with a long history of it. As a boy of thirteen, he created harmless malware, such as a centipede that crawled across the computer display of infected computers, or a rainbow of squares that would take over the screen and flash wildly. This was back in the '80s and was revealed when he bragged about it to the police during the interview I mentioned. You see, in 1987, at the age of seventeen, he was arrested for creating and infecting computers with the "Brain.A" malware, the first virus that took advantage of the boot sector in personal computers. He created a business around it by buying computers infected with his virus, removing the virus, and then reselling the repaired computers for a profit. Believe it or not, that was the first known instance of anyone ever using malware for financial gain. Here's a picture Interpol was able to obtain of him from the arrest."

The photo was of a much younger Strenzke, without the peppered goatee or close-cropped hair he sported in the VKontakte photo.

"His father was a professor at the Saint Petersburg National Research University of Information Technologies, Mechanics and Optics, very prominent. That's likely where Strenzke got his early start in his computer abilities—from his father. According to the interview transcript, when his father first learned of his son's illicit activities, however, which was even before the first arrest, he came down hard on him. Best guess is that it was an embarrassment to the father, and he was furious that his son was using the computer knowledge he taught him for such illegal purposes. Strenzke's mother—again according to the transcript—always stood by her son. She adored him. She didn't condone his activities, but she did her best to protect him from the harsh punishments the father tried to impart, especially when that punishment became physical. When the boy was ultimately caught at the age of seventeen for the Brain.A affair, that was the last straw for the father. He used his connections to help the boy avoid jail time, but there was an altercation between them afterward. Strenzke, however, was stronger than his father, who was in his late fifties, and he nearly beat the man to death in the altercation. The father was hospitalized. The charges against Strenzke were reinstated at the father's request, along with additional charges stemming from the beating the father sustained from the fight. When the mother refused to visit her husband in the hospital, in opposition of his actions toward the son, the marriage ended. Public records show they divorced shortly thereafter. While his son was still in prison, the father resigned his position at the university and moved away, settling in a place called Ryazan, a Russian city located on the Oka River southeast of Moscow. About two years later, not long after the son was coincidentally released from prison, the father was found dead on a local street, mysteriously stabbed to death. The murderer was never found."

"So why wasn't any of *this* information, the stuff about Strenzke's father, found by Big Machine? Surely there were online news reports of that." challenged Corver. He was beginning to be perceived by people in the room as having a somewhat hostile attitude toward the capabilities of the new supercomputer.

"Well, to begin with," began Q-Directorate, "remember, this was a long time ago, before the internet was mainstream. Newspapers weren't online back then, and like the local police reports, I'm guessing all of the old newspapers from that time period haven't been scanned and made available online. There's also another reason." Q-Directorate paused for a moment and fidgeted at the stage a bit. He realized there was an oversight in what he had presented. "I should have made it clearer earlier: the father didn't have the same last name of 'Strenzke.' You see, he wasn't Sergei Strenzke's natural father; Sergei was the mother's son from a previous marriage, and he never took his step-father's name."

Corver said nothing else, a look of exasperation evident on his face.

"Sorry about that. Anyway, getting back to Strenzke himself, something significant happened during that first stint in prison: his mother was killed, gunned down while he served a one-year sentence. The rumor was that the killer was someone from his old neighborhood that was ripped off by the Brain.A scam. As a result of his being sent to prison, and then his mother being murdered while he served his sentence, Strenzke became a different person by the time he got out—more serious, more business-minded, more focused. His hacking methods grew more sophisticated. In 2007, a key-loading virus he created recorded everything a user typed into an infected computer; he saved credit card information entered during online purchases and sold it to others. This was considered state of the art hacking at the time.

"He was arrested again. This time, however, it wasn't for hacking. As I said, he harbored a lot of anger from being in prison, especially because his mother was murdered while he served his sentence. So in addition to becoming more serious about hacking, he also became more ruthless, more violent in nature. He beat in a man's skull with a tire iron. The victim was the person rumored to have killed his mother while he was in jail. A revenge killing. Strenzke was subsequently caught, arrested, and put in prison again. It was during this second stint of one year that he began to form his own criminal gang."

"Wait a minute. How did he get out after only one year?" CIA Deputy Director Ernest McCoy interjected. "He should've been in prison for a lot longer than that for murder. Even in Russia they still generally hold murderers accountable."

"Good question. The answer we got on that is somewhat suspicious. His conviction was overturned; it was determined that some of the evidence used against him was fabricated, and he was released. Our belief is that this wasn't legitimate; there was probably a payoff; someone was able to get him out."

"The record on him becomes quite fuzzy after that, almost non-existent, most of it borderline hearsay. Interpol believes Strenzke runs a highly sophisticated criminal hacking enterprise. There are even advertisements to hire software coders and testers that are attributed to his organization. Interpol has him on their wanted list. Upon further analysis, we believe he still resides in Russia; more particularly, St. Petersburg."

"How do you know this?" came the immediate question from someone in the audience.

"Easy, actually. Here's the only other posting of him from VKontakte: it's an image of his totaled BMW630, with him proudly posing in front of it as it's being hitched to a tow truck, right in front of *Spas na Krovi*; you can see the famous St. Petersburg church in the background. This was in 2013. Obviously his hacking activities were paying off. For Terror, we can't find anything else on him in the internet. Strenzke is almost the same way, but not quite. He's a little cocky. On rare occasion, he'll let something out about himself like this photo. In that one regard he fits the profile of the prototypical hacker: a narcissistic sociopath. Only in this case, it's to the extreme. As we're seeing, he's lethal in the cyber world."

FBI Director Adlai Corver turned to CIA Deputy Director McCoy further down the row and said, "So where does that leave us? Are we on a hunting exhibition? The whole June 6th attack…Ørsted, Frège, it's all Strenzke's criminal organization? The Russian mafia? I kind of find it a little hard to believe, based upon the breadth and sophistication of the attack."

"Our belief is that Strenzke's organization is significant," Q-Directorate quickly responded. "And let's not forget his partner

Terror. Terror must be the architect, the master coder, or something."

"Look, this is great work, Q-Directorate," Corver said. "I don't want to denigrate what's been found. But I just can't see a Russian mafia organization waging the kind of cyber attack that we saw, the hits against significant targets across the country...and remember, they were all synchronous. How would they even recruit the mules to get all the malware into the infected systems, all the way over here in the United States? And then everything was restored at DFW after it all started; there was no permanent damage done. How could they have profited from *that*?" Corver shook his head for a moment. "It doesn't add up. I just don't see it."

"Well, we have no evidence of it yet, but it's possible their organization could be getting help. Maybe a rogue nation is cooperating with them," said Q-Directorate.

"Like Iran or something?" said Holdman.

"Possible...or North Korea, China. We could also be looking at the most sophisticated international criminal effort ever, with the Russian mafia teaming with criminal organizations over here."

"You mean the mob? The mob is cooperating with the Russian mafia?" Holdman said.

Holdman and Corver looked at each other and were incredulous.

Manmoth, ever Q-Directorate's protector, sensed the direction the conversation was taking and turned in his seat and said, "Look, Q-Directorate is just presenting the information. Teams are tackling this as best they can. It's clear we're facing something novel here, and we need to consider all of the possibilities. We're all under a lot of pressure; I get that. Let's keep our cool and think things through. Ideas are going to be floated for consideration, and let's not attack the person throwing them out there." He looked at the audience as he spoke, but the statement was meant for Corver and Holdman, who were becoming almost belligerent in their tone.

"You're right," Corver said, nodding. He raised his hand as if to wave himself off and looked up at Q-Directorate.

After Manmoth turned back around, Director of the NSA General William Powers leaned over toward him, and the others nearby leaned in as well, taking their cue to huddle so they could talk privately for a moment.

"If Q-Directorate is almost done..." Powers started to whisper.

"He is," Manmoth responded. "He's essentially done."

"Okay, good, we need to talk in private. Let's end this and do just that."

"Right," Manmoth said. He looked at Q-Directorate up on the stage and signaled to him. Q-Directorate took the cue.

"Ladies and Gentlemen, that concludes this evening's session," Q-Directorate announced. "Once again, I want to thank you for taking the time on a Saturday night to attend this important meeting. Please continue to monitor your phones and email for messages; if we have more information, we'll reach out to you immediately. In the meantime, continue working on your team assignments."

Everyone left except for the senior representatives of the Intelligence Community, who remained seated in the first two rows. Some of them stood and leaned against the stage. Q-Directorate remained as well.

Holdman waited for the last person to step out of the auditorium, and then he turned to Q-Directorate and spoke. "You said at the beginning that we now have enough information to *act*. What did you mean by that?"

"It means the Secretary of State needs to have a heart-to-heart with our friends in Russia," Freedman answered for Q-Directorate. "We need to chase this guy Strenzke down, get him and his friend, this...*Terror* person, and take them to task. We need to break up their organization and shut it down."

"So we're going to turn it over to Russian officials? Rely on them to fix this mess?" said Corver with a hint of doubt in his voice. "With everything that's going on in that part of the world, and the cold relations we now have with Russia, that seems like a difficult proposition. I'm afraid they'll just laugh at us."

"No, they won't," Freedman answered. "I think we get the Russian Government all over this. Hold them accountable for acts perpetrated against U.S. financial institutions and commercial enterprises. They're already feeling pressure from international sanctions. If we start making public allegations that the Russian Government is openly sanctioning the hacking of U.S. enterprises, that's going to add to the amount of international heat they're feeling. I think we can get them hopping on this one. Meantime, we get our own operation going...move a Cyberknife team out there."

McCoy and Powers nodded in agreement, but Corver said, "Our own operatives in Russia? Are we sure? That would be a huge step; a huge escalation for sure."

"We're working on presidential approval," Freedman calmly responded, a bit perturbed by the question. The issue was outside Corver's domain. "We're going to *need* our own operatives out there, Adlai. Look, our financial losses, the country's financial losses, they're getting too big. It calls for drastic measures, and I don't think anyone wants to trust this solely to Russia. You basically said so yourself."

"I don't know, James," Holdman added. "I'm sort of feeling like Adlai. Russia's motivation to help us is the threat of more international pressure? They've never cared about that before, why would they now? I have a hard time seeing them helping us, especially given the fact that we've already imposed certain economic sanctions against them as we speak."

Freedman became visibly agitated. "Gentlemen, you know as well as I do we've always had a schizophrenic relationship with Russia, at odds with them on some fronts, cooperating with them on others. Hell, we're still using their launch vehicles to get our satellites into space. As far as I'm concerned, Russia helping us to shut down a hacking organization in their own back yard is like them giving us the sleeves off their vest." Freedman paused for a moment and then continued, "You're too new in your position to know about it, Mike, but there's a history of this type of cooperation with Russia. Ask McCoy to tell you about Sabotol later."

"Yeah, but that was a long time ago, James," Corver quickly interrupted. "What about Snowden? We didn't get any help there."

"That's different, Adlai, and you know it," Freedman responded with an intense glare.

The matter was settled. The President would be briefed on the matter the next day, along with the recommendation for a covert team to be sent into Russia. The U.S. would have to cooperate with Russia to obtain as much information and help as possible, but in the end, CIA agents might need to do the heavy lifting.

Q-Directorate spoke. "I need to add another important piece of information." All eyes turned to him. "Everyone knows about the situation in our financial sector: last week alone over two-hundred-fifty million dollars were lost through hacking and system exploits. As was said before, our national banking infrastructure is under siege. And in the background of all this, Big Machine identified another curious anomaly."

"Great. Here we go again," said Corver.

"Yes, well, an unusually large amount of 'put' options are being traded in the stock market. In fact, put options for every Fortune 500 company have been systematically purchased at historic levels. They were purchased under a multitude of shell accounts, via gradual, systematic accumulation. This activity flew under the radar for quite some time because of the stealth fashion in which the options were purchased; it's only now receiving coverage in the investment community. Give or take a few days, all of the puts have the same maturity date, July 28. That's only thirty-one days away!"

"Sorry, I don't make enough money to completely understand the implications. Put options: help us 'laypeople' understand what this means," ventured Corver, never afraid to speak up.

"Basically, put options are bets that the market is going to fall," offered McCoy. "Someone out there, or some entity, is making a huge bet that the stock market is going to go down, and that it's going to happen in the next thirty-one days."

"That's right," confirmed Q-Directorate. "And something would have to cause the market to fall. We believe that something is Frëge—the full-fledged unleashing of it. It will be invoked on a massive scale, wreaking havoc to our country's infrastructure. Thirty-one days is our deadline!"

This new development was news to everyone. It caused complete silence. Everyone remained still for a moment.

"Shit," McCoy finally said. "That's not a lot of time."

"We need to stop Frëge before it goes off," said Freedman, a grave tone in his voice. "I don't care how we do it...decrypt it, find Strenzke and Terror...we can't let Frëge cripple this country. Powers and McCoy, I want you with me and Bradley when we brief the President. We need to get this Russian cooperation going ASAP."

Everyone stood up to leave.

"And one more thing," Freedman added. "You all know this, but I'm going to say it anyway. We need to limit disclosure on this to an absolute minimum. Keep it on a strict need-to-know basis. It can't get leaked. Period."

11

Experimental Quintet

Monday, June 29
[T$_{detonate}$ minus 29 days]

Transcript (Partial): Subcommittee on National Security

Status: Closed session

Classification: Top Secret

Number in attendance: 4
(not including stenographer; fourth person remained silent)

—Redacted per authority under 50 U.S.C. §1 et seq.

.
.
.

Banks: Who was it?

Undisclosed#1: Ralph Bensley.

Banks: Is he dead?

Undisclosed#1: [Redacted]…questioned under the influence of Sodium Pentothal.

Banks: Damn. So it's what we thought. Arthur Spence's murder wasn't just a coincidence.

Undisclosed#1: No, it wasn't. We can put that notion to bed after Bensley.

Banks: Still, it's curious to leave such a "calling card" with Arthur. It put us on alert. It's as if someone wanted us to be aware of it, throwing it in our faces if you will.

Undisclosed#1: A mind game; took Gordon's shooting of the agent in Russia and threw it right back at us in the form of Spence's mangled body. That was your theory in the first place. Clearly someone devious is calling the shots on this one. What's concerning is the larger implications of it all. The brazen nature of it is alarming, not to mention the fact that results are being obtained. They're making their way up the chain until they find what they need. Spence was out of it for twenty years; now they got to someone in active service. And the speed, just as disturbing. Phone records for cell-sites covering both areas are being checked, all registrations during the time periods in question tracked down. There has to be someone that's verifying names. Spence and Bensley were good; they knew they couldn't give anybody up. They must have gotten to a point where they couldn't fake it. Verification...from the inside.

Banks: [Redacted]...It's possible this isn't under official sanction.

Undisclosed#1: True. Could be someone going rogue. It doesn't really matter, though, does it?

Banks: Sure it does. It makes all the difference in the world.

Undisclosed#1: [Block Redaction].

Banks: Angstrom needs to be notified of that. We need to tell him. He can't be blind.

Undisclosed#1: [Block Redaction].

Banks: Well then, the question is whether we should move her. [Unintelligible]...target?

Undisclosed#1: [Block Redaction].

Banks: He won't go for that. He's developed a significant emotional attachment to her. That's clear. They even went skiing together. There's no way in hell he'll agree to that. As soon as he finds out...[Interrupted].

Undisclosed#1: [Block Redaction].

Banks: Are you sure? Can that even be done? In all my years...

—*Request for counsel noted; request deferred*—

Undisclosed#2: [Redacted]...legal review...[Redacted]...already obtained anticipatory declaratory judgment from FINT per Title 50.

Undisclosed#3: Fred, you understand this is a unique situation. We're covering new ground here. Critical to national security.

Banks: Of course. Certainly. Tell me, exactly how would you like me to put it to him?

Undisclosed#1: [Block Redaction].

Banks: Should I leave that part up to him, or is someone else making that call? I would suggest...[Interrupted].

Undisclosed#1: [Block Redaction].

Banks: Got it. We'll need to monitor it closely...monitor them. He's one of the most loyal we've got, but everyone has his limit. By the way, let the record reflect that my request for counsel was rescinded based upon the assurances I received as part of this discussion, which I understand may ultimately be redacted.

Undisclosed#3: Noted.

—*End of transcript*—

* * *

"So how's my man in charge?" Gordon said as he entered the small conference room.

"Gordon, a pleasure, as always," Angstrom said as he stood and shook Gordon's hand.

The formality was somewhat tongue-in-cheek, and they grinned at each other as they sat down. Angstrom and Gordon had known each other a long time, having been on many missions together over the years. Both had been top field operatives on Garrett's small team; they last worked together on the mission that brought Davis to the United States, which was right before Garrett retired.

Gordon was one of the few truly good friends Angstrom had— one of the few people he really trusted. That trust came gradually, only after having been on countless missions together, overcoming severe challenges and relying upon each other in the direst of situations.

Gordon was almost as good a field operative as Angstrom was: intelligent, daring, and having that special instinct that only the exceptional few possessed. One difference between them, however, was their physical stature. While Angstrom was tall, thick-boned, and muscular, Gordon was of average height and build, much more flexible and quicker than Angstrom—a power hitting right fielder versus the agile shortstop. Their looks differed all the way down to their hair styles (which, in essence, reflected their respective personalities). Angstrom had black hair combed formally to the side and back, with slightly graying temples, a gel holding it neatly in place, whereas Gordon had brown hair kept loosely to the side and left to move about freely.

Their demeanors were different as well. Gordon was lighthearted and had a sense of humor, one of the few people who could even evoke humor from Angstrom. There was often a banter between them, even under extreme circumstances. It seemed like the more the pressure involved, the more the banter, as if their exchanges were demonstrations of strength, an ability to not crack under pressure and maintain one's composure even under the most severe situations. It caught others off-guard when they witnessed it, not so much with respect to Gordon, but definitely with Angstrom, as the joking was so unlike his otherwise reserved, serious nature.

One peculiar aspect regarding Gordon was that no one knew his real last name—not even Angstrom. Angstrom wasn't even sure "Gordon" was his real *first* name. His background was completely erased from records. The last name "Levitt" was displayed on his employee badge, but it wasn't real. He took whatever identity was necessary for a particular mission, and the CIA fabricated the documentation to support it. Angstrom learned of this fact about a year after Gordon joined Garrett's team: Angstrom decided to do his own background check on him and couldn't find anything. Gordon wasn't listed in any of the accessible databases, not even the one used to obtain a colleague's office telephone number. When Angstrom did a search in publicly available records, there was nothing but the superficial for a man named Gordon Levitt. Ultimately Angstrom approached Garrett about it, and it was then that he was informed of Gordon's "bleached" background. It was something new that Garrett had done with Gordon when he recruited him. When Garrett originally suggested to the administration that Gordon's identity remain a secret and that his background get bleached, they liked the idea and approved it, even adopting the technique for a select number of other specialized agents that met certain criteria.

Only in some obscure, highly guarded location could Gordon's true background be found. Angstrom supposed that in his new role he could access it if he wanted to, but he didn't. It was better that way.

Sometimes Angstrom wished the bleaching would have been done for him too, but he had too much history and extended family for that to have been possible. Garrett intimated as much. Gordon was a special case: no family, low profile, a loner in college. So one day some ten years ago a man showed up in Garrett's organization, from nobody knows where, and went by the name "Gordon."

Another key attribute of Gordon was his ability to speak fluent Russian in several dialects. It enabled him to do a lot of work on missions with a Russian slant. He was the one who went into Russia to help Davis defect and ended up shooting an FSB agent twice in the process: once in the elbow, once in the opposite ankle (a strategic measure to incapacitate without killing).

"Our first *team* meeting, eh?" said Gordon. "I finally get to meet the rest of my new friends, after all this time—after all those closed door interviews that you never invited me to, all those expedited background checks and security clearances."

"That's right. I didn't want you to scare any of them away before they got here."

"Heh, funny. I would've loved to have seen you interview them; what a sight that would've been. And to think, they still wanted to join us even after that."

"Careful, Gordon, I can still slam your ass to the mat anytime I need to."

"Sure, sure, I get that. Sure." They both gave a short chuckle, and then there was silence for a moment. Gordon noticed the thin folder resting on the table in front of Angstrom. "What can you tell me about them before they get here?" he said, nodding to the folder.

"Three new additions: two male, one female." He opened the folder slightly, glanced at it, and then said, "The woman's name is Gwen Stafford. She's twenty-seven. Been at the Chicago branch of the FBI for the last five years." He looked up at Gordon, "You want her measurements?"

"Hmph, clever. What happened, did she get tired of fighting gangs…or maybe taking out corrupt politicians?"

"Something like that, actually. She wants international experience, international matters. She's a solid recruit, excellent undercover background, with some intelligence work—domestic, of course."

"What's her strong suit? Does she have a specialty of some kind?"

"Just a solid overall background—impeccable track record. She knows how to handle a weapon; has several kills to her name. Also been on quite a few raids."

"How'd you even find her?"

"Someone higher up dropped her file on my desk."

The two stared at each other for a moment.

"She's solid. This isn't a favor for anyone. I didn't just rely on a paper file; I had HUMINT interview several of her colleagues. I personally talked with her current manager."

"You're okay letting her move into a group like ours, straight from the FBI? That's quite a jump." There was a note of concern evident in Gordon's voice.

"Look, Gordon, we're rebuilding here, make no mistake about it. We've had a lot of time in the field, and the opportunity will definitely be there for more of that. But we need to start growing the team back to strength—to something sustainable. That's not going to be easy or just happen overnight, it's going to take patience. We're going to have to start mentoring, sharing our expertise. We'll do what's prudent, of course, in terms of how much responsibility we give them out in the field, but we need to develop them. I looked at the applicants and their abilities, not just where they're currently at in an organization, and I'm confident these three people"—Angstrom tapped the folder—"are the best options."

"Okaaay…yeah…well, I'm cool with ya' John, you know that, but hell, I don't want to get killed. You know?" Gordon paused for a moment. "Anyway, what kind of missions are they going to throw at us with a team like that, with so many new recruits?"

"That's not going to be an issue, Gordon. In fact, I'm going to talk about that during our meeting today."

Gordon pondered the situation. He still wasn't convinced. Finally, Angstrom said, "Trust me, we're not going to skip a beat. We're going to get our missions."

Gordon took a deep breath. He was trying to get a sense as to what he was getting into. He liked Angstrom—had a great amount of respect for him—but he was concerned about the direction the new team was taking.

"Hey," Angstrom said, "Just remember what you were like when *you* joined Garrett's team way back when: you weren't exactly Jack Reacher."

Gordon still said nothing. Angstrom shrugged his shoulders and said, "Bottom line, you can always go back to Franklin's group. I know you miss that already."

That was enough to prompt Gordon to break his silence. "Yeah, right. Okay, so we're on a *journey* here. Tell me about the other two. Maybe I'll feel better."

"Well, one of them is Thomas J. Reed."

"Ah, the one touted as a young John Angstrom."

"Very funny."

"I'm serious. That's what people call him...well, some people. He's not exactly your look-alike, but he's developing an early track record like you. Anyway, he's a good pick. I'm impressed. And I like how you're poaching him from Franklin."

Angstrom smirked.

"They're going to allow it? I mean, taking someone from Franklin's team?"

"I've been given authority to go inside or out."

Angstrom, Gordon, and Franklin all used to be colleagues in the same group under Garrett. When Garrett started to contemplate his retirement, he needed to pick a successor. When Angstrom experienced a nervous breakdown, Garrett had no choice but to promote Franklin, and people were moved under him. Meanwhile, Banks and Garrett secretly monitored Angstrom's recovery as he toiled away in a temporary desk job. When it was believed that Angstrom had recovered sufficiently to return to duty, he was given a small mission as a test, partnering him with his old friend Gordon to see how he would perform. After the completion of that mission, Banks and Garrett were convinced Angstrom was ready and immediately slated him to replace Garrett (unbeknownst to Franklin). Banks would have to play a more direct role in grooming Angstrom because Garrett retired sooner than expected for health reasons.

"Have you ever worked with Reed before?" Angstrom asked.

"Just once, but he was on the periphery. I didn't really get a chance to see him in action."

"His record is impressive."

"Like I said, people are starting to talk about him like they used to about you. Mind you, he's still young."

"I know, but he's already served key roles in some important missions. He's got excellent field experience."

Just then two people appeared at the door. One was Gwen Stafford, the other, Thomas J. Reed. Stafford knocked on the door. "Hello. Looks like you guys beat us here. Can we come in?" she said while chewing some gum.

"Hello, Gwen. You bet. Come on in. Gordon and I were just catching up on some things," Angstrom replied.

Gordon studied Stafford and Reed as introductions were made. He studied Reed first—the man whose reputation preceded him. He seemed young. Confident, but young. Reed realized he was being watched, and while Stafford spoke, he nodded to Gordon, who did not return the gesture and instead turned his attention to Stafford, who was busy explaining her background. She was about 5'9" with red hair, slightly curly, falling a couple of inches below her shoulders. A few freckles dotted her cheeks. She had large, deep-blue eyes and somewhat thick eyelashes. She also had a "killer" body, obviously the result of a lot of workouts. Not bad, Gordon thought, quite a beauty. Stafford continued to talk while he studied her. The red hair was striking; he couldn't get over it. Then something dawned on him: she had red hair just like Angstrom's ex-wife Breann used to have, even styled the same way. He immediately turned to Angstrom, who was already looking at him like he was reading his mind.

Angstrom continued to watch Gordon and ever-so-slightly nodded, as if he were saying: *Has nothing to do with it, don't even go there.*

Gordon gave a slight smile.

Stafford noticed the exchange and said, "I'm sorry, did I miss something?"

Gordon became slightly embarrassed. He underestimated her and didn't think she would've noticed the subtle exchange between Angstrom and himself. Angstrom chuckled and waited to see how Gordon would wiggle his way out of it.

Gordon was just about to say something but stopped when he noticed someone else at the door. The others turned to look, and Stafford's eyes opened wide, unable to control her initial surprise at seeing the man.

It was Magdos. His entire frame filled the doorway, and he said nothing as he stood there. The small conference room suddenly seemed cramped.

"Ah, everyone, I'd like you to meet Gino Magdos, another member of our team," said Angstrom as he reached over to shake his hand. "I guess that completes the quintet."

No one caught Angstrom's jazz reference. They were too preoccupied with comprehending the new person that had entered the room.

As Stafford and Reed introduced themselves to him, Gordon shot a subtle glance over to Angstrom. This time there was no smile, just a raised eyebrow, as if he were asking: *Where'd you find this guy?* A look of satisfaction came over Angstrom.

When introductions were over, Angstrom jumped to a new topic, Cyberknife. He gave them the background on the original cyber attacks, the ongoing financial assaults, and the recent clues found by a supercomputer the government simply referred to as "Big Machine."

"Secretary of State Mark Creighton is meeting with the Foreign Minister of Russia to discuss some of the evidence that's been uncovered," Angstrom continued. "We're lobbying for Russia's cooperation and permission to have our personnel there to help."

"You're kidding," said Reed. "Will they agree to that? U.S. agents in Russia?"

"We're not positioning it as agents per se, just government *'officials,'* although we all know they'll be agents. And we're framing the issue as an international criminal matter. The thinking is that Russia's under such international pressure from what they're doing in the Ukraine that they'll jump at the opportunity to help. Cooperating with us to shut down an international hacking enterprise is the least they could do. It would be the classic case of two hostile countries cooperating on a limited, isolated basis, each with self-serving motives. Russia could publicize its 'benevolent' action to the rest of the world, and the U.S. would take down the most sophisticated and dangerous cyber criminal enterprise out there."

"So what does this mean?" said Gordon. "The five of us going into Russia and sitting across the table from them to have a discussion? To help them shut it all down? Find this man *Terror,* along with his friend Strenzke, and put an end to it? Our covers will be blown—our pictures in every espionage database around the world. That's a lot different than the deep cover missions we're used to."

That last statement stung Angstrom a bit, causing a subtle change in his expression. Gordon noticed and immediately regretted saying what he did, especially in front of the others. Perhaps he had gone too far, he thought, but he was concerned about what was being proposed.

"It's not going to involve only the five of us," Angstrom responded. "Part of Franklin's team will be involved as well."

Gordon paused, not wanting to say more with everyone else around, but mentioning Franklin didn't help the situation. Angstrom sensed the tension; he knew that Gordon's being aligned with him over the years caused the friction between Franklin and Angstrom to spill over to Gordon by association. That was why Gordon didn't hesitate to switch from Franklin's group when the opportunity presented itself.

"Gordon, you and I can talk more about the politics of this later. For now, I want to get into how this is going to work. I think you're going to like what you hear."

Angstrom pulled out a small map from his folder and a black marker from his pocket. The map was of the far northwest region of Russia. "Okay, let's talk about our role in Cyberknife.

"Two Navy SEALS will covertly transport Franklin and me into Mys Peschanyy via the Gulf of Finland." Angstrom drew the symbol of an antenna on the map to mark the location. "Mys Peschanyy's surrounded by an extremely rural area—mostly forest interspersed with vast oil fields. It's only about ten miles outside of the northernmost perimeter of St. Petersburg, but it's separated by a pretty thick forest. The SEALS will set up an IAD outpost there, including a scrambled, low intercept link to the K-Com satellite network."

K-Com: the new military satellite communications network that went live last year. The system comprises ten Ka-band satellites flying in geostationary orbit around twenty-two thousand miles above the Earth. Each satellite supports ninety separate Ka-band beams for channelization, providing download speeds of over 65 Mbit/s to a 24-inch dish. Voice and data transmission involves state of the art coding, compression, authentication, and encryption for hyper-secure links as compared to the previous-generation system. When it was first launched there was no way to keep such a system completely secret, and it was vehemently opposed by Russia and China, with concerns raised about spying; cameras on that many satellites was excessive and unwarranted, they claimed. But there *were* no cameras on the satellites, the United States responded—it only handled voice (data transmission wasn't mentioned), and the system was strictly for "peacekeeping and emergency relief" purposes. When the first high-bandwidth, full-duplex communication was made last year, it was the culmination of an intense development effort. From inception to completion, K-Com is a technological marvel not only because of its technical specifications, but also because of the relatively short time it took from development to deployment, all within budget and with relatively few glitches along the way. It marked a new highpoint in the government's procurement of space system technology.

"The equipment we'll use at the IAD outpost, including the K-Com transceiver and two ruggedized laptops, will contain special electronics and software: if it isn't addressed with a pass-code at a predetermined repetition, a wipe of the firmware will occur, and then a physical burn will be self-triggered via a low-volume composite. This way, if something happens to us, there's no chance of operable equipment falling into the hands of Russia."

"So you're physically participating in this mission as well?" interjected Gordon.

"Yes, I am. Initially I'll be at the IAD outpost with Franklin and the two SEALS. That situation will change, however. I'll eventually move to a safe house in Untolovo where I'll serve as a center of operations for you guys. I'll communicate with you from there. The safe house is a small cabin off the Glukharka

River." He drew a symbol of a small house on the map to denote the location.

"There's going to be a lot more extensive briefings on this, but here's essentially what we envision happening. A small team from Franklin's group, let's call them the Franklin contingency, is going over there posing as U.S. officials. They'll continue to exchange intel on the cyber attacks with Russian officials and learn from them what they know. Together, they'll devise a plan to hopefully track down and stop Strenzke and Terror. The Franklin contingency is going to be staying at the Hotel Astoria in St. Petersburg, where they'll call into Washington every night and provide a status report. Obviously we expect the Russians will be eavesdropping, which is okay. All the Franklin contingency will do is relay information they exchanged with the Russians that day, along with any rudimentary plans that are made. What the Russians *won't* know is that all of those status calls will be replicated and retransmitted through K-Com back to me and Franklin at the IAD outpost. Franklin and I—at least while I'm still with him—will be able to hear everything. But the Kremlin won't know it. With the help of PRISM and Big Machine, all reported information will be further processed, and Washington will be in a better position to help the contingency.

"As for you guys, you'll secretly be in St. Petersburg doing your own thing. I'll provide more details about that later. You won't, however, be making any contact with the Russian officials. That's going to be the sole province of the Franklin contingency. Even *they* won't know you're there. You'll have very limited communication among you via a specialized link on K-Com. It'll be a different access protocol than the one I'll use at the IAD outpost, with a much lower transmit power, thereby enabling your communication devices to be smaller and more portable. For security reasons, I won't be part of your talk-group while I'm at the IAD outpost. I've got a dual-mode transceiver, however, and after I move into the Untolovo safe house, I'll be added to the talk-group and then be able to directly communicate with you. We'll review the communication protocol later; it's similar to comm-sec

1. I'll also have to give you a crash-course on limited vocab communication."

Angstrom leaned back in his chair.

"So, as I said, you guys won't be making any contact with the Russian officials. You're presence won't be known. Needless to say, if you're caught, it won't be good." He turned to Reed and said, "Thomas, you're going to be involved in a secret rendezvous with someone over there; he's going to be feeding us intel. Again, we'll go over the details later."

"How long do we envision this taking? How long will we be over there?" asked Stafford.

"Our best information indicates that Frège is expected to detonate on July 28th."

Gordon quickly did the math in his head. "That's only twenty-nine days away!"

"That's right," Angstrom responded. "There's not a lot of time—we're going to have to move fast. I suppose theoretically we could be there longer, even after the 28th if we haven't found Strenzke or Terror by then, but let's not worry about that right now."

"How are we going to get into the country so fast?" said Gordon.

"The ground work is already being laid. We're going to leverage backlogged identities. Gordon and Gwen, you'll be there as husband and wife, entering from Finland," Angstrom said.

Gordon and Stafford briefly looked at each other. Gordon figured that the arrangement was Angstrom's way of pairing a seasoned operative with a new recruit.

"Lovely," said Stafford, chewing her gum and smiling at Gordon.

He shot a grin back at her and looked directly into her eyes. To his surprise, her smile somewhat disarmed him, causing him to become slightly aroused. There was something in her look; it was electric. Just then Gordon realized that Angstrom was watching him, a faint grin on his face, like he was telepathically communicating: *There's more to her than you think.*

Then Angstrom continued, "So as I said, things are going to be moving really fast; this will be our first test as a team. A significant responsibility given we've never worked together before. We'll show 'em what we're worth."

Gordon watched Angstrom intently. He knew the whole reason their team was being given the assignment was because of Angstrom and the trust the CIA placed in him. Gordon looked over at Magdos for a moment, studying him, observing how he reacted to everything. He noticed how quiet the man remained.

Angstrom grabbed his folder and abruptly stood up. "Let's grab some lunch in the cafeteria. It's on me. Meet me at the end of the hall in about five minutes."

Gordon remained seated as the others rose and left the room. When everyone was gone, Gordon stood up to close the door and then sat back down. It was an invitation to have a serious conversation, so Angstrom sat back down as well.

"What do you think?" said Angstrom.

"I like it."

"I told you. Have a little faith."

"Mm. If you don't mind my asking, who are the lucky ones from Franklin's group?"

"I'm still working on it, going over everyone's file. It calls for a different kind of skill set: diplomacy. I've already noticed in some peoples' long term career goals that they've expressed a desire for doing something like this. Those people are high on the list."

Gordon nodded with comprehension.

"I can't say enough how important Cyberknife is, so picking the right people from Franklin's group is going to be critical," Angstrom continued.

Gordon was impressed by the authority given Angstrom. It made him feel like a sea-change was occurring in the organization, some new, stronger direction.

"Franklin doesn't know everything yet?" said Gordon.

"No. Not yet. By the way, we're going to leverage Redblood."

"Really?"

"Yes. And I'm thinking about letting Thomas drive that."

Gordon was just about to respond when there was a knock at the door. A woman poked her head in. "John, I'm sorry to disturb you, but Fred would like to see you in his office right away."

"Can it wait until after lunch?"

"I'm sorry, he said he needs to see you immediately."

Angstrom and Gordon looked at each other, wondering what it could be. As Angstrom stood up he said to Gordon, "Let's talk more later. Details, I know you want them."

Gordon nodded. He was hoping to ask Angstrom some questions about Magdos. He was curious about him; he wanted to know more about the man who looked so powerful that he could snap a man in two with his bare hands. But now that would have to wait.

Angstrom said to Gordon, "Tell the group I'm sorry for missing lunch. I'll take a rain check."

Then he followed the secretary out of the room.

12

Anne, My Dear

BANKS' OFFICE WAS ONLY A FEW DOORS DOWN FROM THE conference room
where Angstrom's meeting took place. When Angstrom entered,
he noticed immediately that Banks was in a very serious mood.

A predominantly one-way conversation took place, with Banks
doing all the talking. Angstrom struggled to keep his equanimity
as he sat and listened to the details of Bensley's attack. The news
filled him with dread. When Banks disclosed what needed to be
done as a result, the conversation took a turn for the worse, which
was what Banks had feared.

Banks was a career man in the CIA, recruited straight from
college back in 1974. He avoided Vietnam by going to the
University of Virginia, though it was still a close call by virtue of
his having graduated before the war officially ended. He became
a rising star in the CIA, excelling in Russian intelligence at the
dawn of the collapse of the Russian "sphere of influence," a
period in history marked by one arms treaty after another. He
was recognized early as a strategic thinker—some claimed he was
the one who popularized the old Russian proverb "Trust but

verify," even before Reagan. It wasn't before too long that the CIA let him form his own group, along with the authority to set its charter.

Garrett was his first hire, a man who quickly established a reputation for his excellent field work and tactical skills. He was the perfect complement to Banks, and they were a formidable team. Eventually a whole division was created around them, with Banks at the top. He regretted losing sight of Garrett's old group over the years, thereby allowing it to decline as it had. Only after it was too late did Banks realize the true nature and extent of Garrett's physical decline. Angstrom would be the new beginning.

Banks' time in the CIA, however, was long in the tooth. He expected the proverbial tap on the shoulder at any moment, polite and respectful though it may be—he would welcome it if he were completely honest with himself. The field-ops aspect of Cyberknife would likely be the last big responsibility he'd have under his division. He knew, however, that something else would serve as the last thorn in his side: the issue revolving around Spence, Bensley, and Anne Davis, a spurious after-effect from Davis' defection.

Banks knew Angstrom wasn't going to like the news on Bensley, but it was even harder to deliver the instructions of what would follow. When Angstrom strenuously objected, it wasn't a threat that came from Banks, it was a warning—an admonition as to what would happen should Angstrom refuse. None of it was good in a lot of different ways. It was the most uncomfortable conversation Banks ever had to have, professionally or otherwise. He knew it was necessary and that there was no choice. He needed to help Angstrom come to the same conclusion.

For Angstrom, it felt like he was hit with a ton of bricks, shocked as he was by what he heard.

How could it be expected? It was ludicrous, this proposal. When Angstrom challenged the authority behind it, Banks slid an official document in front of him, an instantly recognizable signature at the bottom. Angstrom became incensed, feeling like a trapped, frustrated animal, frantic to escape yet helpless.

In all his years, Banks was never so unsure as to what would happen next in a conversation. He sensed the fury within Angstrom. Angstrom glared at him for a long time in silence.

Banks felt feeble in the presence of Angstrom's intense glare. It was the first time in a long time that he felt his age. Just when Banks thought something would happen, like Angstrom would explode, the opposite occurred: Angstrom's shoulders relaxed, his fists unclenched, and he left without saying another word.

After walking some distance down the hall, Angstrom stopped to think and collect himself. He couldn't fathom it. It was as if everything he had done up until that point, all the service to his country, didn't matter. His breathing was still heavy, his pulse elevated, and there was a slight tremor in his hands. How dare they, he thought. There was a sudden urge to go straight to Adam Wright, to hear it straight from him. But then he thought Wright wasn't high enough. This was too important. He needed to go to McCoy himself. Does McCoy even know what's going on? The threats that were made? He closed his eyes and ran his hand through his hair in frustration. Of course he did; that document wouldn't have been signed if he didn't.

Someone walked by and asked him if he was all right.

"Yes, yes, I'm fine. Thank you."

He walked back to his office feeling somewhat dazed, and when he got there he closed the door and fell back into his chair. He sat there alone for a long time thinking the whole thing through. He couldn't get Davis' image out of his mind; she had become everything to him. He'd never felt like this before about anybody, not even Breann when they first met. And now there was this.

The more he thought about it, the more torn he became. If he stepped back and looked at everything objectively, it was clear that an issue of national security was at stake—as Banks put it, nothing as significant since the Golos Affair. If he was completely honest with himself, he'd have to admit that they cut him a lot of slack already, first by letting her live with him, and then by letting him continue in his current role. Besides, deep down he knew this was coming. As soon as he learned of Spence he knew it wasn't going away. He even started preparing for it. He just didn't think it would have come so soon or that it would lead to this. He could feel himself calming down the more he thought about it.

Still, it was the woman he loved.

"Gordon," he said over the phone. "You busy? Good, come on over." When Gordon arrived, Angstrom said, "Come in. Close the door. Do me a favor, lock it."

A serious look came over Gordon as he sat down. "What's going on? Everything okay?"

Angstrom paused before responding. "What do you think of the team so far? You've been to lunch with them, had a little time to consider it, what's your impression?"

Gordon was surprised by the question. "Good…a good start." He knew his old friend. He could tell that something else was on his mind, maybe his conversation with Banks, but he didn't say anything.

Angstrom took a deep breath, letting the tension release with his exhalation. Finally, he reached down into his desk drawer, grabbed a bottle of single malt scotch, and put it on the desk, along with two glasses.

"You're kidding. I thought you gave up the stuff. I didn't even think you kept a bottle around anymore," Gordon said in disbelief. He looked at his wristwatch: 3:40 P.M. Then he saw something in Angstrom's eyes, some sort of pain. Even without knowing what happened to Spence or Bensley, Gordon figured Angstrom was under a lot of pressure because of Davis. "Oh hell, why not? Pour me one."

Angstrom poured, and they each raised their glass. Gordon drank right away, but Angstrom hesitated for a moment, took yet another deep breath, and then drank.

"Tell me what you know about the people in Franklin's group," Angstrom said. "I need to pick some people to form the contingency. I've read their files, but I want your opinion."

Angstrom slid a small stack of files across the desk toward Gordon.

Gordon could tell that this wasn't what was bothering Angstrom, but he figured that talking about the contingency might help, so he gave him his thoughts. The more they talked, the more relaxed Angstrom became. When the conversation progressed to Cyberknife overall, Angstrom was almost his old self.

He put the scotch away, and Gordon was relieved.

* * *

By the time Angstrom finished talking with Gordon he felt better, the conversation having forced him to forget for the moment about the earlier discussion with Banks. Unfortunately, the feeling was only temporary. By the time he was able to finish everything he had to do that day it was after 7 P.M., and as soon as he got into his car to drive home, there was a sharp pain in his stomach: nerves settled in as he thought about the prospect of facing Davis that evening.

The house was dark when he got there; she wasn't home yet. He knew it was supposed to be a late day for her; that was why he had no qualms about getting home so late himself. He appreciated the fact that he was going to have some time alone— that is, until he realized it was his turn to be responsible for dinner. He would've picked something up on the way had he remembered.

After putting on a Thelonious Monk CD and turning up the volume, he checked the refrigerator to see what was available.

Steamed shrimp left over from the previous evening. He would make shrimp scampi. A pot of water was put on the stove for the pasta, and then he went upstairs to change.

"Well, this is a wonderful situation to come home to," Angstrom heard as he came down the stairs. Davis was sitting on the couch in the small living room with her shoes already removed; her bare legs were crossed and propped up on the coffee table, a glass of red wine already in her hand. "I took the liberty," she said, holding up the glass. "Come, join me."

"Let me check the water first. I want to see if it's boiling."

"I already did. The pasta's in. Come on over."

Angstrom grabbed the glass she handed him.

"Isn't this wonderful, John? Us coming home and being together like this?" They clanked their glasses together. "I haven't been this happy in many years...maybe never. Every day is—how should I say it?—exhilarating, even just the ordinariness of it. Then, to come home to be with you...I couldn't ask for more."

Her voice sounded as beautiful as ever; he never got used to it. He smiled and sipped his wine.

"Is everything alright? You seem nervous or something," she said.

"No, no...I'm fine. Tough day at the office, you know." He took a deep breath. "I'm happy to be with you too. So tell me, how was your day today? Was it Bobby, or maybe Young-Su? Which star pupils did you teach today?"

"Both," Davis said. "Oh my God, you wouldn't believe what happened. So, I was giving Bobby his lesson, and of course his mom was there as well, sitting in the room with us. The only problem was that they arrived for the lesson ten minutes late, so I decided to run Bobby's lesson a little over. I like Bobby; he's a good boy, and I was helping him prepare for a solo he was going to perform at his school."

"Yeah, so what happened?"

"Well, Young-Su comes with her mom, and you could see the mom, right at four o'clock sharp, starting to peer through the door window. She kept doing it, anxious for her daughter's lesson to start. Then it became ten after, and she starts knocking on the door. Real loud. She comes in, and then she started saying how it was time for Young-Su's lesson. When I told her we were just finishing up, she became angry, started lecturing me on how it was important to stay on schedule. Then Bobby's mom tried to say something to calm her down, and that made it worse." Davis took a sip of her wine.

"This doesn't sound good," Angstrom said.

"All of a sudden, Young-Su's mom started saying, 'I going to tell Mr. Shulman about this. He won't stand for it. Not in his store.' By then Mr. Shulman was *at* the door. He must have heard everything because he said, 'Mrs. Lee, don't you worry about it. We'll give you an extra fifteen minutes, free of charge. Please don't worry about it.' Then he winked at me."

"And did that fix it? Was Mrs. Lee happy?"

"Sure she was. She settled down. But it was very uncomfortable at the beginning of the lesson. She sat there glaring at me. I was angry as well. I couldn't believe the woman. Mr. Shulman later calmed me down, told me not to worry about it. He said she's always like that, been so for years with the other instructors. He's about had it with her, he says. He told me if it ever gets to be too much, just tell him, and he'll terminate her contract, pick up a new student."

"Wow. I suppose you meet all kinds at that shop."

"It's funny, though, as soon as we got underway with the lesson, when my mind was on the work, it was okay. Isn't it strange how when you focus on the work, the brain, it just blocks that other stuff out?"

"Yes, it is. Listen..." He looked at her for a moment then changed his mind. He finished his wine and stood up. "Let me go cook the pasta. You relax. Change your clothes and take a shower if you want."

"Thanks, I think I will. By the way, this music—it's Monk, right?"

"That's right," Angstrom responded, still standing there.

"What song is this?" she said.

"It's called *Ruby, My Dear*. That's Coltrane on the saxophone."

"I thought so. It's beautiful. I love it. So simple, but there's so much in it, you know?"

"Mm."

He went into the kitchen and Davis went upstairs. The kitchen was small, but he liked it. He liked everything about the old house—small and intimate, just perfect for the two of them. The inside was completely redone by the previous owner, newer white cabinets, black granite countertop.

The pan was hot and made a sizzling sound as soon as he put some shrimp into it. *Crepuscule With Nellie* played in the background. He looked through the kitchen toward the stairs, up to where Davis had gone, and then poured himself another glass of wine. It was the most he had drunk in one day in a long time.

Angstrom had the table set by the time Davis came back down. Her hair was wet and she had changed her clothes.

"This is magnificent, John. And candles, no less! Perfect. It sets the mood," she said as she sat down and put the white cloth napkin on her lap.

"Here's some more wine," he said as he poured her a glass, standing at her side. Just as he sat down, new music came on.

"It never entered my mind," she said.

"Pardon?" said Angstrom, looking up at her after putting his napkin on his lap.

"That's the name of the song: *It Never Entered My Mind*. Right?"

"Oh...yes. That's right. Impressive."

"Thank you for putting it on. It's one of my favorites." She raised her glass to him.

"I think you say that about every song I put on: 'It's one of my favorites,' " he said with a chuckle.

"So what if I do? It's part of you, and I love that you share it with me. I want to know all about you, John, everything…at least, everything that I can." Angstrom didn't say anything and just looked at her. "Anyway, it really is one of my favorites."

They both started eating, and they ate in silence for a while, decompressing from the day, enjoying the food and wine, and the music. They were happy to be in each other's presence, and sometimes for them, that was enough, without any words needing to be said.

"Anne?"

"Yes, what is it?" She could tell there was something not right that evening. As beautiful as it was, she knew something was bothering him, but she resisted the urge to pry.

"Listen. You're…I want you to make sure that you watch yourself."

"Huh? What do you mean?"

"You know, like we talked about. We've made this decision to live like we are, and I…you just have to remember to stay vigilant. Right? Be careful, observe things around you, make sure no one is watching you. Just like we said before. Use your training, look for any telltale signs that something isn't right."

"Of course. I always do. Why, has something happened? Is there a reason you're telling me this?" she said with a look of concern.

He knew they were listening.

"I care about you, Anne…more than anything on Earth."

She was startled by such a profound statement.

"I don't want anything to happen to you, so I just want you to be careful, okay?"

"I will, John. Of course." She put her fork down and looked at him.

She knows, he said to himself. She knows something is wrong, but she won't press me. He squeezed his hands together under the table, rubbing them nervously.

"Listen. I have to go away for a while. I can't say where, and I can't say for how long. It's work."

She watched him, still not picking up her fork.

"I hate leaving you, I'm realizing that now," he said. "I'm not sure I can do this anymore—be separated from you."

"John, I'll be alright. This is your job. Your career. It's okay. You go. And when you come back—*you will come back*—we'll pick up right where we left off. In the meantime," she looked around the room, "I'll fix this place up some more. Make it more of our own. And you make sure you *dodge all ze bullets*," she said jokingly in an exaggerated Russian accent. She hunched over and pointed her thumb and forefinger into the shape of a gun, grinning, with a sinister look on her face.

"Anne, please, don't joke like that," Angstrom said from across the table. There was no smile on his face.

She realized how bothered he was—bothered by what she thought was his having to go away.

Angstrom stood up from his chair. Davis was surprised and watched him. The music played in the background.

He walked over to her. She didn't understand what he was doing at first. He knelt at her side, put his hand on her knee, and looked right into her eyes.

"Anne, I love you."

She smiled and they held each other's gaze. After a few seconds, a tear fell on her cheek.

"I love you too, John."

His head fell on her lap, and she caressed him.

001000110

000110011

PART TWO

110110001

101011100

011010111

001101011

13

Installation

SEVEN DAYS—NOT BAD, ANGSTROM THOUGHT, EVERYTHING considered. He figured it would've taken much longer than that to get into Mys Peschanyy, what with all of the up-front planning and authorization involved, but there he was.

Tacit Gray didn't hurt. The "drop-and-deliver" small-hull boat plane, developed specifically for the Navy SEALS, was an engineering marvel. A precise compromise between power and sonic acoustics, the propulsion system could carry the aircraft and its cargo (up to ten passengers and a quarter-ton equipment payload) over medium range distances while producing an extremely low sonic profile. The plane was made of a composite material with an angular design to refract EM radiation, yielding a stealthy profile. It also had a state-of-the-art hull with a specially-scooped belly for skimmed amphibious landings and flotation. Needless to say, it took one hell of a Navy pilot to fly it. Some pilots even insisted Tacit Gray was still only a prototype and

159

questioned its readiness for actual missions, but that didn't deter Angstrom and Franklin, or the two SEALS accompanying them.

The plane had already lifted off by the time they had made it to shore. After tripping the quick release valve to let the air out of the inflatable boat that quietly motored them to shore, they hid it among the brush. The plan was for Tacit Gray to return when signaled, and the boat would then be re-inflated with a portable hyper-pump.

"Angstrom, you're not panting, are you?" Franklin said as he stood on the muddy shore and adjusted his rucksack.

With no moon visible and the thick forest only twenty feet farther inland, they were in total darkness, such that Angstrom couldn't see the grin on Franklin's face. None of them could see much of anything.

"Quiet!" Angstrom sternly whispered. "Let's not talk from here on out!"

Fortunately for Angstrom, Franklin's assertion wasn't true; he *wasn't* breathing heavy. Since the skiing trip with Davis and how difficult it was to keep up with her, the intensity of his daily workouts had increased, both for cardio and for strength. Weeks later, and after a lot of pain and soreness, he was in much better shape, and the unloading of equipment, first from Tacit Gray and then the small boat, didn't faze him.

In addition to the modified M16 and ruggedized laptop each of the SEALs carried, they were responsible for the components of the disassembled portable land station—a portable satellite dish and K-Com transceiver—which was around 45 pounds total. Angstrom carried a special weapon in his ruck.

The hike through the thick forest was challenging to say the least. They were in total darkness, the foliage was dense, the terrain hilly and unpredictable. One of the SEALS, Lieutenant Roy Grahame, periodically checked his GPS readout and intermittently turned on a red-phosphor lamp in short bursts to check conditions ahead. Angstrom and Franklin followed in succession. Brad Gentry, the SEAL who would serve as the comm-tech for the mission, was last. Each of the first three men had a small glow stick dangling from his ruck so the next person could follow.

The air was chilly, and even though any exposed skin had been sprayed with insect repellent, Angstrom could still feel something biting him every so often.

It was hard for him to block thoughts of Davis from his mind. He had been successful at it until just then; the physical exertion reminded him of their skiing trip. It was about 2 A.M. where he was at, which made it about 6 P.M. back home. He wondered what she was doing—probably walking home from her cello lessons. He was worried about her. While he slept on Tacit Gray he even had a dream about her. It was vivid. A Russian spy broke into their home and shot her. He could see the bullet travel through the air in slow motion, stirring him awake the instant it penetrated her skull. It seemed so real, like he was actually there.

Focus, he said to himself. Focus. Focus on the forest...and where you're at...and what you'll be doing when you get to where you're going. Focus.

They hiked for about an hour when they finally reached a clearing. Grahame signaled for them to stop, and they all got their bearings. They were at the edge of a cliff, with a small, sparsely populated area extending out in front of them in the valley below.

The landing in the Gulf and their movement through the forest had been precise, Angstrom thought. He could tell they were almost exactly at the point where they needed to be.

Over the expanse before them, maybe ten homes could be seen dotting the countryside, with oil drilling installations further off in the distance. There seemed to be no end to them; the cantilever masts extended across the land. Although none of the lights were on in any of the houses, lights on the drilling stations provided some illumination, even as far away as they were.

Grahame motioned for them to continue. They hiked for another forty-five minutes along the edge of the clearing until they reached a point near the target house. Grahame stopped, raised the back of his hand to the others, and pointed down to the house. It was situated on around four acres and could barely be seen through the heavily wooded and rocky terrain. Large, jagged boulders protruded from the ground like giant bones, with trees sprouting from among them.

The house was actually owned by the U.S. government through a deep shell account, secretly acquired years ago for just such clandestine purposes. The team carefully descended the cliff and made its way across the field, ducking into tree cover whenever possible. As they hiked, Angstrom noticed many fallen trees—massive, petrified trunks with large root systems extending into the air, like statues of dead soldiers knocked over.

When they got closer they came upon a gravel driveway that wound around boulders and fir trees, leading upwards to the small house at the top. The men carefully traversed the driveway, making sure the area was safe with no booby traps or interlopers. The gravel made a slight crunching sound under their boots. When they reached the house, it was just as the satellite images had shown (as much as could be captured through the many trees): a small, one-bedroom, non-descript home with white, heavily worn clapboard siding. An old barn was in the back instead of a garage, which could have been utilized if a larger deployment was called for. Gentry went to the utility box and shined a red light on it, then connected a test box to check that the house had electricity. Grahame traversed the perimeter, M16 in hand, looking into the windows to see if he could see anything. By the time he made it back around, Gentry turned and signaled to them that the electricity was on, and they all went inside.

As they began to remove their packs, Franklin asked, "How long before the satellite link is established?"

"Shouldn't be too long," Gentry responded as he handled pieces of the land station. "Maybe an hour, at most. We'll need to route Cat-5 from it into the house and set up the laptops through a wired router. That'll be a bit longer, not much, provided there are no snags."

"Do you need any help?" offered Franklin.

"No, we're good. Thanks."

Gentry worked for about an hour outside.

"K-Com link is established," he eventually said while kneeling on the ground, not bothering to look behind him at Grahame. "Good thing we found a clearing through the trees on this side of the house. We've got a good line of sight to the satellite, which will make the link much more reliable. He held a small, battery operated LCD meter connected to a test port directly on the land station.

"Sufficient bandwidth?" Grahame whispered.

"About forty meg down."

"Shit, you must be using two channels."

"Nah. At this speed, we only need one. It's more than enough."

"What will it translate to inside the house?"

"Pretty close to that. We shouldn't see much degradation."

"Let's get back inside and set up the laptops."

"Right."

Angstrom was already seated in front of one of them, its screen emitting a blue glow in the room.

"You should get ample bandwidth when you're connected. Is the computer ready?" Gentry said as he entered the house.

"I just finished booting it up," Angstrom said.

"I've got the router going too," Franklin said. "All we need is the pipe."

Gentry went over to it and connected the cable he had unrolled into the house. Then he leaned over Angstrom's shoulder to observe the PC's screen.

Angstrom was already appreciating the abilities of Gentry and Grahame. They're good, he thought. Professional.

"Okay, let me sit at the terminal for a minute and make the initial connection," Gentry said as he took Angstrom's place.

In the meantime, Franklin and Angstrom went into the small bedroom to talk. They kept the lights off. Angstrom carried one of the phosphor handheld lamps to provide a small amount of light.

"So, the rest of the group arrives early next morning," Angstrom said.

"Yeah," Franklin said. "I'm anxious to get the laptops set up so we'll be ready for their reports. The team should arrive at the hotel tomorrow; I'm sure they'll be calling Washington some time after that."

"Gentry'll get it working. What do you think the odds are this will amount to anything?" said Angstrom.

"What, you mean whether or not we get the two, this Terror and his partner Strenzke? Hard to say. I'll have a better read on it after the first day's report tomorrow."

"Agreed. You happy with the people I selected?" Angstrom said.

He noticed a slight squint in Franklin's face after he asked that. He could see Franklin's face pretty clearly because his eyes had adjusted to the darkness.

"So how the hell did that come about, anyway, you selecting people from *my* team?"

Angstrom was wondering when Franklin was going to say something about that. So here it was, he thought.

"Just following orders. Those were the instructions, and I went by them. Did you object?"

Angstrom knew he had, but he also knew Franklin wouldn't acknowledge it.

"Look, it is what it is," Franklin answered. "Now that it's done, we focus on the mission. Right?"

"Of course."

"How'd *Davis* take your leaving?"

This time it was Angstrom who felt a little sting.

"She's fine. Why?"

"Fred briefed me."

Angstrom didn't respond. He held firm in the darkness.

"He had to," Franklin added. "Someone in my position has to know what's going on."

Angstrom took a deep breath and looked away from Franklin.

"She'll be fine, John. Don't let it get to you. You can't. We have to stay focused over here."

"I know. I'm good. It's been a long time since we were on a mission together, hasn't it?"

"It has," Franklin responded. "This one's gonna go better than the last one."

"There's no choice," said Angstrom.

Just then, Gentry popped his head in and said, "K-Com is live on the PCs. We're on."

"I'll go validate the protocols," said Franklin.

"Thanks," responded Angstrom. "Give me a few minutes and I'll be right out."

14

Cold Handshake

St. Petersburg, Russia
Tuesday, July 7
[T$_{detonate}$ minus 21 days]

THE MORNING AFTER ANGSTROM'S LANDING AT MYS PESCHANYY marked the arrival of the so-called Franklin contingency in St. Petersburg. A black limousine pulled into St. Isaac's Square and dropped the five weary travelers off at the front entrance of the Hotel Astoria. It was just before dawn. Cyrillic letters forming the hotel's name—астория гостиница—shone blue on an electric sign at the top of the six-story building, lighting the dark sky around it. Grand pillars rose upward along the building's stone and concrete facade.

St. Isaac's Square is a sprawling area with many historical buildings of impressive architecture. St. Isaac's Cathedral is situated at one end, its famous neoclassical exterior styled after a Byzantine Greek church with a large golden dome at its center and four smaller ones surrounding it; strategically placed spotlights cause the domes to glow majestic in the darkness. The Mariinsky Palace stands on the southern end of the square. It's adorned with Corinthian columns and a reddish-brown stone facade that gives it a more formal, administrative appearance consistent with its current function. In the center of the square stands a bronze, equestrian monument of the Russian Emperor Nicholas I, a prancing knight seemingly guarding the whole area.

"The hotel looks beautiful," Jane Wykoff commented to the others as she approached the front entrance. A doorman stood waiting and opened the door for them as they neared. "This whole area is quite incredible," she said as she took a last look around before stepping inside.

Wykoff was the most senior person of the contingency and was chosen to lead it. Angstrom was somewhat intrigued by her profile and planned to monitor her performance closely. She was thirty-eight and had short brown hair in a tight curl that was trimmed short around the sides and back. Her black-rimmed glasses finished a look that conveyed authority.

The next most senior person was Stuart Ackman. He was a couple of years younger than Wykoff. While fairly effective in his current role as a field ops agent, he really excelled as an intelligence analyst. He was in the Russian and European Analysis Section of the Intelligence Division for years before transferring into Garrett's group, thinking he needed the broader experience to boost his career. He also thought he might like doing field work. He was wrong. At least he was honest about that fact when he was approached about Cyberknife; Angstrom appreciated his candor. After discussing Ackman's long term career aspirations, they both agreed his time in the Division had run its course and a transfer was in order. Angstrom, however, floated the idea that Cyberknife was the perfect exit point: diplomacy would be needed above all else, and it represented an excellent segue to new opportunities. Ackman agreed.

Angstrom had noticed a similar type of situation when he reviewed the files of the other four members making up the

Franklin contingency. That figured prominently in his selection of them for the assignment.

The front lobby of the Astoria had an eclectic feel to it. The floor was of parquet wood. Floor-to-ceiling silver curtains with black horizontal stripes lined the walls and completely covered them except for where there were windows. Black chairs with a golden crescent moon pattern were placed in groups in several areas of the lobby, along with angular, modern-looking coffee tables and end tables, thereby forming intimate gathering spaces for guests. Overall the lobby was quite impressive with a sort of whimsy to it that otherwise belied the building's more formal exterior. The sensory experience somewhat revived Wykoff and the rest of her team, groggy as they were from the flight from Washington; in total the trip had taken over 24 hours. Fortunately they were able to sleep on the flight.

After all five members of the team checked in, an older gentleman from the hotel, short and bald in appearance, met them at the front desk and gestured them toward the elevator. As they stood waiting for it to arrive, the man said in English, but with a heavy Russian accent, "Your bags will be brought to your rooms. Then we will serve breakfast for you in restaurant. Please be there at nine o'clock. It is on main floor." He motioned toward the direction of the restaurant.

"Excellent. That gives us some time to get freshened up a bit," Wykoff said as she checked her watch.

"The meeting will begin at 10:30 A.M.," the old man said. "Someone will be here to escort you to the other hotel."

"Other hotel? What do you mean?" interjected Ackman with surprise.

"To the meeting place," the old man responded.

"But the itinerary indicated that we were going to meet here, at *this* hotel," Wykoff said with a look of confusion.

"Meet in hotel, yes, but not this one," the old man said. "You will be taken next door to a conference room in a nearby hotel — the Angleterre. No conference room here."

"Ah, that makes sense," Wykoff said sarcastically as she turned to her colleagues.

A bell rang and the elevator doors opened. When everyone entered and stood in the small, cramped compartment, Wykoff leaned over and sarcastically whispered to Ackman, "They must have more sensitive bugs at the Angleterre."

The old man turned and looked at her. If he overheard what she said, he didn't acknowledge it.

It turned out to be the old man from the Astoria who escorted them to the Angleterre. They walked outside and followed him on the sidewalk through the heart of St. Isaac's Square.

Jet lag was beginning to affect them.

"At least the sun's out," Ackman said to Wykoff. "The fresh air feels good. This is kind of crazy, though, that we have to do this."

"Stay alert. I think the Russians are playing games with us, trying to gain an advantage. They know we're tired, so they're trying to disorient us a little. Let's not let them."

When they arrived at the lobby of the Angleterre, the old man bowed and said, "Please, have an excellent meeting. Good day."

The lobby was just as striking and impressive as that of the Astoria, although with a much different feel to it: a shiny black marble floor was complemented by sleek, brown leather chairs and red cloth sofas in the middle of the lobby. White, life-sized marble statues of historical figures from ancient Greece lined the walls. The lobby mixed modern with old to provide a unique ambience.

A man rose from one of the couches and approached them, somehow recognizing them for who they were. "Hello," he said in English but with a much lighter Russian accent as compared to the other man. "My name is Oleg Medlikov, Russian representative from Interpol. You may call me Oleg. I will take you to the conference room. It's a pleasure to meet you."

"Interpol?" Ackman said. "What is this? We didn't contact Interpol about this meeting. We don't want Interpol involved at this point."

"It's okay," the man responded with a smile. "They will not know. Please, come this way." He turned and walked away, expecting the others to follow.

Wykoff cast a raised eyebrow toward Ackman, this time unable to suppress a grin, like she wanted to say: *What the hell did that mean?*

Almost as if Medlikov read her mind, he turned to her as he walked and said, "Representatives from the OMSN, one of our Special Police Units, will be meeting with you. They are a unit of the Russian Interior Ministry, with a focus on fighting the organized crime. Yes?"

"Excellent. Thank you," said Wykoff.

The rest of their walk was in silence as they followed Medlikov through the hotel. When they reached the conference room, Medlikov stepped aside and extended his hand toward the door, inviting them to enter. Wykoff, being the only woman in the group, entered first. It was a fairly large room, with floor-to-ceiling mirrors completely covering the walls and red, regal carpeting on the floor. A long, ornate table extended down the center of the room and had elaborate chairs around it. A crystal chandelier hung from the ceiling. Wykoff counted ten men already seated on one side of the table; the room was heavy with cigarette smoke. A few of the men, but not all of them, rose with icy expressions on their faces as they saw her enter.

They were there reluctantly, Wykoff thought. Tension between their two countries was high, and they didn't relish the idea of helping the United States on a criminal matter.

After everyone entered, Medlikov closed the door and went to the lead position of his side of the table. He then referred to himself as the head of the OMSN and proceeded to quickly introduce the rest of the team. Medlikov's identification of himself as head of the OMSN instead of as a representative of Interpol, as he previously referred to himself, confused Wykoff and Ackman and made it hard for them to follow the hastily made introductions.

Wykoff, sitting directly opposite Medlikov, introduced her team as well. Then she said, "Thank you again for having us here for this important meeting. As you know, the United States is being subjected to a massive amount of cyber attacks. The nature of the more recent attacks is different than those of the past, their frequency increasing at an alarming rate. It's gotten to a critical point for us. We're prepared to share with you what we know, including evidence pointing to two individuals in your country, as well as information that is dictating the urgency of the situation. We therefore very much appreciate your willingness to meet with us and help put an end to this matter."

A translator repeated everything that Wykoff said. The men on the other side of the table all nodded after they heard the translation. Medlikov responded.

"Russia does not condone this criminal activity. For us, our willingness to help you is self-serving: we want our country to become recognized as a center of international commerce, and that cannot very well be if we are also known as the center of international cyber crime."

A mechanical screen was set up at the front of the room, and a projector was put on the table. The United States was expected to present first.

Wykoff attached her laptop and called up a PowerPoint presentation. Then she methodically went through some of the information regarding the attacks, focusing mainly on overall statistics and financial ramifications as opposed to the technical details. Her information was more focused when it came to the evidence pointing to Strenzke and the man who referred to himself as "T3RR0R," or "Terror."

When she was done, Medlikov nodded to someone from his team, and a man rose and went to connect his laptop to the projector. A litany of information was then presented—many slides worth. The man spoke of the general capabilities of the Russian police, their success in stopping cyber crime, and general information about hacking activity around the world— information already known from publicly available sources.

Wykoff's team got more and more exhausted as time passed. She insisted upon meeting with the Russians that first day in order to get the introductory formalities out of the way, and given the rather pedestrian nature of Russia's initial presentation, Wykoff was glad she did, brutal as it was sitting through the meeting.

"Thank you for that introduction, Oleg. Let's proceed with the details of what you know about Strenzke, Terror, and their hacking organization."

"Yes, of course. I must say though, you look very tired—your whole team looks tired. We'll have plenty of time for this tomorrow. Are you sure you don't want to wait and get some rest?"

"Thank you, Oleg, that's very considerate of you, but as you saw from the stock trading intelligence, we've got a very tight deadline we're dealing with, and time is of the essence. Please, let's continue for a while longer. We're anxious to begin learning about the intelligence that you have so that we may begin to form a plan with you. In the meantime, when I feel like we've reached our limit for the day, which admittedly may be fast approaching, we'll let you know."

"Very well," said Medlikov.

Medlikov nodded to a different man on his side of the table, and another presentation was shown: photos, images of different documents, printouts of internet network activity, even short snippets of video footage from stakeouts, the relevance of which completely escaped Wykoff's team.

Collectively it was still not much help—facts were disjointed and did not seem to relate to each other, and none of it related to Strenzke or Terror, or any connection to the cyber attacks occurring in the United States. Wykoff's team took notes and asked questions, and the answers were almost always nonresponsive, sometimes with only little relevance to the questions, other times not at all. This continued into the late afternoon, with no lunch served, and only short, periodic breaks every two hours. Members of Wykoff's team occasionally closed their eyes as they fought sleep, their heads bobbing as their chins fell to their chests and stirred them awake. At one point coffee was brought in on a pushcart; it was deep black and had an awful taste; no one drank it except for the Russians, who seemed to savor it. Needless to say, the bewilderment resulting from the Russians' disjointed presentation was exacerbated by the jet lag, which had become acute, as well as by the fact that they weren't served anything to eat all day, so they were starved.

This was not the case for the Russian team. Every time they reconvened from a break they seemed more refreshed than ever. Sometimes Wykoff could have sworn that different people had replaced some of the previous participants, but she couldn't tell for sure because they all seemed to look alike: same color hair, same height, no distinguishing features. They were even dressed alike, each wearing similar dark suits and ties.

Wykoff grouped her team during one of the breaks in the afternoon.

"This isn't much help," Ackman offered.

"I know. That's why we have to do this today," Wykoff responded. "We have to get this bullshit out of the way. It's what we expected, right?"

"It is, but that doesn't make it any easier. I don't know about you guys, but I'm about dead," Ackman admitted as he looked at the others. They all nodded in agreement.

"Ms. Wykoff, I'm sure your team is completely exhausted by now, and certainly this information is overwhelming after your being exposed to it for only the first time. I hope you feel that our first day was a fruitful one, yes?"

"Yes, Oleg, you're very perceptive. Our team *is* exhausted. The jet lag is well upon us. May we continue again tomorrow?"

"Yes, of course, that is the plan. For now, we will have you escorted back to your hotel. An excellent dinner will be waiting for you there."

It was music to their ears.

"Thank you, Oleg. We appreciate that."

Everyone stood, and the Russians came from around their side of the table to shake hands with Wykoff's team. When they exited the conference room they met the old man from the Astoria waiting for them. "Madame, I will be happy to take you back to hotel."

When they were gone, Medlikov turned to his team and said, "Well done. Well done. We've had our bit of fun. Tomorrow we get to work."

* * *

When Ackman dialed Washington that evening to report on the day's events, the call was routed from Washington through a ground link to the K-Com satellite system, which was then retransmitted back to Mys Peschanyy. A message appeared across the two ruggedized laptops as a notification of the pending transmission. One of the laptops was folded shut, and Angstrom and the others gathered around the other laptop to listen to the report.

Wykoff didn't pull any punches, even though she was well aware that her call was being intercepted by the Russians. She described the Russian team that attended and the information that was exchanged. In addition, however, she dropped a few coded phrases which only Washington could decipher. "No rain that day, but overcast" may have seemed like innocent banter, but the Americans listening knew what it meant. Other phrases were much more obscure and didn't even fit with the rest of the report.

"What do you think?" Franklin said when he and Angstrom were later alone.

"I think it was a 'kiss your sister' event," Angstrom replied.

"That's what it seems like. Tomorrow should be better."

"It better be. This is too important for it to be a drawn out affair. Tomorrow's meeting will be after a full night's sleep. Let's see how the team does then."

"You're not blaming the team for the slow start, are you? This was just the first day."

"Not at all. But it'll be extremely important how they perform tomorrow. They'll need to take control, put the Russians on the spot, not move off subject until an issue's been fully vetted. You've been in these situations before; you know the drill."

"Yeah. They're going to have to press for useful information, and then get right into a plan of action."

Angstrom agreed. He had talked about this with Wykoff in advance, coached her on what to expect and how she should react. The first day went just like Angstrom thought it would. Now it was her turn.

Wednesday, July 8
[$T_{detonate}$ minus 20 days]

Wykoff took the initiative the next day. She informed her team that they were moving "off schedule." They showed up for breakfast at the Astoria's restaurant earlier than the time arranged for them. The restaurant staff was caught off guard, having been told in advance what was expected to happen. It caused a delay in Wykoff's team getting their meals. Wykoff calmly indicated that her group was perfectly happy to leave without being served if that's what the Astoria wanted. The food was promptly served.

Meanwhile the old man was notified, and he appeared at their table about twenty minutes later.

"You must have been extremely hungry this morning," he said. "I'm glad the food is to your liking."

"Thank you," Wykoff responded. Everyone at the table kept eating. "We've got a long day ahead of us with a lot of work to do, so we're eager to begin."

"I will be ready to escort you when you are finished."

Ackman looked up from his bowl of oatmeal. "We'll be ready soon. We'll meet you in the lobby in about thirty minutes."

"Certainly. Certainly." And with that, the man left.

As soon as he was gone, Wykoff said, "You guys just about finished?"

Everyone indicated he was.

"Okay, let's go."

They left so suddenly that the old man wasn't even in the lobby, which was their intention. They left the hotel and walked to the Angleterre by themselves. Their arrival was a surprise.

"Please inform our host that we are ready when they are," Wykoff said at the check-in desk. "We will be waiting in the conference room. Also, do you have a menu from which we can order snacks?"

"Yes, yes, of course," the startled woman at the counter responded. She scurried for a restaurant menu to show Wykoff. The manager of the hotel by that time saw what was going on and approached.

"Good," Wykoff said. "We'll take some Arabica coffee. Please have it brought in immediately; don't hold it for the snack cart. We'll also take a new pot every hour. In addition, we would like snacks brought in every *two* hours." She proceeded to choose items from the menu and instructed the woman as to which snacks should be served and when. "We will have lunch at noon," again selecting menu items. "Of course, please bring enough for everyone."

"A lunch was planned for you anyway," the manager said, aggravated.

"Excellent. My team has certain food requirements, and we would appreciate your delivering what I requested."

"As you wish," he said, bowing his head.

After that, the team went to the conference room. A hotel employee scurried to get to the front of them and escort them. The hotel manager quickly made a phone call.

It wasn't too long before the Russian team arrived at the conference room, but not everyone appeared at once; some were as late as forty-five minutes, looking a bit harried and hastily dressed as they arrived.

"Good morning, good morning," Medlikov boisterously said as he entered. He shook hands with Wykoff. "Today's meeting will be different, eh?"

"We're looking forward to a very fruitful discussion," Wykoff said as she looked into the eyes of Medlikov, "including the plan to capture Strenzke and Terror."

"Yes, yes, of course," he said with a slight bow of the head while still holding her hand. "Let us begin, shall we?"

"By all means."

The presentation began, and right from the start Wykoff noticed more "substance" in the material. She and the other members of her team took pains to ask questions and slow the presentation down anytime something was unclear. Medlikov could see that the Americans were fully rested and alert and that there would be no room for further delay. He moved directly to the pertinent points of the presentation.

It was several more hours of background material and intelligence before Medlikov finally said, "So, as you have seen, we have a lot of information beyond what you have already uncovered. As for the man you refer to as 'Terror,' we have developed a good read on him as well. He is not nearly as obscure as you think. We traced him through his hacking, and by some of his, shall we say, recruiting activity. As to his specific whereabouts, we have identified what we believe is his primary center of operation. We are not one-hundred percent sure, however, and so our superiors have instructed us to not reveal that yet—not until we get more verification. We just need more time."

Ackman became agitated. Being second chair on the team was frustrating enough—he thought he should be leading the initiative—and he wanted to play a more active role in the current discussion. What Medlikov just said exacerbated this feeling, and Ackman was eager to say something to help advance the conversation. He was about to speak when Wykoff nudged him under the table. He turned to her and she furrowed her brow in a way that communicated: *Not yet. Stay cool.*

"Oleg," Wykoff then calmly said. "It is our expectation, the expectation of the United States, that we be *more* than just innocent bystanders—more than just diplomats who meekly stand by and listen to the information as it trickles in. We're here not only to listen, but to act—to participate in the tracking down of these two individuals and taking them into custody. We have a lot of questions to ask them. Furthermore, as was already communicated to your government before we arrived yesterday, we expect to be on an expedited schedule while we are here. This is not an exercise in formality; this is a critical situation requiring the expertise and cooperation of both of our countries. Share with us what information you have, and we will deliberate *with* you in determining its veracity—and in determining the feasibility of any operation—an extension of your own force, if you will."

Without hesitation Medlikov let out a short, deprecating laugh and said, "Ms. Wykoff, you are on Russian soil. You have no authority here, and we intend to *give* you no authority. We are sensitive to your country's plea for help, and that is why you are here, but make no mistake, you are here to observe and to learn— it is *we* who will make the decisions and decide the course of action. In the meantime, we will share whatever information we deem appropriate, and only *when* we deem it appropriate. We will find these men, and we will bring them to justice, but do not feign to believe that you are experts here. You're out of your element, and you will follow our lead. There is no other choice. You see?"

15

Confrontation

FRANKLIN BECAME ENCOURAGED WHILE LISTENING TO WYKOFF'S report that evening. She included a little bit of the blow-by-blow between her and Medlikov. The response from Washington was encouraging, but Angstrom detected subtle notes of disappointment in their voices. The last thing they said to Wykoff was a revelation: *The aches and pains are getting worse; time continues to be of essence.*

Everyone was huddled around the ruggedized laptop listening to Wykoff's report, and they nervously looked at each other when that last piece of news was delivered. As it stood, it was only twenty-one days until theoretical detonation. That didn't leave much time.

"I'm going to transmit," Angstrom suddenly said.

"Gonna have your own conversation with the sky, eh?" Grahame responded without skipping a beat.

Franklin, however, was surprised by Angstrom's announcement.

"What for? We're not supposed to use bandwidth unless it's absolutely necessary!"

Grahame sensed the tension, and he nodded to Gentry for both of them to step outside in order to let Angstrom and Franklin talk in private.

After they left, Angstrom said, "Tom, you heard it yourself, things are getting worse by the day!"

"John, this is only the second day of meetings. Christ, the first one was just a formality. Our team did better today. You heard Wykoff—she took control. Tomorrow it'll be even better. We're on this."

"Yes, she did do better. And to her credit, she didn't sugarcoat Medlikov's response: the Russians will do things on their own terms and at their own pace. It's not clear to me whether they're going to help us or not. Meantime, we've got a ticking time bomb ready to go off and do Lord knows what in the United States. For all we know the Russians *want* Frége to go off. Maybe that's been part of the plan all along."

Angstrom regretted saying that last part. He had let himself get goaded into saying more than he wanted to without any real effort on Franklin's part.

"C'mon, John, you heard it today—in only one day Wykoff got the Russians completely turned around. Tomorrow we'll learn even more—press them, just like Washington urged Wykoff tonight. Then Medlikov will reveal the plan to grab those bastards Terror and Strenzke."

It all sounded so easy, so convenient, Angstrom thought. Wrapped up, tied in a bow, and handed to them. He was suddenly reminded of those countless rounds of butting heads with Franklin over the years. No matter what he tried—passive-aggressive, firm, aloof—Franklin was hostile to the core. Angstrom had no patience for it.

"I hope you're right," he said. "You probably *are* right. But I'm still going to transmit. Now, I need to ask you to leave while I do so."

"What? The hell I will. I'm in on this too."

"Tom!"

Franklin was incredulous, but he ultimately went outside with the others, furious. He knew what his instructions were; he knew who had the lead.

Angstrom put on the headset, adjusted the mic, and began the process of establishing a K-Com link with the Pentagon.

He was alone for about twenty minutes before he went outside to tell everyone he was done.

"Well, how'd it go," Franklin anxiously whispered. Grahame and Gentry watched Angstrom as well to see what he would say. It was dark outside; everyone could barely see each other.

"Stay the course."

"That's it? You were on for close to half an hour and that's all you have to report? Stay the course?"

"Yeah, well, I wasn't talking for all that time. I stayed inside for a while and thought about things afterwards," responded Angstrom, which wasn't true. He *had* been talking with Washington all that time.

"So, stay the course," Franklin said as they all went back inside. "That's what I thought. I still can't get over how quick on the draw you were. I didn't think that was your nature, John. Doesn't seem like you."

"Mm," Angstrom murmured. He rubbed his chin for a moment while everyone looked at him. "I'm going back out for some air."

"Don't get lost," Grahame quickly said. He could tell Angstrom needed some space, like something was bothering him.

Before stepping outside, and while everyone continued to observe him, Angstrom sarcastically said to Grahame, "If you don't hear from me in thirty, send out the rescue team."

Thursday, July 9
[T_{detonate} minus 19 days]

When the Russians arrived at the conference room the next morning, Wykoff and her team were already seated and having breakfast. They all stood momentarily to acknowledge the arrival of the Russians, then took their seats again and continued eating. Medlikov's team, surprised at finding the Americans already there, arranged themselves on the other side of the table. Medlikov was miffed that the Americans weren't following the schedule established for them.

When Wykoff saw that Medlikov was settled, she pushed her plate forward and said, "Oleg, we're ready to hear your plan on how you're going to get Terror and Strenzke."

It was like a grenade tossed into Medlikov's lap first thing in the morning. He was taken aback at such a bold pronouncement. He'd thought his parting words the evening before would have made his position clear. He now realized he was wrong. But he wanted to see how serious she really was, how firm was her resolve. After all, what leverage did the Americans have to justify taking such a posture?

"Ms. Wykoff, as I said yesterday…"

"With all due respect," Wykoff firmly interrupted, "I can't place much credence in that. Our country sent us here with an expectation—an expectation for results. Cooperation by the Russian Government figures prominently into those expectations."

"And as I was about to say…"

"Furthermore, if your position is that you're going to do that at your own election, at your own sweet pace, frankly we don't have the time for it. If that's going to continue to be your intention, simply inform us right now and we'll be on our way. Only, I can assure you, the powers-that-be in my country will take careful note. If we have to return empty handed, and so soon, it will not be viewed favorably."

Medlikov already knew the United States was not pleased with the rate of progress after the first two days of meetings. Based upon what he heard from the wiretapped phone conversations, he knew the Americans could not be pushed much further.

"Our countries have certainly had their differences," Wykoff continued, "but there's a history of cooperation between us. Reference is made to the Sabotol Affair; we would think your country would have a great affinity to help us after all we did for you on that." She paused for dramatic effect, and then she stood up as if she was prepared to leave. She was on a roll, caught up in the moment. "I don't think more needs to be said. So, Oleg, tell me: What's it going to be? Are you intent on continuing to play these games with us, wasting our time with this slow pace of disclosure? Because if you are, we've got better things to do. Just let us know."

Ackman was flabbergasted by the bold position his colleague took. They hadn't discussed such a maneuver in advance, and it was a huge risk. If the Russians called her bluff they'd be out on their asses without anything to show for it. She was speaking on behalf of the entire country, risking her whole career in one fell swoop. If it backfired, she could kiss her career goodbye. The plane wouldn't have landed at Dulles and the Pentagon would have had her head on a platter. All of these concerns instantaneously ran through Ackman's mind, but he forced himself to remain calm and maintain his composure. He had no choice. Her strategy chosen, there was nothing else to do but play along, so he turned his attention from Wykoff back to Medlikov.

Medlikov tensed, clenched his fists, and glared at Wykoff across the table. While keeping his eyes on her, he said to one of his colleagues further down the table, "Put up today's information. Skip the first thirteen slides; go straight to the stuff on Bladlikov." The projector was turned on, the instructions followed. Medlikov and Wykoff continued to stare at each other as this was done. "Please, sit down, Ms. Wykoff. I'm sure you will be very pleased to hear our plan to capture Terror. This will occur day after next, if this meets with your approval."

It was Wykoff's turn to be caught off guard. Such a reversal by Medlikov—to the point of saying that Terror would be captured in two days—was an extreme departure from the slow pace of the last two days. She couldn't believe how effective her strategy was; it was a thrilling feeling. She forced herself to remain calm, however, suppressing any outward appearance of emotion.

"Thank you, Oleg. We would be pleased to hear this information," she said as she sat down.

Slides were skipped, the presentation advanced.

"This is Bladlikov," Medlikov said as the image of a man was shown on the screen. "He is Russian secret police. He has been undercover, posing as—how would you Americans say it?—a disenfranchised youth. He has tremendous hacking skills, and he used them to get a job in Terror's coding organization."

"Has he met Terror?" said Ackman.

"Please, patience!" Medlikov said in an annoyed tone. He glared at Ackman for a moment. "Now, as I was about to say, Bladlikov has been in Terror's organization for over two years. It goes without saying how difficult it was to get him into it and how long it took.

"Bladlikov has legitimate hacking skills; he's part of a new, undercover segment of our police force: highly educated, with an emphasis on technology, more specifically, coding and hacking. Due to this fact, his stature has grown within Terror's organization. Over time he was moved from one physical location to another, each time moving into roles of increasing responsibility. For a long time he didn't even hear of anyone referred to as Terror, nor were we aware of such a person. Then, about four months ago, Bladlikov was moved yet again. This time it was to a significantly larger compound, the largest we know of in the organization. It was then that Bladlikov became aware of a man referred to as Terror; his name started to come up frequently in discussions. But in addition, Terror made frequent visits to the compound. Everyone deferred to him, clearly the man in charge of everything."

Wykoff and Ackman were on the edge of their seats, fascinated by what they heard.

"It was through Bladlikov's excellent police work, including much information that he was able to provide us under dangerous circumstances, that we learned of the true identity of Terror."

"You know who Terror is?" Ackman couldn't help but interject. When Medlikov provided no response, Ackman said, "Incredible."

Wykoff was aggravated by Ackman's interruption. She was almost deferential when she looked at Medlikov and said, "Please, continue."

A new photo was displayed. It was the photo of a man from the shoulders up, very formal in nature, with nothing in the background, like a passport photo.

"This is Ivan Terrebenzikov, also known as Terror. He was a young man freshly graduated from the Saint Petersburg National Research University of Information, Technologies, Mechanics and Optics when this photo was taken. He was recruited into the KGB. This was back in 1988. After the failed coup d'état of 1991—the *August Putsch* to wrest control from Mikhail Gorbachev—our intelligence forces unfortunately suffered through many difficult changes. Upon the dissolution of the Soviet Union in 1991, Boris Yeltsin became President of the new 'Russian Federation,' and he dismantled the KGB. Terrebenzikov was moved to the newly formed FSK, the Federal Counterintelligence Service. He apparently became disenchanted with the disarray that he saw all around him. In 1995, when President Yeltsin yet again reorganized the FSK into the FSB, Terrebenzikov was put into our Signals Intelligence Division. People still in the FSB who knew him back then have said that Terrebenzikov became disgusted with the direction of the FSB, the whole country for that matter. It wasn't long after his placement there that he quit."

"That was in 1995, some eighteen years ago. That would make him close to fifty by now," Wykoff said.

"Forty-eight," Medlikov responded.

"Ah, right," Wykoff said. "Listen, I'm sorry for the interruption Oleg, but this is simply incredible. Excellent police work. What do you know of him between then and now?"

"Not much, as you might've guessed. As I say, it was only through Bladlikov's excellent undercover work that we discovered Terrebenzikov was this person known as Terror. Our search of official records shows nothing, like he ceased to exist after he resigned from the FSB. We now know, however, that he is the technical genius behind a large, powerful, sophisticated cyber criminal organization that spans the globe. It was only after the United States contacted us that we realized just how expansive it was."

Medlikov waited to see if Wykoff or Ackman would say anything, and when they didn't, he continued. "Bladlikov is watched very closely. We have only limited contact with him. Nevertheless, it is because of him that we have learned the location of Terrebenzikov's compound—the central hub of the operation, the place where the most sophisticated coding and hacking occurs. It has been under our surveillance now for quite some time.

"The photo you now see is the front of the compound. It's in an industrial part of St. Petersburg—lots of large, old warehouses, many of which are empty and unused. In fact, this is why we chose to meet with you here in St. Petersburg instead of Moscow." An aerial image of the compound was displayed. "The warehouse takes up a whole city block, and it is filled with Terrebenzikov's hacking organization. This is the very core of the operation, and it's right here in St. Petersburg."

Wykoff's team was silent, staring intently at the photo. The building looked like a fortress. Guards stood ominously on the outside, in some cases with weapons visible—even on the roof.

"The compound is under electronic surveillance. It leaks signal all over the place. Now, I want you to watch closely. This is the only video we have of Terrebenzikov. As you can see, it's not much, but it's him."

The image was jerky and blurred, such that not too much could really be seen of him.

"He has been going in and out of the compound more often lately, as if something important was developing."

Wykoff wondered why they had only that single, shitty video of him if he was entering and leaving so often, but she let it pass. Medlikov was on a roll; she didn't want to interrupt him.

As if Medlikov read her mind, he said, "We have not been able to track him when he comes out; the multitude of warehouses in the area is like a...a labyrinth. He darts in and out of them, often surrounded by people, obscuring our line of sight to him. In addition, it is our speculation, though we have not confirmed it, that old, underground tunnels are being used for secret passage between the various warehouses. These buildings are very old— over a hundred years—and there are no blueprints of them on record anymore. The underground tunnels connecting the warehouses were used at one time for industrial purposes. Not so much anymore, but whenever city inspectors have checked such warehouses in the past, they found such tunnels.

"Anyway, as I said, we know from Bladlikov that Terrebenzikov goes into the compound much more often now, and because of this, we established a way for Bladlikov to signal us whenever he does. A pattern was identified, certain times of the day when more likely than not Terrebenzikov was in the compound." Medlikov turned from the screen to Wykoff. "So you see, we have been very busy, even before your country's plea for help. We have our own concerns to think about, and a hacking organization on a scale of this one will not be tolerated in Russia."

"What about Strenzke," Ackman said. Wykoff turned to him and nodded, and then back to Medlikov with an inquisitive look.

"We find no strong link between the two men. Strenzke was even in prison for a while not too long ago. We cannot find any ties between them other than the photo you pointed out to us, the validity of which we would question."

Wykoff, other than raising the corner of one of her eyebrows, said nothing. Medlikov was compelled to say more.

"We think it's nothing to be made of—a red herring, as you would say. No, our focus has been on Terrebenzikov. He is key."

Wykoff wasn't sure what to make of Medlikov's comment about Strenzke. The CIA had information on him, knew his background. She saw the Interpol report herself. But she wasn't going to challenge Medlikov, not after all he had disclosed. They were making great progress, and she needed to follow through on Terrebenzikov. Strenzke could be dealt with later.

"Okay, so now what? What do you propose be done about this?" Wykoff said.

"We go. We verify Terrebenzikov is there through Bladlikov, and then we storm the compound. We get him and shut the operation down, give you access to it, yes? Day after tomorrow; we already have a plan."

Wykoff was very pleased with this development but refrained from showing it. A break was called. The Russians left the room and a tray of pastries and coffee was carted in for the Americans. The team was clearly pleased with the sudden turnaround in Medlikov, including his sudden sensitivity to the urgency of the situation.

Wykoff wasn't quite sure what to chalk it up to, whether it was her own performance during the meetings, or just an otherwise inevitable progression of events, the pace of which was planned all along by the Russians. In any event, significant progress was made, and optimism resulted, even confidence. Just a little more fight was necessary, a little more pushing for Wykoff to get what she wanted. She was almost there.

The American team stretched their legs, one-by-one making their way to the refreshment cart. Nothing was said by any of them at first. Eventually they broke into a couple of small groups, with Wykoff and Ackman forming one of them. They stood next to the cart.

"Excellent work, Jane," Ackman said as he took a sip of his coffee. "Where do you think we should go next?"

Wykoff shook her head slightly as she chewed her food, raising a forefinger to her lips. She didn't want to talk. It was likely anything they said would be overheard by bugs planted in the room. For all they knew there was one right on the cart. Ackman silently acknowledged, and they finished the break without talking.

When Oleg's team returned, Wykoff decided to engage in a little small talk. A courtesy extended to the other side, a gesture of appreciation for the progress that had been made.

"Oleg, this square at which we are located, St. Isaac's Square, it's quite impressive."

"Ah yes, thank you. St. Petersburg is a beautiful city; it doesn't always get the recognition it deserves, unfortunately, because of the bad...press that our country sometimes receives."

"What's the statue in the middle of the square? The man on the horse?"

"That's a monument to Nicholas I."

"Very beautiful. And how about the big building to the south?"

"That's the Marinsky Palace, where our Legislative Assembly holds session. The hotel you are staying at is very famous as well; it used to be one of the most luxurious hotels in the Russian Empire back in the 1900s."

"It's very nice. Thank you for such fine accommodations."

"You're welcome."

"Well," Wykoff then said. "Please share with us the plan we'll use to get Terrebenzikov."

"Excuse me?" Medlikov responded.

"The plan. Let's discuss the plan we'll use to get him. We want to know all the details, from start to finish, so we can be most effective in helping you."

"No, you misunderstand, Ms. Wykoff. There will be no helping. We do this by ourselves. This is a Russian matter involving a Russian citizen. I'm sorry if there was a misunderstanding, but you won't be actively participating. We could not allow it."

Wykoff paused, framing her position in her mind before she spoke. "Oleg, this isn't just a Russian matter. Look, see that man at the end of our table?" She gestured to the man sitting at the far end of her side of the table. "Adam Sircy—a cyber forensics expert. He needs to talk with Terrebenzikov. To interview him as soon as possible. We need immediate, direct access, right at the premises of the compound. There are some algorithms Sircy wants to discuss, things we need to learn about. He's going to want to tap into their computer network right on the spot. So," Wykoff said, turning from Sircy back to Medlikov, "as you can see, we need to be there when this happens."

"Hmm," was all Medlikov could immediately say. He looked over at the others sitting on his side of the table. "Perhaps," he finally said, "we should take another break. I need to discuss this. What you are asking is unusual to put it mildly, and I don't know if we can allow it."

Wykoff was about to say something when Medlikov held up his hand to stop her. "We will see," he said.

His team rose and once again left the room.

"Ms. Wykoff, I will be frank with you, I am quite surprised at the news that I have to deliver."

Wykoff's team braced themselves.

"My superiors would first of all reiterate that we want to cooperate with the United States. Despite the differences that our two countries have had, and that we *still* have, we feel that in regards to this matter it is important that our two countries are aligned. Therefore, it is with great pleasure, and as I said, to my complete surprise, that we can allow you some level of participation in what we do. Of course, we expect your country to appreciate this heightened level of cooperation by Russia."

"Thank you, Oleg. I can assure you that we most certainly do. First of all, your hosting us as you have and exchanging information with us has been of vital importance. And now, to take such immediate action on the information...my superiors will be very pleased."

"Good," Medlikov said. "I should tell you that we have had this plan for Terrebenzikov for some time now; your visit here is therefore quite fortunate in terms of timing." He turned to the last person sitting on his side of the table and said, "Have Captain Kreschenko come here immediately, along with the materials to explain our plan." Then he turned to Wykoff and said, "Your team may be in a position to *observe*. That is as far as we can allow. You will not, however, be part of the actual assault on the compound. I'm sorry, but for your own safety we must insist. This is non-negotiable."

Wykoff thought about this for a moment. Then she turned around in her seat so that her back was to the table and invited Ackman to do the same. She wanted to huddle with him to discuss a few things without being overheard by the Russians.

"Do you want us to leave the room for a moment?" Medlikov offered.

"No, that's okay," Wykoff replied. "Just give us a minute."

After discussing matters between them, Wykoff and Ackman eventually turned back around.

"That would be fine, Oleg," she said. "As long as we then get immediate access to Terrebenzikov, right there at the compound, that would be acceptable to the United States—and most appreciated. Thank you. Now, please share your plan."

Testimony

Before the Committee on Banking, Housing, and Urban Affairs
U.S. Senate, Washington, D.C.
Governor Daniel F. Goldman: *Change in Cyber Attack High-Profile Targets*
July 9 [Excerpt]

Besides the increasing frequency, the scope of high-profile targets has changed. Figure 1 shows the top targets for the previous year. The goals of these attacks are evident by virtue of their categorization.

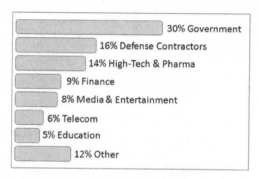

FIGURE 1

Figure 2 shows that over the past year attacks against financial institutions and commercial enterprises have surpassed everything else at an alarming rate. While some of these attacks were merely intended as disruptions to business in the normal course, the vast majority were promulgated for theft.

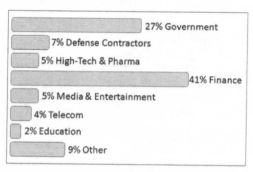

FIGURE 2

Through its oversight, the Federal Reserve has instituted procedural measures to help protect against circumnavigation of protective security measures. Moreover, the National Institute of Standards and Technology is creating a cyber security framework...

16

A Whisper into the Sky

Thursday, July 9—Evening
[T$_{detonate}$ minus 19 days]

IT WAS COLD OUTSIDE, THE AIR WAS MOIST, THE SKY DARK; stars shone brightly. Angstrom looked around at the small backyard of the house, closed in as it was by densely populated fir trees: the ground was covered with white gravel packed firm in the hard dirt; small weeds sprouted; the barn was overgrown with vegetation, its wood heavily weathered.

They had heard another briefing from Wykoff that evening at around 7:30 P.M. Plans for a raid were revealed. Angstrom then had another of his own conversations directly with Washington. Franklin, for his part, was incensed at being excluded again, which was of absolutely no concern to Angstrom.

It was now 11:30 P.M. and everyone besides Angstrom was inside the house asleep. Angstrom walked from the back door of the house for some distance and came upon a large boulder protruding from the ground. Although it was cold to the touch it didn't deter him, and he scooted on top of it, his knees bent so he could put his arms around them. It reminded him of something he had heard many years ago while visiting an ancient temple in Nara, Japan: the belief that such boulders were the "bones of the earth." It seemed like that to Angstrom just then.

A woodpecker sounded, crickets chirped. It was eerily peaceful. He turned his back to the house, looked up into the sky, and became reflective.

Wykoff was asserting herself in the meetings, he thought. Maybe she was worth a chance in his group after all. A second look to say the least. Angstrom made a mental note of it.

But then he stopped himself; he didn't want to think about Cyberknife that evening—not Franklin, not Wykoff, not any of it.

It was late, so dark that he could barely see the house when he looked over his shoulder at it.

His eyes went back to the sky and he contemplated it. The vastness...the infinite space...he gazed at it for quite some time; it affected him and altered his perspective, or perhaps, helped illuminate a different perspective that had been developing in him. For a moment there was a sense that what he was doing in Russia—everything involved for that matter—was trivial. Those stars...his subconscious kept pondering them.

And there was Anne, a meaning in it all. She penetrated the void. She was the bridge from that boulder on the ground to the stars above him.

He wondered yet again what she was doing...he couldn't get her out of his mind. It was around 11:30 P.M. where he was at; that would make it around 3:30 P.M. in Washington. He imagined her eating the afternoon snack she liked to have at about that time of the day, usually some type of energy bar or a piece of fruit. His mind could see her clearly, like he was sitting at the table across from her. He watched her chew, the black birthmark at the corner of her upper lip moving with the motion.

How could he be here, stuck in this lonely, God-forsaken place, while she was there, alone, so far away from him? He never felt like this before on a mission. He used to miss his two girls sometimes, especially when they were much younger, but he never felt this way about his ex-wife Breann. Things were different now—he was different. He realized that. From the time of his mental breakdown until now, his inner being continued to evolve—evolve in a most profound way. Like the progression of Miles Davis from the stark, singular tones of his cool jazz period to the much more complex, seemingly confused nature of the *Bitches Brew*—one completely unrecognizable from the other.

He took a deep breath—the fresh air felt good—and continued to focus on the stars. He could see Ursa Major; there was Alkaid at the end of the bear's tail.

Then he imagined Davis later in the day, walking on 35th street, walking home from the music shop. The image was vivid in his mind. An uncomfortable feeling came over him. His imagination projected someone else in the image: a stranger. A man following her. A spy. An assassin. Then the perspective of Angstrom's view changed: he was looking over the assassin's shoulder; the mysterious man approached Anne, almost within her reach.

Angstrom grew tense. He couldn't see the stars anymore. He was looking at them, but they weren't there. As he stared into the sky, he whispered to himself, *"Anne."*

Grahame's voice suddenly interrupted his thoughts: "John, you okay?" Grahame realized he had startled Angstrom. He had encroached on his space and didn't realize until too late that Angstrom was deep in thought.

"Huh, yeah, yeah. Hey, Roy," Angstrom hastily said as he realized where he was. "Beautiful night, isn't it?" He wondered if Grahame had heard him say Anne's name out loud. He wasn't really sure if he *had* said it out loud. He was disappointed in himself for not having heard Grahame's approach. It wasn't like him. His mind was clouded, his senses dulled. Concern for Anne Davis was affecting him.

"You sure you're okay?" Grahame said.

"Yeah, I'm good. Just getting some fresh air—good for thinking."

Grahame didn't immediately respond, fully conscious now of having intruded. Finally, he said, "Look at those stars."

Angstrom could tell that Grahame was the type of man who, under different circumstances, he could have become friends with. But in the lives they led that would have been difficult, if not impossible. Still, the notion, upon thinking about it, caused him to become more open.

"A strange mission, this *cooperation* with the Russians," Angstrom said. "Not my normal game. Takes a little getting used to, and I can't say I have yet."

"I know. I'm feeling the same way." A pause, then, "What's the deal with Franklin? Is he solid?"

"Yes, he is. He's excellent in the field. He can get on your nerves every once in a while, but don't take it personally. It's just how he is."

They were both quiet for a while. Grahame took a sip of coffee from the mug he was holding. Steam rose upward from the hot liquid.

Angstrom wanted to say more, to share his feelings, his fear for Davis' safety, but it was against his nature. He was an incredibly private person. Finally, he said, "How long have you been doing this, Roy. I mean as a SEAL...how long have you been one?"

"About six years commissioned. Lifespan's not great in this field, one way or another. It's physically and mentally demanding—nothing else like it."

Grahame knew the kind of thinking that went behind Angstrom's question. He could sense that Angstrom was in some kind of a reflective mood, but he didn't press the issue.

"Are you married?" said Angstrom.

"Nope. Never have been. Maybe some day; I won't say it's out of the question. Certainly not compatible with my current lifestyle. You know what I mean?"

"Yes, I do."

Quiet again. Then Angstrom said, "You can't talk much about your work—certainly with others outside of the force."

"Right. That doesn't make it any easier. I suppose it's the same for you."

"Maybe even more so."

"I don't know, I'm still enjoying the hell out of it...and I know I'm doing good for the country. The physical and mental exertion is an incredible high in its own right, and I work with a tremendous team; we'd do anything for each other. Once this is over, it's over. Can't do this kind of thing forever. That's why I tell myself there's time for the other part later."

"And the occasional screw to tie you over?"

"Heh, heh. No. I'm not like that." Grahame thought about what he'd just said and continued, "I mean, I'm not hard up for it. If something like that happens every now and then, it happens, but I'm not out there prowling for it. To be honest, I really don't have the time or energy for it...I can't allow something like that to cause me to lose focus."

Angstrom moved and got off the rock. He stood right next to Grahame, but they could barely see each other's faces in the darkness.

Grahame heard him say, "You've been fully briefed, right?"

"Yes, I have."

"Alright, let's go back inside. I'm starting to feel a few bugs nipping at me."

"Yeah, sounds good. I can feel 'em too."

"I'll transmit when I get there—should take around 4.5 hours."

"So you're leaving tonight?"

"Yes."

"Does Tom know?"

"No."

A grin appeared on Grahame's face. Somehow he liked that fact.

The next morning when the team awoke, Angstrom was gone. As promised, Angstrom transmitted to Grahame from the Untolovo safe house at around 5 A.M.

* * *

Line Intercept
Report Date/time (U.S. Washington, D.C.): July 9/9 P.M.
Priority Level: High-Immediate
Geodata:
Source- Lat: 66°26′19″ N, Lon: 71°39′16″ E (Untolovo, Russia)
Destination.- Lat: 68°27′34″ N, Lon: 73°35′25″ E (Mys Peschanyy, Russia)
Link: U.S. K-Com v.23 "Prine"
U1 ID: John Angstrom
U2 ID: Lt. Roy Grahame (SEAL)

U1[072314 0430]: *Radio sync. Verify.*

U1[072315 0432]: *Repeat. Radio sync. Verify.*

U2[072315 0432]: *Ten-ninety-two. Sync confirmed. Over.*

U1[072315 0432]: *'Bout time. Over.*

U2[072315 0432]: *Hey, wasn't sure exactly when you'd complete the hike. Over.*

U1[072315 0432]: *In position. Repeat. In position. Will beacon others. Over.*

U2[072315 0432]: *Roger. Didn't take you too long. Over.*

U1[072315 0432]: *Would rather be on that rock, looking at the stars. I'll relay details of raid to others. Min necessary. Will instruct to deploy. Observe only. Over.*

U2[072315 0433]: *Roger. Over.*

U1[072315 0433]: *Change protocol. Immediate. Over.*

U2[072315 0433]: *Confirmed. Which one? Over.*

U1[072315 0433]: *Trans schedule as follows: 5 "B" as in bravo…"A" as in Adam…"K" as in kite. Will initiate link to others via group-com. Over.*

U2[072315 0434]: *Confirmed. Over.*

U1[072315 0434]: *Bugs were bad. Worse than first night. Over.*

U2[072315 0434]: *Should've used DEET. Told 'ya. Over.*

U1[072315 0434]: *Sign out. Scan sync trigger. Over.*

U2[072315 0434]: *Scan sync ready. Over.*

U1[072315 0434]: *Scan sync 5-4-3-2-1-register. Out.*

17

Tuned and Primed

Friday, July 10
[T$_{detonate}$ minus 18 days]

EARLY THAT SAME MORNING ANGSTROM RELAYED the information on the planned raid of Terrebenzikov's compound—date, time, location—to the rest of his team in St. Petersburg via the ad hoc group link over the specialized K-Com channel.

"That's day after today!" Stafford said excitedly after the communication was over.

"That's right," Gordon calmly responded, turning off the portable communication unit and putting it back into its small case.

"That doesn't leave us much time to prepare."

"It's enough. Things will move fast sometimes; you'll get used to it."

Gordon and Stafford had checked into the hotel in St. Petersburg together as a married couple under fabricated identities. Gordon was sitting on the edge of the bed, and he looked over to Stafford, who had gone to sit at a small desk in the main room. He couldn't help but look at her fiery red hair, even after she had cut it short for the mission. He was still fascinated by her appearance, and he was finding that she had a fabulous personality to boot. She was the full package as far as he was concerned.

It was Angstrom beguiling him, he thought. Angstrom put her on the team to torment him with her beauty. Gordon knew that was absurd, but the thought made him chuckle just the same.

"What's so funny?" Stafford said from the other room.

"Huh? Oh, uh, anyway," he said, "we'll be ready. The plan is for you and me to observe the raid without being seen, so we're going to need to scout for a location. The Franklin contingency is going to be there too. We don't want them to see us. It's going to be tight."

"I have to admit," she said as she came back into the bedroom, "I'm used to a lot more disclosure on the details than this. I don't even..."

Gordon looked at her, his head tilted slightly sideways, waiting to see what she would say. She caught herself mid-sentence. She knew things were going to be different than at the FBI and that she needed to learn fast. It was a new set of rules, and the last thing she needed was to start complaining.

Gordon looked at her expectantly, waiting for her to finish what she was going to say.

"Okay, never mind. Strike that. I'm fine. So how should we approach this?" she finally said, shaking her head with a somewhat disappointed look on her face, aggravated with herself.

"No problem." He went over to the suitcase and pulled out a book of maps, each page covering a small section of St. Petersburg. Squares and rectangles with names on them denoted buildings. "Here," he said, pointing to the map. "Somewhere around here is where we'll need to be. This is where Terrebenzikov's compound is located, and over here is where Wykoff was told they'd watch from. So, we're going to go check out this area over here," he said, pointing to an adjacent area.

"Hopefully there's a suitable location for us. It may be tricky; I don't know what's there. It's not clear from the map, and I couldn't get any more details. Unoccupied warehouses, operating businesses, we'll have to go check it out. Even that's not going to be easy. According to John, the compound is swarming with guards."

"Okay, well, let's do it. I'm ready," she said eagerly.

He hesitated. "Hmm, I don't know. Maybe...maybe I should do this alone. Just to be safe, so we don't attract a lot of attention."

She was stunned but kept a straight face.

"I'm kidding, I'm kidding. But we have to go shopping first."

"Shopping?"

"Yeah, we're gonna need a pair of binoculars, and we don't have any. We'll go to a store in the main square and pick up a pair." Without her having a chance to think about it, he said, "Okay, let's go. We'll discuss our approach on the way."

As they prepared to leave, Stafford asked, "What about Thomas? When will we hear from him...to make sure he's okay?"

"Don't worry about that. He's doing what he needs to do. When the time comes, he'll be where he's supposed to be."

Gordon's response surprised her. For the moment he wouldn't even tell her where Reed was or what he was doing.

A satellite image with more detail of the compound would have been nice, Gordon thought, but there wasn't enough bandwidth in their link for it. Instead they had to rely upon a description from Angstrom, who had gotten a satellite image through his higher bandwidth link on K-Com. Because of what Angstrom relayed to them, they would be able to move through the area more safely and hopefully find a suitable vantage point.

A taxi cab dropped them off about 2.5 miles from the location, in an area that was at least a little more cosmopolitan as compared to the industrial section of St. Petersburg for which they were ultimately headed. Their clothes were ordinary: blue jeans, pullover shirt for him, same with a short-sleeve blouse for her. She wore flats, making the walk through the city easier.

Gordon carried nothing with him except a small shopping bag containing the binoculars they had purchased. He had no gun. It would have been too risky moving through the city with one.

It was a strange feeling, something he wasn't used to, this walking through St. Petersburg out in the open and unarmed. The vulnerability was not a feeling he liked, which he took the trouble to tell Stafford. They held hands as they walked on the sidewalk through the throng of people, playing the part of husband and wife.

"We can't go any farther together," he whispered to her all of a sudden after they stopped in the middle of the sidewalk. "Give me a kiss, and then go across the street and wait for me in that crowded coffee shop over there. Here, you take the bag with you."

Stafford looked across the street and then back to Gordon.

"Listen, don't speak to anyone while you're there; not even the waitstaff. Act like you're mute if you have to; just point to something on the menu and order. You've got the Russian rubles I gave you before, right?"

"Yes, of course," she responded, reflexively patting the small white purse that hung on her shoulder.

"Alright, good. I'll come back and meet you there when I'm done, okay?"

"And you feel I can't come?"

"It's like I said, the surroundings are going to change pretty significantly. Our husband and wife routine won't look right in that area; it's too industrial."

She nodded in comprehension but wished it weren't true. She wanted to be a part of as much as she could on the mission, to soak it all up and learn.

"Now, give me a smile like you love me, and a short kiss," Gordon whispered, smiling as if to mask the very instructions he gave her. The kiss wasn't absolutely necessary, but he couldn't resist.

Gordon hastily walked in the direction of the compound. Halfway there the surroundings changed; there were fewer shops and restaurants and an increasing number of old buildings. When he was only a few city blocks away, it was all industrial: delivery trucks, shipping platforms, and one after the other of large, old warehouses. His casual attire stood out in such a setting, so he had to move about more carefully. He walked in the shadows as much as he could, or at a minimum close to the interior of the sidewalk, shielded by those few others that passed by in the opposite direction.

He eventually came upon an old, narrow cobblestone street. A building about a block down matched Angstrom's description, and Gordon knew he had reached the destination. He spotted men standing guard at the main and side entrances, so he bent down to pretend to tie his shoe so that he could survey the area. He needed to find someplace where he and Stafford could position themselves in order to observe the raid. There was a fire escape on the building right above him, with windows along the wall. Based upon what Angstrom had previously reported, that was where Wykoff's group would be situated. It had the perfect view. The problem, however, was that there wasn't any place else evident where he and Stafford could go.

He had to stand up; he could only tie his shoe for so long before it looked suspicious. He turned in the opposite direction of the compound and walked along the narrow street. The outside wall of the compound itself was made of dark brick and extended all along the street as Gordon walked. It seemed to go on forever. About fifty yards farther there was another building on his side of the street—smaller than the others and only two stories high— that caught his attention. Even this far away from the compound's front entrance, the wall of the compound still continued across the street from where he stood. He turned to look toward the front entrance of the compound; the view wasn't great, but one side of the main entrance could still be seen, as well as another side door about a hundred feet closer. He turned his attention back to the two-story building and figured it might be just what they needed. It looked like an old abandoned store. There was an old wooden sign with faded writing on it attached to the front facade. The front windows were boarded up, the door chained shut. Looking upward, he saw that the windows on the second story were boarded up as well. That wouldn't do. Then it occurred to him: if the rooftop was accessible, it might be the perfect spot.

He went to the rear of the store to check it out. From there he saw that a chain on the back door had been cut. Someone, at some point, had broken into the place, and no one had bothered to replace the chain. This was the spot, he said to himself. Stafford could go to the building's roof and observe the raid from there.

It had taken him a while to get to where he was. Stafford couldn't stay at that coffee shop forever, Gordon thought. But he wasn't done. He wanted to see if he could find a different vantage point with a closer view. He wanted to see if he could actually get inside of the compound. It was so large, maybe he could move anonymously within it, depending upon what the inside was like. He went back and forth in his mind as to whether he should try it. It was risky, but being inside while the raid occurred, not just standing outside watching, could prove invaluable—his trained eye could catch things that others might miss, even in the heat of the action. And he knew that this was probably one of the most important missions he'd ever been on, maybe *the* most important. The higher the stakes, the higher the risks, he thought.

He looked in the direction of the compound and eyed the side entrance, noticing again the two armed guards standing in front of it. There was no chance he could get in through there, no matter how much he thought about it. Then he remembered what Angstrom had relayed to him about the possibility of tunnels below, and how they may connect the compound to the surrounding warehouses. It was worth a shot, he thought, so he continued the walk down the narrow street away from the compound. Eventually he reached a point where the compound's wall across the street ended and the wall of a new warehouse began. It took him almost a half-hour to carefully make his way about its perimeter and study it. He found a delivery dock that wasn't being used but had its large door open, and he slipped inside.

From there it was a circuitous navigation through the various hallways and rooms of the building—trial and error while he took pains to avoid being noticed. There were parts of the building where almost no one was around; other parts had a few people scattered here and there. It definitely didn't seem like a warehouse that was fully operational, Gordon thought.

The route he took was certainly too dangerous for Stafford to come along as well. It didn't matter how good he and she were, there was no way they could both go through that warehouse together and not stand out. But when the time came, he could do so by himself. Stafford could stand on the abandoned store's rooftop while he was inside of the compound. That is, if he could find a tunnel that led to the compound and gain entrance to it without being caught. He needed to make his way into the bowels of the building, find the tunnel if it existed, take it to the compound, and then hope there was no one at the other end to meet him. A lot of risk piling up.

If only he could find the tunnel. The building was huge. It was like finding a needle in a haystack.

It was another half-hour of slow movement through the building, ducking, hiding, and in some cases listening to what others nearby said, before he got the feeling he was close. It was a mental struggle as well: he needed to remember where he was and how he got there so he could get back out, and also to keep in mind the general direction at which the compound resided with respect to where he stood. Time was adding up; he was leaving Stafford alone in that coffee shop for too long.

His sense was that he was right in the middle of the adjacent building, in the heart of it. And there, at the end of a long hallway, he saw a set of large metal doors, both of them open. On either side of them stood two armed guards. His guess was that that was it, the entrance to the underground tunnel connecting to the compound.

Even if he could think of a way to take those two guards out, would there be more of them at the other end of the tunnel? More risk, he thought. He wasn't used to it. He had already gotten an uneasy feeling about openly walking through the streets of St. Petersburg, unarmed no less. Now he was prowling around in a warehouse adjacent to a Russian cyber hacking compound. The more risk that accumulated, the greater the chance of something going wrong, and too much risk was accumulating. Maybe he was taking things too far. He'd have to think about it. For now, he needed to get out of there and back to Stafford. He'd left her alone long enough. She was probably well past her third or fourth coffee, even if she sipped slowly.

He was right in thinking that it would take him less time to get out than it did to get in. The only problem was that when he surveyed the tables that filled the outside seating area of the café, he didn't see Stafford. The outdoor seating area was covered by a plastic tarp to shield the café's customers from the sun, so it cast a shadow over the tables; he could still see clearly enough, and she wasn't there. He was about to go toward the front door to the inside of the place when he felt a tap on the shoulder.

When he turned to look, it was Stafford. Bright red hair and a big smile on her face. She put her arms around the back of his neck and leaned over to give him a short kiss. Then they separated and smiled at each other.

She was playing the part well, he thought.

"I couldn't stay there anymore," she whispered to him through smiling lips. "I was on my fifth refill and two pastries."

"Good. You did right," he whispered back. They turned to walk in the direction of their hotel and held hands as they walked. "So where'd you go?" he asked after they had walked a little farther.

"Oh, there was a small portrait gallery a few stores down, so I spent some time in there. After that I looked around in a book store."

"You didn't pick up anything in English, did you?" he said in earnest.

"No, of course not. I just spent time at the magazine rack, mainly looking at pictures in fashion magazines."

"Smart. That was good." Surprisingly, he was rather enjoying the role of mentor.

She said, "How did it go in there?"

"It went well. We've got a lot to talk about, so let's find a quiet place and talk. Look, there's a bench over there; let's go sit."

"Oh honey," she said in a playful voice, "I just love this vacation we're having together."

He looked at her and laughed.

"I'm sorry, was I playing the part too much?"

"No, that was perfect. Absolutely perfect."

* * *

Grahame communicated with Angstrom that evening over the K-Com link; he relayed Wykoff's latest report she had provided to Washington, doing so in the briefest terms possible (per the limited vocabulary protocol). Angstrom in turn communicated with his team in St. Petersburg over the Ad Hoc group link. He also communicated directly with Thomas Reed during a separate transmission.

Line Intercept
Report Date/time (U.S. Washington, D.C.): July 10/3:15 P.M.
Priority Level: High-Immediate
Geodata:
Source- Lat: 66°26'19" N, Lon: 71°39'16" E (Untolovo, Russia)
Destination- Lat: 59° 53' 39" N, 40° 15' 51" E (St. Petersburg, Russia)
Link: U.S. K-Com Ad Hoc; One-to-one direct; Thread A14.3
U1 ID: John Angstrom
U5 ID: Thomas J. Reed

U1[072315 1432]: *Radio sync. Verify.*

U5[072315 1432]: *Ten-ninety-two. Sync confirmed.*

U1[072315 1432]: *Excellent. Good ship. Have you made connection with Redblood? Over.*

U5[072315 1433]: *Affirmative. Over.*

--PAUSED PORTION; LINK MAINTAINED--

U5[072315 1435]: *Repeat Affirmative. Over.*

U1[072315 1435]: *Good. Good. Does story hold? Over.*

U5[072315 1435]: *Caused surprise. Doubt expressed at what was proposed. Over.*

U1[072315 1436]: *That's what I thought. Gotta move fast. Faster than we thought. Push it, but don't put yourself in jeopardy. Over.*

U5[072315 1436]: Already on it. Positive response to overtures. Potential high for what you proposed. Over.

U1[072315 1436]: *Good ship. Stay on it. Out.*

18

Jam Session

Saturday, July 11
[T$_{detonate}$ minus 17 days]

THE PIECES CAME TOGETHER LIKE A GIL EVANS/MILES DAVIS JAZZ composition: the strings played—the Franklin contingency had its meetings, Angstrom's team got into position; and now it was time for the brass to "weigh in"—the raid.

Wykoff and her team, accompanied by Medlikov and a couple of his men, were perched at the three windows of one of the rooms of the building that overlooked the compound, just as Gordon had figured. There they waited, anxious to witness the sudden onslaught of armed police and the infiltration of the compound. Wykoff still insisted that at least part of her team should play a more active role, but Medlikov remained firm, insisting it was not possible—especially for "diplomats" like themselves.

The Russian police were assembled at a station about a half-mile away, preparing for the strike. During this time, Gordon and Stafford made their way to the two-story abandoned store he had found the day before. Gordon didn't realize how hard he had been squeezing Stafford's hand as they walked; it had been a long time since he held a woman's hand, especially of a woman as beautiful as Stafford.

"Let up a little," she finally said.

He was moving rapidly, concentrating on where they were going and what needed to be done, forgetting that he was even holding her hand. "What? Oh, sorry." He lightened his grip, but then a moment later he released it. "We have to break up here. Give me a hundred feet and then follow."

She stopped and let go of her grip. He moved quickly and with purpose.

When he was about a hundred feet ahead of her, she started to follow him, retracing his path as best she could. And then he disappeared. Stafford was puzzled but continued to move forward. When she got to the point where she believed he had disappeared, there was a narrow passageway leading between two buildings. Bordering one side was the old store Gordon had previously identified. She studied it, wondering. At the end of the narrow passage, which was about thirty feet long, she saw Gordon. He stood there waiting for her, hands at his sides, one foot pointed slightly sideways. The sun was at his back; all she saw was his silhouette, but she knew it was him. As soon as Gordon saw that she had seen him, he moved. She went to where he was standing before and found herself in a back yard overgrown with weeds, a rusty cyclone fence encircling it. As much as Gordon had told her in advance, he hadn't told her about this part, and she was slightly confused by where she found herself.

"Psst," she heard. She looked toward the building and saw Gordon standing in the darkness of the interior, just inside the door. He motioned for her to follow him. She entered and instinctively closed the door behind her. It was too dark to see, almost pitch black. She began to reopen the door to let some light in when he instructed her not to.

The pungent odor of human waste immediately assaulted her senses. She felt a hand grab her arm, and before she knew it, Gordon was leading her up some unseen stairs to the next floor. Then there was a sound and a jarring of her arm, and she could tell that Gordon had stumbled. She heard a growl; it didn't sound like him.

Gordon let go of her arm and there were sounds of a struggle. She quickly realized that a squatter had been sleeping on the stairs and Gordon had stumbled over the person. The struggle was over before it started; there was a muffled sound for a moment, and then silence. Stafford couldn't tell what Gordon had done.

"We won't hear from him again," Gordon whispered.

He grabbed her arm again and led her up the stairs to the second floor. A small amount of light filtered through the wooden slats nailed to the windows. Gordon went to another door in the corner of the room that led to another set of stairs. It was only five or six steps before they reached yet another door. Gordon forced it open and sunlight bathed them. They were on the roof.

"The binoculars?" he said.

"Right here."

There was an urgency in his voice, business-like.

"There," he said, pointing down the narrow street toward the front entrance of the compound. "Look down there and you'll see the front entrance."

She looked through the binoculars.

"Now look closer in," he said. "Look closer in toward us." His finger pointed to the area he was talking about. "That's a guarded side entrance." She saw the two men standing at the side door. "There's bound to be more access points on the other side, loading docks, what have you, so we'll just have to see whatever there is to see from here. So that's the compound, and this is where you'll be with the binoculars."

She nodded.

"Careful for reflections."

"Huh? Oh, you mean the glass on the binoculars?"

"Yeah. Don't hold it at an angle where it reflects the sunlight. You don't want to cause a glare and give away your presence. Now, look over there," he said, pointing down the same side of the street that they were on. "Over by that fire escape, that's where the Franklin contingency will be."

She looked through the binoculars but couldn't see anyone. The fire escape was about fifty yards away in the direction toward the front entrance of the compound.

"Unless they were able to talk the Russians into letting them participate in the raid, which I doubt, they'll probably stay inside, looking out from the windows...but that's where they'll be. If they come out onto the escape, don't let them see you."

She became puzzled. "You mean *us*."

"No, I mean *you*."

Her head tilted as she tried to comprehend what he meant, a puzzled look on her face.

"I'm going farther. There's a tunnel down there that I'm going to try to get into. I think it leads to the compound."

"Gordon, we didn't talk about that. There's going to be a lot of people down there."

"I know. But this is too important for us to just sit back and watch everything from a distance. Trust me. I've got ways to move around in places like that without being picked out. I'll be alright."

"You want me to come with you?"

"No. Too dangerous. With just me moving around in that building, there's a certain amount of risk. With both of us together...that would be too much. You stay here and observe what you can. Look for anything odd or suspicious, any small thing that jumps out at you or stands out. Not even sure what that might be. When the raid happens, it's going to go down fast." He remembered her background and added, "...as I'm sure you know."

Gordon rose and began to move away from the edge of the roof.

"I'm going to lay some things in the way so it won't be easy to get up here after I'm gone. I'll prop some things up against the doors so you'll hear if anyone tries to come up."

She stared at him and said nothing.

"Good luck," he finally said. There was a pause. Then, in an attempt at humor—he could tell she was worried by this previously undisclosed aspect of the plan—he added, "honey."

She smiled, nervously.

That was it. He left. She could hear him moving things around as he made his way back downstairs, placing items in the path just like he said. He searched through the darkness on each floor to find something to lodge against each of the doors before he closed them.

The long solo continued, each note more drawn out than the last. The sparser the notes, the more meaning attributed to each one.

Gordon was in the adjoining warehouse, just like he had been the day before. He moved with more confidence this time, knowing full well where he had to go and how to get there. The people inside the building seemed to move with a little bit more energy, and, it seemed to Gordon, nervousness. They were louder, heavier in their steps, almost like they knew it wasn't a normal day. Gordon moved carefully but with deliberation, doing his best to look like he belonged there, avoiding as much as possible the more populated areas. At one point he had to hide in a small closet off a kitchen while two people lingered in the area. The kitchen was closed, and other than those two people and himself, no one was in it. The man and woman who had ducked into it thought they were alone. Patiently, but apprehensively, Gordon bided his time. The two spoke in Russian:

"Can't you leave her?" the woman said.

"She doesn't deserve that. I'd rather kill her."

They began to grope each other.

"Oh," she murmured, a sound of pleasure in her voice. They kissed passionately. The man's lips moved to her neck. He bit her earlobe.

"Quit it," she said with a laugh.

The man stopped and pulled away. "Can you come over tonight?"

"Will she be gone?"

"She'll be gone for the next two days."

"You're Sure?"

"She's going to visit her parents. She told me again this morning."

"Mm. Perfect."

They fondled and kissed each other a bit longer, with no more talking as they did so, until finally the man said, "Come on, we'd better go. Break time's over." With that, they left.

The rest of the way through the building was not a problem, and eventually he arrived at the location of what he assumed was the entrance to the tunnel that led to the compound. There was only one guard at the entrance this time. That was a relief, except for the fact that the doors were closed. Odd, he thought. What was the reason for that? If they were locked from the other side, that would be a problem. He remained hidden about forty feet from the tunnel's entrance. Boxes and crates stacked seven feet high provided a place where he could monitor the situation without being seen.

* * *

"So how much longer?" Wykoff said to Medlikov. "It should be happening by now, shouldn't it?"

"Patience! Please!" Medlikov said with annoyance. "Patience. We are careful in what we do. Results must come with minimal injuries, for sure. This is a carefully planned operation. You will see firsthand the great planning and ability of our police."

Wykoff shrugged. She looked across the room to where Ackman stood in front of another window.

"And how is your vantage point?" Medlikov said. "Can you see the front entrance all right?"

"Yes, just fine, Oleg," Wykoff answered. "Tell me, what about the other access points. I can see a side door about a hundred feet down with two men standing by it. There must be other access areas around the building, like the loading docks...how are you sealing those off?"

"It is all under control, Ms. Wykoff. You will obviously not be able to see it all from where we stand, but it's being taken care of. Trust me."

"Okay, then let me ask another question," she said while continuing to look through the window with a pair of binoculars (supplied by Medlikov). "Why are we monitoring the front entrance? I don't understand."

Medlikov looked at her curiously, somewhat aggravated.

"I mean, of all places, you're going to storm the front?"

"Just watch. Okay?" he said in a state of aggravation.

It bothered Wykoff that no one on her team was part of the operation, and she subconsciously wanted to transfer some of that annoyance to Medlikov. She was also curious as to why they *were* just monitoring the front entrance. Why couldn't at least part of her team go with Medlikov's men to monitor a different part of the building? She knew, though, that based upon the tone in Medlikov's response that he wasn't going to budge on the issue.

* * *

It was time for the last movement, the coda of the performance.

Gordon knew time was short. This wasn't an exact science, meaning the announced time for the raid was only an approximation. Variables could alter the timing in either direction. Fortunately, there was no one else in the area except for the one guard standing at the metal doors. Otherwise, the area seemed deserted, as if everyone had cleared out. He needed to decide pretty quickly whether he was going to take a chance with that guard or not. He wasn't completely convinced the doors led to a tunnel, or even if they did, whether the tunnel would lead to the compound. Was that possibility worth the risk?

A million permutations ran through his head, variations and

contingencies, all subconsciously leading to a way he would approach the guard. He was convincing himself he would do it.

Gordon grew solemn for a moment. This was the moment of truth; the moment that came at the critical point during the many dangerous missions he'd been on over the years. He thought back to Chechnya. It always went back to Chechnya. Gordon never forgot the words of Angstrom on that mission, right before they made the definitive move: *The risk has to make sense in light of the motivation behind it. Not the goal at hand, but the true, ultimate reason of it all...the reason for our being there.* Gordon remembered it vividly, along with the serious expression on Angstrom's face. The immediate risk, he told himself, was not so great. It was only one guard, albeit with a weapon slung across his chest. He could think of several ways to approach him. The real question was what might follow after that? What would he find on the other side assuming he got in? Still, even those risks didn't outweigh the precarious threat facing the United States—the current attacks, and the doomsday that threatened to follow.

He convinced himself that it was time to move.

He stepped away from the boxes and crates that had provided him cover and went backwards away from the guard. He needed to enter the area from around the corner so when the guard saw him for the first time, it would appear as if Gordon was just another worker casually approaching the area. Before he turned the corner to enter the hallway, he noticed a small scrap heap and grabbed a discarded engine component of some sort.

When he did turn the corner, he was surprised to learn that he had underestimated the distance; it seemed at least fifty feet. Too late to turn back; he was at the point of no return, so he continued at a steady, confident gait down the hallway toward the guard. His head was down while he pretended to look at the scrap component in his hand, studying it as he walked. The guard noticed him immediately but did not appear to be concerned.

When Gordon was forty feet away, the guard asked him, in Russian, why he wasn't at the meeting. Gordon ignored him. When he was thirty-five feet away, the guard yelled, "Hey!"

Gordon looked up but continued walking. He held up the engine component in his hand, like it would mean something to the guard.

"*Ostanavlivat!*" said the guard when Gordon was about twenty feet away.

Gordon could tell the guard was both confused and alarmed. He walked another five feet and saw the guard grab the gun slung over his shoulder. Just then, Gordon began to jog while rearing back the arm holding the engine component. The guard saw this and moved faster. Gordon threw the component with all his might and hit the guard in the shoulder. As soon as he had released the metal object, Gordon moved to a full sprint, and before the guard could fully recover and aim his weapon, Gordon was upon him. Although Gordon wasn't large in frame, he was quick and agile, with finely taut muscles, and the guard was no match for him. With two quick strikes, he incapacitated the man before any shot was fired.

Gordon turned back to look down the hallway from where he came, and there was no sign of anyone. Good, he thought. The engine component had made a clanking sound when it hit the ground, and he was concerned about the noise. He reached for the handle on one of the large doors, bracing himself for whatever might be on the other side. He could tell right away from its construction that it was heavy, so there was no chance he could flip it open quickly and surprise anyone who might be on the other side. Fortunately it wasn't locked, and when it was opened just slightly, he peered in through the crack to see if he could see anything. Nothing, as far as he could tell; just a dimly lit, large hallway, like an extension of the one he was in, with no guards in sight. He pulled the incapacitated guard inside, and using some of the guard's outer clothing, formed a makeshift gag as well as something to bind the man's arms and legs. In order not to take any chances, he went back through the door to grab the engine component lying on the ground, went back to the guard, and with a giant thud, slammed it against the guard's head. A pool of blood started to form, so Gordon dragged him a little further into the tunnel. As a last step, he reached for the gun lying on the ground and then closed the door behind him. When he saw what kind of gun it was—a Saiga 12-gauge shotgun—he realized how close he had come to having his head blown off. He held it up to get a feel for it. It'd been a long time since he fired one. He grabbed the potato grip with this left hand and held it firmly. Just like he remembered it. He wondered whether he'd have to fire it. He hoped not. That would mean all hell had broken loose. Gordon checked the side of it to make sure the safety was disengaged, and then he carefully moved forward, unsure of how far he'd have to go before he came to the other end of the tunnel.

The air seemed to turn eerily still outside, everything suddenly quiet, like the suppressed energy before the final movement.

Russian vehicles suddenly burst on the scene and pulled up to the compound en masse, as if massive storm clouds ominously moved in, reaching forward to the fullest extent before unleashing their wrath. Stafford leaned forward on the ceramic tiles that rimmed the roof's edge and raised the binoculars. Rotating her wrist, she moved them slightly before looking into them to make sure the lenses didn't emit a glare.

She saw armed police everywhere, each with what appeared to be a PP-2000 submachine gun as best she could tell. An armored vehicle pulled right in front of the two guards that stood at the side entrance, and then a police transport vehicle pulled next to it. Police stormed out of it; the two guards were overwhelmed and at a loss as to what to do. They immediately threw their arms up. Something was yelled at them, and they fell to the ground, face down. The raid had begun!

Stafford turned her attention back to the front entrance, where by then there were swarms of police, all in black uniforms, helmets, and bullet proof vests. A ramrod was used to force the doors open, which was also done at the side entrance. Stafford was impressed by the coordinated action. What came next was by the book: flashbangs. Stafford was too far for them to have any effect on her, but she saw the sudden bursts of light that came from the opened entrances, and a second later heard the thunderous bangs. The sounds echoed through the narrow street and beyond.

The police, however, did not immediately charge inside. Some entered, a few, but not the full force.

"Why aren't they charging in?" Wykoff asked Medlikov.

"Some are entering. Scout forces go in first."

"Not enough. That warehouse is huge; there's bound to be a lot of manpower inside. You're going to need more," she said sternly. "They should be moving in, Oleg!"

Medlikov was angered but said nothing as he continued to watch, standing next to Stuart Ackman by a window.

"I don't want to lose him," she persisted. "If we lose Terrebenzikov, that will be a great loss! He'll go under deep cover after this. We'll never find him."

They watched as the police formed a ring around the compound, and then in unison all backed away, their guns held at their hips, aiming at the building.

Wykoff saw this and started to believe that maybe they knew what they were doing after all. If this many guards surrounded the whole building, there'd be no chance Terrebenzikov could escape.

"What about the tunnels?" Ackman suddenly interjected, turning to look at Wykoff. "If there aren't enough men inside...."

Just then there was a loud explosion, much greater than the flashbangs. A burst of fire came shooting out of the front and side entrances of the compound. Debris flew everywhere, glass flying in every direction. All of the policemen fell to the ground to shield themselves.

Everyone observing from the vacant building ducked from the windows and crouched down for cover. Wykoff started processing. Was that one blast or two? It was subtle, but it almost sounded like there was more than one blast.

It happened so fast and was so loud, she wasn't sure.

Gordon was about a hundred yards from the other end of the tunnel when he heard the flashbangs. He could tell there were several of them, all going off at just about the same time, but their sound was distinctive, and the sounds came from the direction he was headed. He started to jog. As he got closer, about fifty yards from the end of the tunnel, he saw two closed doors, just like the two he came through at the other end. He was close. When he was about twenty-five yards away, he slowed down and pointed his weapon. Who knew what was on the other side? And when the effects of the flashbangs wore off, someone might try to come through there to escape. He thought he heard the muffled sounds of voices, men yelling.

When he was within five yards, the explosion Wykoff and Ackman had witnessed blew the two large doors wide open. The force threw Gordon into the air and back fifteen feet. He landed hard. A powerful ball of fire followed, bursting through the tunnel's doors and nearly reaching him before it receded. The heat was intense. Had he been a few feet closer the fire would have engulfed him.

He was on the verge of passing out, dizzy, his ears ringing furiously as he lay on his back. His body wanted to give in to the pain. The urge came over him to close his eyes and let himself pass out. He tried to lift his head to look over his chest toward the opening. His head throbbed. He couldn't see anything, his vision severely blurred. His head slowly fell back down, his neck muscles weak and unable to support the weight. He purposefully closed his eyes. It felt good with his eyes closed. His breathing slowed, relaxing him. He still couldn't hear anything, but he could feel the sensation of his chest moving slowly up and down as he breathed.

Strange images appeared in his mind. Suppressed images from long ago, things he didn't even think he could remember anymore: a child, maybe seven or eight years old, lying in a stretcher; an automobile, the interior badly burned from a fire; two bodies lying on the ground, blankets completely covering them. More images, unconnected from the previous ones: a sandstorm; blood dripping, forming a puddle in the hot sand; a hand grabbed him, and when he turned to look, Angstrom, a serious expression on his face; words spoken, unrecognizable. The images assaulted him at a frantic, dizzying pace, all in a matter of seconds. The image of Stafford's long, red hair; then it was cut short; her eyes peered at him; long, thick eyelashes...

A moment later, his eyes opened. He shook his head a little. It hurt. Throbbing. He could hear yelling coming from the end of the tunnel. He was back to the present.

Gordon forced himself to turn over onto his hands and knees. His head drooped, which made things worse as blood rushed to his brain. With all of his energy, he struggled to stand. His legs were weak and he leaned against the wall for a moment. More voices, louder. The realization came as to where he was, and he turned and ran as best he could. The forced movement further revived him, and other than what was probably a severe concussion, he was physically unharmed. His pace increased, retracing his path backwards. He reached the end of the tunnel where he had entered and there was still no one around. The area immediately outside of the tunnel seemed abandoned.

When he got close to the giant room that led to the outside, a thought occurred: there were probably a lot of police outside, ready to come in. How was he going to get out of there? If he knew anything about police procedure, the place would be surrounded, swarming with police. In his rush to scope the place out the day before, he hadn't thought about that. He was more concerned about getting inside than he was getting out. He remembered thinking there would have been chaos during the raid—that there would have been droves of people scrambling to escape—and that he could have used that to his advantage. The explosions must have changed all that.

He was kidding himself. He really had not thought it through. He was disappointed. Such a lapse in planning wasn't like him. Then he started to hear voices—a lot of voices.

19

Gray Smoke

"WHAT THE HELL WAS THAT, OLEG?" WYKOFF YELLED AS SOON as the debris had settled from the explosion. Plumes of smoke flowed from the front entrance of the compound and into the air. Shattered glass was everywhere. She went over to where Medlikov and Ackman stood.

"I'm not sure. It's clear something exploded, but what caused it, I have no idea," Medlikov responded.

"What do you mean? Did your plan include using explosives?"

"No. Certainly not. I mean, you saw what I did. There were flashbangs, yes, but the big explosion..."

There were eight people in the room. They were all looking at each other, stunned. Wykoff was about to say something when Medlikov's phone rang. He pulled it out of his jacket, checked the caller ID, then raised his palm to Wykoff and said, "Hold on." He walked away from them to talk in private.

"What do you think? Did the police cause the explosion?" Ackman said when Medlikov was out of earshot.

"I don't know. He says no, but I can't get a good read on him. He seemed genuinely surprised," said Wykoff. She turned to look through the window at the scene of the explosion. The police were scrambling, some helping those that were on the ground after having been thrown back by the blast, others running inside to help the few that had gone in before the explosion.

"We've got to get in there. The sooner the better," said Ackman. "Whoever was in that front part of the building was blown to smithereens. Look, there's no shooting or anything going on, no one fighting back. We have to get inside to look for evidence. Let's grab the rest of the team and go."

"Without any protective gear? Are you crazy? I hear what you're saying, but that's a combat zone down there and we don't even have a bullet proof vest!" said Wykoff. She thought about it for a moment. As she continued to watch the scene unfold, she spotted a police officer coming out of the building carrying a piece of charred rubbish—she raised her binoculars to get a better look. It looked like a piece of computer equipment; the police were already gathering evidence and hauling it away. She let the binoculars down and shared Ackman's sense of urgency. "Damn, you're right. We need to get down there. Adam," she yelled over to Adam Sircy, who was still looking out of a window, "come over here."

As Sircy approached, the others on her team gathered as well. "What's up?" he said.

"Listen, we're going down there, right now—you, me, Ackman, the whole team. I want us down there ASAP. You need to look at the computer stuff; find something useful, clues to what we're looking for. Hopefully there'll still be some operational equipment; maybe farther inside the building we'll find something. We need code, algorithms, manuals, documentation, anything. The rest of us will do the same. Look for survivors, someone who can tell us something. We have to get to them before the Russians have a chance to escort them away. I want to conduct our own interviews, not rely upon transcripts from the Russians. We'll get some protective gear when we get down there. We'll insist on it. What're they going to do, force us to leave? We simply won't stand for it."

She proceeded to give them further instructions, directing some to divide up and go deeper into the building right away to find a perimeter of activity and make sure people weren't being taken away through some other exit.

"The building's huge," said Ackman. "We can't cover it all ourselves."

"I know," Wykoff said. "We'll cover what we can and see if we can't work with Oleg and the police to leverage what they're doing...or at least understand it and try to influence them as far as the evidence goes. That's the best we can do, but it's better than standing around here and doing nothing."

She looked at Ackman and considered whether there was anything else they should be thinking about.

"Let's do it," Sircy finally said, anxious to get to the equipment. Sircy was young—ten years younger than Wykoff. He was ambivalent to the historic nature of what they were doing, working with the Russians, participating in a raid, right there in the heart of St. Petersburg. People would be talking about it for years, just like they did after Sabotol. Sircy was more focused on the immediate task at hand: getting to the hackers and their code.

They walked through the large room toward the door. Medlikov, who was still talking on his phone on the other side of the room, saw them and rushed over.

"What's going on? Where are you going?"

"We're going down there," Wykoff said, gesturing toward the window and the compound. "We've got to get Adam in there to look at whatever's left."

"Yes, yes, that's what I was just discussing on the phone. I can take you. It has been cleared. Let's go."

To the group's surprise, Medlikov led them through the building and onto the street. Once there, he spoke to a few officers in Russian and then motioned for Wykoff's team to follow him as he walked toward the building.

"Wait a minute," Wykoff said. "We don't have any protective

gear or anything. We can't go in like this."

"Just follow," Medlikov said. "I've already gotten a preliminary report from inside. "C'mon, you'll see what I mean."

Broken glass cracked under their shoes as they carefully moved forward. Debris was everywhere. The smoke was noxious, like burning plastic. They only made it so far before their eyes started to burn and the chemical smell made it hard for them to breathe.

Medlikov turned to a police officer and instructed him to get gas masks for them. He also grabbed a two-way radio so he could communicate with the police directly. In the meantime, they moved back to the other side of the street where it was at least a little easier to breathe.

There was no major fire emanating from the compound. When Wykoff realized that, she leaned over to Ackman and said, "I wish we had an explosives expert with us. I'd like to understand what could have produced this type of blast."

Ackman raised an eyebrow and shook his head sideways, indicating he had no idea.

"Notice how there's no lingering fire," she continued.

With gas masks on, they proceeded into the building. Before they even entered they could tell that the front lobby was completely obliterated. The wall that separated it from the room behind was also blown away. They passed through the lobby and that first room and came to a second. Standing at the periphery of the second room they could see that it was very large. It was completely dark except for the streams of light bouncing around from police officers wielding flashlights in the distance, as well as the small amount of sunlight that filtered in all the way from the lobby.

They were given their own flashlights, and then they carefully continued forward. The flashlights in the distance hinted at how large the room was—cavernous. Whatever computer equipment had been in there before the blast, it wasn't anymore, thought Wykoff. The cement floor seemed thick under her feet, like the room was originally designed for heavy equipment, but the large space was empty as far as the light from her flashlight could reach. She looked over to Ackman and wondered what his initial impression was.

Wykoff directed two members of her team to proceed farther into the building, as they had previously discussed. With such darkness enveloping them, combined with the Russian police moving around, Medlikov didn't notice that part of Wykoff's team had splintered off.

Wykoff kept walking, with Ackman and Sircy at her side, searching for anything meaningful. As they approached the middle of the room the floor started to slant inward, and it felt rough under their feet, not like smooth cement. The more they walked, the steeper the decline, until finally Wykoff realized they were walking into a crater created from the blast.

"Look how powerful the bomb was," Ackman said to her through his mask. "This is reinforced concrete and the explosion tore right into it."

As they walked, Medlikov came to their side. Russian voices could be heard over his two-way radio.

"Any news yet?" Ackman said.

"Not much. The police are seeing what you are. There's still a sense of shock among everyone."

Wykoff, with a tone of compassion, asked, "How are the police?" She saw the dead officers being carried out while she had entered the blast sight.

"Ah, thank you for asking. There are several casualties so far. As you saw, the blasts occurred after several scouts had gone inside."

"I'm sorry to hear that, Oleg." She paused for a moment. "Wait, you said 'blasts.' So there was more than one?"

"Correct. It's been confirmed." He raised his two-way radio at them. "They were very tightly spaced, hard to tell from where we stood, but there were several."

They eventually got to the other side of the room, and there, against the wall, they saw what appeared to be a large pile of electronic junk. The smoke in that part of the room was heavier, clouding the rays of light from the flashlights. They moved closer to the piles and shined their flashlights on them. Piles and piles of computer displays, keyboards, tables, and large racks of equipment rose to at least ten feet high and for long stretches along the wall.

"The force of the blast must have thrown it all against the wall," said Medlikov.

Everything looked broken, burned, and torn apart. Wykoff tried to grab a piece of equipment and the whole pile started to move, so she stopped for fear of everything coming down on her.

She went over to Sircy and said, "What do you think, any of it salvageable?"

"Possible, but I doubt it. It looks pretty burned and banged up. You want me to start digging?"

"No, let's keep moving. I want to see what else is here." She motioned to Ackman, and the three carefully moved through the darkness, with Medlikov beside them, looking for a door that led to the next room.

As they did so, Ackman leaned over and said to Wykoff, "No bodies."

She searched the ground with her flashlight and realized he was right. Where were all of Terrebenzikov's hackers?

As big as that second room was, the third was even larger. The electricity was out, and there were no windows for natural light to come in, so it was darker than the other rooms, the smoke even thicker. There was also fewer police in that room, with fewer flashlights bouncing around. They walked for quite some time without seeing anything other than the bare cement floor under their feet.

"This place is huge!" Sircy said through his mask. "It must be as big as half a football field! If this was all filled with equipment, there would have been a whole army of hackers."

Wykoff agreed, and the prospect was daunting. But she was also confused—just like the last room, this one seemed devoid of equipment. And again there were no bodies. They came upon another large crater. It was at least seven feet deep at center, larger than the last.

All three heard Wykoff's name called and turned to look in the direction where the voice came from. It was Medlikov some thirty yards away at the other side of the room. He had walked ahead of them and stood near the back wall. When they caught up with him they saw the same thing: equipment strewn everywhere and in the same battered and burned shape as before. The piles, however, were bigger, extending much further from the wall. Computer displays were shattered, computer cases cracked open with the charred PC boards exposed. Sircy contemplated the amount of heat that would be necessary to produce such an effect.

Medlikov directed them with his flashlight to look down further along the piles. Bodies. Wykoff was startled when she first saw them. She walked over and crouched down next to one and shined her flashlight on it; the body was all black, heavily charred, the face indiscernible.

"This is terrible," Medlikov said after Wykoff stood back up. "I don't care what these people were doing, I wouldn't wish this upon anyone."

Wykoff followed the trail of equipment and shined her flashlight on the ground as she walked, careful not to trip over the bodies; they were everywhere, each one the same, burned beyond recognition. She was glad she had her mask on; the stench would have been awful. When she reached the end of the wall, she turned the corner and continued along the next wall. It was the same, with huge piles of equipment. She calculated at least a hundred bodies.

She turned around to go back and was startled to find Medlikov behind her. He had followed her, like he wanted to be so close that he could read her thoughts.

"I don't get it, Oleg," she said to him. "If the police didn't detonate the bombs, then who did?"

"That's what I've been wondering. It must have been sabotage," he answered.

"What, their own equipment?" Sircy said as he approached them.

"I suppose," said Medlikov. "They must not have wanted it to get into someone else's hands."

"I guess I can see that," said Ackman. "If someone got their software, that would be the end of their operation."

"But whoever did it ended up killing their own people," Sircy countered.

"Maybe they were not essential," said Medlikov.

"Wait a minute," Sircy challenged. "That's not what your intelligence showed at the meetings. And that doesn't jive with Bladlikov's reports."

"Your right," conceded Medlikov. "You're absolutely right. I must admit, I'm puzzled myself."

Wykoff remained silent, processing what she heard and comparing it to what she saw. "Oleg," she finally said. "You said Terrebenzikov would be in here when the raid occurred. Your agent, Bladlikov, was supposed to have confirmed that."

"He did. Bladlikov signaled that Terrebenzikov had followed his normal pattern—he was in the building."

"Wait a minute. Where *is* Bladlikov? Is he safe? I'd like to talk to him."

"Yes, he is safe. He left the building as soon as he sent his signal, not wanting to be in the middle of any firefight that might ensue. It's a good thing he did," Medlikov said, looking around at the carnage. "You may speak with him later if you wish."

"Yes, we'd like to," Wykoff responded.

They stood there for a moment as Wykoff contemplated what they might do next. Sircy was carefully rummaging through one of the piles, trying to find a computer from which he might be able to salvage a hard drive, but the prospects weren't good. He tossed the pieces of equipment back into the pile as soon as he picked them up. It was hot to the touch.

Wykoff said, "So how are we going to find Terrebenzikov, or at least his body? I still don't get what the hell happened. Did they get tipped off?"

"Unlikely," Medlikov said. "The place must have been rigged in advance in preparation for any type of raid. Look at it this way: at least the operation is shut down. That should solve your immediate concern, eh?"

"Not really," Sircy said while he was squatting and inspecting something. "For what we've been experiencing in the United States, there had to be multiple installations like this."

"We didn't expect to just destroy a hacking compound, Oleg. We need answers," Wykoff added.

Just then another transmission was heard over Medlikov's radio. "Ah, perfect timing," he said. "They found the room Bladlikov told us about; the room where Terrebenzikov's office was supposedly located. Follow me!"

Medlikov moved quickly to another part of the building. The others followed. The next area was the same as the others, but they didn't stop to investigate. On the way through it they met up with the other two members of Wykoff's team.

From what Wykoff could tell, the next room looked like another large manufacturing floor that was converted into a massive office space. Medlikov led them to a metal staircase illuminated by the flashlights of two policemen. Wykoff shined her flashlight upward and saw that the stairs led to an elevated office high above, with two large openings where there used to be windows.

"The stairs are stable," one of the policemen said, Medlikov providing the translation.

When the team proceeded up the stairs, they were disappointed at what they saw: the office looked as if a separate explosion had occurred in it; all of the equipment was obliterated, much of it blown from the room and down onto the area below. Pieces of what appeared to be two bodies were jammed into corners at the far side of the office. They went for a closer look.

"One of these must have been Terrebenzikov," Medlikov said, refraining from looking too closely at the mangled and burned body parts.

No one said anything. There was no way to verify it. The bodies were once again heavily charred, limbs missing, the head from one of them completely gone. The smoke so high up was rather thick; even their masks could not filter it all. Wykoff and

Ackman looked at each other but said nothing. The sight of the disfigured bodies was gruesome.

Then a thought occurred, and Sircy said, "Wait a minute. This was Terrebenzikov's compound." They all looked at him. "Why would he detonate bombs while he was still in the place? Why blow himself to smithereens?"

Everyone turned to Medlikov.

"I don't know," he said grimly, shaking his head. "I don't know. Maybe he wasn't the one who set it off." Medlikov thought further, then, after a long pause, said, "Maybe he wasn't as indispensable as we thought." When he received skeptical looks, he said, "I don't have an answer right now. None of this makes sense. We will keep investigating."

"Let's go talk to Bladlikov," Ackman said.

"Yes, we should," answered Medlikov. Without hesitation, he led them through the building to the other side of it. Once outside, they saw police everywhere, as well as fire trucks and ambulances.

* * *

Stafford observed what she could from the rooftop. As soon as the bombs went off—there was definitely more than one, she was sure of that—her heart sank and a sense of dread came over her. They were powerful explosions. She was surprised the roof of the compound itself wasn't blown off. Gordon was in there, she said to herself. Depending on how close he was to one of those bombs, he might very well be dead. Something went wrong, the flashbangs, then the bombs. It didn't look like any raid she'd ever been a part of back with the FBI.

She tried to focus on what she saw, but it was hard to concentrate without thinking about Gordon and where he might be. For a moment she thought about going down there and trying to get into the building herself. She knew she couldn't; police were everywhere. More were coming.

Shortly after the explosion, she saw Wykoff and her team go down onto the street. She watched as they put on masks and entered the smoldering building.

Gwen Stafford was completely bewildered. Based upon what she saw, she didn't think the explosions were intended by the police.

About a half-hour later, bodies were carried out on stretchers, blankets completely covering them. There were so many, she thought. They kept coming.

Hours passed without any sign of Wykoff's team again. As far as she could tell, they never came out. Stafford stayed put, waiting and watching. She eventually figured that Wykoff's team must have exited from the other side of the building.

It grew dark; a flood of blue and red lights from police cars and fire trucks glowed along the narrow street. Watching through her binoculars, she estimated at least a hundred and fifty bodies were eventually carried out. The whole area was cordoned off.

By midnight most of the vehicles were gone. It was quiet, and with no vehicles around with their shining lights, she could barely see anything. Only by the faint glow of an occasional burning cigarette did she know that some of the police were still standing down there. After another hour, there was still no sign of Gordon.

Stafford sat down from her crouched position, her back against the short brick ledge that extended around the perimeter of the roof. Her knees ached from crouching for so long. The air had become cooler. She shut her eyes for just a moment to give herself a rest, and they burned. When the burning stopped, it felt good to keep her eyes closed.

She wasn't going to leave him, she told herself. She couldn't leave him behind. It was still too early though. Just another hour, then it would be time. She let her head fall back to rest against the roof's ledge.

Gordon had quickly moved away from where the voices came.

He made his way down a long hallway and found the kitchen he had hid in before. He dashed inside and stood thinking for a moment. On a whim, he went over to the industrial-sized refrigerator and opened it. Cans of Diet Coke. He quietly opened one and gulped it. Then he grabbed a couple of sandwiches wrapped in plastic.

More sounds from nearby. Police must be flooding the area, he thought. The kitchen was not the place he wanted to be with a lot of people lingering around. Time to move. He needed to get as far away from those policemen as possible. Using the area where the voices came from as a reference point, and the direction where the tunnel was as another, he ran in a third direction, thinking that would be safest.

The building seemed to go on forever. It looked like it was being used by some business, but no workers were around, like they had all evacuated the place. He found a hallway with stairs that went up to the second floor. It was quiet upstairs, no people around. Still, he didn't want to take any chances or assume too much. He found a large empty storage closet, went in, and closed the door behind him. It was about thirty feet long with empty shelves on either side. Gordon went to the far corner, sat down, and began to open the first sandwich. After he took the first bite, he realized he didn't have the shotgun with him anymore.

Stafford couldn't tell how long she'd been asleep; it must have been at least an hour. She found herself lying down on the roof, curled up to keep warm. She edged up and looked over the ledge. Nothing seemed to have changed. She was groggy, still half asleep. It was time to move, she thought.

Just then, however, she thought she heard something. The noise was faint and came from the other side of the door that led from the stairs to the roof. Maybe she imagined it. She remained still, listening. Another sound, only the slightest. A feeling of alarm came over her. It could have been anything, she told herself: a rat or alley cat, the wind, the house settling, even a homeless person. She slowly stood up, and as quietly as she could, moved to the side of the roof about five feet away from the door. Her eyes were well adjusted to the darkness and she could see the outline of the door.

The doorknob turned slowly. She glanced around but didn't see anything she could use as a weapon. There was that piece of wood Gordon had leaned against the door so that it would fall and make a warning sound if anyone opened it, but she was reluctant to go that close to grab it. The door slowly opened and a hand appeared. She was about to kick the door shut against it, but then she saw the hand reach around for the piece of wood. Whoever it was knew it would be there. A smile came on her face.

"Redhead?" she whispered.

"Curls," came the response.

It was Gordon. He grabbed the wood and swung the door open. Both looked at each other and smiled in the darkness. Then they hugged.

"My God, I'm so glad it's you!" she whispered excitedly after they separated. "Are you okay?" She leaned back and looked at him, head to toe, to see if there were any signs of injury.

"I'm fine. Probably a grade-million concussion, but otherwise fine. I think most of my hearing has even returned."

"What happened?" she asked. They continued to speak in a low whisper. Gordon told her everything he knew, including how he got out of the building, and Stafford explained everything she saw from the roof.

"I was just about to try and go inside," she said.

"I'm glad you didn't." He paused for a moment and collected his thoughts. "There were a lot of police in there for the longest time. I camped out in an empty part of the building and let my head clear. Had to move slowly. Sorry to keep you waiting."

"Are you kidding?"

Gordon went over to the edge of the roof and looked down.

"You can't see much now," she whispered from behind.

"How about with the binos?"

"Still not much. Officers at each entrance standing guard."

"I'm not sure against what," Gordon said. "There's not much in there."

"Did you go to the compound?"

"I did. I was finally able to make it over there."

"What'd it look like?" Stafford said. "All I could see from here was a bunch of dead bodies being carried out. No equipment or anything like that."

"Yeah, that's about right. We'll talk about it later. For now we need to get out of here. What time is it?"

She looked at her watch. "About 2 A.M."

"Let's get back to the hotel. I'm exhausted and my head still hurts. You must be hungry, too," Gordon said.

"Famished. Aren't you?"

"Here, have this." He pulled out the sandwich he had saved for her. "It's not much, but..."

"I'll take it!" She swiped it from his hand and quickly unwrapped it. After she took the first bite she said, "Mm, heaven."

Gordon smiled and wished he could see her face better.

"C'mon," he said. "We're going to cut through the back and go in a different direction. After we've walked for a few blocks we'll look for a cab."

She took another bite of the sandwich and followed him. As they walked, Gordon reminded himself that he'd have to do a K-Com group call to report what he saw.

* * *

The U.S. NTEG satellite system is comprised of five SE-v2 satellites flying at an altitude of around 200 kM above the earth. The super-high altitude enables coverage of the earth's entire surface with only five satellites. Each SE-v2 is loaded with a payload of the fastest, highest resolution, super spectral imaging capability available. The high resolution technology has a ground sample distance of less than three-tenths of a meter panchromatic, thereby providing the ability to capture data points on the ground that are only about 12 inches apart. By scanning at 25,000 lines/sec, an SE-v2 payload can provide continuous image-scanning across a distance of about 300 miles in less than a minute.

From when the United States first contacted Russia about the cyber criminal activity to when the raid on the compound actually occurred, nineteen days had passed. It was a fast turn of events. And just as soon as Medlikov had revealed the location of Terrebenzikov's compound, the appropriate SE-v2 satellite was quickly redirected by the Pentagon to begin capturing images of it.

And yet, even with such a rapid response it wasn't soon enough. If the SE-v2 had been redirected to begin watching four days earlier it would have captured a series of industrial trucks pulling up to the compound's loading docks. Stretchers with dead bodies covered by blankets would have been seen being unloaded from those trucks, along with rack upon rack of computer equipment, all of it hauled into the compound, the damage to it already done, acidized, burned, and demolished, or at least, helped along its way before the final explosions did the rest of the work. In short, the staging of a fabricated disaster.

As it was, the staging was already complete by the time the SE-v2 satellite was instructed to train its cameras on the compound. The Pentagon missed it.

So had Gordon. If he would have made it past the guards and gone through the tunnel into the compound a day earlier, he would have seen all of the staging before the explosions occurred.

Once the staging was set, all that was left was the setting off of the explosions that served as the capstone to the event, the enactment of the deception to its conclusion. Wykoff's team observed it all without the need for any willing suspension of disbelief, because it all seemed so real and believable, their senses assaulted with so much information of such a startling nature.

* * *

Line Intercept
Report Date/time (U.S. Washington, D.C.): July 11/7:05 P.M.
Priority Level: High-Immediate
Geodata:
Source- Lat: 68°27'34" N, Lon: 73°35'25" E (Mys Peschanyy, Russia)
Destination- Lat: 66°26'19" N, Lon: 71°39'16" E (Untolovo, Russia)
Link: U.S. K-Com v.23 "Prine"
U1 ID: John Angstrom
<u>U2 ID: Lt. Roy Grahame (SEAL)</u>

U2[072615 0550]: *Radio sync. Verify. Search for Applecore.*

U2[072515 0555]: Repeat. *Radio sync. Search for Applecore. Verify. Adam...Baker...Charlie...Davis...Everett. Verify*

U1[072515 0556]: *Sync check. Applecore. Over.*

U2[072515 0556]: *Hope I didn't interrupt your beauty sleep. Over.*

U1[072515 0556]: *No chance. Status update. Over.*

U2[072515 0556]: *Roger. Strange happenings. Raid complete. Several bombs went off. Big ones. Report was that they weren't set off by good guys. About 200 bodies. Massive damage, unsalvageable equipment. Over.*

U1[072515 0557]: *Confirms what was seen by the peanut gallery. Suspect apprehended? Over.*

U2[072515 0557]: *Negative. Believed dead. Difficult to confirm. Over.*

U1[072515 0558]: *Any secret sauce obtained? Over.*

U2[072515 0559]: *Negative. But evidence shows possibility of it being a valid site. Over.*

--PAUSED PORTION; LINK MAINTAINED--

U2[072515 0604]: *Confirm presence. Over.*

U1[072515 0605]: *I'm here. Is contingency done? Over.*

U2[072515 0605]: *Negative. Discussion to follow. They're staying put. There's going to be a meet-and-greet. Over.*

U1[072515 0606]: *Roger. Over.*

U2[072515 0607]: *You're still staying on vacation, right? Over.*

U1[072515 0607]: *Affirmative...We'll be here longer...Scenery too breathtaking. Out.*

20

Vodka, Beer, and Sleep

Sunday, July 12
[T$_{detonate}$ minus 16 days]

SENNAYA PLOSCHAD IS A BUSTLING SQUARE IN THE CENTRAL PART of St. Petersburg, Russia, generally situated at the intersection of Garden Street, Moskovsky Prospect, and Grivtsova Lane. It has a long history, with roots dating back to the early 1700s as a central marketplace where one could buy essentials such as hay, firewood, and cattle (its name translates to *Hay Square* after the famous Hay Market of London). Surrounded by poverty-stricken slums, it was a gathering place for merchants of cheap goods, many of questionable origin, and drew the criminal element. In the early days of Sennaya Ploschad, criminals were publicly flogged, partially as punishment, partially as a form of cheap, public entertainment. The district was so notorious for its seedy nature and slum neighborhoods that Dostoevsky used it as the setting for his literary masterpiece, *Crime and Punishment*. Rodion Raskolnikov, the main character in the novel, lived in an apartment right on Gorokhovaya Street, and it was at 102 Griboyedova Canal where he killed the pawnbroker Alyona Ivanova—bludgeoning her to death with the blunt end of an axe—and then roamed the streets in a semi-delusional state.

In modern times, the area experienced a sort of metropolitan rejuvenation. A major train station is situated there, Sennaya Ploschad Station (taking its name after the square itself), and no less than three metro train lines run through it, all interconnected via a modern, underground transfer corridor. Still, signs of poverty withstood the transformation. About ten years ago the local government decided to address the area's most notable sign of urban blight, the last remnant of the square's market origins, the famed "Kiosks on Sennaya Ploschad." The collection of small kiosks numbered over 150 at its peak. Merchants dealt in cheap goods, stolen contraband, and food long past the "sell-buy" dates; they preyed on the poor. The government forced all of them out and razed the small, dilapidated structures. In their place, they put paved walkways, luscious landscaping, art sculptures, and wrought iron fences.

The government had gone a long way toward reaching its goal of transforming the square, but not completely; a few local businesses held out, resisting all attempts at city cleansing. They were establishments with the right criminal connections, the ability to pay the necessary graft. One of those businesses was a nightclub just two blocks away from Sennaya Ploschad Station; it served as a common stopover for men of a certain disposition; its name, the Apraksin.

It was late at night on a Sunday, yet the Apraksin was busy; busier than other clubs nearby. It was one of the busiest establishments in the area, and that night, two very important men were there.

"So, you were right! The ungrateful bastards...how they turned on us so quickly!"

"Not *us*," Strenzke responded. "*You*. They turned on *you*. It was you they chose to be the sacrificial lamb. It was only because of me, your old friend, that you're still alive."

Strenzke raised his shot glass filled with vodka to Ivan Terrebenzikov, who returned the gesture, and they drank. Strenzke poured them each another. He owned the Apraksin, and both he and his close friend Terrebenzikov used to be regulars at the club. Not so much anymore, especially in Terrebenzikov's case, who, upon his friend's urging, had been keeping a low profile for the last six months.

Apraksin was a large establishment; there was a large bar in the center, with tables and chairs all around, filling the large first-floor room. A small stage, seldom used, was at the back. Prostitutes proliferated—Russian, Finnish—the place teamed with human flesh waiting to devour (and be devoured). Prostitutes easily outnumbered their potential customers five-to-one.

"We've outgrown this place, you know," Strenzke said while looking around. "I can barely stomach it anymore, and I own the damn place."

"I know. But it served its purpose," Terrebenzikov responded. "We built an army, a world-wide network of hackers and coders, and the money from this place helped us get our start. Now it keeps our hackers happy…at least the ones here in St. Petersburg. Their refreshment for a hard day's work, eh?" He looked around and then continued, "A means to an end, as the saying goes."

"Mm, yes, and so it is," Strenzke confirmed.

They both realized that it gave neither of them pleasure anymore, carnal or otherwise. They didn't even feel comfortable *being* there. Not because they were nervous about being out in the open after what happened at the compound—though that was a concern—but because they saw the Apraksin for what it was: dirty, banal, and depraved, a place for the unsophisticated and the desperate, the empty souls. Strenzke and Terrebenzikov were middle-aged, and they realized that it made them both uncomfortable, even sickened them, to be there. Their tastes had changed and had become more refined.

They didn't even need the revenue from the Apraksin anymore. Not since the Kremlin stepped into their lives those many years ago.

But on that night Strenzke had experienced a yearning for the past: a simpler time when all he had to worry about was making money and having fun. What happened at the "compound" the day before was startling and a stark reminder of how deep they were in with the Russian military. It gave them both a very bad feeling. And so, they craved a revisiting of the impetuousness of their youth—the vodka, the surroundings, the filth. One last fling in a period of their lives that they envisioned would soon be gone forever, a long, faded memory.

The smell inside of the Apraksin immediately assaulted the senses if one weren't used to it: hot, sweaty flesh, like the inside of a barn, only the odor was of humans instead of cows or horses— soiled humans, smothered in cologne or perfume as the case may be. It was the smell of animalistic fornication, carnal, pervasive.

Thomas J. Reed was one of those not used to it. The pungent odor hit him as soon as he walked into the place. He could barely summon the strength to sip the beer that rested on the table in front of him. The smell, combined with the heavy cigarette smoke that permeated the room, caused him to lose all appetite. And he was leery of his drink being doped; some drug that would make him more susceptible to the overtures from the women that hovered around him. They lined the walls like vultures; women clearly of a lower class, their clothes a notch below and a generation behind what would have been considered fashionable. Each smiled. Each had her own little something to say as men walked by. Reed felt like they were going to jump him as he walked to his table. He looked at each of them as he passed, their eyes beckoning, some reached for him, stroked his arm, whispering provocative invitations. Like vapid orbs pressed into their skulls, their eyes were eager, sinister, vacuous. The walk to his table seemed interminable; as he then sat there and reflected upon it, he was relieved the walk was over.

He tried to remain anonymous, tucked away in a corner of the room with a shadow enveloping him, barely able to see Strenzke and Terrebenzikov from where he sat. But he did see them, even among all the prostitutes, drinkers, and smokers. He couldn't believe it when he first did, but there they were, like fish swimming in shallow water just below the surface, easy enough to see if one simply looked for them.

"I don't get it," Terrebenzikov continued. "I just don't get it. After all I've done...and before our work is finished. Shit, they haven't even seen it completely work yet, and they risk it all by coming at me. The stupid idiots, pisses me off."

"Oh, it will work, my friend, we know that. It's only a matter of time. What happened in the States proved it. The damned Politburo is chomping at the bit now. And when it finally happens for real, when the full power is unleashed, the world will be changed forever. And we'll get our billions."

Strenzke was pleased to see the anger in Terrebenzikov, the passion. Strenzke had passion too—only it wasn't seeded with anger, but greed, the desire to make all the money he could. "Even if half of it ultimately ends up in frozen bank accounts that we can't reach, we'll still have more than enough for our lifetimes," Strenzke continued. He let out a laugh and then had another shot, tilting his head back quickly. He tapped his empty glass on the table so loud that others nearby turned to look. "To hell with this place. For this one night, let's forget ourselves and drink. Drink to oblivion."

Again they drank. Then they sat in silence for a moment, observing everything. What they had seen so many times before at the Apraksin they observed now with an almost clinical detachment, as if looking at animals in a zoo.

"And the Kremlin," Strenzke finally said, "the bastards, they'll get what *they* want. They'll get what we promised. Whether it's enough for them, enough to help them accomplish what they really want, we'll see. Either way, we'll be long gone, right? You with Catherine, me with Aloysha...that heavenly woman. We'll all be together, far far away from this place, you and me the kings, eh?"

"And you're still sure we're not leaving too soon?" said

Terrebenzikov. "I mean, they gave us a lot, Sergei. Yes, this club helped us get our start, but it wouldn't have been enough. The money we got from the government, along with their help to set up the satellite locations, we wouldn't have been able to do it without them. Shit, you might still be rotting in jail if it weren't for the FSB getting you out."

"True, true," Strenzke responded. "But they got everything they needed from us, and then some—orders of magnitude more than what they put into it financially, and you know it." Strenzke grew serious. He leaned across the table and said, "Listen, I can't stay here anymore. It sickens me. Hell, *we* can't stay here any longer." Terrebenzikov kept looking at him. "It doesn't even feel like we have our own lives anymore, like we've been conscripted into service. The RCA thinks we're part of them."

The RCA: a clandestine part of the Russian military known as the Russian Cyber Army. It's thought to have been formed over ten years ago, with estimates that Russia now spends roughly $10B U.S. dollars annually to develop its cyber warfare capability. A new kind of army for the next generation of warfare; linguists, data scientists, malware coders, network experts, physicists, business intelligence—expertise in all aspects are represented, comprising a holistic coverage of what would be necessary to wage a cyber war.

Terrebenzikov said nothing, looking at the face of his friend.

Strenzke poured more vodka and drank. His tone changed; it became more entreating. "Think of all those years we gave to it, Ivan. The years of toiling, sniffing security systems in overseas networks, logging the thousands upon thousands of keystrokes, writing sophisticated algorithms to search the results for passwords and credit cards, the VPN tunneling...all of it. It was so many years of our lives. The RCA owned us."

Terrebenzikov shook his head as he processed what Strenzke said. "So they have no idea we're getting out?"

"They better not. Not before we're gone, let's put it that way, or we could be fucked. That's why I keep Bredziv and Vanatoly so close now."

Strenzke motioned with his head toward two large men sitting at a nearby table. Terrebenzikov saw them and wondered whether they'd be anywhere near enough if it ever came to it. He kept thinking about the raid, and the great lengths at which the FSB went to stage it.

Strenzke watched Terrebenzikov carefully. He could tell that Terrebenzikov was still conflicted.

"What about Grigori? Look what happened to him," Terrebenzikov finally offered. "He tried to get out. Made his fortune and left, just like we're planning to. The Americans caught up with him—had his ass extradited from the Netherlands. Things didn't turn out too well for him."

"And you think your government is going to protect you if you stay here? C'mon, Ivan, you're not thinking clearly. The vodka's already getting to you. Besides, it's going to be different for us. The Americans will never find us; no one will, not where we're going."

Strenzke stopped talking and studied Terribenzikov.

"Ivan, hey, we talked about this so many times before, long, drawn out conversations. I thought we were past this. If you're having a change of heart, I need to know, because I need you focused one-hundred percent. We're a team, Ivan; I won't do anything without you. And just remember, it's like I said before: the longer we stay here, the harder it will be for us to get out."

Terrebenzikov continued to think and looked directly into the eyes of his old friend. He knew Strenzke was right. It was just that learning what happened at the mock compound, the blowing up of it, rattled him. He had no doubt as to the power of the FSB after that.

Finally, he nodded to Strenzke. He was ready—nervous, but ready.

But then, what happened at the compound, what almost happened to him, was a hit to his ego. He couldn't get it out of his head. "I just can't get over it…how they got you out of jail in the first place, set us up with all that money and resources, gave us all of that assistance, and then they were willing to do away with me, just like that. *Me!*"

Strenzke realized that his friend's ego was bruised even more than he thought. He would have to be brutally honest with him. "Look," he began, "the FSB has its head up its ass. It wouldn't recognize genius if it was staring it in the face. You want to know what they said to me? Huh, you really want to know?"

"Of course," responded Terrebenzikov.

"Here, drink first," Strenzke said, pouring another shot. "Now, you want to know? Okay, fine. 'He's peaked,' they said. 'That algorithm was his crowning achievement, and that was over three years ago. He'll never do anything like that again.' That's what they said to me. Can you believe that shit? The Deputy Prime Minister himself, right to my face!"

The vodka flowed. Their senses became dulled, which was what they wanted. No one would bother them in Strenzke's own bar, no matter how inebriated they were.

"You spoke to the Deputy Prime Minister? Who else was there?"

"I didn't know them all. Not this time. There were too many. Lots of military. General so-and-so. Bullshit. It's big. This is big, Ivan," Strenzke said. "They all tried to gang up on me, strong-arm me. They could try all they wanted, they weren't going to break me. I held to it."

"So what did you say when they said that?" Terrebenzikov said, grabbing the bottle of vodka from his hand.

"I told them to fuck off!"

"Really," Terrebenzikov said, laughing incredulously. He rubbed his sweaty wrist across his mouth. "You said that with all those uniform shits in there?"

"No, my friend, I didn't. I may be crazy, but I'm not stupid." Strenzke tilted his head back to drink, and then a boisterous laugh came from both of them. "Anyway, in the end I convinced them that without both of us, me *and* you, they were shit. Only *we* knew the intricacies of how our code works—the really important parts of it; they know we didn't walk them through all the source code. And sure, the RCA runs the other networks now—

Hungary, Belarus...all of them—but we supply the critical code, the secret sauce. They think they know, but they don't. Only we know. In some ways we are more important to the Kremlin than their own RCA." Strenzke laughed again, and Terrebenzikov followed, intrigued by what his friend said. "Bottom line, without us, they're screwed, and without you, they don't have me. That's what I told them. All of them, right to their faces. The shitheads, they're not going to take us out."

Strenzke's speech became slurred. Even as seasoned a drinker as he was, the vodka had caught up with him. Both of them had trouble speaking in complete sentences anymore, but they could still follow what the other said. They knew each other for so long that they knew how the other thought. They could almost finish each other's sentences whenever they were drunk.

"Well, anyway, it's fixed. They should be happy," said Strenzke. "Now they have both of what they wanted: the Americans off their asses for a while, and me and you still in their service."

"Raise your glass, Strenzke. It's okay. They got enough out of us, and we from them," said Terrebenzikov. Their shot glasses clinked. "They fail to understand that it is only the truly brilliant, like me and you, that make it possible...the brilliant do not become replaceable." Terrebenzikov's thoughts became more addled by the minute the more the vodka took its grip of him. The emotion was there, but not necessarily the meaning, but still Strenzke understood, and he nodded gravely. "They don't realize what more they could have had: the power!" continued Terrebenzikov. "Their grip could be even tighter. Shit, if we were in the States, think of what we could do."

"But I realize, Ivan...I realize."

"Drink with me again, Sergei."

"Of course."

"To the man who saved my life!"

"Only listen," Strenzke said, leaning over the table. "We have to be careful now. I don't trust them anymore. If they were willing to take you out so quickly, to offer your dead body up to the Americans, they could get that idea again. We must be paranoid from now on...until it is over...and then we are gone."

"By the way, did they tell you how the Americans found out about us?"

Strenzke remained serious, but his expression changed. "Yeah, that damn VKontakte page!"

"Aaah, ha, ha, you're kidding me! It comes back to haunt you!" Terrebenzikov laughed and reached across the table to squeeze his friend's shoulder. "I thought you were going to beat Aloysha when you found out she created that page for you."

"I would never lay a hand on her; you know that. She...she didn't know what she was doing. She thought she was doing something special for me, a surprise...that heavenly twat."

"Ha, ha, the surprise is on us, eh?"

Just then the manager on duty, Vladimr Kronzev, came over to them. "Hey, hey, what's all the noise about over here?" he said with a smile.

Strenzke looked up at him and then put his arm around the man's waist. "Sit down, Vladimir," he said boisterously. "Have a drink with us."

"Certainly. I do not hesitate."

There was laughter around the table as the vodka flowed.

"Vladimir, have I ever told you how Ivan and I met?" Strenzke said, his eyes half-closed due to his intoxicated state.

"No, ha ha, not yet," Kronzev said. He was happy to have been invited to join them and quickly fell into the mood.

"Listen," Strenzke said as he leaned over the table like he was passing a grave secret. "We go way back, me and Ivan. We are like brothers. Close to forty years, we go." Terrebenzikov listened intently, Kronzev with curiosity. "Both our fathers were professors at technical university. One day we see each other when we were with our fathers. We were only little boys then, right Ivan."

"Ah, that's right. Our fathers instructed us to computers, heh heh." Terrebenzikov was so drunk he forgot about the hatred he held for his step-father. "Hey, how old are you now, Sergei?"

Kronzev quickly turned to Strenzke to see what he would say. Rare was the occasion when he was made privy to such personal information about his boss. He was eager to hear the answer.

"You know how old I am! What do you ask me? I'm forty-eight, three years older than you."

"Hmm, we're not young boys anymore, are we?" Terrebenzikov said. Out of nowhere the melancholy phase of intoxication had suddenly surfaced. The mood became somber.

"No, we're not," Strenzke responded. "That is why it is time."

Strenzke and Terrebenzikov raised their glasses once again, this time with a serious look on their faces. Kronzev had no idea what they were talking about, but he joined in the toast nonetheless.

Reed watched intently from his table. Time and again he had to wave the prostitutes away, their overtures seemingly coming more frequently, each a different woman from the last. There were so many, he thought. He was on the edge of his seat knowing how drunk Terrebenzikov and Strenzke were; he could take them out himself, as soon as they walked out of the place; follow them and drag them into an alley, then roll them without a struggle they were so stoned.

He knew he wouldn't. That wasn't the plan, and there was no accounting for it. And he knew whose turf he was on. There were others in the room guarding the two. Reed could pick some of them out: there was the one sitting at the bar smoking a cigarette and constantly turning to watch Strenzke and Terrebenzikov; then there were the two large men sitting at a table nearby (they also declined the invitations of the women, the few who were too new and didn't know any better); and the goons at the door, they didn't even feign to hide their firearms.

No, he would do as he was told: wait and watch. He wasn't seasoned enough for the type of improvisation that his new mentor, Angstrom, was famous for.

There was another matter, more immediate, that Reed was going to have to deal with. If he didn't do something soon, at least invite one of the prostitutes to join him at his table, he was going to start looking suspicious. This was not the type of place to just come alone, sit at a table, and drink a beer. Yet that's what he was doing. The men watching out for Strenzke and Terrebenzikov would become suspicious of him, if they hadn't already.

As if on cue, a woman approached his table once again. She seemed younger than the others, purer, relatively speaking. Certainly less offensive to his taste.

"How are you enjoying your evening?" she said.

Reed redirected his attention from Terrebenzikov and Strenzke to the woman. "Please, join me," he said in perfect Russian, even including the subtle aspects of the dialect associated with the local area. He held his hand toward the empty seat.

She smiled as she sat down, revealing a small gap between her two front teeth. Her hair was blond and was shoulder length. She wore a bright red dress that fit her body tightly. It was difficult for her to sit, her dress was so tight. She crossed her bare legs and faced him, the short skirt covering even less of her thighs after she did so. He momentarily saw her panties as she crossed one leg over the other.

She was younger, he decided, but still experienced; there was a way about her. She probably charged more than some of the others because of her good looks and her youth. It turned his stomach to think of all those women prostituting themselves, and with who knows what kind of men. They probably didn't even get to keep a good portion of what they made. They were screwing their lives away.

"What's your name?" she said.

"Rubin."

"I haven't seen you here before. Where are you from?" she said.

Reed was not about to answer personal questions. "What can I get you to drink?" he said, deflecting her question and holding up his hand to signal the waitress.

He carried on a conversation with her for quite some time,

making sure he was the one asking the questions. He had to think of how he was going to get out of that place, and so far every scenario that came to mind involved her, which he desperately wanted to avoid. Paying a woman for sex was bad enough, but doing so in that place was tantamount to gross negligence.

He drank at a measured pace, mindful of how much he consumed. He acted, however, like he drank a lot more than he actually did. A purposeful slur appeared in his speech, his eyelids appeared a little heavier. The eager woman bought into it, excited that her handsome prey was within her grasp.

"So how did they fool the Americans?" Terrebenzikov said to Strenzke, his guard completely down from all the alcohol he'd drunk.

"Vladimir, leave us," Strenzke suddenly said.

Not only was Strenzke three years older than Terrebenzikov, he could hold his liquor better too. He was conscious of the fact that no one outside of a select few in their immediate organization knew what was really going on. After Kronzev left, Strenzke leaned over the table and said, "You heard about the bodies carted out after the explosions?"

"Yes, of course, we heard about it together."

"What you weren't told, my friend, was that the bodies were carted *in* several days earlier. Hundreds of them, straight from the morgues."

Terrebenzikov stared at him, comprehending what was being said.

"The dead were killed again," Terrebenzikov said stone-faced. The liquor colored his mood.

A short time later, Reed saw out of the corner of his eye both Terrebenzikov and Strenzke get up and leave. Reed's job was done for the evening. Terrebenzikov being alive was confirmed, just like Redblood had postulated. Now he needed to get out of there. But he couldn't just get up and leave. It wouldn't look right. He'd have all kinds of people on him.

And so he stayed. The woman at his table kept drinking

expensive, overpriced drinks, running up the tab. He stuck with beer. He asked for another, continuing to insist to the waitress that he open the bottle himself. Something about the pleasure of it, he said. It was really for the purpose of making sure nothing was put into it. He drank enough to make someone believe a person of his physical size might be drunk. The whole time, however, he never lost his faculties.

She quickly grabbed the fresh bottle he had just opened and held it up to his mouth. "Here, drink more," she said. Then she tilted the bottle and poured the beer into him, like she was filling up a car with gasoline. While she held it to his mouth, she put her other hand on his thigh and squeezed. As he drank, she moved her hand on top of his crotch, caressing it. He drank as if he were a baby drinking from a bottle. He even became slightly aroused during this strange process. She was getting bold, he thought. Good. He decided to move the process along even faster.

When the bottle was empty he wiped his mouth and said, "Let's get together." He looked at her eagerly.

She smiled like a wolf ready to eat its prey. "Let's go upstairs," she said. "Come on."

She put the empty bottle on the table and wiped the beer dripping down his throat with her hand. Then she stood up and kissed him on the neck. Kissing was generally frowned upon, but she couldn't resist; she was attracted to him. After that, she grabbed his hand and urged him to follow, but he stopped her and said, "Wait, let me get a beer to go."

One more beer, he thought, just to make it completely convincing. When the waitress came, he fumbled through his wallet to pay the tab, tipping her generously.

He held the fresh bottle in his hand while she led him upstairs. They walked past a line of other women, all of whom smiled and looked at him. "Have fun, Kristy," one of them said. "He's a handsome one."

Slowly they walked up the old, rickety wooden steps. He felt like he was in a saloon in an old western movie. He purposefully wavered in his gait, even stumbling once as they climbed the steps.

There was a hallway at the top, with several doors on each side. A man sitting on a stool held up five fingers to the woman. Room five.

Reed knew it was important for that man to see him as he wanted him to: drunk, close to passing out. He let his head slump forward, chin to chest. Then he started to lean on the woman, putting his arm around her shoulders. Wavering, Reed bumped into the wall as they walked.

"Kiss me again, Kristy," he said loudly, making sure the man would hear him. He stopped and put both arms around her, trying to kiss her right there in the hallway.

"Easy, Rubin, I don't want you hurting yourself before we get started," she said. "I'm looking forward to this."

She stopped at door five, pushed him against the wall, and complied with his request, kissing him. This time it was on the lips, which as a prostitute she never did with her clients. But she made the exception because of how attracted she was to him. She was going to enjoy her time with him for as much as she could.

As they kissed, he put both of his arms around her, and his hand reached for her ass and squeezed it.

She led him inside the room. It was small; a double bed and a tiny, adjoining bathroom. No decorations, nothing adorning the walls. The walls were dirty and cracked in many places. One area was plastered over where it looked like a large fist had gone through it.

"I have to go to the bathroom," he said in slurred Russian. He ran his hand over his face and then through his hair, mussing it.

"Don't you pass out on me, Rubin."

"I'll be right back."

He closed the door, put his bottle down on the dirty porcelain sink, and looked at himself in the mirror. After urinating he went back to the sink, rubbed cold water on his face, and then poured all but a small portion of his beer down the sink. As he exited, he drank the rest, making it look like he had drunk it all himself.

She was sitting on the edge of the bed waiting for him. When he appeared, she slowly lay down, the whole time looking earnestly into his eyes. She rested her head on the pillow and spread her legs apart, forcing her short red dress to rise above her hips and thereby reveal her panties. Reed went to her and sat on the edge of the bed.

He caressed one of her legs, squeezing her flesh. Then he bent over to kiss her and got on top of her without even taking his clothes off. She wrapped her legs around his waist. Reed rolled sideways to lie on his back, and she followed his lead and got on top of him.

She straightened at her hips while sitting on him and removed her skirt over her head. He looked at the black-laced bra covering her breasts and fondled them. The white skin on her abdomen had several birthmarks. She lowered her head and started kissing his neck.

"Mm," he said, raising his hands over his head and under the pillow. She unbuttoned his shirt, kissing him some more. He lay there like that for a while, occasionally letting out sounds of pleasure as she kissed and fondled him.

This went on for just enough time that Reed saw his opportunity. He closed his eyes, and as she continued to enjoy his body, he gradually feigned falling asleep.

"Wake up," she said when she eventually realized what had happened. She nudged him.

He turned his head to the side and continued to act like he was sleeping.

She slapped his cheek. "Wake up, damn it! You can't fall asleep on me. Wake up"

"Huh, what," he groggily said, his eyes slightly opening to look at her.

"You can't sleep in here. Are we going to do it or not?"

"No...no...too tired. Let's just lay here." He turned his head sideways on the pillow again, a dreamy expression on his face.

"Listen, you have to pay me!"

"What?" he said, his eyes remaining partially closed.

"My time. Either way, you have to pay. If you don't, it's big trouble."

"Fine."

He motioned over to his wallet on the end table next to them. It was an old, well-worn, black leather wallet, overstuffed with rubles. She leaned over and grabbed it while still lying on top of him, thumbed through it, and took out a wad of bills.

"That should cover it," he said smiling, watching her through half-closed eyes.

"Hmph," she said, taking the bills briskly. She hadn't had a client as young and good looking as him in a long time, and she had become incredibly aroused. She was looking forward to screwing him. Now she was incensed by the realization that it wasn't going to happen.

"Listen, can we stay here for a few minutes before I leave?" Reed suddenly said. "I don't want to walk out now; it would look embarrassing, you know?"

She couldn't believe what she was hearing. "Yeah, sure, fine," she said, still counting the bills. It was way more than she'd hoped for. "Sleep. I'll wake you up in fifteen minutes. But that's all you get."

She squirmed off of him and went to the bathroom to fix herself up.

"Thanks," he said, turning onto his side.

* * *

As much as Davis loved the Georgetown home she lived in, it felt empty without Angstrom there. The inside was small and intimate, but each room felt bigger, somewhat strange with only her there.

The food she prepared tasted blander by the day, healthy yet uninspired. The ritual of preparing it was gone without the prospect of sharing it with him.

She came to realize that there were virtually no pictures of Angstrom anywhere in the house; a few framed photos of his two daughters, and that was it. She knew it was due to his profession and the corresponding desire to have as little information about him as possible lying around the house, but she wished she had at least one framed picture of him now that he was gone; something to hold and to look at.

In addition to feeling lonely and isolated at home, she also felt uncomfortable about venturing outside. When he was there, it wasn't a concern. Now, however, going out seemed different, like it was a major event. She was okay once she got to where she was going, but the walk to get there was the problem: she was out in the open and vulnerable. Her specialized Russian training, involuntary as it was, should have given her the courage to overcome her fear and insecurity. It didn't. She knew what the FSB was capable of. She knew her leaving probably stung them hard.

And so the anxiety she felt stemmed from the very circumstances under which she gained entry into the United States, and the retaliation the FSB might seek.

The nervousness was stimulated not just by Angstrom's leaving, but by the manner in which he acted right before he left. He never said anything was wrong, but she got the feeling from him that there was. Something in the way he said goodbye to her. That last night together was so remarkable, one she would never forget—he said those words to her: I love you—but after he left, she began to process it all, piece it together, the words he spoke, what he did, and how he did it.

It had been almost two weeks since he left, and she grew more anxious by the day. She couldn't stop thinking about the different ways the FSB might come after her.

She fought against fear on a daily basis. Certain parts of the day were worse than others: lying in bed at night, walking alone to work, and in the evening when she had to walk home. Walking home was the worst.

She ran through the whole thing in her head a million times. John wouldn't leave her alone if he thought she was in danger, especially without saying anything. Was the FSB tracking her?

All the way to the United States, right in the backyard of the nation's capital…and the Pentagon itself?

She checked all the first floor windows to make sure they were locked, and then she drew the curtains when she went to bed. Each night was more terrifying than the last, staring at the ceiling, becoming alarmed at any minor sound she heard in the house, a car she heard driving by outside.

She started to stay until closing every night at the music store just so she didn't have to be alone.

"You don't have to stay so late," Shulman would say, but she insisted. Even when there were no students to teach, she stayed, doing anything that needed to be done around the shop; odd jobs to keep herself busy until closing. Shulman began to insist upon driving her home. It was the least he could do if she was going to stay so late and keep him company. She was relieved at this development, eagerly taking him up on his offer, because she had become paranoid: the first evening he offered to drive her home—that very same day—she thought she saw someone following her as she walked to work.

21

FRËGE

Monday, July 13
[T$_{detonate}$ minus 15 days]

WHEN IT HAPPENED, IT WAS SUBTLE AT FIRST: obscure, seemingly random and disjointed events, like small trickles of water that washed onto shore, a precursor to the great waves that followed.

Fred and Elisa Banks lived in Chevy Chase Village, Maryland, one of the most affluent cities in the United States. It's a small area—just over two-thousand people—surrounded by many other affluent communities. They chose it over thirty-seven years ago as a place to live and raise their children. Back then land prices were expensive, but not nearly as pricey as they are now. He and his wife fell in love with the area as soon as they discovered it. Houses were generally of a colonial or Georgian style, but other classical architectures were evident as well. Banks' house had a beautiful, wrap-around porch on the front. An elegant white balustrade encircled it, and it was furnished with wicker furniture.

It was tremendous foresight on Banks' part in choosing the area. As a young recruit just starting out at the CIA, he knew he'd also spend a lot of time at the NSA in Fort Meade, as well as in Washington. If a triangle were drawn on a map connecting Langley, Fort Meade, and Washington D.C., his house would be close to the center of it, a reasonable commute to any of those locations.

5 A.M.: an early start even by Banks' standards; the sun was not yet out, and less than a smattering of cars were on Western Avenue as he drove to CIA headquarters. Charming homes lined both sides of the street. He was pondering what he had just heard from the latest Wykoff report. The Russians had come through after all. They got Terrebenzikov and shut down the compound. But he wasn't satisfied. They didn't get any algorithms. No solution to crack Fröge's encryption or solve the mystery of Ørsted. They had nothing—nothing on how the malware worked, what was in it, or the ultimate damage it could unleash.

Maybe interviews of the few prisoners taken during the raid would yield something, or perhaps the undercover policeman, what was his name, Bladlikov? He doubted it. He had a feeling that the Ørsted algorithm was a closely guarded secret, not made widely available to others (at least in source code form). The clock was ticking; $T_{detonate}$ was getting closer, and they were no closer to an Ørsted/Fröge solution.

As he continued to drive along Western Avenue, his thoughts turned to Angstrom. Whenever Banks had a problem to solve or some issue to consider, he always "waited" on it, mulling it over again and again, sometimes subconsciously without even realizing it, before he ultimately made a decision or came to a conclusion. Sometimes he waited so long that people thought he was avoiding the issue, even abdicating his responsibility. Other times he waited so long the issue seemed to take care of itself or just go away. There were three places where he did his best thinking in this regard: in bed at night, in the shower early in the morning, and in his car during his drive to work.

At this particular moment, it wasn't a decision that had to be made, or a question that needed to be answered. A decision already *had* been made, but Banks continued to think about it. He was struggling with how much of a break in protocol it was for someone at Angstrom's level to go out on a mission like he had. It was approved mainly because of Banks himself. He advocated for it over the strong objection of others as soon as Angstrom proposed it. His thinking was that it would further demonstrate Angstrom's return to strength, his being ready for the larger role they envisioned for him: Banks had told Deputy Director Ernest McCoy that Garrett's elite team would be rebuilt around Angstrom. Even if nothing came of Angstrom's efforts in Russia, his carrying out the mission would still be to Angstrom's credit, a reaffirmation of his overall stature within the Division. If Angstrom's team actually *did* accomplish something, like perhaps capturing Strenzke, or maybe even miraculously getting a solution to crack Frëge, there could be no doubt that Banks had backed the right horse. Besides, Angstrom had been out of circulation from being a full-fledged field agent since only two years ago, a relatively short time in the grand scheme of things. It wasn't like he was completely out of practice or forgot how to do things. He was the best at what he did, and those kinds of skills don't atrophy overnight.

And then for Banks, retirement. Banks sighed as he thought about that elusive goal. Retirement, comfortable in the knowledge that his legacy within the organization—his division that included the special team originally led by Garrett—would survive. Banks was so deeply involved with these ruminations that he hardly paid attention to his driving. He'd made the drive for so many years he was basically on autopilot.

When he approached the River Road intersection and saw that the stoplight wasn't working, he didn't give it a second thought. The next one at Massachusetts Avenue wasn't working either. It wasn't until Watson Street that he realized all of the stoplights were out. They weren't flashing or frozen on any particular setting, they were completely off. It hadn't stormed overnight, so that couldn't have been the cause, he thought. He assumed it was a glitch in the system and thought nothing further of it, except for the fact that it was an annoyance—commuters had to treat each intersection like there was a stop sign instead of a fully functioning stoplight: stop, go, stop, go, each driver having to wait his turn. He wished the other drivers would follow the proper protocol and go when they were supposed to, but that never seemed to happen.

Just after his car made it through the intersection his smartphone, which sat in a dock attached to the dashboard with a suction cup, made an unexpected sound. He looked and saw that it somehow had gone into speakerphone mode and was dialing a number. He reached over and pushed the icon to stop it, puzzled by how that could have happened. As soon as he turned his attention back to the road, however, the same thing happened. A slight concern came over him. He looked up and saw that the stoplight he was approaching at Canal Road wasn't working either.

It was too early, he said to himself; too early for this to be happening. By Q-Directorate's calculation there were still fifteen days left before Frëge was supposed to go off, if it ever did.

He pulled onto the shoulder just before he got to Chain Bridge so he could grab his phone and make a call; his schedule might be changing. If an attack was really happening—he still had his doubts—he wouldn't go to his office at Langley. Instead, he would call Q-Directorate and meet him at NSA headquarters. If it was starting, he wanted to be at the NSA Control Center, the best place to be to get the most comprehensive information. He attempted to dial Q-Directorate's home, but something was wrong with his phone. He looked at the top and saw there were no bars—no connection to the network. Damn, he thought. Damn, damn, damn. No network. Not good. He never had bad coverage on this part of the drive; not since he switched carriers.

Then something else happened with his phone: a strange pop-up message flashed across the screen, something indiscernible. Images began to successively open and flash on the display. He recognized them as photos from the SD card. Then icons or images from web sites he had previously visited flashed across the screen, one after the other; the photo-viewer had opened and was displaying remnant screen shots of web pages. Self-invoked actions happening right before his eyes. It was as if the operating system was acting on its own, or...had been hacked.

If this was the depth with which Ørsted and Frëge could reach—down to an individual's cell phone—there was no telling its ultimate power. Banks got nervous.

He tossed the phone onto the passenger seat, turned his car around, and spun the rear tires of his BMW 530i. It would take him close to an hour from where he was at, but he needed to get to NSA headquarters. If Frëge was detonating, it would be everywhere, and he knew Q-Directorate would already be at the Control Center without even calling him.

Damn. Much too soon, he thought, gripping the steering wheel tightly. And still, after all this, no one had a clue as to why, or who.

Retirement. Maybe he'd have to stop thinking about it. A feeling of dismay came over him. It was time for someone younger to take the reins—someone who relished it. He just didn't have the energy for it anymore.

"Hank, it started, didn't it?" Banks said as he took off his navy blue sportcoat and threw it onto one of the nearby chairs. The Control Center was Q-Directorate's domain, one of the few places where he was referred to by his real name, Hank Bingham.

The room was large, about the size of a small auditorium, but because of the sheer amount of electronic equipment packed inside of it, it felt cramped. Several large screens lined the walls, each with the ability to display multiple sub-screens simultaneously; they were directly linked to Big Machine and PRISM, displaying massive amounts of real-time data and analysis. Smaller computer systems were situated throughout the room, row upon row of them, with a system analyst manning each one, each able to tap directly into one of the main cores of Big

Machine and display processed analysis mid-stream. Complex software enabled graphical output of the real-time processing, formatting it into a human-readable representation.

Another part of the Center was interconnected with key IT infrastructure throughout the country, both private and public. It was a small fraction of the data pulled in by PRISM, selectively chosen at any particular time by analysts in response to particular situations being investigated. Banks always thought of the place as a type of "Situation Room" on steroids, the only difference being that in some cases active intervention could be invoked as opposed to just passive monitoring.

Bingham was looking over an analyst's shoulder at a computer screen, pointing to it, when he heard Banks' voice. Bingham wore a colored tee shirt, faded jeans, and Docksiders with no socks. His hair was mussed and unwashed. He looked much younger than the forty-two years that he was—certainly younger than he seemed at the formal briefings.

Bingham turned to Banks to respond, a coffee mug with the Baltimore Orioles logo in his hand. "Yeah, it started. We're seeing it across the country."

"You got here early," Banks said. "How'd you find out so fast? I only experienced traces of it this morning on my drive in."

"You're kidding, right?" Bingham said as he turned back to the display he had been studying. "Big Machine flagged the first instance of it at around 1 A.M. I got the call. Been here ever since."

"But what happened? The attack isn't supposed to occur for another two weeks! What the hell's going on?"

"Not sure. No one is. Looks like that date was a false one, lulling us into a quasi-sense of security by making us think we had more time."

"This isn't good. We'd better get the word out."

"Already done. We're following the Holdman Protocol[2]. Flights at all airports are already canceled, incoming international

---

[2] The Holdman Protocol was devised by Mike Holdman, Director of Homeland Security in the event that Ørsted and Frège detonated and caused the considerable disruption to society predicted by the NSA.

flights redirected when possible. Police and fire were alerted across the country, as well as hospitals. Emergency standby power is deployed and ready at critical institutions. The National Guard has been notified."

"Hmm, and you guys are sure about this?"

"Of course. Freedman was already briefed and gave his approval."

"I see." Gesturing toward the coffee mug in Bingham's hand, Banks said, "Got any more coffee?"

Bingham was bothered by the question because he was anxious to get back to work, but he did his best to hide his aggravation. He turned and yelled across the room, "Someone get this gentleman a cup of coffee, would you? Thanks." He turned again to the screen. "Has it got it?" he said to the analyst whose shoulder he was looking over.

"Nope. Looks like the penetration wasn't deep enough, again," the analyst responded.

"Well, we'll get it. I know we will. Just a matter of time," Bingham said, still watching the monitor.

"What's up?" Banks said as he moved closer.

This time Bingham didn't even try to cover up his aggravation at being bothered at such a crucial time. "We're monitoring a particular thread of Big Machine's," he said, pointing to a graph displayed on the computer screen. A line was slowly being drawn, moving upward and to the right on the graph. "You see, when we predicted Ørsted's next major attack, we did more than just alert the IT community and provide prevention and remediation guidance. We set traps for it."

"Traps?"

"Yes, traps, or as we like to call them, 'honeypots'—holes in software to detect unauthorized intrusions. They look like part of a network, but they're actually isolated areas that contain information a hacker would want to steal or attack. With the cooperation of companies and agencies across the country, we inserted honeypots in various computer installations and software, such as at DFW Airport. It's very complex, multiple levels deep. At each level, more of the Ørsted and Frëge code proliferates, moving further and further into the honeypots, until finally, we hope, enough will be captured for Big Machine to analyze and crack the encryption. With that, we'd be able to diffuse Frëge, as well as identify the algorithm that disassociates and reassembles Ørsted, hides it, or whatever the hell it does."

"Fascinating," Banks said. "Have we ever done this before?"

"Yes, we have. The use of honeypots is common nowadays. Ours, however, are more sophisticated and more powerful, hot off the press from DARPA."

"So how broad is it so far?"

"Huh, what do you mean? The honeypots?"

"No. Frëge. How much has it gone off out there?" Banks said, pointing to one of the giant displays on the wall that was displaying a computer generated map of the United States.

"Ah. Well, so far, it's what you see. Each star represents an auto-detected instance from sensors we had installed in places across the country—all part of the Holdman Protocol. Didn't you read the technical note in the appendix?"

"Not all of it. It started to go over my head."

"Hmph. Well, anyway, those stars over there," Bingham said as he pointed to the state of Maryland, "represent the attacks on the cellular networks in our area. Does your cell phone work?"

"No, it doesn't. In addition to the fact that it's acting goofy, it constantly shows no bars."

"Yeah, the whole network is down."

Banks looked back at the map. "The stars...they're appearing at a pretty noticeable rate," he said. "Those are new reported incidents?"

"Yes, but not necessarily 'reported' in the usual sense," Bingham said. "They're auto-reported from the embedded sensors. Manual reports can't come in that fast." He suddenly stood upright while looking at the giant map and said, "Look!"

Everyone in Control Center, close to a hundred people, heard Bingham and looked up at the map. The rate at which the tiny stars appeared dramatically increased. Clusters began to form. Tension grew in the room.

"How are the reports going to come in if communications get knocked out?" Banks said.

"At some point they won't—not from areas hit hard enough."

Everyone continued to watch as stars populated the map at an alarming rate. The clusters became denser; in certain areas whole cities were completely covered.

"My God, New York will be overtaken!" said Bingham. "The stars just represent samples where we had sensors inserted. Actual proliferation will be much greater than that."

"There're no more updates from New York," one of the analysts said, turning to face Bingham.

"Same for Boston," said another.

Bingham turned to Banks and said, "That means all electronic communications in two major cities are already out." He turned back to the map and said, "Extraordinary. The synchronous nature of it! The speed! The power!"

Stars continued to fill other portions of the map; other major cities were overtaken. And then it all suddenly stopped; it was as if the screen had locked up. No one said anything and just watched.

"The updates seemed to have stopped," Banks said. "What happened? Did the screen freeze or something? I don't understand."

"That's it," Bingham said, stunned. "Frëge must have detonated so fast, at so many places at once, that the entire communication infrastructure in major cities across the country has become inoperable—there are no means by which our sensors can send us data. That's why the stars suddenly stopped growing. We've been cut off from all the sensors."

There was continued silence in the room. Everyone remained still, trying to comprehend the magnitude of what was happening.

"Mind you," Bingham added, "this isn't just DDoS carpet bombing hitting everything, this is Frëge detonating on a massive scale...not something temporary that can be fixed by a simple system reboot."

"I've got to go," Banks suddenly said. "They're going to need to meet about this *yesterday* with the President."

As he began to leave, Bingham said to him, "Grab one of the K-Com units. Remember the channel selection per the Holdman Protocol."

"Right," Banks stopped and said. "Where's the closest place I can get one."

"C'mon, I'll show you," Bingham said as he ran up the carpeted steps to catch up to him. He suddenly stopped in his tracks, turned to the analyst he was talking to when Banks first entered the Control Center, and said, "What does Big Machine say? Did it trap enough before all hell broke loose?"

"It's processing. Analysis must be massive. The graph is barely budging," the analyst said, staring at his screen. "Got to be an incredible amount of data for the chart to be moving this slowly. It's processing, though. I can tell."

"Good. Keep at it. The minute it finds anything, reach me. You guys know my code."

"Got it," the analyst responded without turning from his monitor.

With that, Bingham ran up the rest of the stairs and left with Banks.

* * *

Davis was up early that same morning. Sleep was difficult for her anymore. She walked down the steps from the bedroom, hoping the paper had been delivered, but she doubted it given that it wasn't even 5:30 A.M. yet. She looked out of the front window toward the street, but nothing was there.

She sleepily ground some coffee beans and started brewing a pot of coffee. After that she walked to the small living room and curled up in a chair with a novel she had been reading: *The*

Beautiful and Damned. Angstrom had recommended it to her. F. Scott Fitzgerald, one of the finest, he said, a writer from the Jazz Age. Despite the fact that the story made her sad, she liked it. Anthony Patch and Gloria, she thought, what a pair, and what an America. She was two-thirds of the way through and dreaded the ending. She couldn't see how things were going to turn around for Anthony Patch.

She started to read part three, A Matter of Civilization. Soon the aroma of coffee was in the air. At the last few hiccups before the machine was done, she rose to pour herself a cup. A short time later she decided she wasn't in the mood to read; she was restless. She replenished her cup and went outside, taking a seat on the top step of the front stoop. Sooner or later the paper would arrive. The coffee tasted good out in the fresh morning air, and she became more relaxed.

By the time she finished her cup she figured it must have been after six. Usually the paper was there by then. Strange, she thought, the man that delivered it was usually very reliable. With empty cup in hand she went back inside and turned on the television, thinking she'd watch the news for a while. To her surprise, there was nothing but a blank screen—that meant the monitor couldn't detect a signal; the cable was out.

She looked around the house wondering what she should do. She was wide awake and didn't want to go back to sleep. A jog was out of the question. She did that yesterday, five miles. Her muscles needed a rest.

Finally, she decided to go to work. She never went that early. Mr. Shulman would really be surprised, she thought, if not aggravated. Tough, she was going.

"Anne, you are here so early!" Shulman said as soon as she knocked on the door at 9 A.M. "Is everything okay? I'm getting concerned you work so much."

"Not as much as you," she said, smiling.

"Yes, but for me, I'm old, and this is my shop. I *must* be here."

"Mr. Shulman, you never take a day off. You should, you know…at least every now and then. I'd be happy to watch the store for you." Davis, despite Shulman's request to call him Nik, or even Nikolas, insisted on calling him Mr. Shulman.

He looked at her sideways. "Anne, tell me what's wrong. Love problems?"

Davis laughed and said, "No, Mr. Shulman. Let's just say my 'male friend' is still out of town, so I'm on my own. I like it here, and I like your company. Is it okay if I work? You don't even have to pay me for all the hours; I just want to be around."

"Of course I'll pay you. Well, maybe I'll let you keep all the money from the Katy lesson today, how's that?"

"That's fine Mr. Shulman," she said laughing. "It's more than enough. Now, how about I look at those books for you?"

It wasn't too long, however, before it became clear that things were not right.

"Hmm, that's strange," Shulman said out loud to himself.

"What was that you said Mr. Shulman?" said Davis from the back office.

"Huh? Oh, I said 'strange.' You see, I can't get a station on the radio. Usually I listen to the Polish station in the morning. But it's not on. In fact, there are no stations at all. Maybe this old radio is finally on the fritz."

Davis appeared from the other room, her eyebrows furrowed.

"It's been a strange morning," he continued. "Have you noticed? All the traffic lights were out on the streets. Like there was a big storm or something, only there wasn't."

"Yes, I noticed that too. And cable T.V. was out at my house."

"Yes, for me as well at my house." He banged on the top of the radio, hoping that would fix it. "Maybe I turn on the television for a little bit, before any customers come. See what the news says."

But the television didn't work either. There was nothing on the small, nine-inch CRT screen (with the special cable box to convert the digital signals to analog).

"Hmm, it looks like the cable's still out," Davis said as she pointed to the television.

He shrugged his shoulders, and they both went back to work.

About twenty minutes later the woman who owned the flower shop next door, Elaine Swenson, came inside. "Nik, where are you?"

"That you, Elaine?" came a voice before the person. Shulman was in the back, looking over Davis' shoulder at his ledger. He appeared with a big smile on his face. "For what do I owe this pleasure?" he said.

"Nik, have you heard?"

"Heard what?" The smile disappeared. "What's wrong?"

"You haven't had any customers yet, have you?

"No, of course not. It's too early. You know that. Why? What's the matter? Is everything okay?"

"No, it's not. There's something wrong. Nothing works...T.V., radio, phone, nothing. Internet either."

"Bah, the crazy internet. It's always down."

"No, really, something's not right."

Davis came out from the back as well. She had heard everything and had a concerned look on her face.

"Oh, hello, Anne. My, you're here early today." The sight of Davis so early in the morning temporarily confused Swenson, especially given everything else that was happening.

Just then the city's emergency alert system sounded outside. It wasn't time for a regularly scheduled test, which meant the powerful siren was signaling a real emergency.

"What's that?" Swenson said. "That's not supposed to go off now." She looked at her wristwatch to confirm it.

"This is strange indeed," Shulman said. He walked out of the front of his store and looked around outside. Others were standing around on the sidewalk as well.

Soon a police car slowly passed by on the street. The police officer driving the automobile spoke over the car's intercom system:

ATTENTION. ATTENTION. ALL RESIDENTS ARE ASKED TO IMMEDIATELY RETURN TO THEIR HOMES. AN EMERGENCY ELECTRICAL MALFUNCTION HAS OCCURRED ACROSS THE STATE. FOR YOUR OWN SAFETY, YOU NEED TO RETURN TO YOUR HOME. PRESERVE FOOD AND DRINKING LIQUIDS. REPEAT...

All three looked at each other, bewildered. The police car didn't stop and continued to repeat its message as it slowly moved forward. Some people ran alongside it asking the officer questions through the opened window.

That was how Davis experienced the beginning of it. With Angstrom leaving under mysterious circumstances and this strange thing being announced by the police, along with the emergency alert system sounding off—all of which couldn't be explained or understood—she became very troubled. She was used to taking care of herself; she was strong and had faced much adversity in her life. But now there were too many odd things happening, too many unaccountable events accumulating. In her experience that was when bad things happened. She felt like she didn't have adequate control of the situation. She was so troubled that she did something that surprised even herself.

When Shulman, Davis, and Swenson went back into the store, Davis said, "Mr. Shulman, I hope this doesn't sound strange..."

Shulman looked at her for a moment. "Hmm, what is it, Anne?"

She looked at him for a moment, hesitant. Swenson watched her too.

Finally, Shulman said, "You don't want to be alone, do you?"

"No, I don't."

"Neither do I. You come to my home. It's okay, you come. We'll keep each other company."

The siren from the emergency alert system sounded again. Shulman and Davis looked at each other.

"Thank you, Mr. Shulman. Are you sure it's okay?"

"Of course. Let's go. We close up shop, then I drive you to your home to get whatever you need. And if this siren still going off at night, you sleep in extra bedroom. It's okay, my wife is long dead, rest her soul."

"Mr. Shulman, you're so kind. How could I ever thank you?" She hugged him suddenly. She was grateful to have found this man—someone she felt an affinity for in her new, adopted country. And her desire to be in his company just then was also out of necessity: she needed time to assess what was going on around her—to figure out what all these strange occurrences meant—and while she did that, she thought it best that she not be alone. The way Angstrom had said goodbye to her had put her on alert—almost like a signal that maybe someone was trying to find her and get to her. If that were the case, she would be less vulnerable if she wasn't alone. With another person around—a witness to what might otherwise happen to her—there was less of a chance a potential assailant would try to attack her. Perhaps she was being paranoid, but with her background and training, better to be that than the opposite. She knew that this could actually be putting Shulman at risk, but she forced that concern out of her mind, which wasn't easy, because other than Angstrom, Shulman was the closest to family she had.

Shulman patted her on the back as they hugged. He was happy too, not just because he liked her and wanted to make her happy, but because he was old and was also disturbed by what was happening.

"Hey, what about me?" Swenson suddenly said. "Can I come over too? Just until my husband comes home?"

She reached into her pocket and took out her cell phone to call her husband. Then she remembered it wasn't working, and an exasperated look came over her.

Shulman and Davis looked at her. They had forgotten all about her while they were hugging each other.

"Yes, Elaine, of course," said Shulman. "You come to my home too. We'll play cards for a while, make a time of it."

"Thank you, Nik," Swenson said while continuing to fidget with her phone. "It's funny, but my phone won't work." There was a nervous frustration in her movements.

Davis watched her and glanced at Shulman. She was glad she wouldn't be alone. Nothing seemed right anymore.

22

The Unthinkable

WHAT INITIALLY SEEMED LIKE RANDOM SPORADIC EVENTS of Ørsted and Frëge turned into a great Tsunami, a full-scale cyber attack on the United States, non-stop, inexhaustible, horrific in scope. The DFW attacks from before were now promulgated a thousand-fold; virtually no type of entity, public or private, was spared; institutions around the country were inflicted and crippled. This time, however, there was no automatic resetting or restoration of systems. This time the full power and magnitude of Ørsted and Frëge was revealed.

The DHS National Cybersecurity and Communications Integration Center (CCIC) had earlier warned companies and government agencies across the country of an attack that might occur at a certain date-time predicted, and many businesses hinted that they might shut down on that date in anticipation of such an event. The public was also provided with vague warnings of a new type of Y2K-type problem that might occur on a certain date, and caution was urged. Assimilation of all available information, however, including leaks of the more detailed CCIC tech bulletins describing potential cyber attacks, eventually put the general public on notice of the true nature of the warning.

But now the actual attack happened too soon for anyone to react. It caught everyone off guard. What's more, a majority of the general public still couldn't believe it when they heard the warnings, the overblown original Y2K predictions still fresh in their minds even after all these years.

Therefore, no one was truly prepared for it. And despite all the warnings, no one truly comprehended what was to come.

U.S.—State of Washington
Grand Coulee Dam—Third Power Plant

The Grand Coulee is no ordinary hydropower plant; when it was first activated back in 1980, it was the largest hydropower plant in the world. It's still the largest hydropower facility in the United States. The Third Power Plant, the largest of the three powerhouses located at the Grand Coulee Dam, has a total capacity of 4,215 megawatts and generates almost two-thirds of the dam's total power.

Alison Kendrick, Chief Facility Engineer for the generators supported by the Third Power Plant, was standing in the main control room. She stood behind Arturo Bendez, who was sitting at the main console.

"Took me over an hour to get here this morning," said Bendez as he watched a multitude of monitors displaying sensor data from readings throughout the plant. "I got here a little before you did."

Kendricks said, "I know. And it didn't help that cable T.V. was out. Normally I watch traffic reports as I get dressed; if I knew all the traffic lights were out I would have left earlier. Alex and Jay were pretty pissed when I got here. Did you see their faces?"

"Yeah. But at least all you got were nasty looks. You should have heard what they said to me before you got here."

"Well, they'll get over it," Kendricks said. "When they see the traffic on the way home they'll understand. I mean, that's the first time I've been late for my shift in a long time, you know?"

"Mm."

Kendricks sipped her coffee as she stood behind Bendez. "How's everything look?" she said.

"Perfect, like always."

"How about turbine speed on G24? It's been a week since the main overhaul was officially complete. It's still riding steady, right?"

"Readings are perfect," Bendez responded.

"They better be. After five years of work I still can't believe the overhaul is finally done."

Kendricks glanced at the readings for the G24 governor. Bendez wasn't exaggerating: speed was right in the center of optimum ranges.

"What kind of coffee is that?" Bendez said without turning around. "Smells like…"

Just then there was a loud explosion. The whole room shook and Kendricks' coffee spilled as she lost her balance. Readings on all the monitors went haywire.

"What the hell's going on?" Kendricks said.

The voice of a hydro-mechanic was heard over Kendricks' two-way radio holstered to her hip: "EXPLOSION AT G24!"

"Jake, is that you?" Kendricks shouted into her radio.

"YEAH. G24 IS DOWN [coughing]…HIGH POWER THYRISTORS MUST'VE GENERATED WAY TOO MUCH CURRENT….SLIP RINGS TO THE ROTOR BURNED UP…I SAW IT HAPPENING RIGHT BEFORE THE EXPLOSION."

Kendricks said, "Is everyone alright?"

"YEAH…YEAH…I THINK SO…[coughing]…SMELL IS AWFUL."

Bendez immediately triggered the emergency alarm, confused that it hadn't gone off automatically. He turned around to look at Kendricks, who nodded.

"Listen, Jake," she said over the radio, "institute emergency shut down, and then invoke emergency procedures. Make sure non-essential personnel get out of there and that the emergency crew puts on safety equipment. We're dispatching fire now. You're sure no one's hurt at this point?"

"...ACTUALLY, I CAN'T TELL...TOO MUCH SMOKE. LET ME GET ON THIS."

"Right. Stay in radio contact."

She turned to Bendez and said, "Dispatch emergency units."

"Already done."

The two exchanged glances for a moment.

"What the hell happened?" She said. "I was looking at the readings for G24 myself—the exciter voltages were fine!"

More people rushed into the control room. There was a general state of confusion; the landline phones were out, and no one's cell phone could get a connection. Just then someone reminded them of the Holdman Protocol.

Kendricks couldn't believe what had happened—her worst nightmare. Judging by what she heard over the two-way radio, the 2000-ton G24 rotor was probably out of commission, damaged beyond repair. The whole Pacific Northwest would be without power, and a generator that had been through a five-year overhaul had just self-destructed.

The malware had been installed some time ago through a vulnerability created during the G24 overhaul itself. Frëge had direct access to the operational controls of the turbine: the nominal governor speed was increased beyond safe levels, the DC exciter voltages raised above proper settings. Once this was done, it was only a matter of time—a very *short* time. All of this was masked because Frëge had tampered with the safety sensors and alerts. To Kendricks and Bendez, as well as the electricians and hydro mechanics located at the G24 site itself, everything looked fine.

Yet this massive blow that would incapacitate the entire Pacific Northwest represented only a small fraction of the overall power of Frëge.

New York, New York

Bob Heggerts was sleeping late. After a long, monotonous day at a kitchen appliance tradeshow at Javits Center, he had hooked up with a woman working at another one of the booths. They had dinner together and then took cabs from one nightclub to another until finally, at around 2 A.M., they ended up at his hotel room. After a few more drinks, plus some marginal sex, they both passed out—so much so that they never heard the loud pounding at the door at 10:15 A.M.

A little past 11 A.M. he awoke with a massive headache. The woman, whose name he remembered as Bridgette, had her back turned to him, still sleeping. He could have sworn she had brown hair, not the long blond hair that was now spread out across the white pillow.

He sat up on the edge of the bed. Water, he thought to himself, water was always good for a hangover.

As he ambled toward the bathroom, he spotted a piece of paper lying on the floor at the base of the front door. Thinking it was the hotel bill, he bent down to pick it up. That was a mistake; his head throbbed as blood rushed to his brain.

To his surprise, instead of a computer printout, there was a handwritten message on the paper:

> POWER OUT. WATER NOT SAFE TO DRINK. SEE
> FRONT DESK ASAP.
>
> —MANAGER

Aw shit, what the hell's this about? he thought to himself. He leaned around the corner to look at Bridgette sleeping—she was out like a light. He wasn't getting her up anytime soon.

Heggerts put his jeans on and threw on a tee shirt. He didn't bother about his hair; he could care less that early in the morning. After grabbing his wallet and the room's card key, he opened the door to go to the elevator.

The hallway was dark; only the emergency lights were on at each end of the hallway. Although Heggerts noticed this, he didn't give it much thought given the state he was in. He stood at the elevator for quite some time before he realized the numbers above it weren't changing; none of them were even illuminated. The elevator wasn't running. His head drooped as he contemplated going back to bed instead of down ten flights of stairs. The handwritten note under his door was odd, though. Fuck it, he thought to himself, the exercise would do him good after drinking so much the night before. Maybe he'd even get himself some breakfast while he was down there.

He passed a few people going in the opposite direction on his way down. Strange looks on their faces, he thought. They acted liked they'd seen a ghost. Maybe he looked a lot worse than he felt, though that hardly seemed possible.

When he finally reached the front lobby, what he saw seemed odd, although he couldn't immediately put his finger on why; something didn't look right. A lot of people were milling about, more than he would have thought normal. There were no lights on anywhere; even though it was daytime and natural light filtered through the windows and glass doors leading to the street, there should have been *some* lights turned on—front desk lights, end table lamps, illumination around some of the wall art— something.

Heggerts made his way through the crowd toward the front desk. There was a long line. He sighed.

Just about when he was ready to give up and go to the restaurant, he spotted a poster resting on a metal easel; a hotel manager stood near it. A group of people were gathered around him, peppering him with questions. Heggerts moved closer. The message on the poster was handwritten in black marker. Something about an emergency...no need to go through official checkout process...computers down. Heggerts listened to what the man said.

"Yes, ma'am, this is happening all over New York, not just the hotel. Power is out everywhere. That's why we're saying our computers are down."

"So you can't check me out?"

"What I'm saying, ma'am, is if your okay with it, you can leave the hotel by noon and we'll automatically bill your credit card when our system is back up. If you wish, we can send a copy of the bill to either your home or email address. We're also waiving extra fees you may have incurred—like the room bar—as long as they're less than fifteen dollars. If you don't feel comfortable doing this, you can wait in line at the front desk and we'll give you a handwritten bill."

Another man asked, "What if our checkout date is not today?" "Can we still stay here?"

"Of course. We're still open, but please understand that power is out all over the city. Our restaurant is closed, there's no television, the phone lines are out...the city has already sent a bulletin that they're experiencing problems at water treatment facilities, so as I've said, there's a drinking water problem. What comes out of the tap is not safe."

Hearing that the restaurant was closed was a huge downer for Heggerts; he was starved. Everything else the man said almost didn't register after that.

Shit, Heggerts thought, I've heard enough. I'm going to the airport to fly standby...get the hell outta here. New York without power is the last place I wanna be.

He turned to look back at the door from where he came and sighed. The stairs—he took a deep breath as he contemplated going back up them.

He suddenly turned to the man answering the questions and without thinking blurted, "Where's the complementary coffee?"

Everyone turned to look at him with incredulous looks on their faces. Heggerts felt embarrassed.

"Sorry, never mind," he said with a wave of the hand. He headed toward the door to begin his long climb up the stairs.

"Bridgette...Bridgette...c'mon, you have to get up," he said, gently rubbing her shoulder as she lay on her side.

"Mm...what is it? Oh...my head," she said as she turned over and rubbed her eyes.

"Yeah, I know, me too. Listen, there's a lot going on..."

Slowly she opened her eyes so that Heggerts could explain the situation to her, as well as what he intended to do. Although sensitive to her feelings, he was in a hurry; he wanted to get out of there and to the airport as soon as possible. As Bridgette stirred awake, he made some coffee using the small brew-system provided in the room; coffee always came first as far as he was concerned, and whatever's wrong with the water, the hell with it.

Had Heggerts bothered to listen to more of what the manager had to say when he was down in the lobby, he would have learned that the subway system wasn't operating. The bus system wasn't running either. Many of the cab companies were closed for business, their dispatch systems inoperable. There was no mass transit available out of the city or to the airport. All flights were canceled at the airports anyway. New York City was essentially in gridlock.

Instead, after shuffling Bridgette out of the room, he packed his travel back and hurriedly stepped out of the hotel onto Seventh Avenue. He couldn't find a cab to hail; traffic was barely moving. He figured if he walked a little bit more that maybe he could find a cab farther down the street. It was then that he realized all the traffic lights were out. All electronic signs on buildings were turned off. None of the stores or restaurants was open for business. People were walking around in a state of veritable confusion. Police were noticeable in number.

It was going to be a long time before he would be able to get out of New York. If he was smart, he would run back to his hotel to try and secure a place to stay.

* * *

All across the country it was the same: airports came to a standstill, factories ground to a halt, businesses were closed. How could Ørsted and its payload Frëge have proliferated so profoundly, through so many different types of IT infrastructure? It was a technical marvel, yet a tremendous, awful nightmare.

People panicked, fearful of what was happening. This was not Y2K, they asserted, this was something much, much worse. This was chaos.

All television was shut down, cable or otherwise; no cryptic message flashed across the screen like the CNN telecast; no color bar code displayed, no public warning message, nothing. Just a blank screen. Even satellite television didn't work; the ground stations were corrupted, leaving no programming to relay. Radio stations couldn't transmit, their transmission towers rendered useless because their computer controlled equipment was infected.

In New York, Los Angeles, and Chicago—all the major cities—power was cut to skyscrapers. Even with emergency standby power, the elevators wouldn't work: the programmable logic devices controlling them had been corrupted. Buildings were therefore closed; those people who were able to drive into the city for work were turned away at the doors and told to go back home.

Traffic in major cities was in total disarray. SCADA systems for all electronic traffic control equipment had been hacked and disabled.

Of course credit cards couldn't be processed: no power, no network to communicate over. Even if there was power, many of the point-of-sale terminals at business establishments were plagued by Frëge; credit card information wasn't stolen, it was simply not read. It was as if the hackers wanted all commerce to come to a grinding halt. Even gasoline couldn't be pumped at gas stations for lack of power to the pumps.

Stock markets never opened. The computerized trading equipment was already inoperative before the first trade was attempted.

By around 3 P.M., when it became readily apparent how widespread the problem was, the rioting began. In areas all over the country, lawless, crazed people took advantage of the situation and robbed stores wherever they could. Emergency personnel were unable to keep up with the mayhem, even after the National Guard was deployed.

Institutions thought to have had the most sophisticated cyber attack prevention and remediation systems—power utilities, water treatment facilities—could not withstand the onslaught. Whenever possible, critical defensive measures were undertaken. A subset of the overall Holdman Protocol, wherein resources were completely decoupled from IT infrastructure by literally unplugging it from the internet, was instituted, but it didn't help. The systems themselves were already infected.

Overall, it seemed as though in just one day Armageddon had come. There was something terrible happening that the average person could not comprehend. The scope and depth of Ørsted and Frëge went far beyond anything anyone had ever seen before, far beyond anything the country had ever contemplated.

23

Damage Report

IN ACCORDANCE WITH THE HOLDMAN PROTOCOL, Q-DIRECTORATE used the K-Com network to page the senior members of the Intelligence Community to set a briefing for 6:30 P.M. The list of invitees was purposefully small, and only the first two rows of VENOMA were filled. All of the senior members of the Intelligence Community were in attendance. Even Defense Secretary Charles Bradley was there. He sat right next to Director of National Intelligence James Freedman in the front row.

"Good evening," Q-Directorate began. There was a somber tone in his voice, a downtrodden look on his face. "So, Ørsted was triggered this morning, much earlier than expected." His voice was monotone, lifeless, like the wind had been knocked out of him. "Our sensors…"

Just then the door to VENOMA swung open and Director of Homeland Security Mike Holdman appeared. He was talking on an N5 portable satellite communication unit of the K-Com system, and everyone turned to look at him as he entered.

"Yes, Mr. President, I know," said Holdman, speaking into the N5 unit. He looked at the others in the room and waved his hand, signaling an apology for the interruption. They all waited for him.

"I'm just walking into the briefing as we speak," he continued. "What? No, that wasn't the intention. Have them speak to General Hendstrom. He's coming up with a new plan for New York. Los Angeles and Chicago will follow the same plan...yes...we'll set one up to meet with you after we break from here...yes, certainly...thank you, Mr. President."

He tapped a button on the N5 to end the link and then looked over to Bradley and Freedman. "Sorry about that."

"The President?" Bradley asked.

"Yes."

"It's not working in New York, is it?" said Bradley.

"No. We're going to have to change what we're doing. It's not enough. General Hendstrom's working on it right now."

"Are we meeting about it?"

"Yes. The President wants a meeting as soon as possible after this briefing."

"Okay, then let's not waste any time," said Bradley. "Q-Directorate?"

"Right." He had been listening to everything, and for whatever reason, he all of a sudden felt energized. "As I was about to say, our selectively placed sensors identified the first abnormality at just after 1 A.M. This was at O'Hare International Airport in Chicago. In less than seventeen minutes, reports from our sensors strategically placed at other major airports showed similar activity. Our sensors were installed at O'Hare and Midway in Chicago, LaGuardia and John F. Kennedy in New York, San Francisco and Los Angeles International in California, Logan International in Boston, DFW and Austin-Bergstrom in Texas, Dulles and Ronald Reagan in D.C., as well as Philadelphia and Miami International Airports. The attacks had the same profile as before, only this time, as you know, there was no recovery."

A map of the United States was shown on the screen behind Q-Directorate. "What you're looking at is a pictorial representation of the sensor reports of the initial attack."

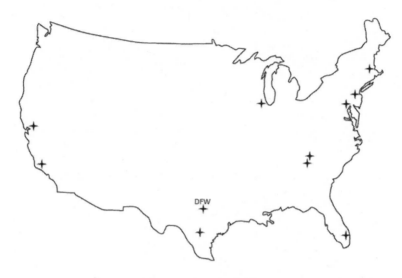

1:30 A.M. Attack Metrics

"In all cases, airport infrastructure was attacked first. Each initial attack started at about the same time, just after 1 A.M. As you can see, other than from the airport sensors, there were no other reports that came in between 1:00 and 1:30 A.M. It was somewhat fortuitous that the attacks occurred at the airports first."

"Why's that?" interrupted FBI Director Adlai Corver, purposefully slowing the presentation down to make sure he could keep up with what was being disclosed. "First of all, how do you know the attacks started at the airports? I mean, in case you haven't noticed, all hell's broken loose out there. It seems to me like it could have started anywhere."

"Fair question. I should clarify that our best indications are that the attacks started at the airports first. It's possible there was early sporadic activity elsewhere, but for the most part, it started at the airports. And we know this because of the placement of our sensors. As shown on this first map labeled 1:30 A.M., the stars designate the first attacks detected and reported by our sensors. When you look at the progression of the attack in the next map, the one labeled 5:30 A.M., you start to see representation from sensors installed in other high profile targets, such as rail transportation hubs, power generation facilities, federal, state, and local admin buildings, and so forth. So we know, at least in these major metropolitan areas, that the attacks essentially started at the airports."

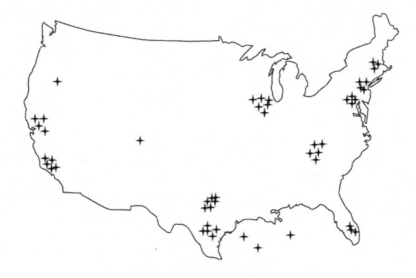

5:30 A.M. Attack Metrics

"I see," Corver responded. "And why do you consider that fortuitous?"

"Well, in the first place, the fact that it all started so early meant that there weren't a lot of planes in transit—mainly just international and freight. Therefore, when the attacks *were* detected, the airport authorities were able to handle the few incoming flights and prevent departures from taking off. And secondly, with the attacks starting at the airports, that gave airport officials early notice of what was happening, thereby allowing them to shut down facilities and get a head start on sending out flight cancellations before the airports were fully populated, all in accordance with the Holdman Protocol. There was virtually no one except for late night services in the airports at that early in the morning. As it is, a lot of people still showed up at the airports because they didn't receive the messages that the airports were closed."

"Got it," said Corver.

"What are those representations in the Atlantic?" asked DHS Director Holdman, taking advantage of the slight pause in the presentation.

"Those are oil rigs. Recall the attack on the Loixe Oil rig the first time around. Despite best efforts, including reinstallation of a lot of system software, that rig was hit again, along with two others off the coast of Louisiana."

"There doesn't seem to be much growth in those areas judging by the 5:30 A.M. map," Holdman said.

Q-Directorate looked back at the map, then said, "Ah, that's because there's nowhere for Ørsted to go. The rigs represent isolated targets in the Gulf of Mexico."

"Hmm, I wonder why anyone would bother attacking them at all then?" Holdman continued. He wasn't thinking clearly, his mind exhausted from the stress of working non-stop since early that morning.

"Well, think about what happened at the Third Power Plant at Grand Coulee: sensors and alerts were sabotaged, the whole system destroyed before anyone knew what was happening. Something similar could have happened at these rigs; they represent huge ecological threats if an attack proved lethal. Oil would gush into the gulf and cause incredible ecological damage before anyone realized what was happening and was able to manually shut down the system. This is one of the few areas where we consider ourselves fortunate: due to the fact that the workers at the oil rigs were on high alert—thanks in large part to the Holdman Protocol—that didn't happen. Drilling operations were suspended as soon as manual site inspections spotted non-standard pressures; almost no overflow oil was dumped into the Gulf."

Holdman was satisfied with the answer. It didn't hurt that reference was made to the protocol he had developed; he could use all the positive reinforcement he could get at that point.

CIA Deputy Director Ernest McCoy took the opportunity to ask a question. "What about those two points inside of the country?" he interjected. As closely as McCoy had been working with Q-Directorate, this latest briefing represented information that was news even to him. "It looks like...part of Northern California, and maybe...some part of Colorado. You didn't mention any airports from there, and they seem to be isolated incidents—no growth in stars from the first map."

Q-Directorate didn't have to look at the map this time before responding, "Yes, that's correct. Those represent the two targets that were hit the first time: the PacNorthern Rail depot and the cable television distribution hub in Denver, Colorado. We had a sensor installed at each, but only at those two locations. Since they were hit before, we thought it made sense to put at least one sensor at each, but no surrounding sensors were installed in that geographic region. That's why there are no more stars there."

"Hold on a minute." The order came from Freedman. Everyone turned to look at him. His voice was calm but powerful, dripping with authority. "Does that mean your maps show only those places where you had sensors installed?"

"Yes sir, for these first two maps, 1:30 and 5:30 A.M., that's correct. These representations only depict those locations where we were able to install the sensors and get auto-reports. We had to work with many different kinds of entities, both public and private sector, in order to get permission from them to have sensors installed in the routers of their networks. And then we had to actually install them. Not super difficult—they're software based—but it did take time and resources."

Freedman raised an eyebrow, concern evident on his face. Everyone in the room knew how bad it was across the country, but seeing it depicted on the map, even the preliminary status as of 5:30 A.M., was distressing. He took a deep breath and signaled for Q-Directorate to continue.

"Two points should be understood from what I've shown so far. First, each designation on the map represents one sensor, but we estimate that each sensor represents about a hundred square miles. That means everything in that particular area was probably hit, eventually. Second, the progression of Ørsted is most certainly much worse than what is depicted here. As I said, we could only do so much in the short time we had to install theses sensors—you can see that we were able to get a lot of coverage along both coasts. The progression of Ørsted is obviously much, much worse than what is depicted in this 5:30 A.M. map."

"Which, of course, we all know," interjected Holdman in a highly aggravated tone. "Listen, we all *know* how bad it is. Christ, all you have to do is look outside; this is a national catastrophe of the highest proportion. But show me the data; show me the scientific results...the hard facts. You must have it. Show me the progression to where we are now."

"Mike, take it easy..." Manmoth quickly said.

"The hell I will! The whole nation's burning—we got caught with our pants down—and you want me to take it easy?"

There was silence in the room. No one moved. The frustration was clear in Holdman's voice; everyone essentially felt the same way. Q-Directorate certainly wasn't offended. The situation was grave, and in a sense, they felt helpless.

"Well...I'm sorry to say," Q-Directorate began, "that from a technical standpoint, we can only estimate. This is because of everything essentially being 'down.' Anyway, we took a shot." Q-Directorate was glad he took the time to create the next map. Others on his staff didn't want to do so because it required manually entering called-in reports, assimilating K-Com data, and making certain assumptions, but he felt at the time that it was imperative. "Here's a simulated 11 A.M. update: manually entered data, along with certain assumptions and extrapolations, have been overlaid on top of the sensor data. Every place you see a star you can assume a massive attack has occurred, rendering computers and computer-operated equipment essentially inoperable."

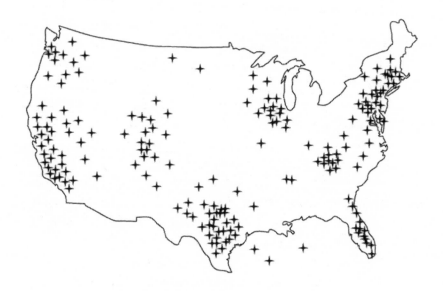

11 A.M. Attack Metrics: Postulate

Everyone stirred in the room. They knew of the turmoil occurring across the country, but seeing the updated map was alarming.

"And of course," Q-Directorate added, "things have gotten significantly worse since this."

Freedman leaned his head back, looking up to the ceiling. Then he turned to the map again and put his hand across his mouth and chin, something he always did when he was deep in thought. No one in the room said anything.

"Obviously July 28th wasn't the real $T_{detonate}$," Freedman finally said.

"No, it wasn't," answered Q-Directorate.

An exasperated Holdman said, "I still don't get it: why create such an elaborate construct, making it look like the 28th was the day, when it wasn't?"

"It's classic warfare," said Sam Neles, Director of the CIA.

"Exactly," added General William Powers, Director of the NSA. All eyes turned to him. "Whoever heard of signaling to the enemy when one was going to attack? It'd be ludicrous."

"Then why'd we believe it?" Holdman countered.

General Powers responded, "Well, just between us girls, we were dumb. Got caught with our pants down...led to believe in a false date, a ruse." He looked up at Q-Directorate on the stage. "Gentlemen, we've just entered a new age, a new type of warfare. The manual's still being written on it, and let's just say we don't have all the plays."

Freedman looked at General Powers. "Warfare? So you think it's military?"

"In my mind, there's no doubt," responded General Powers. "We're being attacked, as in war. When we talk to the President and the Security Council, I'm going to recommend that our military be put on high alert. This could be Pearl Harbor in spades. None of us wants that on our hands."

Holdman ventured, "Some would argue we've already got it."

"Now hold on..." General Powers began, glaring at Holdman.

Bradley was listening and thinking ahead. "Wait a minute," he interrupted. "We're going to have to bring some of our fleet back to the coasts. We can't take any chances. We need to get with the Joint Chiefs of Staff, ASAP." He turned to Q-Directorate and said, "Still no direct evidence pointing to the source of the attack, correct?"

"Not yet."

Silence in the room.

"It's Russia. Got to be," said General Powers. "From the reports I've heard from our team over there, it sounds like Russia's pulling the wool over our eyes."

"I'm not sure I agree with you," said Holdman. "Whether it was successful or not, they agreed to help us get one of the individuals involved...that Terrebenzikov. They haven't admitted to anything other than the fact that they knew about Strenzke and Terrebenzikov. How do you get it's Russia from that?"

"Mike, we have reason to believe the Russians lied to us over there," McCoy interjected. "They led our team down the garden path, but it was all a lie."

"You're sure? I mean, you know this without a doubt?"

"I haven't had a chance to update you yet. Let's talk after this meeting so I can give you some of the details."

Holdman pursed his lips.

"Look," General Powers said, "the only other country large enough to launch a cyber attack of this scale is China, and nothing points to them...nothing. We found that link to Terrebenzikov in the code, right? And the Russians don't deny the existence of Strenzke and Terrebenzikov. And the message that streamed across the CNN telecast, that was in Russian. I mean, sometimes you can't ignore the obvious."

Again there was silence in the room as everyone pondered the situation.

As if sensing the grave mood in the room, Q-Directorate said, "We're all over this. Big Machine has a lot of data to work with now. We've captured infected code at different sites that are only microseconds apart. We're going to crack this thing, and soon. My only fear is that Big Machine doesn't burn itself out in the process. It's having a field day processing the data."

"Better than sex, I'm sure," said Corver, flatly.

"Listen, gentlemen," said Freedman. "Unless there's something else useful to add..." he glanced up at Q-Directorate, who shook his head in the negative, "I suggest we let this man tend to his work. Q-Directorate, if there's anything significant, any new piece of information you think we should know about, page us on K-Com. All of us. You know the drill, just do it. In the meantime," Freedman rose and everyone in the audience followed, "we'll leave you to your work."

24

FRËGE: Refrain

In the very near future, many conflicts will not take place on the open field of battle, but rather in spaces on the internet, fought with the aid of information soldiers. This means that a small force of hackers is stronger than the multi-thousand force of the current armed forces.
— Former Duma member Anatoly Kurjanovich[26]

Tuesday, July 14

CYBER ATTACKS HAD BEEN SYNONYMOUS WITH CYBER CRIME. It was an affliction that the average person was accustomed to hearing about because it happened so often. But the damage wrought by Ørsted and Frëge across the United States changed all that; its scope, and the amount of damage it inflicted, was unprecedented. It was a veritable cyber nuclear bomb that crippled the nation.

The hope was that with Terrebenzikov's death, the ultimate launch of Ørsted and Frëge might have been forestalled. Clearly that wasn't the case; it came even earlier than expected, and the most recent intelligence out of Russia, that Terrebenzikov wasn't even *at* the compound during the raid, now seemed more plausible.

And with that realization it became immediately clear that it wasn't just Strenzke and Terrebenzikov, along with their cyber criminal organization, who were behind everything. Now it was unanimous: all fingers pointed to the RCA. What no one could immediately fathom, however, the big question in the room, was *why*? Was something more horrendous to follow? Not since the Bay of Pigs had a U.S. President been on such edge, the military on such high alert.

By the middle of the second day of the onslaught, in the midst of all the havoc, the answer came.

Reviewing the facts as later assembled, the cyber attacks in the United States occurred almost exactly twenty-four hours before those that followed across Eastern Europe (demonstrating again the ultimate level of synchronicity involved). Ørsted attacked without warning, detonating Frëge on a lethal scale: the Ukraine, Georgia, Belarus, Romania, and Moldavia. The Baltic States, for some inexplicable reason, were spared.

Even as crippling as the attack against the United States was, those across Eastern Europe were worse. This was due to two primary reasons.

First, those five countries expected nothing. There were no dry runs beforehand, no DFW-type small-scale attacks that then self-corrected themselves, thereby raising eyebrows and placing government officials on high alert. There was no ominous, wholesale shorting of stock at the Ukrainian PFTS that would have hinted at a "D-Day." And the United States did not share what little intelligence it had with those five countries, including what might be coming, because it had no reason to. So there was no preparation by those European targets, no protocol established to address what might come.

Second, the IT infrastructure was not as advanced in those countries as it was in the United States; equipment and software were older and less sophisticated, not hardened and patched to survive the attacks that came. This made it even easier for Ørsted to proliferate, and spread it did, like the plague. The whole orchestration of the attack on Eastern Europe could be likened, in a very ethereal way, to the seminal jazz album *Bitches Brew* by Miles Davis: a cacophony of seemingly random, unrelated noise upon first impression, chaos, wherein only later, upon further inspection, an order is revealed, deep, rich, and complex.

Nothing seemed beyond the reach of Ørsted—microprocessors, programmable logic devices, microcontrollers—the older the target, the quicker and more easily it succumbed to the assault.

The first human casualties attributable to the cyber attacks in Eastern Europe occurred on that first day at Henri Coandă International Airport in Otopeni, Romania. Air traffic control computers became infected, rendering the system inoperative. But before any message could be relayed to planes in flight (even the separate radio communication system didn't work), two incoming planes collided on the tarmac after making emergency, unguided landings. Knocking out tower control communications at the exact same time as the air traffic control system itself was not intended, but despite all of the careful planning, the RCA did not foresee just how easily their code would penetrate the Romanian systems.

On the contrary, deaths were meant to be kept as low as possible. In fact, they were emphatically discouraged. The Kremlin stressed that as few deaths as possible should directly result from the cyber attacks. There was a purpose to the edict: without any deaths directly attributable to the cyber attacks, Russia could ultimately hide behind the murky argument that *even if* it were involved in the attacks, the lack of casualties meant the cyber attacks could not be considered an act of war (any deaths "proximately" caused would be argued away as not truly stemming from the cyber intrusions). This was extremely important to Russian officials, because ultimately they knew that there *would* be kinetic attacks, there *would* be boots on the ground—but only in Europe, not in the United States. That was the lynchpin to Russia's diplomatic strategy, for it would later be argued that under the Hague Convention the cyber activity that took place in the United States was not an act of war. There were no directly attributable deaths, no infiltration of soldiers, no (kinetic) munitions fired.

The Kremlin knew their "position" was tenuous, but that never stopped them before.

And so, when the cyber attacks hit those Eastern European countries, none of their governments knew or suspected what was happening. None of them, that is, except for one: Georgia. That was because it was only as recently as 2008 when Russia had launched a cyber attack against Georgia, the first of its kind in the world, as a precursor to Russia physically invading the country. During that cyber attack, the Georgian Government's internet systems were completely incapacitated. In an extraordinary turn of events, U.S. private companies responded to pleas for help made by the Georgian Government and helped restore its systems, even to the point of allowing Georgia to relocate physical internet assets inside the United States—data centers, servers, switches, etc. The United States Government later censured those companies on the grounds that no permission was sought prior to providing such aid to a foreign government. No legal action was taken, however, because laws on the subject were too undeveloped and unclear at the time. Federal laws have since been passed on the issue, and to provide such foreign aid now required extensive levels of government review and approval.

At present, the point was moot. There was no hope for such aid to be provided to Georgia. The United States, including the technology companies within it, were deeply embroiled in their own defense against Ørsted and Frëge, along with remediation from the resultant damage.

The attacks against the Eastern European countries were technologically similar to what happened in the United States, with one critical difference: after the cyber bombing that occurred on that first day, soldiers came the following day. Photos later smuggled out of Kiev showed the first signs of them dressed in black with ominous black hoods covering their faces. The CIA identified the weapons they carried as AK-9 silenced assault rifles, standard issue for the Russian GRU special operation units. It was proof of what the CIA already knew, and what the Ukrainian Government had been saying for a long time: Russia had spent years building a network of sleeper agents in the Ukraine.

They came amid the chaos: the *maskirovka*, or "disguised warfare" as the CIA later referred to them. After Kiev, reports of the same came from Kharkiv, Donetsk, and Odessa, major cities in Eastern Ukraine. Several hours later there were reported sightings in the western parts of the Ukraine, including L'viv and Rivne. All during the second day, the wave continued and expanded its reach. Belarus was attacked, as well as Georgia, Moldavia, and Romania. What the CIA didn't know, what it could never have fathomed until it actually occurred, was that Russia had established sleeper networks in *all* of those countries.

The Russian bear of the taiga had seemingly been woken, only to reveal that it was never really asleep in the first place. Instead it had been secretly planning, lying in wait, preparing for what now came.

Everywhere was the same. The cyber assault came first, destabilizing the government, the military, and society in general. Then came the masked soldiers, seemingly from nowhere, as if they rose from the very ground itself, like black devils of destruction and terror.

And there was no resistance. There was too much damage to infrastructure, too many basic services no longer available, too much disorder and disarray. Russian extremists, planted months if not years in advance, fostered riots, tearing into storefronts and fomenting anarchy. Those that resisted were gunned down. People feared for their lives. The fear and panic in the United States stemming from the cyber attacks was nothing compared to the absolute shock and horror felt by the people of Eastern Europe. The new, rudimentary status of their existence due to lack of basic essentials—power, sanitized water, etc.—was compounded a hundredfold by the terror caused by the Russian soldiers that controlled the streets.

This was nothing like Russia's military action against Georgia in 2008. Russia was better organized this time, better prepared, and the power of Ørsted and Frëge much worse.

By only the third day following the initial cyber attacks in Europe, a military force of 45,000 Russian soldiers was immediately deployed from the Russian border and into the region. Armored vehicles arrived in the Ukraine first. More were airlifted into the other countries. Russia played the white knight, claiming the Russian military was necessary to restore order and safety to the region. Just like that, the Blitzkrieg was over, and the borders of Russia were instantaneously extended on many fronts to that of the cold war era Soviet Union.

Pictorial representation created by Defense Secretary Charles Bradley of the Russian cyber attacks on Eastern Europe, and the physical invasion that followed.

Photo from Operation Cyberknife files

In hindsight, the press of the United States, as well as government leadership, all recalled and made reference to the ill-omened statement the President of Russia, Vladislav Selkin, made at the Munich Security Conference a year earlier: "The breakdown of the Soviet Union was the biggest tragedy of the last century." Selkin had been obstinate and aggressive for several years, but no one fathomed it would lead to this. As a result, the United States realized that it could not remain neutral any longer. Foreign diplomacy, which President Wilson once stated was one of the President's greatest powers, would no longer be enough, nor would economic sanctions.

Russian tanks and other armored vehicles dominated the attacked countries. Checkpoints were seized without resistance. Airdrops continued, both in terms of human capital and Russian hardware.

Selkin continued to proclaim, mainly through the press of an unaffected Western Europe, that anything happening in the four countries was by the will of its people, and that Russia must be there to facilitate the "renaissance" that was occurring. Air travel into or out of the countries was banned, again in the name of safety. Any flights over the affected countries would be shot down as hostile, no questions asked. "It is necessary because of the dangerous situation. Russia will supply forces in those countries to observe, and to help those in need."

It was the doubletalk for which the Kremlin was famous. No news or pictures from the region were allowed. With the IT infrastructure rendered useless, nothing could be uploaded to remote news agencies, and borders were quickly manned with Russian military to prevent unauthorized crossings. Only satellite images from the United States' NTEG system were available to document the invasion as it occurred. (None of them, however, were shared with the rest of the world because the United States did not want to reveal the true extent of the imaging capability of the system.)

Within a matter of days, it was clear that any resistance was futile. The desolation of the infrastructure was too severe, the

Russian forces too great in number, with all in-country defenses captured or rendered useless. The Soviet "Sphere of Influence" had been re-created, reaching all the way to the border of Poland. All of Western Europe watched in horror, fearing that it was only a matter of time before they might be next.

And at least for the moment, there was no great power of the United States to turn to for help, for it had its own masterwork of a problem to contend with and comprehend.

In the United States, people felt like they had gone back in time, maybe even to a different place. After three days, there was still no television, radio, or phones. Still no power. A state of emergency for the entire country had been declared. Families gathered, neighbors huddled, food was shared, candles burned. Few cars were on the street; to the extent possible people remained in their homes. Emergency vehicles were the norm— police, fire, ambulance, as well as the National Guard and the United States Army.

Martial law was declared.

001000110

000110011

PART THREE

110110001

101011100

011010111

001101011

25

Integrity

CIA Headquarters
Friday, July 17

SAM NELES STOOD AT THE WINDOW OF HIS OFFICE, HIS BACK to the door, peering out of the one-way, bullet-proof glass with his Bushnell 12x50mm binoculars. As director of the CIA, his office was the largest in the building. It was on the top floor and faced the front of the campus. At 7:30 P.M. there was still enough light outside to see a good distance. From as high up as he was, he could see over the forest that stood across from CIA headquarters all the way past the George Washington Memorial Parkway to the Potomac River.

He saw someone at the edge of the river; actually it was two people: an old man and a woman, presumably his wife, she sleeping in a lawn chair, he sitting beside her with a fishing rod in hand. On a normal day Neles would have thought nothing of it, but given everything going on in the world, a man fishing out of the river struck him as odd—almost primordial. The man was fending for his own food. Neles tilted the end of the binoculars slightly downward and saw a cooler resting next to the man's feet, and on the ground around him was what looked like empty beer cans. He tried to look closer to see what brand they were.

"You ready for us, Sam?" came a voice from behind.

He turned, put the binoculars back into his desk, and said, "You bet. Come on in."

CIA Deputy Director Ernest McCoy entered, and behind him was Fred Banks.

"Where's Freedman?" Neles asked.

"Still with the President. You want to wait?"

"No. We're on the same page; let's do it," said Neles. "Please, gentlemen, have a seat."

When Banks pulled out one of the chairs in front of Neles' desk, Neles said, "Let's go sit over there."

Per Neles' request, Banks and McCoy took a seat on a light green, cloth-covered couch on the other side of the room. Its armrests were squared, the back rectangular in shape, a modern style. Neles sat across from them on a chair made of maple wood and having a cherry colored leather seat. An antique, nineteenth century coffee table separated them. The furniture didn't match, but every time he saw it, Banks always thought it went well together.

"So, how're you holding up?" McCoy said to Neles.

"Not so well on a number of fronts. Holdman's been a big pain in the ass. Trying to pin everything on us."

"Yeah, well, he's got to really be feeling it right about now. Director of Homeland Security...tough spot to be in," McCoy responded.

"We're all knee deep in it," responded Neles.

"Quite so."

Banks didn't normally venture anything when he was meeting with superiors unless first spoken to. He broke with protocol and ventured, "How many deaths so far?"

"Too many," Neles gravely answered. "The country has been turned upside down in a matter of days. Power grids are a mess—still no power across large regions of the country. Hospitals are operating on emergency backup generators. This is just..." Neles stopped himself.

McCoy and Banks nodded.

"Is it true," McCoy ventured, "that Japan is supplying disaster relief experts to help us?"

"They offered, and we'll probably take them up on it. They've got the best processes and procedures in the world for this kind of thing. There's so much to be done, no permanent solution in sight. This is going to easily cost the country hundreds of billions of dollars. We're meeting with the President again in two hours; it's going to be bad. He's at his wit's end."

"Mm, I can imagine." McCoy said. "FEMA is doing all it can, but it just wasn't built for something like this."

"Yes, well, there's going to be a huge ramp up in spending after this; whole new departments for R&D," Neles continued. "This was a wakeup call that came too late."

"More R&D beyond what DARPA's already doing?" asked McCoy.

"What DARPA's doing now is going to look like kindergarten compared to what's coming. This is a whole new frontier. If there were any doubts about it before, they're gone now. Hell, the entire country's been brought to its knees by a two-pronged cyber attack named after a Danish physicist and a German mathematician. We're going to need whole new divisions in our military, drastically different skill sets."

Neither McCoy nor Banks responded for a moment.

Finally, McCoy said, "What'd the President say about Europe?"

Neles shook his head. "Not now. We'll talk about it later."

McCoy momentarily glanced at Banks.

"Let's talk about Cyberknife," Neles said. "The part dealing with our people in Russia. Where are we on that?"

"John Angstrom and his team are still in St. Petersburg," Banks responded, leaning forward slightly, like he was poised and waiting for the question.

"They're separate, right?" Neles asked. "I mean, they're not all together over there. Or are they?"

"No, they're separate...somewhat. John's alone. The others aren't far away. They're communicating on K-Com Ad Hoc. Working perfectly, I might add."

"McCoy told me it was quite a deliberation as to whether someone at Angstrom's level should even be there. Garrett didn't used to do that, right?" Neles turned to McCoy and said, "Sorry for the tangent."

"No, it's okay," said McCoy. They both turned to Banks.

"That's correct," Banks responded. He was somewhat amazed that Neles would bother to ask a question about that. In the grand scheme of things it wasn't just down in the weeds; it was far below the surface, at the roots. But Banks knew that that was one of the hallmarks of Neles: to keep a lot of plates spinning, some big, some not so much, and they all got their due attention. The topic of Angstrom being out in the field—someone of his position within the organization—was getting its fair share at that particular moment. "Someone in Angstrom's position," Banks continued, "wouldn't normally go out on a mission like this. This is different. Angstrom's different. He brings something special to the table, that intangible element that no one else possesses. Hard to duplicate. For a mission as critical as Cyberknife...well, I was the one who recommended that he go. And he really wanted to go; felt like he had something to prove."

"He's got nothing to prove, and he should know that," Neles said, looking at McCoy as well. "Well, anyway, McCoy briefed me a couple of days ago. He told my about Thomas Reed's report. There's no chance he's wrong in what he saw, is there? I mean, he really saw the two together, this Strenzke and Terrebenzikov? I know that Wykoff's report on the raid is now in question, but she still stands by what she saw."

"No, it was bogus," Banks answered. "Strenzke and Terrebenzikov are both still alive."

"But Thomas never saw either of them before. There were no pictures, except for the one, and Terrebenzikov was in complete shadow," Neles pushed back. He already had this conversation separately with McCoy, but he wanted to hear it first-hand from Banks.

"You're right, there was only that one picture of Strenzke," Banks said. "But it was enough for Thomas. He claims with one hundred percent certainty it was him. And the other man matched the description of Terrebenzikov perfectly: approximately forty-five to fifty years old, tall, lanky, thin brown hair in a ponytail, thick eyebrows. It was them."

"You got that description from Redblood, right?"

"That's right."

"Renke?"

"Correct."

"And that's how Thomas knew in the first place that they'd be in that bar?"

Banks said, "Yes." He sat silent for a moment then added, "Renke's been instrumental. It's nice to see the investment paying off after all these years. Without a doubt, it's his moment to shine, and he's living up to it. Thomas chased down a lot of info Renke got us, and it all checked out."

"Good," Neles said. "I can use some good news these days; I'll take it where I can get it."

McCoy and Banks adjusted themselves in their seats, mentally preparing for what might come next.

"He's been undercover over there for a long time," Banks said all of a sudden. "We're going to have to watch him."

"Who? Renke? Why? What's happened?" McCoy said, turning to Banks with a curious expression on his face. This was something they had not discussed in advance. "Are they onto him?"

"No, not yet. But he's been over there for six years. That's a long time for someone in his situation. History tells us it's getting to around the time when bad things start to happen. I'd recommend not risking it if we don't have to," Banks said.

"But the informants...the ones that Renke is tapping...they're good?" Neles asked.

"Rock solid," Banks responded. The questions were trending toward his area of direct responsibility, and he always made sure under those circumstances to answer for himself. McCoy was used to it and didn't mind in the least. That wasn't always the case with some of the other deputy directors Banks had reported to over the years. Some preferred that he keep his mouth shut in front of senior management, letting them do all the talking.

"Okay, well, before I forget, I agree. Let's start the extraction on him. Is that something under you, Fred?" said Neles.

"Technically, no," Banks responded. "He's not from my division. He'll be offered a slot—I've got a lot of respect for him— but he doesn't report to me right now. He falls under Russian Infiltration."

"Okay, well, see that the process gets started," Neles said. He returned his attention to McCoy. "He deserves a good bump when he gets back, along with a good vacation." Neles stood up all of a sudden. "Sorry, I need some coffee. You guys want any?"

Banks and McCoy each nodded yes. Everyone was living on caffeine ever since the cyber attacks had begun.

Three cups were brought in.

"The thing that still puzzles me...I don't get why the Russians did what they did," Neles said as he stirred his coffee while sitting down. McCoy and Banks looked at him slightly puzzled, unsure of what exactly he was referring to. "This 'low level' in our organization that they had under their control over here, the double agent, why use him up on some woman who defected from Russia?"

McCoy and Banks realized that Neles had made a transition to a different topic: the Russian killer tracking Davis (and the low-level CIA double agent who aided him).

"Why even have someone tracking this woman down, this Anna Czolski, all the way over here in the United States? You said it yourself, Ernest, she doesn't *know* anything. No names, no org structure, nothing—other than, perhaps, the latest in FSB assassination techniques. They haul her ass off to a training compound and keep her captive there for two years, doing their best to turn her into some kind of...FSB female killing machine, and then when she's let out, she bolts. So they track her down all the way over here? For what, tradecraft knowledge? *Killcraft?* Are we sure we're not missing something...like maybe there's more to this?"

"We don't think so," said Banks. "We vetted her thoroughly. She let us go as far as we wanted, even consenting to Sodium Pentothal. I don't think she knows anything beyond what she's already told us. If she does, she beat the hell out of the Sodium Pentothal—we gave her a pretty high dosage, barely kept her conscious." Banks took a sip of his coffee and then continued, "As far as the FSB's motive in coming after her...we don't know for sure. We've got theories."

"Like what? Give me an example," Neles said.

"Well, for one, to discourage other FSB agents from doing the same. As you know, they take that kind of thing seriously. They have to, given the way they treat their agents by using terror and fear as a means of controlling them. We also think it's possible she may have really angered someone. I mean, really pissed someone off. Not just the leaving after all the time and energy expended on her. More like something personal...like perhaps someone had fallen for her and took it hard when she bolted. She's quite remarkable looking, you know."

"I saw the video footage of one of her interviews," Neles acknowledged. "Striking, I'll agree. But that would have to be one powerful son of a bitch to order a hit on her all the way over here in the United States...just to get revenge because his pecker was jilted...and exposing a double-agent in the process. Personally, I don't see it."

They all sat quietly for a moment, uncomfortably letting Neles' opinion linger in the air like an uninvited guest. McCoy and Banks sensed that there was another transition in the conversation that needed to take place. They each sipped their coffee.

"So," McCoy started. "I think we need to follow through with this in Russia. I mean, getting back to Angstrom. You agree, right?"

"Without question," Neles responded. "With what's happened here and in Eastern Europe, we've got no choice. Even if we crack the code on this...Frêge. For all we know, Strenzke and Terrebenzikov could be working on something else; some other cyber threat. If getting them puts a dent in the RCA's capabilities, we've got to do it. Get them...take them out...either way," Neles said sternly. He took a long sip of his coffee, peering over the cup into the eyes of Banks. Banks watched in silence; they were on the same page.

After a moment, Banks turned to McCoy and inquired, "What about Renke? Should I roll his extraction into it? Even if he isn't exposed after this, the mental strain on him will be tremendous."

"I agree," McCoy said, turning to Neles. "Unless you disagree, Sam."

"No, I don't."

"Alright then, let's get him out," McCoy said.

Neles put his cup on the table and said, "And if that weren't enough, we've got that *other* problem, don't we." He stood up and walked over to a bookshelf lining one of the walls.

"You mean the double agent, the mole in our organization?" McCoy responded.

"Yes, the mole. Where are we at on *that*?" Neles reached and grabbed a book from the shelf, a large hardcover, and sat back down at his chair. Banks looked down and recognized the cover. It was a history on Russian spies. Neles began thumbing through the large glossy pictures of captured spies.

"As you know," said McCoy, "we've now checked all phone records, both cell phone and landline, made during the murder of Arthur Spence and the kidnapping of Ralph Bensley. After what happened to Spence, and then Bensley, we knew the killer must have been getting help. Spence and Bensley would've done their best not to give up any real names—at least, not right away. The killer figured the same thing, so he had someone on the inside check the names Spence and Bensley gave him—had the names looked up in our database to make sure they were legitimate."

Neles rubbed his forehead with his thumb and forefingers. It pained him to think of what happened to Bensley. He knew it was a mistake not to have had a bodyguard with him, but he got tired of bickering with the man about it. Now this happened. McCoy and Banks watched Neles as he sat silent in thought. Eventually, Neles said, "Please, tell me it's not someone in HUMINT."

"The double agent? No, he's not," McCoy said. "At least, not directly. He's a low level in Support. What happened, though, was that he got in bed with a *woman* in HUMINT—sorry, no pun intended—and that was the access. The double agent talked her into the name checking."

"You know this?" Neles said, agitated. "Why didn't you tell me sooner?"

"I literally just found out this morning, and with so much going on, this is the first chance I got."

"Alright, alright." Neles said, holding up his hand. "So, what else? What now?"

"We've already got the double agent and the woman in custody. Unfortunately, the double agent insists that he doesn't know the identity of the killer. We haven't gotten much of anything out of him. I don't think he knows too much. So far he's withstood all manner of interrogation."

All three looked at each other for a moment.

"Contact with his runner in Russia sounds like it's really weak and tenuous, at best. All he knew was what he was supposed to do: make sure he had access to the database at precise times on certain dates, and he did that through the woman. Needless to say, the killer used a disposable cell phone, so there's no use tracing it."

"And how did the Russians get to this double agent? Do we know that yet?" Neles said.

"We're still trying to find out," McCoy responded. "We're still interrogating."

"What's the double agent's name?"

"Bergman. Emory Bergman," McCoy said.

Neles searched his memory, then said, "Never heard of him."

"There's no reason you would. He's low level."

"And what about the HUMINT woman. What's her story?" Neles was distressed by what he heard.

McCoy took his glasses off and rubbed the inside corners of both eyes with thumb and forefinger. "It's pretty sad. Alison Kane, early fifties. Husband died several years ago of pancreatic cancer."

"So she had a high risk profile," Neles added, finishing the story.

"Exactly. And...we missed it. Needless to say, we're trying to keep this quiet."

"If she's from HUMINT there's no telling what else this killer may have been told...the names."

"Alison Kane insists it was only two names, first when Arthur Spence gave up Ralph Bensley, and then the name Bensley gave up."

"Mm-hmm. And why kill Spence but let Bensley live?"

Banks offered the answer to that one.

"We believe Arthur Spence was in retribution to what we did in Russia to get Czolski...Anne Davis...out. After that, not sure. Maybe because Bensley was still in active service while Spence was retired? An attempt to avoid escalation? At this point we can only speculate. Our post-interview with Bensley, including deep sub-conscious probing, indicated that the information he gave up was limited to the circumstances surrounding Davis. That's all he was asked about."

Neles said, "That's still too much. And did Angstrom's name come up?"

"Yes."

Neles looked sternly at McCoy and said, "I'm sure you're all over this."

"Of course," said McCoy. "We can talk more about it when you have the time."

They all glanced at each other.

Neles tossed the book onto the coffee table, causing a loud thud. He took a deep breath, slapped both of his thighs as he stood up, and said, "Alright, gentlemen. Carry on. Banks, I'm expecting to hear news as soon as you get it. We need to get those bastards in Russia—both of them." He turned to McCoy. "And keep after Bergman. I want to know how they got to him in the first place, and what they do to contact him now. And then we can talk about Angstrom."

26

Calm before Culmination

Russia
Saturday, July 18

THE PLAN HAD ALREADY BEEN ESTABLISHED, OR AT LEAST, the high level architectural elements of it, before Angstrom and his team had set foot in Russia. He viewed it from the beginning as a mission of elimination rather than extraction. When the two options were originally presented to Angstrom, he knew immediately which it was going to be. The high caliber targets involved, as well as the short timeframe, made the decision a fairly easy one, grave though it was. Banks certainly thought so; Angstrom could see it in his eyes when he originally presented the mission. It was one of the reasons Angstrom wanted to participate himself: the sanctioned assassination of two high value targets, right in the heart of Russia, would be the most serious undertaking in his career. The mission had to succeed. Furthermore, there could be no direct evidence tying it to the United States. Otherwise there was no telling what the ramifications might be. The two countries were already at the tipping point. That's where the covert nature of it came in; the suspicion could be there, but not the overt proof. The Russians could figure it all out, down to the last bullet, but there should be no way for them to prove the United States had anything to do with it. As far as the United States was concerned, the Franklin contingency represented the only American officials that were there in Russia.

The finer points of the mission, the when and the where, that would be worked out later, after Angstrom and his team had more intelligence. Sometimes that was the only way to do it, especially on such short notice and without any of the groundwork having been laid in advance. That was how Garrett would have done it: the situation needed to be meticulously analyzed and vetted, nothing by the seat-of-the-pants if it could be avoided. The only difference now was that the people in the seats had changed, Angstrom taking that of Garrett's, and Gordon moving into what used to be Angstrom's role, sort of.

By now, Reed had already done most of the legwork. He met with Renke, who in turn tapped into several of his most reliable informants. That was what brought Reed to the Apraksin the other evening. And after Reed confirmed that Terrebenzikov was still alive, the team knew they were gold with the information they were getting. It flowed from informant, to Renke, to Reed. Renke was calling in all of his favors, using all of the silver bullets he had saved up.

As for Gordon, he knew the minute he heard Angstrom was coming along on the mission that it was going to be a big one. And with respect to Angstrom's purported role on the mission— acting as a "center of operations" from the safe house in Untolovo—Gordon knew that that wouldn't be the full extent of it. He knew it would involve more. No one travels all that way on this kind of a mission just to be a center of operations, the so-called man behind the curtain. They certainly never did it that way before. When Gordon learned that Angstrom would be carrying a CS5, he immediately understood what was coming. It made perfect sense.

* * *

As Gordon lay awake in the bedroom of the hotel in St. Petersburg, there was a knock on the door. It was Stafford.

"I thought you'd be ready by now," she nervously said.

"I am," he responded, turning to look at her but not getting up.

He had gotten a few hours of sleep after being awake part of the night monitoring the K-Com channel on the N5 satellite communication unit. He and Stafford took turns doing so in shifts during pre-arranged times when protocol windows were set for communication.

"Listen, there was a transmission from Angstrom a couple of hours ago."

"Again? Why didn't you get me?" he said, rising quickly and sitting on the edge of the bed.

"You took a lot of hours last night. I thought it was important for you to get some sleep," she responded.

There was a disappointed look on Gordon's face.

"I asked John if I should get you, and he said no, the message was short, and that I could easily relay it to you."

"Alright, alright. So what is it? What's the message?"

"He said to tell you that Redblood's coming with us. He said you'd know what that meant."

"Wow. That's a bombshell," Gordon said.

"Why? Who's Redblood?"

"He's one of us. Been undercover over here for a long time."

Stafford watched Gordon and waited for more. Gordon wasn't sure how much he wanted to say. There was always a question as to how much one needed to know.

"Name's Theodore Renke. He's a good agent. An excellent agent. Made a lot of good contacts and connections over here; got us a lot of excellent intel." Gordon ran his hand through his hair. "I guess it's time. I hope he's not in danger. Angstrom didn't say anything like that, did he?"

"No, that was it."

"Nothing? You're absolutely sure? I mean, we talked about the sparseness of the messaging and how any little thing, no matter how small, could mean something."

"I know. That was the whole message about Redblood...I mean Renke. There was one other thing, though. Angstrom said 'the franks and beans are gone.' Then he signed out. My interpretation of that is that the Franklin contingency has left."

"That's right. Well, let's get going. We have to go to the drop and get the M9s. Did you already take apart the N5 after the last transmission?"

"Yes. And I already dropped the acid on the comm chip."

"Good. We'll shatter the plastic and scatter it in a few dumpsters on the way. From here on out, no more wireless. Now it's all perfect coordination...and the targets being where they're supposed to be."

It was only five days after Ørsted and Frège had detonated in the United States, four days after Eastern Europe. With no more wireless to rely upon, everyone on Angstrom's team knew that the schedule was going to be tight for the rest of the mission. No one wanted it to last any longer than it had to. Having to revert to backup communication would be incredibly risky.

That same morning, Angstrom awoke from his sleep at the safe house in Untolovo and moved quickly to prepare for departure. It was very early, still completely dark outside.

Only he among the team knew the calamitous state the United States and Eastern Europe were in. With his N5+ unit, he had the added ability to communicate directly with Grahame on a different portion of the K-Com spectrum, and he got the update from him. As for Angstrom's team, however, the state-owned news agencies in Russia suppressed all mention of the cyber attacks. Nothing was transmitted over television, nothing appeared in newsprint. The whole matter went unacknowledged. No one heard mention of it. Angstrom had made the strategic decision not to inform his team so they wouldn't get distracted. They needed to be completely focused on the matter at hand.

It did, however, influence timing. As soon as Angstrom heard from Grahame what had happened, and that the Franklin contingency had left, that's when Angstrom knew they had to strike.

The latest intel from Renke made that decision seem like a foregone conclusion: who would've known that Strenzke and Terrebenzikov would want to flee Russia? Angstrom was surprised when Reed first gave him the intel. He would have thought they'd want to stick around and bask in the glory of their efforts, at least for a while. The intel said otherwise, and Renke's informants were continuing to prove very, very reliable.

Angstrom looked around the single room of the safe house. It wasn't actually a house so much as a cabin, even down to the log construction. He left everything as he had found it. The green-canvassed cot was slid back into the corner with the two blankets folded and piled at the end of it. There was nothing much else in the place, save for a few toiletries in the small bathroom. He stepped outside, into the chilly darkness of the forest.

The last thing he had to do before he left was destroy his N5+ device. There would be no more communication over it for the rest of the mission. He would be cut off from his team, cut off from Grahame, cut off from the world. An uncomfortable feeling came over him as he held it in the palm of his hand and looked at it. It represented the only way to theoretically hear any news of Davis. That same feeling came over him as when he had to say goodbye to her: confusion, apprehension.

There was a metaphysical struggle occurring in him, one first revealed when he had to leave Davis; now it was reaching its peak.

On the one side he would ask himself why he needed to be there in Russia. Why did he insist upon it? He should've remained in the States, orchestrated the operation from there, trusted his team to perform, and then waited for news of the results. That way he could have stayed with Anne, protected her.

He did not want to be separated from her, or to leave her alone.

Yet there was a part of him that wanted to be where he was, to participate, to not separate himself from the person he used to be. Yes, Garrett would've stayed behind, but Garrett had a strong, experienced team, one that included both Gordon and himself. Angstrom had a new team (with the exception of Gordon). So Angstrom wanted to control everything and make sure the mission went according to plan. It was too important. How could he do that if he was back in the United States? Maybe Banks thought that as well; maybe that's why he advocated so strongly for Angstrom to go as soon as Angstrom proposed it. After all, he surely had studied Angstrom's psyche profile; he knew how he was wired.

Angstrom went deeper and deeper into thought, recalling his own first mission and the faith Garrett had placed in him and Gordon. He realized that Garrett must have experienced the same mental struggle, yet he was able to withdraw from it, able to let Angstrom and Gordon go it alone.

The urge to turn back—to hike back to Grahame's post and compel the return of Tacit Gray so he could go back to the States, back to Davis—almost overtook him. It was a soul-struggle.

His fingers separated the plastic of the N5+ chassis, making a loud snapping sound, and the small pcb broke off from its screw junctions. He placed drops of acid onto the small communication chip, watched it dissolve before his eyes, and then held the scraps in his hand. After hiking for about a hundred yards along the bank of the Glukharka River, he flung the components into the water. He heard plop sounds as they dropped but couldn't follow their trajectories very far in the darkness. The water had a foul stench.

He looked down at his watch: roughly 2:10 A.M. That would make it 6:10 P.M. in Georgetown, he calculated. He wondered what Davis would be doing and where she was; normally she'd be in the midst of an evening lesson with one of her students. Now, with what was happening in the United States, the mayhem, there was no telling. He kept reminding himself of her survival skills, her uncanny instincts, and her "training." He tried to use those thoughts to set his mind at ease, but it didn't work. He better than anyone knew that being in the midst of chaos made it easier for a hunter to catch his prey. After a while he realized he had been standing there at the river's edge lost in thought for quite some time, and he forced himself to refocus on the matter at hand.

The ground was rough with no path to follow on the route he took. Mosquitoes were out as well, in full force. He was glad there was a bottle of insect repellant in the cabin.

The only item he carried was the rucksack on his back. It held a McMillan CS5 (Concealable Suppressed) subsonic/supersonic sniper rifle. The shoulder stock, quick-detach sound suppressor system was disengaged to make the stubby, 12.5 inch barrel configuration even more compact while he carried it. A long range, variable zoom scope was also in the ruck, which ultimately would be attached to the Picatinny rail at the top of the receiver. The CS5 was the optimal sniper rifle for what Angstrom had to do: monitor from a distance and then silently invoke the weapon, right in the middle of an urban environment.

The rest of the team would be carrying M9 semiautomatic pistols. That was Gordon's choice. Each M9 would be equipped with a suppressor to lower its sound signature, which would be of vital importance given where they planned to hit Strenzke and Terrebenzikov: two blocks from the Sennaya Ploschad Station; two blocks from the hoard of people at Sennaya Ploschad itself; right in front of the Apraksin. In order for them to get out of there after the hit, they couldn't afford to draw a crowd with loud gunfire, which, unfortunately for Gordon, ruled out the Desert Eagle 44, his preferred weapon of choice.

Delivery of the M9s had been pre-arranged by Renke. Per instructions, they would need to enter an old, shuttered building from the back entrance, where an unidentified individual would be waiting with the guns. Only one person would enter at a time, the others keeping a safe distance away but within eyesight of the entrance, in case it was a trap. It was unlikely they would be able to do anything if it was, but at least only one person would be put in such a position. Given the reliability of Renke, however, there was little doubt that things would go as planned.

Another member of Angstrom's team had his own special task that same morning; it started at just about an hour after Angstrom had set foot on the bank along the Glukharka.

Thomas Reed was on Bolshay Street, the side street on which the Apraksin was located. It was just after 3 A.M. The Apraksin was closed; very few people were out and about. There was still the occasional late customer who stumbled out of the place, inebriated, wavering on his feet. Otherwise the area was quiet, desolate. All of the business establishments nearby were closed as well.

The Apraksin was situated on a plaza, wherein an area of about four-hundred square yards of cemented space extended in front of it. Long ago the building used to be a theater that hosted live performances, and the plaza served as a gathering place for patrons. Not so much anymore. No one wanted to be seen entering or leaving the Apraksin, and the area was known to attract the criminal element, such that even during prime business hours not too many people gathered on the plaza itself.

Reed went back to the Apraksin that morning to validate one more time what he had remembered about the area. He needed to study every detail, every geographic point of interest. Nothing could be left to chance. He looked carefully before his approach, making sure no one suspicious might be around watching him. A low, heavy fog aided his ability to move without being noticed. He moved slowly along the sidewalk across the street, keeping as far away from the front of the Apraksin as possible, out of view from the two security cameras he spotted on the corners of the building.

As he observed the area, he was reminded of the most basic, readily observable aspects first. The large, open space comprising the plaza extended in front of the Apraksin. Beyond that was Bolshay Street, and on the side of the street nearest the plaza there was a parking lane where a row of cars could park. Bolshay was a two-way street with one lane in each direction. On the other side of it there was a sidewalk, which is where Gordon stood. Beyond that was Nab Griboyedova Canal, about 200 feet wide. And beyond the canal were a lot of large office buildings.

The canal made the situation almost perfect, because it made it impossible for people to linger directly on the other side of Bolshay Street.

When the time came for the hit, Gordon, who would be in the immediate area, would need to plant two remotely activated Improvised Flash Devices (IFDs) outside the front of the Apraksin. A magnesium-based device was unlike a standard hand grenade, which produced a *detonation* that propagated through supersonic shock. A flash device produced a *subsonic combustion* that propagated through heat transfer; the end result is a quiet but brilliant burst of light, temporarily blinding those close enough to witness it.

The plan called for two such IFDs situated in the a ninety-degree assault configuration. Angstrom had developed the technique over seven years ago for an assault in Egypt. The configuration required the IFDs to be strategically placed to produce a barrage of light from two forty-five degree angles on-center, which in this case would be directed from Bolshay Street to the front of the Apraksin. A shooter needed to be just in front of the IFDs with his back to them. That would be Gordon. The bright light emanating from behind him would temporarily blind those who were bathed in it, yet there would be no sound of an explosion to draw the attention of those in the surrounding area. Gordon would only cause detonation of the IFDs if it was absolutely necessary; everyone hoped it wouldn't be.

Another person, in this case Renke, acted as the roamer. The roamer served as the timing element. His exit from the Apraksin would serve as a signal that the targets would soon follow. He would continue to some point on the perimeter of the semi-circle formed by the radius extending from the front door of the Apraksin to the IFDs. From there, one option would be for him to turn and wait for the targets, serving as another shooter. That wouldn't be necessary because Angstrom would be the second shooter. Moreover, they were in an urban environment and would need to get out of there quickly. Therefore, Renke wouldn't stop at the IFD perimeter; instead, he would keep walking and go to his car, which would be parked along the line of cars at the edge of Bolshay. That would be their getaway car. In addition, Renke was told to make sure that when he first exited the Apraksin there was a distance between him and the targets. Otherwise the timing wouldn't work and he would be in danger of getting shot. Gordon learned that lesson the hard way, taking a bullet to the shoulder on a mission in Lebanon some years ago. Angstrom chastised him for it, saying never again.

Reed was glad that the area was just as he had remembered it. There were two large cement planters near the edge of Bolshay, with a little space between them and the street. Boxwoods and prairie grasses were planted in them, causing the greenery to reach four feet high from the ground. It was the perfect place for Gordon to place the IFDs when the time came: they were at almost forty-five degree angles from the center of the front door. The tall plantings would even provide cover for him.

Reed turned and looked back down Bolshay Street in the direction from where he came. About a hundred feet away there was a bus stop with a glass shelter. That would be where Gordon would sit and wait for Renke's exit when the time came.

All Reed needed to do now was walk past a few more buildings to get to the end of the block. From there he would go around the corner to inspect the alley that led to the back of the Apraksin. That's where he and Stafford would be. He wanted to check it out one last time. Before he did so, he turned and looked in the direction opposite the Apraksin. Beyond Nab Griboyedova Canal was Voznesenskiy Street, which ran almost perpendicular to the canal, but not exactly; it extended slightly to the left, such that the front of the buildings on the right side of that street could be seen for some distance away instead of each building's face being hidden by the one in front of it. His eyes followed the street for two buildings. The second was the Grafton Hotel, six-stories high. His eyes went to the top floor, then from the right side of the building toward the center. Because Voznesenskiy Street was at a slight angle from center as it extended from the canal, Reed could see the entire length of the building, as well as all of the windows of the rooms. He found the room that had been rented for Angstrom. He could see that there was a good-sized balcony with wrought-iron rails extending on the outside of it. Reed didn't stop to look for too long for fear of being noticed by some straggler, or someone peering out from the Apraksin.

He could tell, though, that Angstrom had planned it perfectly. To the unaided eye, Angstrom's balcony was a long distance away from the front door of the Apraksin. It was within perfect site, however, for someone looking through the high-powered scope of a sniper rifle. Reed could envision Angstrom lying on the ground of the balcony, the CS5 stabilized on a tripod, peering through the scope between the wrought iron bars of the balcony's railings. The arrangement was perfect, as long as the person behind the rifle was skilled enough. Reed wished that he was going to be at the front of the building instead of the alley so he could see it all unfold.

27

Fire Brew

RENKE ENTERED THE APRAKSIN THAT NIGHT AT 11:30 P.M., A TIME AT WHICH he was told by a key informant that Strenzke and Terrebenzikov would be there. According to the informant, it was to be their last time at the Apraksin; they were fleeing the country, cashing in their chips as it were, living off the fruits of their labor. He learned from another of his informants, one fairly high in official rank, that the FSB was also aware of this information and were none too happy about it. The sentiment within the FSB was that Strenzke and Terrebenzikov were divorcing themselves from the RCA much too quickly, that they treated the cyber assaults as just an opportunity to financially rape the United States and enrich themselves, ignoring the true historical import of what was happening: the creation of a new world order. That wasn't financial enrichment, that was expansion of power, the beginning of a reconstitution of the great Soviet empire. Jeopardizing such a historic event by leaving before the work was done, before it was all carried out to its logical conclusion, was selfish, unpatriotic. Renke had also received some additional, almost indecipherable information concerning Strenzke—some vague notion about missing money, stolen funds. It all added an additional sense of urgency to the mission; there was no telling what the FSB might do based upon this new information.

Renke had parked his car on Bolshay Street much earlier that day in order to make sure he got a space near the front of the Apraksin.

He was seated at a very good table, which was fortunate, because the Apraksin was packed that night. A steady stream of customers kept the club filled to capacity. Even by the Apraksin's standards, business was good that evening, and Renke had to pay handsomely for his table. It was situated near the front of the establishment, part of a row of tables that sat along the side wall. What helped was that the row was positioned on a sort of raised platform that slightly elevated his row of tables above the rest of the room. This gave Renke a great view of the entire area. He could see everything.

A waitress brought a bottle of *Baltika No. 2 Lager* and set it on the table in front of him. The green bottle was already dripping with moisture. He looked at it and wished it were a *No. 6 Porter* instead, a dark, heavy beer that was his favorite. He remembered, however, the label on the *No. 6 Porter*, which indicated that it was "not less than 7% alcohol," something he certainly could not tolerate that evening. In fact, based upon past experience, he always thought the alcohol content in the porter was much *greater* than 7%. Even with his high tolerance for alcohol, a couple of *No. 6s* would've had him under the table.

He grabbed the *No. 2* and drank it as his eyes surveyed the room, searching for Strenzke and Terrebenzikov. If they were there, they'd almost certainly be on the main floor. There was no private dining upstairs anymore; the dining room was converted to a special suite long ago, one designated for the high-paying customers who enlisted the services of more than one woman at a time. Renke also knew it was unlikely Strenzke and Terrebenzikov would be upstairs with anyone; it was common knowledge that they stopped partaking of the Apraksin women a long time ago.

A dancer was on the small stage at the back of the room, an anomaly. The Apraksin stopped hosting nude dancers years ago under pressure from local officials. Being only two blocks away from the sanitized Sennaya Ploschad, a prostitution house flaunting its services with naked dancers pushed things too far.

The nude dancing gave the place a different feel, more festive, like it was a special evening that night. Renke wondered if the dancers were perhaps at the request of Strenzke himself, part of a last "sayonara" before leaving the place for good.

The music was louder than usual—a powerful thumping sound filled the air. The dancer on the stage held Renke's attention for a moment. She wore a silky pink bra with black lacing, a pink g-string, and pink, four-inch, patent leather heels. Her blond hair was drawn tightly into a ponytail behind her head, like a young cheerleader's, only she wasn't young. Renke estimated that she had to be at least in her early thirties. She had a deep suntan, causing her blond hair to glow as it fell against her dark skin. What really caught his attention, though, was her physique: she was muscular, with strong thighs and powerful calves, a slight v-shape from chest to torso. She removed her bra, revealing full, firm breasts. Renke recalled watching a female bodybuilding competition many years ago on ESPN and how none of the woman flexing their muscles on the stage had large breasts. The announcer indicated that the reason for the small breasts was a combination of low percentage body fat and pumped muscle. Renke recalled thinking at the time that it was a strange topic for the announcer to even be commenting upon. That's what seeing the nude dancer reminded him of—a female bodybuilder—though her muscles were not nearly as exaggerated, and her breasts were much larger. Must be implants, he figured. She removed her g-string and tossed it onto the floor. Her movement was slow, measured. The men sitting around the table seemed in awe of her. She had high cheek bones, no smile on her face, completely devoid of emotion. No money was tossed onto the stage, none was waved in the air; it wasn't allowed. If a man wanted her attention, he would have to pay for it by renting one of the expensive rooms upstairs. No doubt the fee for a dancer with her looks would be much greater than normal.

Renke turned his attention from the dancer to the people in the room; his eyes slowly moved outward from the stage, following the customers sitting at each of the tables.

He saw them! Strenzke and Terrebenzikov were at a table two rows from the stage, one dressed in a black turtleneck sweater, the other a blue blazer with a white T-shirt underneath. There was no doubt in his mind; it was them. Strenzke still sported the peppered-gray goatee and close-cropped hair.

Without letting it be obvious, he kept an eye on them at all times. Every so often one of them would lean over to hear what the other had to say over the din of the loud music. Otherwise, they rested comfortably and observed everything around them, as if they were soaking it all in for the last time.

When Renke spotted them, he knew he had to stay in the club. His doing so would serve two important purposes.

First, it acted as an initial signal for Angstrom and Gordon. If Renke had left the Apraksin shortly after entering, rubbing his forehead as he came out, that would mean the targets weren't inside. In that case, he would have to walk around outside, only to return an hour later to repeat the process. He would continue doing that, as inconspicuously as possible, for the rest of the evening. If, on the other hand, Strenzke and Terrebenzikov *were* inside, he would remain inside himself, thereby conveying the important message to Angstrom and Gordon that the targets were there. Second, Renke, as already mentioned, served as the roamer and the timing element in Angstrom's assault configuration. He was responsible for informing them when the targets were leaving the Apraksin by his coming out ahead of them, a closed fist to the mouth serving as an extra level of the signal so there could be no doubt.

Stafford and Reed would be in the alley guarding the back door, so they of course wouldn't see any of this activity. They would be kept abreast of the situation in a different way.

So once again the information Renke got from his informants proved accurate: Strenzke and Terrebenzikov were there. Renke looked down at his *No. 2* and told himself he was going to have to nurse it slowly. There was no telling how long it would be before Strenzke and Terrebenzikov decided to leave.

It was a thrilling moment for him, not only because he knew what soon would follow, the taking out of Strenzke and Terrebenzikov, but also because it marked the beginning of his return home. At long last, his time in Russia would be over!

Gordon was situated about a hundred feet west of the front entrance of the Apraksin. He sat and waited at the bus shelter. A shopping bag holding the IFDs rested beside him on the bench. The M9 was tucked in his waist under his sportcoat, the silencer not yet attached. He sat facing the street with his back to the Apraksin. The canal was just beyond him on the other side of Bolshay Street. Boats periodically passed by, their tiny green and red LED lights visible in the darkness, as well as the faint outline of the boats themselves as light from the surrounding area— streetlamps, some of the windows of the office buildings overhead—provided slight illumination at various points along the canal. There were just enough pedestrians walking around so that Gordon didn't stand out. The area was exactly as Reed had described it. Gordon saw the two large, cement planters across from the Apraksin. Reed was right; they'd be the perfect place for the IFDs.

Gordon was already in position when Renke first appeared at the plaza. There was no mistake in Gordon's spotting him because Renke wore a black jacket with a red knit shirt underneath so he'd be easily recognized. Gordon saw him approach by foot from the other end of the block. Just as casually as any other customer, Renke nodded to the man standing guard at the front door of the Apraksin and went inside.

After about a half hour had passed, Gordon thought something might be up, because Renke didn't come back out. Gordon considered the fact that there might have been some delay in Renke's getting seated at a table, so it was too early to draw any conclusions. After another fifteen minutes had passed with still no sign of Renke, Gordon became more alert. After a whole hour had passed, there was no doubt about it: the targets were inside.

It was starting. After all the planning and preparation, it came down to this. Gordon began to perspire a little. His heart rate increased. He momentarily looked across the canal to the top floor of the Grafton Hotel far off in the distance. The balcony where Angstrom was supposed to be was completely dark—no sign of anyone. Gordon turned again to look over his shoulder toward the Apraksin.

Calculations went through his head. He hoped Strenzke and Terrebenzikov had already been inside before Renke got there. Otherwise, given that Gordon didn't see them enter from the front, that meant they would have entered through the back. If that were the case, they'd most likely leave through the back—not what anyone wanted. Stafford and Reed were back there in the alley, but their encountering the targets was not the desired outcome. If Strenzke and Terrebenzikov *did* leave through the back, Gordon and Angstrom would know about it by Renke's exiting from the front with both hands in his pockets. Obviously Stafford and Reed would see the targets when they appeared.

Gordon waited for quite some time without seeing Renke come back out. At one point, a man and a woman came near Gordon and sat on a bench a few feet away. The man was older, in his late fifties. The woman looked to be in her early thirties. At first they just talked. Eventually, the man put his arm around her shoulders and moved his other arm around her abdomen. They kissed with an almost animalistic passion. Not long afterward, they left. A paid escort, Gordon figured. He was glad they were gone.

Looking at his watch, he saw that it was getting late and that he'd been sitting there for quite a while. He looked toward the club and saw that there was still only one man standing guard. Gordon was getting anxious.

At about the same time as Gordon first positioned himself at the bus shelter, Stafford and Reed were around the corner at the entrance to the alley that led to the back of the Apraksin.

"You go in first," Reed said. "I'll trail by about thirty feet. After you've walked for a while, look around and make sure no one else is there, then attach your silencer. Keep it stowed but ready for use. If the targets come out, it's going to be without warning. They may not be alone. Like I said before, you'll see an area about twenty feet past the back door where the wall from the adjoining building juts out. Keep behind that. I'll be on the other side of the door crouched in a corner behind a large dumpster. You can't miss it when you walk by. When you see a green dumpster with a red stripe at the bottom, that's it. The back door to the Apraksin is right after that."

Stafford followed his instructions and found that it was just as Reed said. She took her position and waited, watching carefully as Reed approached and ducked into his position. Now they wouldn't be able to see or talk to each other. They would have to wait, watch, and listen.

One of two things would eventually happen. Either Strenzke and Terrebenzikov would come out, in which case they'd have to take action, or they'd hear someone yelling from Renke's car at the end of the alley where they came from. That would indicate that they needed to run back and get into the car.

It was an odd experience for Stafford to be waiting there in that dark alley as she was. She was in position to potentially assassinate two people, two high-value targets, all the way on the other side of the world. It was a far cry from the raids she used to go on in the south side of Chicago. She couldn't believe how quickly her life had changed (and the confidence Angstrom had placed in her).

"Sergei, you're right, we *have* outgrown this place. I won't miss it," Terrebenzikov said, shouting over the music.

"Me neither. It sickens me, really, to be honest. We'll have our dinners, take care of business, and then get the hell out of here."

Both had *No. 6s* in front of them. Vodka was out of the question. They needed to remain sharp. The beer was really just a placeholder, something to have in front of them while they sat and observed, something that wouldn't knock them out.

"What do you think of that woman on stage?" Terrebenzikov said with a smile.

Strenzke turned and looked at her. The pink bra and g-string were already strewn on the floor.

"Not my type," he said.

"Hah. What, are you afraid of her? Maybe she's too strong for you, eh, beat you up," Terrebenzikov joked.

"Hell yes. As a matter of fact I *am* afraid of her," Strenzke said, laughing. "Look at her."

Dinner was brought to them a little later; the Apraksin was known for its prostitutes, but not its food, so one of the employees went out on a special run for them. Each had a large steak and a baked potato with all the trimmings.

While they ate, a young woman approached their table. She was relatively new to the place and was never told who Strenzke and Terrebenzikov were.

As she came within several feet, two large men at a nearby table, Bredziv and Vanatoly, stood and prepared to stop her. Strenzke noticed and waved them off without the woman ever noticing the difference. He and Terrebenzikov returned their attention to their meals, acting like they didn't notice she was there.

"Well, look at you two," she said, "having a special dinner brought to your table. Steaks, no less. I guess you're not satisfied with what you already see in here, huh?"

Vladimir Kronzev, the manager of the place, noticed what was happening and began to come over with an angry look on his face. Terrebenziko waved him off. Again the woman didn't notice.

"You see," Strenzke began, a boisterous tone in his voice and a purposefully dumb look on his face, "seeing all of these beautiful woman in this place makes me very hungry. I can't help it." He rubbed his belly.

Terrebenzikov watched, amused.

"Mm, maybe I can help you with that," she said, sitting down next to him with a sparkle in her eyes.

"Eh? Maybe you can. How much do you charge for your services?"

"Shh, quiet," she said, looking around nervously. "You're not supposed to offer money like that. We go upstairs, and you rent a room."

"Oh, I see, I see. Well, I don't need a room." He leaned back in his chair and raised his hands behind his head. "I'm not bashful. We'll have our little fun right here."

Terrebenzikov laughed. The woman was taken aback and a little aggravated, feeling like she was being laughed at.

"What do you mean by that?" she said, a questioning look on her face.

"I mean, whatever we do, we do here." He patted the table. "I don't need a room. That just costs extra. Let's cut the overhead; I'll give *you* everything. See, straight to the bottom line." He leaned over and twiddled two fingers up her thigh with a flirtatious look on his face.

She smiled at him, happy that she had found her first customer of the evening. She figured she had snagged a big one, what with his having dinner from the outside brought to his table. Strenzke turned to look at Terrebenzikov for a moment, and then he looked back at the woman and squeezed one of her breasts.

"Hey, listen. You can't touch me like that here. It's against the rules." She became more animated, anxious to reign in her prey. "Come on, I'll take you upstairs." She grabbed the hand that had fondled her breast and started to get up.

"No, no, I mean it. There's no need to go upstairs. We do what we do right here." He motioned toward the naked woman on the stage and said, "We'll put on our own show for everyone, right here. Who needs a room? What do you say?" Strenzke gripped her hand tighter and pulled her back to her seat.

"Are you serious?" She looked over at Terrebenzikov and saw

he was laughing. "You guys better not be laughing at me. Women get treated with respect in here, you know? You need to learn that."

They stopped laughing a little.

"Oh, oh, I see. My apologies. I didn't mean to upset you," said Strenzke, putting his arm around her and giving her a gentle squeeze.

That lightened her mood again. "Mm, I really like you," she said. "Really, let's go upstairs." She grabbed his hand and held it.

"Hey, stand up for a minute. I want to get a full view of you," Strenzke abruptly said.

In a normal place such a statement would have been met with scorn. Not at the Apraksin. Such a request was common. She stood up and posed for him, turning all the way around. This was progress, she thought, confident in her appearance.

"Ah, very nice, very nice. Do me a favor, I really want to see what I'm getting for my money. Take your clothes off."

Terrebenzikov laughed, this time louder. He was enjoying his friend's little tête-à-tête. The young woman, however, wasn't sure what was going on and didn't know how to take Strenzke.

"Right here? I can't do that. Not in front of everyone else."

He again gestured toward the naked woman dancing on the stage.

"Why not?" he said. "Look at her. Well, okay, I'll tell you what. Go up onto the stage and do it. Take your clothes off right here and walk onto the stage. You know how to dance, right?"

Now she thought they were making fun of her again, and she became livid.

"Listen, you keep this up and I'll call the manager over. Believe me, you don't want that to happen. Harassing a woman in this place is the last thing you want to do."

"Oh yes? Well, I'm not so sure. Do me a favor, go find this manager, and then tell him to go fuck himself."

Strenzke laughed at his own statement, and Terrebenzikov was almost in tears by the woman's shocked reaction. By that time, one of the woman's friends saw what was happening and came over, apologized for the interruption (Bredziv and Vanatoly let her approach), and whispered something into the woman's ear. A look of embarrassment came over the young woman and she put her hand over her opened mouth.

"I'm so sorry, I didn't know who you were," she said while anxiously standing up.

Strenzke smiled at her and said, "Ha, it's okay. Here, take the night off. Go enjoy yourself." He stood up, reached into his pocket, and took out a wad of rubles the equivalent of five-hundred U.S. dollars. The woman stared at it.

"I couldn't take that, sir. It's not…it's okay. I'm very sorry to have disturbed you."

She began to leave again.

Strenzke grabbed her arm and stuffed the money in between her breasts. Then he looked into her eyes intently and said, "It's okay. Take it." He softly kissed her on the cheek, sat back down, and resumed his meal, not looking up at her again.

Terrebenzikov saw this and slowly stopped laughing. A more serious look came over him, and he began to eat as well. The woman walked away with her friend, stunned.

Strenzke and Terrebenzikov grinned at each other when she was gone.

After some additional time had passed, a man approached their table; Bredziv and Vanatoly let him pass. With a big smile on his face, the man reached to shake Strenzke's hand, but just at that moment Strenzke had turned in the other direction. Terrebenzikov, seeing this, nodded to the man and then nudged his partner. Strenzke turned and immediately saw the man, an old friend of his, and a big smile appeared on his face. He stood and hugged the man. Terrebenzikov followed suit, and they invited the man to join them.

Renke watched from a distance, wondering who the man was.

The three visited for close to an hour; by then it was 1:30 A.M. The man finally stood and said goodbye, giving Strenzke and Terrebenzikov vigorous hugs.

After that, Renke saw Strenzke raise his hand and motion

toward the back of the club to where Vladimir Kronzev, the manager, was standing. Kronzev immediately came over, and Renke saw Strenzke motion for the man to take a seat.

Terrebenzikov watched from across the table, amid the pounding thunder of the music, as Strenzke spoke at great length into the ear of Kronzev, who was leaning over so Strenzke could do so. At one point Kronzev pulled away and looked at Strenzke in disbelief.

Strenzke turned to Terrebenzikov and nodded, who in response pulled out a one-page document from his breast pocket. He handed it to Strenzke, who flattened it on the table and slid it over in front of Kronzev.

"Are you sure, Sergei?" Kronzev said loudly.

"Of course I'm sure," shouted Strenzke.

"It's not necessary. I...it's hard for me to accept such an extravagant gift...it's too much. I don't deserve it," Kronzev said into Strenzke's ear.

"It's okay, Vladimir," Strenzke said, patting his friend on the back. "Ivan and I are tired of this place. You have it. I don't want it anymore, and I don't need it. I have all the money I need."

Vladimir Kronzev was stunned. He looked at Terrebenzikov with a perplexed look. Terrebenzikov returned his pleading gaze with an assured smile, nodding his head to the pounding beat of the music.

Then Strenzke reached with his pen and signed the bottom of the paper. The deed to the Apraksin was transferred to Kronzev.

"Take it, my friend," Strenzke said. "Go put it in the safe in the back. I've already informed security of my intentions; they now answer to you...except for Bredziv and Vanatoly." Strenzke motioned toward the two security men sitting at the nearby table.

Renke watched as Strenzke, Terrebenzikov, and Kronzev stood and hugged each other, vigorously patting each other on the back just like Strenzke and Terrebenzikov did with the other man. Then Kronzev disappeared. Strenzke and Terrebenzikov, still standing, signaled to Bredziv and Vanatoly, who then stood as well.

That was it, Renke thought, they're leaving! He watched to see what direction they went, and then, after leaving money on the table for his tab, quickly rose and left, making sure to get ahead of Strenzke and Terrebenzikov.

Gordon, who was looking over his shoulder, saw Renke when he appeared at the front entrance. As he came out he held a closed fist to his mouth as if he were clearing his throat. That was the signal, Gordon thought to himself, the targets were coming out!

He quickly rose and moved along the row of parked cars toward the cement planters directly across the front door. Meanwhile, Renke continued walking from the Apraksin toward his car; he saw Gordon out of the corner of his eye as they passed. A few pedestrians were milling about in the area, and the one guard stood at the front door, but otherwise there weren't many people around; the inside of the Apraksin was still packed, but the steady stream of new customers approaching from outside had subsided.

Still no sign of the targets, Gordon thought as he kept watching while he walked, the bag containing the IFDs held at his side. That was good—Renke was able to get in front of them a safe distance.

Gordon made it to the first planter, walked in front of it, and lodged an IFD at the inside edge facing the Apraksin. He continued walking to the second planter, glancing at the guard to make sure he wasn't watching. He wasn't; two women from the club had come outside to talk to him. Gordon placed the second IFD in the other planter, and then, instead of continuing to walk, he circled back around it and stood behind its tall foliage for cover. It was all done with such fluid movement that no one paid any attention to him.

Renke got into the driver's seat of his car and waited without starting the engine. He was about seventy-five feet to the left, four or five car lengths in front of the bus stop's pickup zone.

Gordon peered over the boxwood and clearly saw that the guard had a Vityaz-SN submachine gun holstered across his shoulder, not even attempting to conceal it. His heart sank. A Vityaz-SN could fire close to eight-hundred 9×19mm Parabellum rounds a minute. Reed hadn't mentioned anything about that. It must have been a sign of heightened security. With a magazine holding 30 rounds, the guard could easily pulverize Gordon's body with bullets. Gordon felt like his M9 was a pea-shooter compared to what the guard had. It complicated things. The flash devices and his skill with the M9s would have to make up the difference. That, and Angstrom.

A moment later the guard's head turned and the front door to the Apraksin opened. One of the security men, Bredziv, stepped outside holding another Vityaz-SN. Gordon took out his M9 and, as inconspicuously as possible, quickly attached the silencer. He recognized the next man who came out as Terrebenzikov, followed by the other security man, Vanatoly, once again with a Vityaz-SN. That meant three armed men, plus Terrebenzikov.

But where was Strenzke?

Gordon was assigned to Strenzke, and Angstrom's CS5 would be trained on Terrebenzikov. Gordon was supposed to start it all by taking the first shot, but his target wasn't there. If only one of the targets were inside, Renke would have given a different signal coming out of the place. He didn't. They were both in there, but only one came out.

Therefore, Angstrom would start the assault. That was the plan. Gordon would need to switch to one of the armed guards as his first target. He still wasn't going to trigger the IFDs unless absolutely necessary. They all agreed it was cleaner that way. He moved to the corner of the planter and knelt down, putting his left hand under his right elbow to support it as he held the M9. Being over a hundred feet away and partially hidden from view, no one saw him. He aimed directly at one of the guards. With his intense focus, everything seemed silent around him.

Angstrom had been watching through the scope of his CS5. He was out on the balcony lying prostrate on the cement floor, a blanket underneath him for warmth, a tripod attached to the under rail of the rifle to support it. The tip of the silencer at the end of the barrel protruded through two metal balusters of the wrought iron railing. The lights of his room were turned off such that he was enveloped in darkness. Each side of his balcony had a solid wall extending floor-to-ceiling; no one could see him from the adjoining units, even if they were outside on their own balcony. He calculated the bullet's drop, factoring in the decreased velocity due to the silencer attachment.

Angstrom saw Terrebenzikov exit the front door without Strenzke. He also took note of the three armed guards and the weapons they carried. He wondered if that would cause Gordon to trigger the IFDs. It still wasn't necessary, Angstrom thought. He hoped Gordon felt the same.

The air was relatively calm, but at his height, he still needed to account for drift. It wasn't a straightforward shot by any means. Fortunately for Angstrom, Terrebenzikov stood relatively still. He must have been waiting for his friend. That allowed Angstrom to switch the 14X variable zoom of the scope to the higher magnification.

Angstrom didn't think he could wait any longer. He took a normal breath, then held it. The trigger was pulled.

Terrebenzikov silently collapsed, blood spurting from his head as it shattered under the impact of the .50 caliber bullet fired by the CS5. He was killed instantly.

Gordon immediately fired his M9 and took out Bredziv, the nearest guard.

The two other guards realized what was happening. One of them, Vanatoly, fell to his knee and looked outward, searching for where the bullets came from. The other had already spotted Gordon by the planter and moved to point his gun. Gordon, having the advantage of being partially hidden, aimed quickly and pumped two bullets into the guard's chest, causing him to stagger backwards and fall to the ground. Vanatoly saw this, and while still kneeling trained his gun on Gordon. All of a sudden, without any perceptible sound, the front of Vanatoly's skull shattered—Angstrom had shot him. Gordon's silenced M9 fired more bullets into the body of the guard he had initially shot to make sure he was dead. Then he replaced his clip.

The few pedestrians who were out on the plaza watched in horror as Terrebenzikov and the guards fell to the ground, heads shattered and pools of blood forming around them. Screams were heard. People ran for cover. One man spotted Gordon, and their eyes met. Gordon wondered for a microsecond if the man was going to shout something, point him out.

After waiting a short moment to make sure the shooting was over, Renke started his car and pulled out onto the street. After pulling almost directly in front of Gordon, however, he slammed on the brakes, fearful of what he saw. He quickly put his car into park and lay down on the passenger seat. That was all he could do in preparation for what he knew would come next.

Strenzke was only a few steps behind Terrebenzikov when they were exiting the building. He stopped at the door, however, to say one last goodbye to Vladimir Kronzev before stepping outside. They hugged. Kronzev begged Strenzke to stay a little longer, but Strenzke declined, affectionately slapping the man's cheek. They smiled and looked at each other, knowing they'd likely never see each other again.

When Strenzke opened the front door, he immediately saw the dead bodies lying on the ground and slammed the door shut. It was clear to him what had happened.

"Vladimir, they're dead! Someone's out there. Get the guards. Quick!"

Several men were summoned and quickly rose from their seats. Although some of the customers noticed this, they weren't too alarmed, thinking it was probably just a rowdy customer that had to be dealt with.

"Send some of the men through the front," Strenzke instructed after all the guards were assembled. "The others take the service door." He pointed at two of the men and said, "You and you come with me."

"Who do you think is out there?" Kronzev asked.

"I'm not sure."

Kronzev quickly went behind the front counter and reached into a large cabinet below. He pulled out AK-47s and handed one to each of the men. He gave Strenzke a handgun per his instructions. The two that Strenzke had fingered followed him to the back door.

Some of the closest patrons saw the guns and immediately became alarmed, but they did nothing, frozen in fear. The majority of the customers were oblivious to what was happening; even after they saw a man holding a pistol dash to the back, with two armed guards following, they didn't know what to make of it. The loud music kept thundering, a nude dancer kept dancing, the alcohol flowed, and the multitude of prostitutes kept customers engaged. There was too much of a visual, intoxicating feast occurring inside the Apraksin to place much credence in what they momentarily saw. It was as if Strenzke and the guards had quickly flashed across the television screen above the bar, happening in the background as it were, with no one really paying much attention.

At the front of the Apraksin there was a service door about twenty-five feet to the side of the main entrance. Two armed guards emerged from this side door first, hoping their appearance would be a surprise to whoever was out there.

It was. Gordon was caught off guard. A slight instant later, two more armed men emerged from the main entrance. They held their AK-47s at shoulder height, ready to fire. Then Vladimir Kronzev himself came out, an AK-47 also in his hands. He owed his life to Strenzke, and he would fight for him now.

This all happened in a matter of seconds. Angstrom saw it unfold. Renke, too; it was what caused him to stop his car in the middle of the street. There were now five armed men against Gordon. One of them spotted Gordon standing some hundred feet away by the planter, pointed at him, and yelled something.

Do it, Angstrom said to himself, quick, before it's...

Gordon had already grabbed the detonation device from his pocket. He fell to the ground and closed his eyes the instant he triggered the two IFDs.

A burst of white light filled the plaza. There was no sound, such that it was like a star had exploded in the vacuum of space. All of the guards had been looking in the direction toward Gordon and therefore looked right into the light. They were blinded, as were the few terrified pedestrians who were still in the area frozen with fear.

With some of the glow still present, Gordon opened his eyes, the brilliant light from the burning magnesium emanating from behind and above him. The guards were stunned. While lying on the ground, Gordon watched the guards and quickly considered what he should do. For an instant he thought about making a run for it. But he knew that was a risk; he couldn't take the chance, small is it may be, of being shot in the back...or being followed. He really only had one option: he outstretched his hand and fired the M9. Two shots to each of the guards at the main entrance, and they were down. Kronzev sensed this and instinctively fell to the ground and rubbed his eyes, desperately trying to restore his sight. He began to squirm away backwards, hoping to get back inside the front door. Gordon saw this and shot him twice, right into the top of his head.

The three men at the main entrance were dead.

Angstrom was able to do the rest. Although the two guards that came out of the side entrance were further away, they were still bombarded by the brilliant white light. They dropped to their knees, their eyesight only partially impaired. Their eyes burned, but they struggled to see. They couldn't see Gordon from the bright, white light that still shone behind him. It didn't matter. Angstrom easily took them out with two shots from his CS5.

Renke, eventually sensing from his car that the burst of light was gone, gave it a few more seconds and then carefully raised up to look out of his car's window. He saw all of the dead men on the ground and spotted Gordon, who was looking right at him. Gordon ran to the car.

"Move, move!" Gordon said after he got in. "Drive around to the alley. We still haven't got Strenzke."

"Damn! You think he might still be in there?"

"Don't know. Come on, move!" Gordon said, pointing forward through the front window to emphasize the point.

"I'm not sure if anyone's going to be back here or not," Strenzke nervously said to the two armed men that were accompanying him at the back door. "We're sure as hell not going to stay in here."

"We'll go out first," one of them said. "If it's clear, we'll call you."

Strenzke nodded. He squeezed his Pistolet Besshumnyy and waited as the men carefully went outside.

When Stafford and Reed saw the back door begin to open, they gripped their weapons firmly and leaned back behind their cover. They listened carefully without looking. They heard a first person slowly come out. The door didn't close. Footsteps. The sound of a second person. The footsteps went from the door to the middle of the alley.

Two men, Stafford calculated. She leaned tight against the wall so as to avoid being seen, her gun ready at her side.

There was a whisper: *"Sergei, it's clear."*

Stafford and Reed both heard the name "Sergei." It was then they knew it wasn't just employees taking out the trash. Sergei Strenzke was there with two other men. Adrenaline flowed. Either Reed or Stafford could start the process as the opportunity presented itself.

"Come on, let's go," Strenzke said.

More footsteps.

Stafford ever-so-carefully glanced around the corner and saw them walking away. Based upon the descriptions she'd been given, she distinguished Sergei Strenzke from the two men at his sides; she didn't recognize either of the other two as Terrebenzikov. She had to quickly decide a course of action. Shooting someone in the back wasn't an easy proposition, but it was what had to be done; she quietly raised her weapon, took a breath, and shot Strenzke twice.

Strenzke felt the pain in his chest and fell to the ground. He looked behind him and saw Stafford holding the M9.

The two other men turned as well. They were almost right in front of the dumpster. Reed heard what had happened, sprung from his position, and saw the two men carrying the AK-47s. They were turning toward Stafford. He shot one of them, hitting him in the shoulder. Taking advantage of the element of surprise, he aimed and shot the second guard, hitting him in the side of the face. Stafford and Reed each fired several more rounds into the guards to finish them off.

When they thought it was clear, they darted out from behind their cover and over to the man they knew was Strenzke. Stafford kneeled down beside him and looked into his eyes. There was no expression on his face, no sign of any thought he wished to convey. This man who she did not know—who she'd never seen or met before—lay on the ground before her, dying.

Strenzke couldn't believe he was shot; who was this strange woman looking down at him? He was confused; there were no thoughts in his head, just a sensation of the blood flowing out of his chest, and the knowledge that in a moment he would be dead. It was difficult to breathe; he didn't want to die and tried to fight it, but it was too much. The woman continued to stare at him, doing nothing; he looked deeply into her eyes and wondered if she held concern for him, and then, a short moment later, he expired.

Tires screeched at the end of the alley. They heard a yell: "Come on! Move!"

It was Gordon's voice. They recognized it and ran.

"Hurry up, get in," Gordon yelled through the open window.

Stafford and Reed got into the back and crouched down. Gordon closed his window, and Renke drove at normal speed away from the scene.

"Did he come out?" Gordon turned and asked.

"Yeah, we got Strenzke," Reed said. "Along with two guards.

No sign of Terrebenzikov."

"We got him out front. Stay down until we pick up John. We need to get out of the immediate area. This place is going to be crawling with police."

28

Giant Steps

RENKE CROSSED THE CANAL ON DEMIDOV BRIDGE and drove to the Grafton Hotel. He bypassed the main entrance and instead entered the parking lot on the side of the building. After turning the car around so it faced the street, he pulled up next to a metal service door. It was there they waited. Renke's fingers nervously tapped the steering wheel; Gordon had to reach over and put a hand on them to stop. It was only then that Gordon was reminded of the fact that this was not the kind of field work that Renke was used to. Developing deep relationships, fostering clandestine networks, assimilating intelligence, that was his true forte. But he did good, Gordon thought; he did what was needed.

Stafford and Reed sat in the back seat. Gordon cracked his window to allow some fresh air to enter; people were breathing heavily, and the air was getting stale.

Angstrom appeared about a couple of minutes later. Gordon and Renke watched as he exited the building with a bag slung over his shoulder. They were relieved to see him. The car's trunk was popped, and Angstrom put the bag holding the disengaged

CS5 inside. When he opened the back door, Stafford and Reed made room for him.

"Everyone all right?" Angstrom said.

"Yeah, we're good," Gordon responded from the front. "Nice shooting."

"Thanks. You too. How about Strenzke? Did he come out?"

"Yeah, we got him," Stafford said. There was a determined look on her face.

Angstrom looked into her eyes. He'd seen that look many times before.

"Good. Let's go," he said. "We have to get out of here. Don't drive crazy." Angstrom thought for a moment as Renke put the car in drive. He leaned forward and put his hand on Renke's shoulder: "Good to see you again, Redblood, after all these years."

Renke nodded as he drove, a slight smile appearing on his face.

The plan was to split up and rendezvous at the cabin in Untolovo. From there they would hike to the safe house in Mys Peschanyy, where Grahame, Gentry and Franklin would be waiting for them. Renke dumped the car at the border between Untolovo and St. Petersburg, and the team separated to hike through the forest. Moving through it at night was going to be difficult, so the plan called for traveling along either side of the Glukharka River in order to use it as a guide. It wasn't easy, especially after all they'd been through, but their energy didn't waver. They were wide awake, the adrenaline still flowing.

Angstrom took the lead and made it to the cabin first. As a precautionary measure, he hid in the forest about 50 feet from the front door of the cabin and waited for each person to arrive. He watched through an IR scope he had attached to his CS5 to make sure that no one was followed. Renke was the last to arrive. Angstrom watched him closely as he quietly knocked on the cabin's door, waited for it to open, and then entered. Angstrom remained outside for over an hour after that and sat in silence, listening for the slightest sounds, scanning the area for movement.

When he was sure no one had followed, he moved from

position and went inside. The room was pitch black.

"Excellent job, everyone," Angstrom said as Gordon let him in. "Perfectly executed."

"Yes," Renke said, standing up from the chair he was sitting on, "the FSB did not want Strenzke and Terrebenzikov to leave, so we did the job for them."

Gordon moved closer to Renke and put his hand on his shoulder. "Welcome, my friend. Welcome back to the world."

Renke was grateful, almost moved to tears. He reached and patted the hand on his shoulder. "Thank you. I can't quite believe it yet. I'm in a state of shock. If feels good to be speaking English again."

They all remained silent for a moment.

"How many went out the back?" Angstrom eventually said.

"Strenzke and two guards," Stafford offered.

"You okay?" he asked, looking right at her in the darkness.

"I'm good."

Angstrom knew that what she and Reed had done, killing people in cold blood, was not an easy thing to get over. He'd been through it too many times himself not to realize that.

"It's going to feel strange for a while," he said. "It can catch up to you without your even realizing it. If it does, don't hesitate to see me. Okay?"

"Thanks. I will."

Gordon added, "We should all probably get post-op counseling with psyche, just to be safe."

Angstrom said, "Agreed. Everyone do that when we get back. Meantime, Gordon, let's you and I step outside for a minute. We need to talk."

Angstrom led the way and cracked the door open. He peered through the opening and listened for noise. Everyone remained still as he did so. After about a minute he was satisfied that it was clear and went outside with Gordon. They moved a few yards away from the house so no one inside could overhear them, moving slowly to minimize the sound of their footsteps.

"Excellent job, as always," Angstrom whispered.

"Thanks. You too. I have to admit, this one had me on edge. I was sweating it the whole time."

"I know. I could feel it from where I was. You did good. Reflexes were sharp."

"I wasn't even sure if I was going to shoot those guards after the flash—at first I thought about just running."

"No, you made the right decision. Almost always better to shoot and *then* run."

Gordon said, "So, you're not ready to mothball me yet, eh?" He thought he saw a grin on Angstrom's face, though he couldn't tell for sure because the forest was so dark.

Angstrom didn't immediately respond after that. They both paused and listened for any noise. It was instinctive for both of them. Eventually Angstrom said, "Let's keep going."

"Huh? What do you mean?"

"To Mys Peschanyy...let's go there tonight."

"You're kidding, right?"

"No, I'm not."

Both paused and stared at the faint outline of the other in the darkness.

"I don't know, John. Everyone's exhausted. Hell, you've got to be exhausted yourself. You made a round-trip back to this place all in one day!"

"I know, I know." Angstrom hesitated. "It's just that...I don't like being here with everything that's going on."

Gordon was puzzled. "What do you mean? You mean what we just went through? You think someone may find us out here? It's not likely, John. Not for the short time we're going to be here. You saw where Renke dumped the car; they're not going to find it for a while. And first thing tomorrow, we're gone."

"No, it's not that."

"Then what? What is it, John? Are you talking about the States? It's not time yet. And we took Strenzke and Terrebenzikov out before the deadline. Shit, nothing may even happen now."

Angstrom proceeded to update Gordon as to what had

happened in the United States and in Europe; there was no need to keep him in the dark any longer. Gordon was stunned.

It was the next part, however, that really drove Angstrom's current thinking.

"Gordon, I'm worried about Anne. I'm worried she may be in danger."

"What?" It took Gordon a second to transition his thoughts to what Angstrom said. "Why? What's happened?"

"It's the Russians; they've come for her in the States."

"You're kidding. Shit, what for? What happened, John?"

"I can't say anything else. I just want to get back to her as soon as possible. With what's happening back home, it makes it even worse. Everyone's focused on the big picture, and rightly so, but that leaves her extremely vulnerable."

Gordon was shocked. He had no idea Angstrom was carrying this weight on his shoulders. He felt badly for his old friend. He felt bad for Davis. He tried to set Angstrom's mind at ease.

"She'll be okay, John. Hell, with her training anybody should be afraid to come up against her. We'll be there in no time. Military transport is going to take us directly home once we get to Finland. It's just a little while longer. Why risk it by pushing too hard?" He reached out through the darkness and put his hand on Angstrom's shoulder. "Come on, John. Let's get some rest. That team in there has been through a lot. Hell, Renke's probably beside himself."

Hesitation. Gordon could feel the pain and concern emanating from Angstrom as he stood with him in the dark.

"If anything happens to her, Gordon, I'll never forgive myself. I shouldn't have left her alone. I shouldn't have left her."

"John, don't beat yourself up. You did what needed to be done. Don't think about it. She's going to be fine. As soon as we get to Mys Peschanyy we'll radio Washington; we'll check on her."

Angstrom appreciated what Gordon said, but it didn't set his mind at ease. He knew, however, that Gordon was right: it didn't make logistical sense for them to keep hiking through the forest.

"Yeah...you're right," Angstrom finally said. "But we're leaving as soon as possible, and then it's double-time."

"You bet," Gordon said, patting his friend on the back as they turned to go back inside. "In the mean time, come on in and congratulate your team. They did a hell of a job!"

29

Sanctuary's Repose

THE TIME IN RUSSIA WAS EIGHT HOURS AHEAD of what it was in the Washington, D.C. area. Therefore, it was around 6:30 P.M. in Georgetown at the height of what happened at the Apraksin. Davis had been staying at Nikolas Shulman's home for the last five days. The turmoil occurring across the United States had not subsided, and it was difficult for anyone to really know the full extent of what was going on for lack of news distribution resources. But Davis was beginning to feel like she had become an imposition on Shulman. She didn't really know how long Angstrom would be gone—he couldn't say for sure at the time of his departure—but she decided that it was time to be back in her own home. She had been keeping a watchful eye during every waking moment, using all of her skills, and there were no telltale signs of anyone following her, no trace of anyone suspicious; as far as she could tell, no one was watching her. She convinced herself that she must have imagined that she saw something before.

Shulman and Davis had decided earlier that day to check on

his shop. No customers were expected, but they had gotten a little stir crazy spending so much time at Shulman's house; they needed to get out and do something. They also wanted to make sure the store was okay. Their drive to the shop was surreal to say the least, with few cars on the road and few people outside in general (people were allowed to go outside as long as it was still daylight).

Shulman had been tidying up a bit and filing papers at the shop, while Davis serviced some of the stringed instruments and cleaned as well. Eventually Davis decided that she'd had enough and was ready to go home.

"Goodbye Mr. Shulman. I'll see you tomorrow," Davis said to Shulman from the front of the store as she prepared to leave.

"Wait Anne, just a minute," said Shulman, rising from his chair in the back office and rushing, as fast as a man of seventy-six could, to the front. "Wait, wait." He had to be careful as he made his way to the front because with no power, the back office and hallway were dark; a few burning candles served as the only source of light. The front of the store was better, being lit mainly by the daylight that shone through the large storefront window.

"Mr. Shulman, what is it? Take your time."

He was slightly out of breath when he reached her.

Davis and Shulman had taken an immediate liking to each other ever since the first day she had set foot in his shop. Several aspects of their lives drew them together.

Nikolas Shulman had emigrated to the United Sates from Czechoslovakia close to fifty years ago with his now-deceased wife, Livia. He worked for years as a painter and craftsman at a ship-building company in Maryland but always dreamed of one day owning his own music store. They lived frugally when they first came to the United States, always living below their means and saving everything they could. They had no children because Livia was physically unable to bear them. All they had were each other.

She was a talented violinist and gave private lessons out of their home. Word spread of her teaching talent, and for decades she ran a healthy studio business out of the basement of their modest home. Everything she made was extra income that went straight to the bank. Simple, compounded interest caused their money to grow into a sizable sum over the years.

Eleven years ago Nikolas Shulman retired; he had worked for over thirty-five years at his company. A decent pension awaited, along with a lot of free time. It was then that Livia urged her husband to finally pursue his dream. He had worked tirelessly as a painter all those years, she insisted, and now it was time to reward himself. He deserved it.

Many of her students from the old studio followed her to the new store when it opened. Soon their small shop in Georgetown was the place to go for private violin instruction.

When Davis first walked into Shulman's store, she immediately reminded him of Livia. Her accent, though not the same, still harkened back to his old country, and to Livia. Davis had dark hair just like Livia did back when Shulman and Livia first met. Oh Livia, he thought to himself, with that deep black hair, you were a goddess.

Davis asked to teach cello in his store. Just like that, out of nowhere, she came into his life. She was a godsend.

That they both came from where they did helped form a bond between them; they grew fond of each other in a familial way. Her staying with him at his home for the last five days only strengthened that bond.

He liked to talk with her about the old country; how he met Livia and the things they would do together in their home town of Liberec. He laughed when he told her one evening about the time when he took Livia out on a small rowboat on the Lusatian Neisse River. She took a parasol and he did the rowing, just like a Monet painting.

"Are you sure you're ready to return home, Anne?"

"Yes, it's time Mr. Shulman. Although things are still a mess out there," she glanced out of the window momentarily, "I miss my home. I don't like being home alone, but I don't like being away from it either. It makes me feel like I'm even further away from John."

She had told Shulman of a man in her life named John; a man she lived with and who worshiped her. It made Shulman happy to know this.

"Are you in a hurry to go?" he said, rubbing his chin nervously. "I know we've had no customers today, but with the power out, what else is there to do? Do you mind staying with me at the shop for just a little longer today? Come on, it's Saturday."

She looked into the warm eyes beseeching her.

"Sure," she answered, "I'll keep you company for a while longer." She turned and looked out of the front window. "It should still be daylight for at least another hour."

"Oh, don't worry about that. I'll drive you home."

"No, Mr. Shulman, you've done enough, and you need to conserve your gasoline. Anyway I *want* to walk home. I'm looking forward to it. I can't keep scurrying around meekly like a mouse the whole time John's gone. That's no way to live."

"Very well, my sweet girl. Let's go sit at the table."

He gestured toward a small, circular table with tiles embedded into its surface, along with two metal-framed chairs with circular seats. They reminded Davis of the cafés and bistros of St. Petersburg. It was arranged at the front of the store among the various instruments on display, so they could look outside through the large front window as they sat.

"Wait here," he said to her all of a sudden after she sat down. He came back with two small glasses and a bottle of port. He set them down and went to the door to turn the sign around to indicate "closed."

A sheepish grin appeared on her face: "Are you sure everything is okay, Mr. Shulman."

"Yes, yes, of course. I just thought I'd make it nice for us. You like the port, no?"

"Of course. You know I do."

"Good." He sat down and poured. "Anne, I enjoy your company. With Livia gone...I don't have anyone to talk to anymore. I enjoyed the time we spent together these last few days. I'm going to miss not having you in my house."

She was touched. She couldn't resist the charm of the old man. It was a godsend for her as well that they had met; there was something about him that reminded her of her father: a link to the past, a love of the "old" country. He filled a part of her that was left void when her parents were killed.

"Well, what should we talk about?" she said, sampling the port. "How about Liberec? Tell me more about your home."

"Ah, Liberac, it was beautiful." A serene smile came upon his face. "Surrounded by mountains. The Jizera Mountains on one side, the Ještěd-Kozákov Ridge bordering another." He still had a slight tinge of an accent, even after all those years. It seemed to become more pronounced, she realized, whenever he reminisced about Czechoslovakia—and also after drinking some port.

They often talked about the places they were from, and what they missed about them. Shulman was fascinated by her and couldn't help but ask questions. It was a topic she knew she should avoid, but she couldn't resist talking at least a little bit about it; he was such a warm, genuine person. But she made sure to not let it get too personal—not too much about her parents, nothing too sensitive.

"So tell me, my sweet Anne...tell me about when you would go to the Marinsky Theater."

Mention of that theater took her back in time; memories flowed. It was her father's favorite, and he took her there many times when she was a young girl.

They talked for a long time. The bottle of port was almost empty by the time they were through visiting, though Shulman had done most of the drinking. As much as she would have liked to, she couldn't let her guard completely down. As it were, she felt a little light-headed after just the two small glasses she drank on an empty stomach.

Sitting at the table and looking out of the large storefront window, along with the port Shulman served, made for a pleasant experience. Sitting in front of that window, however, also had another effect: it made it easier for Davis to be watched.

Even after the five days since Frëge had detonated, pedestrian traffic along the sidewalk in front of the music store was minimal. People ventured out for the necessities—cars were on the streets during the day—but things were nowhere near normal. A nondescript, black Chevy Malibu was parked across the street from the music store; it was several car-lengths away and nestled between a couple of other parked cars so as to avoid being noticed. There were two men inside of it; they had been watching—and listening.

"The view is good," said one of the men, the younger of the two, who was sitting in the back seat.

"Shh," the other said, the one behind the steering wheel—the one with the dirty blond hair. "I can't hear when you talk." He adjusted the earpiece in his ear and turned the volume up on the receiver. He was listening to the channel associated with the bug planted closest to where Shulman and Davis sat. After a few more minutes he said, "We do it tonight."

"Tonight? Are you sure? We didn't say this would be the night," said Treshenko.

"I'm saying it now: we do it tonight. She's going back to her house," said Mitslov.

"Shit...you're kidding!" He reflected for a moment on what he just heard and then said, "That makes it easier for sure."

"Shh, I said be quiet. It sounds like she's going to walk home by herself."

Treshenko, sitting in the back seat, became pensive. He sat for a long time without saying anything, clenching his fists nervously as he thought about things. After a while he ventured, "We go home after this, right? I mean back to Russia."

Mitslov looked at him in the rear-view mirror. He ran his fingers through his tousled hair in frustration as he held the gaze of his partner. With no change in expression he said, "Maybe, Treshenko, maybe. I don't know. Sometimes I begin to think we'll never go home."

Treshenko became perplexed at this new revelation; he wanted to say something, to pursue what was just said, but Mitslov anticipated this, held up his hand, and then said, "Get out. Go over to the place we talked about. I have to move the car before she comes out. Hurry."

After Treshenko got out, Mitslov put the car into drive and moved.

It was dusk when Davis left the store. She felt warm after drinking the port, and when she stepped outside the fresh air felt good. She looked intently into the sky and took a deep breath. Then she looked all around her; a few empty cars parked along the street, but that was it. No one else was around. She began to walk, cautiously observing everything in her proximity.

Across the street from her there was a row of beautiful old brownstones. Treshenko stood in a gap formed between two of them. He watched Davis and let her walk a good distance before he came out from his position and carefully followed her.

They knew her route. They could anticipate where she'd be before she ever got to any particular point. Even when she took a turn in an unexpected direction, purposefully changing things up in case she was followed, it didn't matter. The two men had worked it out in advance: there was an alley she would have to pass in order to get to her house, no matter what route she took. It was the perfect place. Mitslov pulled the car into the alley and parked just beyond view from the sidewalk, far ahead of Davis. Then he got out and stood behind the corner of a building that abutted the sidewalk; there he watched and waited.

Davis noticed that it was getting dark fast. The quietness all around her felt ominous and set her even more on edge. She could hear her own footsteps as she walked. She filtered out the sound and concentrated: there was a presence near her—at first it was just a sense, a feeling. The sight of the man in her peripheral vision when she looked over her shoulder confirmed it. She tried not to become alarmed, but she clearly saw someone. As if he noticed he was spotted, the man fell farther back, but she knew she was being followed: when she turned a corner, so did he.

She wondered what he would try to do. It would've been easy enough to have just killed her if that's what the intention was. A silenced bullet to the head was all it took. But she knew it was more than that; they wanted information; they wanted back from her what had been taken. They needed her alive—at least for a while.

But then she started to doubt herself; she started to doubt whether the man really *was* following her. Maybe she was just being paranoid. His technique certainly seemed odd enough, or sloppy to say the least. Maybe he *wasn't* an assassin. Perhaps he was some random pervert or petty criminal trying to take advantage of the situation. She reached inside of her purse; she knew the large knife would be there, but she wanted to feel its handle to confirm it. It was all she had to protect herself. Getting a gun, at least legally, was out of the question given her overall circumstances, and she dared not ask Angstrom for one.

She summoned her courage and turned to once again look in the man's direction. A slight look—one meant to appear casual and unintended—but long enough to allow her to see him clearly. Her heart sank; it was certainly no ordinary man. He carried himself with a sense of purpose, and he had a strong, imposing physique. This time he didn't even bother to look away when she looked at him; he looked right back at her, a dark figure in the twilight.

So it was true: they had come for her. She felt it in her bones. They weren't going let her go. But how could they have found her? She realized that John hadn't told her everything; things must have been going on in the background that he couldn't share with her; that's why he said goodbye the way he did.

But why didn't the man turn away when she looked at him? He let himself be spotted. She stopped walking to think. She was right in front of the store where Angstrom took his clothes for dry cleaning, but it was closed. Everything was closed. She looked into the glass and could barely see her predator's reflection in the darkness. She watched as he kept walking until he was directly across the street from her. It was brazen of him to reveal himself that way, to allow himself to stand out, so why would he do that? She tried to think of what his plan might be. Of course, she suddenly realized, the alley! It was only about ten feet away. The man was closing in on her so that he could grab her and force her into the alley. She couldn't let that happen. She had the knife, but even with that plus her training she feared it would not be enough if she ended up with him in that alley. She had gone through enough sparring exercises to be able to quickly size up a formidable opponent.

She could turn back and go in the direction she came from. Perhaps she should start breaking windows in all of the nearby businesses and houses, screaming at the top of her lungs, thereby attracting attention to herself. She ran through all of the options in her head. In the end, she knew there was only one that she could pursue. She wanted a life free of them; she wanted it to be over and final. They couldn't keep coming after her forever; not in this country, and not at such great risk. For this man to have tracked her down and found her, some chips must have been cashed in, some favors called. This was their one, big shot to get her. If she could survive it, if she could kill this man before he killed her, she felt like the odds were good that that would be the end of it. Therefore, she had to confront him.

And so she turned to face him, and they stared at each other in the silence. She was going to approach him—to walk right up to him. She would grab the knife from her purse as she neared and do her worst before he got close enough to reach her. Five to seven feet, that's all she needed. Get within that distance and her knife would do the rest. She was an expert at it, lethal. But just before she was about to take a step, she saw him move toward her. *He* was taking the initiative. Once again she called upon all of her exhaustive training; she had encountered this scenario over and over again during her instructions; she could still recall the instructor's words pounded into her brain. She prepared herself, planting her feet and positioning her body. The man kept slowly walking toward her. He was about twelve feet away. She grabbed the knife by the blade and held it up to throw it. Just a few more feet and he would be within striking distance. Why didn't he stop? He must have seen the knife she was wielding, but he kept coming. It was no matter, she thought to herself, it was his death. She flexed her arm and was about to throw.

Before her arm could move, however, there was a slight "thwirp" sound and she felt a sharp sting in her thigh. It startled her, and there was an intense pain that followed.

It was Mitslov. He had appeared from around the building where he stood and shot her with a rubber bullet from a silenced handgun. She glanced over to where he stood and saw him.

There were two of them, she thought to herself in an instant, two! She turned back to the man on the street coming at her, who had just then started to run. She had to deal with him first; it was the only choice. Then she felt another sting against her body—shot again. The rubber bullet, the velocity of which was slightly reduced from the silencer, was not lethal, but it inflicted great pain. Treshenko was within striking distance; as fast as she could she threw the knife, but she was off. She had lost her stance and her concentration, and therefore her aim. Treshenko lunged and tackled her to the ground. Then he held her down. Mitslov ran over to help. She tried to struggle, but the two men were too powerful. Mitslov jammed a needle into her thigh and injected a chemical into it; he wasn't going to take any chances. He tossed the syringe onto the ground, and Treshenko hurriedly picked it up and ran over to the car parked in the alley.

Mitslov held Davis pinned to the ground with a hand over her mouth so she couldn't make a sound, thereby giving the chemical time to course through her body and have its effect. Treshenko pulled the car to the curb next to them, shielding them from view. Davis tried to bite Mitslov's hand, but he pressed his other arm against her neck and choked her against the ground. She was helpless. There wasn't enough training in the world that would enable her to get this powerful man off of her. Soon her brain began to feel like it was freezing; there was an intense rush, and she became dizzy. He relaxed the pressure after a few moments when she stopped resisting, and after several minutes, the drug rendered her unconscious. He threw her into the car and then looked around to make sure no one was around to see them. Before he got into the car, he went and retrieved her knife lying on the ground several feet away.

30

Soul Difference

> Kojiro had put his confidence in the sword of
> strength and skill. Musashi trusted in the sword
> of the spirit. That was the only difference
> between them.
>
> *Musashi*, Eiji Yoshikawa

WHEN DAVIS AWOKE, SHE FOUND HERSELF IN AN OLD, dingy factory. The windows had steel cages over them, and they were located high up on the walls. Industrial lighting hung from the high ceiling, and rusted metal chains dangled from various points. The building had several such rooms, and she was situated in the one at the rear of the building. Although there was nothing visible to confirm it, Davis had the feeling that the building was located somewhere along the Potomac—some unused or abandoned building along its bank. It was dark inside with no power for the overhead lights. But a brilliant full moon shone through the high windows whenever it occasionally appeared from behind the clouds. In addition, a large thick candle burned as it rested on the floor about ten feet from Davis.

Her hands were tied behind her back and she was lying on the floor against a brick wall. The ground was dirty; there were oil stains all over it. Trash littered the dark, gloomy area.

Mitslov sat on a chair that was turned backwards, his hands resting on the chair's back; he was situated directly in front of Davis, no farther than ten feet away. He watched her with an impassive look on his face, his blond hair as disheveled as ever.

She didn't recognize him.

She continued to watch, and her eyes slowly gained focus. Anne Davis forced herself upright and sat against the wall.

She was in stark contrast to the grunge all around her. Her physical beauty and overall way of dressing set her apart even from the man who sat in front of her: he looked to be of a completely different social class in comparison. Almost as if he realized this, his eyes squinted, a slight look of resentment appeared on his face.

"Who are you?" she said in Russian with a firm tone.

He stared at her without responding. It was the same question he would always get. When he didn't say anything, she took the opportunity to take further stock of her surroundings. A large tool bench abutted one of the walls, empty metal shelving was scattered about, and several long, industrial tables stretched across the room.

"There is no one here. Your screams would not be heard."

He spoke Russian. It was confirmed: FSB.

She tried to stand up, but the drug had not completely worn off, and she slumped back down.

Mitslov rose and removed the light coat he wore. His movements were slow and methodical; he watched her the whole time. The Makarov-style sidearm that fired the rubber bullets was holstered around his shoulder and under his arm. No doubt it was now loaded with real bullets. He saw how her eyes went straight to it, and it gave him pleasure. He walked across the room toward one of the old metal tables; his hard-soled shoes clapped against the cement floor, sounds of grit being crushed under his feet. After carefully laying his jacket on the table near where another candle burned, he un-holstered his gun, the silencer still attached to it. As he caressed the barrel he said, "This is for later, when we are finished." He re-holstered the gun, removed the leather holster from the side of his chest, and laid it onto the table, watching her the whole time. Then he pointed to the gun, snickered, and said "You will never get close to this."

He reached into a small leather bag and grabbed a syringe. After a pause, he walked back toward her. He stood over her for a moment. She was weak, groggy, and barely able to hold her head up to look at him. "You don't mind a little Sodium Pentothal, do you?" he said. Then he bent down and injected the needle into her arm, grabbed her under both arms, and dragged her onto the chair. After taking a step back to look at her, slumped in the chair as she was, he changed his mind: it was too early to let her sit. So he picked her back up. She couldn't support herself and fell over his shoulder. She was confused as to what was going on and felt the first rush from the Sodium Pentothal. All of a sudden, she was violently thrown against the wall like a sack of potatoes. With her hands tied behind her back she couldn't brace herself, and her head slammed against the brick wall. She fell to the ground.

"Easy!" a voice could be heard saying. "We need to get information out of her first."

It was a different voice. Treshenko's. He stood in the distance.

"Quiet!" Mitslov responded.

Davis had not noticed Treshenko before, and in her dazed state she couldn't locate him. She was bewildered. She began to call upon her training, mentally focusing, trying to stave off the effects of the Sodium Pentothal. Keep your mind focused on something, she was taught—stories, songs, memories—something to minimize the effects of the drug.

She could feel herself being picked up again and put back onto the chair. Mitslov grabbed a clump of her hair, pulled her head back, and stooped down to come face-to-face with her. He sniffed her neck, smelling her sweet perfume, and the sensation transfixed him; he took another deep breath. A look of lust appeared on his face. Being in control of a woman of such beauty and smelling so sensuously overcame him.

He caressed the side of her face. He moved closer still and rubbed his nose against the soft skin of her neck. Then he began to fondle her breasts over her shirt.

"Mitslov, what are you doing?" Treshenko said incredulously.

"Shut up!" he turned and yelled. "No names, damn it. Get out of here. Go stand guard. OUT!" Mitslov pointed to the door with a furious look on his face.

Treshenko remained where he was, startled. The two stared at each other. Finally, Treshenko relented. Mitslov waited until he was gone.

"Why...why are you doing this?" she whispered, her head still held back by the hair.

Mitslov continued to fondle her. His breathing became heavy; she could hear it; he panted through his nostrils as he feverishly labored over her. He pressed his cheek against hers.

"Why do they even care? I don't know anything," Davis pleaded. She spoke softly as he groped her. "Please, let me be. I don't know anything."

She started to cry. Focus, she reminded herself. What could she think of? Jazz songs...jazz artists...*John Coltrane...Dizzy Gillespie...*

Mitslov stopped and looked into her eyes. His instincts told him to ignore her pleadings, but she was beautiful. She beguiled him, and he was feverishly aroused. It was the first time he was so close to her, and he was unprepared for the effect she had on him. Of course he had seen pictures of her, and he'd been trailing her for a while. But none of it prepared him for how he felt now, being so close to her, and having her within his power. Her beauty was truly unparalleled when viewed from so close. Besides, he thought to himself, he had a lot of time invested in her—too much time—tracking, hunting, lying in wait. His cover was at risk because of her. Therefore, he didn't want to rush the process; her death would come soon enough. He earned the right to savor the moment. Just this once he would enjoy a verbal interaction with her, respond to her appeal. He became intrigued with the prospect of having a conversation with her.

"You caused a lot of damage when you ran away. Three agents dead in Russia, two by the blade of your knife. You used your training well, by the way. Only, you shouldn't have used it against us." With a querying look on his face he said, "Where *is* that knife?"

He walked over to the table again, grabbed her purse, and rummaged through it. He pulled out the large knife. "Ah, here it is. You're favorite toy." He went back to her and touched her cheek with the side of the blade; she felt the cold metal against her skin. For some reason he didn't like the image of the knife against her face, so he flung it away, causing it to scuttle across the floor.

"I was...just trying to save my father." She felt lightheaded. Focus.

"Yes, and that's when you killed Raskalnikov, a more senior agent. A shot to the head, I understand."

She remained silent, unsure of what to say.

"But your damage extended far beyond just the killing of those three men. You see, you wounded the spirit of an organization— of certain individuals *within* the organization. One in particular. A powerful man. A man who had intentions for you. Heh, heh...looking at you now, I can see why. I'm sure it would be easy to become obsessed with a woman like you."

Davis' mind raced. What was he talking about? Who was he referring to? But then she told herself that maybe she shouldn't try to think about it. Maybe she should stay focused on the jazz...*Miles Davis*...*Cannonball Adderley*—who else could she think of?

Mitslov watched her; she looked lost. He knew she was fighting it.

Try as she might, the drug kept working against her; her mind went back to what he said: *a man who had intentions for you*. It was someone from the training compound, she concluded. Her thoughts returned to those two years of her life that she so desperately wanted to forget. The man who oversaw her training was in his early fifties. Dark hair with graying temples, he had a dignified look about him, like he was part of the upper class of Moscow. But he wasn't; he was a hardened killer, an instructor, there to train her and others like her. It was him, she realized. He had become infatuated with her, maybe even had plans for her. His ego must have been bruised beyond measure. She suddenly looked up into Mitslov's eyes with the realization.

"Yes, you remember, eh? Ha, ha. You shouldn't anger a man like that. He has friends in powerful places, I can assure you. And of course you must understand," he continued, the grin disappearing from his face, "a lot of time was invested in you, a lot of training and resources. You returned the favor by tricking people, betraying them. Russia put its confidence in you—and you stabbed it in the back."

"I didn't want it. Any of it. I was forced."

"It's not so smart to spurn the man you did, the *way* you did. A man like that becomes bitter, lets his dick think for him. He would even disobey orders, and protocol, just to seek his revenge."

Mitslov paced, slowly walking around her in the chair like a lion circling its prey before devouring it. He walked up close to her again, put his hand on her shoulder, and leaned down to look deeply into her eyes.

"But in this case, there is no need to disobey orders..." He began to fondle her again. "Mm...no need to break protocol." He let her hair run through his fingers and smelled it. She tried to turn away, but he grabbed her chin and turned her toward him. He pulled her thighs apart and got down on his knees between them. She was wearing a skirt with no stockings. He put his hand on the calf of her leg and caressed her soft skin. His hand slowly traced the outline of her leg, up to the inside of her thigh, and he squeezed her flesh. She tried to press her knees together, but he forced them apart.

"You embarrassed people—important people." His voice was distracted now, less anger was in it. His focus was on her body, and lust began to overtake him. His voice took on an almost soothing tone, clinical, as if he were a doctor examining his patient. He made perverse sounds under his breath as he talked and fondled her. "A lesson must be set for your actions. It must be demonstrated that your brazen flight from our country would never be tolerated. People must know what would happen— other people in our organization who are weak, like you, and have their doubts. People who refuse to serve, and to do their duty."

"You do this on American soil...it is a grave mistake!" she suddenly exclaimed. With all of her ability she was forcing herself to stay alert. "Your FSB will be sorry for such an escalation."

Her admonition momentarily snapped him out of his lustful reverie. He looked up at her, but seeing again the beauty in her face, and the glassy, drugged look in her eyes, he ignored her comment and continued to fondle her. His head moved down between her legs, and his nose pressed into her panties. Then, as if to heighten his enjoyment, he looked up into her eyes and held her gaze. "And of course," he said, "there's the issue of what you took. Of course we must have that back. *That* is your greatest sin."

A sense of dismay and desperation came over her. She was losing it; she couldn't think of jazz anymore. This monster was having his way with her body. She resisted with the last ounce of her strength: "I don't know what you're talking about. There must be some mistake."

"I'm sure," he said with a laugh as he returned his attention to between her legs.

She knew it was hopeless; it was a miracle she lasted as long as she did; any normal person would have already succumbed to the full power of the drug. She had gone through the struggle once before—the struggle to shield her thoughts and memories from the intense probing of the CIA. She couldn't do it again. In her stupor she looked around the room at potential possibilities, trying to figure out what she could do. Her hands were tied behind her back, and nothing, no weapon, was within reach. She looked down at the man kneeling in front of her, his hulking frame, and knew that he was too large and too powerful to resist. A head butt would've been useless; the action would've knocked her out cold.

What if she raised her legs and tried to get him into a scissors hold? Again, hopeless. She was at a loss, but she had to do something. She knew she would end up talking, and then…perhaps rape, death. Her only hope at that point was to avoid getting raped. If she could do that, then she felt like, in some small way, it would have honored the man she loved.

She spread her legs even farther apart and raised them into the air. Mitslov deluded himself into thinking that she was enjoying herself. He made another purring sound and helped hold her legs in the air as his face remained buried in her panties.

With all the strength she could muster, she closed her legs around his head and squeezed them tight, grunting loudly. That was the first part.

Now came the insults, the blows to his ego. She had to egg him on.

"You filthy beast, I want no part of you. You are ugly, just like the men I killed!" She tilted her hips sideways, forcing his head to the side while remaining between her legs, until finally she fell out of her chair and onto the ground. She held her vice-like grip around him, and her dress rose above her hips so that the top of his blond hair was visible. She spit on it, making sure the sound was loud enough for him to hear her doing it. "I'm glad I ran away from you all; you are pigs, not men. Ugly, stinking pigs."

Mitslov used his hands to separate her legs from around his head and then stepped away, standing over her as she lay helpless on the ground. It was a far cry from the calm, usually blank expression that would be on his face just before a killing. The insults she had lodged against him infuriated him, and he became deranged.

He beat her. He inflicted great harm to her body, breaking her. She writhed in pain, and still he continued. It was intense, clinical, and she was powerless.

She was on the verge of blacking out. She could barely see so badly beaten was her face; everything was a blur. She didn't even know where she was anymore. There was no beauty to her now; her bloodied, swollen face resembled nothing that Angstrom would have recognized if he saw her.

Mitslov was done. She was close to death. "Where is it?" he said. He kneeled down beside her, grabbed her by the hair, and pulled her head back. "If you want to live, tell me where it is. You know what I want."

She struggled, her neck straining because of how far back he pulled her head. She mustered what little energy she had and tried to speak. It was a wonder that she could formulate any manner of thought because of the severity of her injuries. She willed herself and weakly said, "To...hell...with...all of you."

That was it. Mitslov could do no more. He was convinced she wouldn't talk. It was time for the ceremonial bullet to the head.

He was just about to walk over to retrieve his Makarov when a loud sound came from behind him. He turned to look, and a metal door had slammed open: a figure stood in the doorway, in the darkness of shadow—the silhouette of a man.

Mitslov was startled. "Who is it?" He broke protocol in the confusion and called out, "Treshenko, is that you?"

There was no answer. Only silence. A stillness.

Mitslov struggled to focus, but he could only see the trace of a man. It wasn't his partner; he was sure of that. But Treshenko was supposed to be standing guard just outside of the large room. Where was he?

He watched the figure, and still there was no change.

It was then that the moon outside moved from behind the clouds, and light shone through the windows from high above. It was just enough to illuminate a portion of the man's left arm: blood dripped from the clenched fist held at his side.

It was an ominous sight, unsettling. Mitslov understood what it meant. Treshenko was gone. How could that be? Treshenko was strong, a trained killer, lethal. There were no sounds of a struggle.

"What are you doing here? What do you want?"

No answer.

"I suggest you leave, my friend. I'm a lot stronger than the man you met outside."

Still nothing. The figure in the doorway stood motionless, his hands remaining clenched at his sides.

Mitslov's mind raced, and he quickly assessed the situation. There was about twenty-five feet between him and the other man. The shadow in which the man stood made it difficult for Mitslov to clearly make him out. What about the Makarov? He could make a run for it. But it was too far, and he didn't know whether the other man had his *own* gun.

"Who are you?" he finally said.

So many times Mitslov heard those words from his own prey. Now it was him asking the question. The irony bothered him.

Suddenly there was a movement, a feeble sound from behind Mitslov: "John…John…is that you? Please…help me." Davis struggled to see, to remain conscious so she could see his face.

Mitslov heard this but did not turn to look at her. He held his position and remained focused.

The other man took one step forward, out of the shadow. It was not John Angstrom.

It was a face she didn't recognize. Or was her sight so distorted, her vision so blurred that she couldn't see clearly, recognize the man she loved? Was it him or not? As she lay on the ground she became confused and started to cry. It was all too much for her, both physically and emotionally, and so, she submitted to the darkness.

Mitslov could now clearly see the man and took survey of him: his frame was large, his stature imposing. It surpassed his own. A look of powerful concentration exuded from the man's visage. There were two large bruises on his face, and blood.

Treshenko had connected with some blows before he died, Mitslov thought to himself. A slight grin came to his face. He told himself that he was not going to be intimidated. He was the one to intimidate—to strike fear in his victims.

"Get the fuck out of here," he said.

The man didn't move. He was prepared for what would happen next, his own assessment of the situation already complete. He had worked it out in his mind and knew what was to be done. It was like a game of chess, the moves already planned, the outcome already determined: all that was left was for the moves to be made.

"I'll ask you one more time, you shit-bag: Who are you?"

And then, finally, a response. Only one word, a name.

"Magdos."

This disarmed Mitslov. He didn't actually expect the man to answer. There was a confidence in the man's voice, in the one word spoken. The fact that the man gave his name unnerved Mitslov. He already figured the man must have been some type of agent—CIA or something. Yet the man made no attempt to disguise his identity—no attempt to remain anonymous. It was a signal—a message meant to convey the notion that Mitslov was going to die, so it didn't matter what he knew.

Then Magdos did something else that disarmed Mitslov: he began to walk straight toward him. It was a steady walk, no hesitation, no attempt to take position for battle.

Mitslov quickly prepared. The fool could try anything he wanted, he thought. The closer he got the better. He readied himself to fight, taking an aggressive stance. As soon as he knocked the man down, Mitslov told himself, he'd make a run for the gun—no use taking any chances at that point. His adversary looked formidable.

When Mitslov threw his punch, it was precise and powerful, all of his training and technique summoned and consummated in that single, quick strike.

But it wasn't enough; it wasn't even close. Magdos was too fast and his method too unorthodox, unlike anything Mitslov had ever encountered before—a true soul's force countering the soulless. At the precise moment Mitslov threw his punch, Magdos let out a loud, piercing scream. It was a terrifying sound, distorted, inhuman, that went straight to Mitslov's brain, and from there to the very nerves in the arm that threw the punch, thereby affecting it.

There was an ever-so-slight quick slant sideways, while in the same motion, both of Magdos' forearms caught Mitslov's arm in mid-air, parrying it sideways. The two forearms continued their fluid movement, taking Mitslov's arm in a direction it was not intended to bend, and the arm snapped at the elbow almost instantly, like a twig.

Mitslov shrieked in pain, falling to his knees. Magdos moved fast, and Mitslov's face became pinned to the ground—a knee clamped down on his neck, a knuckle jammed into his temple, pressing upon it. Mitslov thought it was going to penetrate his skull. Veins in his forehead protruded from the physical stress inflicted on him.

Magdos looked over and saw Davis lying helpless on the ground, disfigured by her beating. He was sorry for her; sorry he couldn't get to her faster. Trailing the two men without being seen was difficult enough, requiring him to stay a good distance back. Then he had to get into his car as fast as he could and follow them, remaining far enough behind so that he wouldn't be noticed. Fortunately he knew in advance where they were going from having followed them before and seeing the warehouse they had set up for this. Getting past Treshenko, however, took even more time.

Seeing her condition just then, with her face all swollen and bleeding, beaten to a pulp, affected him, incensed him. His teeth clenched tightly as his face moved only inches away from Mitslov's. When Magdos spoke, his voice sounded eerie and disturbing, like controlled rage incarnate: "Let's see how much *you* can tolerate."

This time it was Mitslov's turn to receive the pain. The screams were loud, but it was as Mitslov said: there was no one around to hear them. There were only his piercing shrieks of pain echoing throughout the dark emptiness of the cavernous room.

There would be nothing about this turn of events in the news; Mitslov and Treshenko would disappear forever, never to be heard from again. There'd be no inquiry from Russia—nothing as to the whereabouts of two missing men. In fact, if it were ever pressed on the issue, Russia would deny any knowledge of the men named Mitslov and Treshenko.

As for Mitslov, he may have gotten a name or two out of Spence and Bensley, but that was nothing compared to the information the CIA got out of him during their "interrogations."

31

In Case of War

Sunday, July 19

Six DAYS AFTER ØRSTED AND FRËGE DETONATED in the United States, which was five days after the eruption in Eastern Europe, the K-Com page went out at around 9:45 A.M. A meeting was set for 2 P.M. Everyone paged attended. VENOMA was packed.

Q-Directorate stood in silence at the podium, waiting for everyone to get settled. When the room was quiet he said, "Gentlemen, we've found Ørsted, gained an understanding of its basic operation, and cracked Frëge."

He waited for a few seconds, letting the magnitude of what he said sink in.

"We know how Ørsted propagates, how it replicates, and how it hides itself."

Not a stir in the room; everyone was on the edge of his seat, hanging on every word Q-Directorate said. The words seemed mysterious to them. Q-Directorate took a moment to look into the audience. He got the impression that everyone was shell-shocked, unable to respond. Even Corver said nothing. Q-Directorate's confident and deliberate demeanor was in stark contrast to the mayhem that was occurring outside, all over the country, all over Eastern Europe. His message was like an oasis in the desert, water for thirst. They waited for more, eager to hear everything. Hopefully they comprehended what he had just said. Whether or not they did, he decided to launch into the details.

"Let me talk about Ørsted first. As we all know by now, it's incredibly complex and multi-layered. In actuality, we should think of Ørsted as not just a single piece of malicious software, but rather, as a whole malicious system, multifaceted, with many different components and modules, each serving its own special purpose, each invoked at a specific point in time or under a predetermined set of conditions. It's truly remarkable; only an organized army of cyber experts could have devised such a true cyber weapon.

"I'm going to try to break this down into very high level concepts so that you'll understand what's going on and what we're dealing with. In order to do that, I'm going to discuss the operation of Ørsted in the context of a single point of reference: the infection of a normal, everyday personal computer. Keep in mind, this is only one example of how the malware system works. There are many different aspects to it, many modes of operation that we are only just beginning to understand. The good news is that it's coming together very quickly after our initial breakthroughs.

"To put it succinctly, Ørsted attacks the PC at its most basic functional level: the BIOS on the motherboard."

"You mean like the Michelangelo malware?" came the sudden interruption from someone at the back of the auditorium.

"It's much more sophisticated than that, Jim," Q-Directorate quickly replied, surprised at the question.

Just then, Lieutenant General Harold Manmoth stood up from his seat in the front row and faced the audience. "Folks, we're at a very critical point here, and Q-Directorate has a lot of complicated information to present to us. Let's let him have the floor for a while so he can make it through his presentation. There'll be time enough for questions after that."

He took his seat and nodded for Q-Directorate to continue.

"Thank you. As I was about to say, for a PC, Ørsted starts by actually replacing the BIOS. It substitutes a malicious version for the valid one. To accomplish this, Ørsted utilizes four malicious sub-modules that we've named as follows:

1. *rootkit,*
2. *fpxe,*
3. *remote BIOS,* and
4. *bootkit.*

"As you'll see, you can think of the BIOS replacement as a sort of virtual flash, first because it's done without ever having physical possession of the computer, and second because the process involves booting the computer from a remotely located malicious BIOS stored on a Command and Control (C&C) server.

"This virtual flash occurs as follows. First, Ørsted infects the PC by installing *rootkit.* This is a stealth software module that enables a remote hacker to have admin privileges on the computer. Unfortunately, we've been learning that this was done remotely through a couple of new zero-day vulnerabilities which we're now having fixed. Keep in mind that the remote hacker doesn't have to be human; it can be an automated, remote hacking system.

"After this, the remote hacker installs the *fpxe* module onto a PC card of the computer. In essence, *fpxe* is a malicious bootloader, and upon a subsequent re-boot it causes PCs with a Preboot Execution Environment to boot from the malicious *remote BIOS* off of a C&C server rather than its own valid BIOS.

"I should add as a side note that once Ørsted caused the systems subject to the June 6th pre-attacks to restore themselves, the link to the malicious *remote BIOS* was severed, thereby leaving no trace of it in the computer; all that remained was a portion of *fpxe* in the PC card, and because scanning the firmware of the PC cards was not part of the standard malware scanning process, that's one of the reasons why we didn't initially find anything. Moreover, in some cases, especially at DFW, *fpxe* wasn't even installed on the PC: it was dynamically linked to a remote library; upon the system restore, that link was severed, again hiding the existence of *fpxe*."

Q-Directorate looked into the audience to gauge reaction; no one said anything. He coughed a little out of nervousness before resuming.

"Anyway, for the full-fledged attacks that started last Monday, in most cases *fpxe* was permanently flashed onto the PC card's firmware. Importantly, the peripheral device where this was done was the PC's network card."

"Hold on a second," Adlai Corver interrupted, "I have a question."

"Yes, what is it?" Q-Directorate was glad to receive a question; he was fearful that his presentation was going to be so overly-technical that he would lose some of the people in the audience. He decided in advance that he was going to take that risk rather than the alternative of erring on the side of not providing enough information. Corver's question signaled to him that at least some high-level people were engaged with what he said, at least up until that point.

"If the BIOS wasn't permanently replaced," said Corver, "and PC card firmware isn't normally scanned, how *did* you find this...this *fpxe*?"

"Ah, it was a painstaking process. After we knew we had trapped the software in a completely infectious state through the use of honeypots, we took apart the computer and examined all of the components, including the network card. Knowing the operating environment made it possible to disassemble the firmware, and then we compared it to virgin code we got from the PC card's manufacturer. It was then that we found the entirety of the *fpxe* malicious code."

Paul J. Bartusiak

netCard_PO_VIS_I2ML2bin Z:\Orsted_netcard\div2\revese	Offset	0	1	2	3	4	5	6	7	8	9	
	00000000	A7	E0	0F	00	1F	F0	00	98	9F	14	........................0......
	00000010	22	32	AA	87	07	93	37	00	1C	00	...y....................
File size: 512KB	00000020	E2	SA	00	00	00	00	FF	F0	E0	00	....
0.51152 Megabytes	00000030	34	00	1C	FA	DF	6B	AA	FB	34	10	....
	00000040	97	95	33	00	14	8F	E8	14	83	0A	.....0....c.
File name: fpxe_sub	00000050	F0	4F	EE	34	00	0B	A0	94	F7	00	..#...@@....|.|.........
	00000060	DD	10	21	34	00	22	22	2F	44	00	◻αε◻◻εε◻◻э◻......◻◻◻
Default Config	00000070	40	10	FF	04	4A	00	EF	E4	40	00	β◻.2..ε.τ◻ψ◻.B◻B◻◻α◻
Attribute: 14	00000080	80	00	A0	43	83	3A	C5	A0	0A	00	...Pρτ◻τω◻◻...oι[◻......
code set: 3	00000090	0F	83	0E	23	E0	E6	E1	00	3F	00	...i...7....4G......z...dew.
	00000100	BF	FA	F7	08	E1	38	00	00	26	0F	..#..βμμ◻........Aδδ...◻.
Mode Text	00000110	EF	00	18	00	1C	08	8F	34	00	5A	6•◻κκκξ◻◻..............
Character set: ANSI-ASCII	00000120	3A	EE	10	22	09	19	1A	04	0F	0C	........EE....xc.1...G.....
Offsets: hexadecimal	00000130	6B	1F	0A	00	00	E0	8F	F0	FA	0A	....#....ψψ....|.|..........
	00000140	E6	00	00	00	17	18	E1	83	83	83	##...$$...vμ#.....................
Bytes per page: null	00000150	80	34	00	00	18	20	C5	0A	E0	E1	.............υ..о◻.λλ..........

Depiction of a small portion of the initial code dump of a network card's firmware containing the *fpxe* malware. The *fpxe* module may be embedded into the firmware or alternatively dynamically linked to a remote library (severing the link would essentially remove any substantive trace of the *fpxe* malware itself). The *fpxe* module causes the PC to boot from the *remote BIOS* malware on a C&C server instead of the PC's own BIOS.

Declassified from Operation Cyberknife

Corver was satisfied with the answer so Q-Directorate continued.

"As I was saying, with *fpxe* installed on the network card, and after a subsequent re-boot of the computer, *fpxe* causes the PC to boot off of the *remote BIOS* from a C&C server, thereby bypassing the valid BIOS of the computer. With a fast internet connection, the resulting temporary slowdown is barely noticeable to the average user. Moreover, for the attacks that started last Monday, *fpxe* contained an additional instruction set that caused the CPU to permanently replace the BIOS with the malicious *remote BIOS* after yet another subsequent reboot. At that point, the actual BIOS on the PC is permanently replaced with the corrupted one."

"The process doesn't stop there, however. The final part is the loading of the *bootkit* module. This module executes right before the computer's operating system does, again making it undetectable by standard security software. Ørsted uses *fpxe* to download *bootkit* from a C&C server and load it into RAM when the computer boots. It goes without saying that this happens—in fact, the whole process occurs—when no type of DoS attack is

382

taking place; otherwise it would be impossible to connect to the C&C server.

"Now, *bootkit* causes a modification of the kernel of the operating system. Once that's done, Ørsted causes the *bootkit* to be wiped from RAM. A virus scan of the RAM won't detect the malicious *bootkit*, because it's gone! Same for the kernel mod. You can see why we were postulating that Ørsted kept disaggregating and reconstituting itself.

"After this, there's corruption of both the BIOS and the kernel of the operating system; the PC is at the complete mercy of the hackers, or more precisely, the Frëge payload that would follow."

Q-Directorate paused to take a drink from the bottled water that sat on the podium. He also wanted to provide some time for everyone to reflect upon what he had just explained.

"Admittedly, this is a lot to comprehend all at once. I'm going to stop for a moment and take some questions, if there are any."

Someone from the back of the room, one of the coding experts, asked a question: "Q-Directorate, I don't understand how the pxe stack of a PC's network card can become corrupted. I mean, the firmware for PCI network cards is very vendor specific; a generic program would be ineffective. Furthermore, most of the network cards nowadays have a physical security switch that needs to be moved in order to effectuate a re-flash."

"Excellent points," responded Q-Directorate. "The vendor-specific issue is handled by the C&C server. The *fpxe* module causes the Organizationally Unique Identifier (OUI) of the target network card to be sent to the C&C, making it possible to determine the make and model of the card at issue. The appropriate *fpxe* firmware is then utilized. As for the part about the physical switch, the *rootkit* module has a PCI extension embedded within it that takes precedence over the physical switch, thereby circumventing it. In fact, this same PCI extension is used to circumvent BIOSs that require an actual digital signature.

"I'd also like to add that Ørsted is so sophisticated that the user is totally unaware of what's happening during this whole process.

This is because *remote BIOS* even has code to duplicate normal BIOS load screens, making it appear to the user like everything is functioning as it should while the PC is booting.

"What's even more alarming is that Ørsted can copy the malicious *fpxe* from a PC's network card onto the firmware of the other peripheral devices for redundancy. So even if someone tried to re-flash the original BIOS to fix the PC, *fpxe* stored on the network card or some other peripheral device would cause the malicious *remote BIOS* to be installed all over again."

Q-Directorate paused again to see if there were any questions; there were none. He looked down from his position on the stage at the faces of the people in the front row. As far as he could tell, it still looked like he hadn't lost them. Just a little more, he wished he could say, hold on a little bit more; I'm almost through with the main points, the most important information.

"Now, the problem with all of this," he continued, "and without getting into even more technical detail, is that the only way to get rid of Ørsted on the PC is to manually re-flash every peripheral device that has firmware—a herculean task for sure."

Q-Directorate paused to take another drink of water.

"Hold on a minute," Corver interrupted while slightly raising his hand, "this is excellent work, and your explanation is very thoughtful and clear. I appreciate that. However, that last part is quite disturbing. You basically just indicated that a solution to Ørsted isn't feasible. Am I missing something?"

"Mm, thank you for the question," said Q-Directorate as he screwed the top back onto the bottled water. "I have to apologize, because I just misspoke. Or at least, I wasn't precise enough in what I just said. Manually re-flashing everything *isn't* feasible. We have, however, discovered a better solution."

"I'm glad to hear it," Corver said. "What is it?"

There was nervous laughter in the room.

"We've found a way to scan the firmware of infected systems and detect the outer boundaries of Ørsted, or more precisely, the boundaries of the *rootkit, fpxe,* and *bootkit* modules."

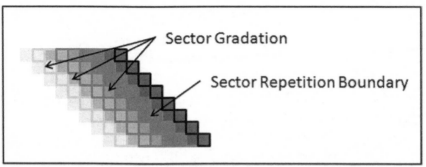

DeGroot Filter analysis of compiled code yields identification of Sector Repetition Boundary bordering malware.

Declassified from Operation Cyberknife

"What you're now seeing is a graphic representation of the boundary of a sample firmware code set. Mind you, we're looking at machine language of compiled code. Viewing it, figuratively speaking, through a new type of lens developed over the last forty-eight hours—what we've come to call a DeGroot Filter after the coder who recognized the key point from the analysis Big Machine spit out—we can see what we call a "Sector Repetition Boundary" in the binary. In plain words, this shouldn't be. Wherever this repetition exists, it means there's an infection in the firmware. The repetition boundary delineates the first instance of the Ørsted module. The DeGroot Filter keeps scanning until it sees this overlap again at another point in the binary; that delineates the other boundary. It's not really binary of the firmware, it's just...well, never mind that part.

"To remove it, it's nothing more than marking the boundaries and deleting the corrupted portions, and then, poof, Ørsted is gone!"

Silence. A room full of people with serious expressions on their faces, numb.

"Q-Directorate, maybe using the word 'poof' in the context of everything that's happening is a bit...ill advised," Manmoth said.

"It's okay, Harry," said Freedman. "The man's under a lot of pressure, hasn't had a lot of sleep. That's fairly obvious from just looking at him up on the stage. Go ahead, Q-Directorate, continue."

"Uh...thanks...I guess."

Slight laughter in the room.

"Well, anyway, Ørsted is removed from the infected system."

Q-Directorate was excited to have just revealed all that he did and naively thought others in the room would feel the same. He quickly realized that no one was interested in the historic aspect of what was being presented: that a new type of cyber weapon more powerful than anything ever seen before had been launched against the country, and that the secrets behind it had already been unlocked, a solution to a major part of it already found. It was all too new for them, the wounds still too fresh. He plowed through his presentation, moving faster so he could get to the remaining salient parts.

"Similar to the hierarchical structure of Ørsted with its systematic invocation of modules, the DeGroot filter would need to be implemented in a similar fashion. The good news is that as complicated as the DeGroot process is, it's all done autonomously, just like, uh, the infection itself. There's no manual intervention required once it's loaded during a boot sequence. Of course, we can't do that for the BIOS itself. That's going to have to be done manually, thereby causing a little more aggravation. The two procedures have to be done in parallel, with a handshaking that continually occurs between the BIOS re-flash and the DeGroot process. Special restore points also have to be created so all the work isn't lost in the event the process is unintentionally interrupted. Anyway, from start to finish the process should take around four to five hours for the average PC."

"Q-Directorate, I have a question." It was DHS Director Mike Holdman. "Am I to understand that this...that what you just described, the whole thing, is what Ørsted is? What I mean to say is, all of the malicious attacks that are occurring out there," he waved his hand, "what you just described is it?"

"Um, no Mike, it isn't," responded Q-Directorate. "That's an excellent segue, though. What I just described is one facet of the whole Ørsted system. Remember, it was a description of Ørsted and its operation in the narrow context of a normal PC. Variants of this are used for different computer systems, such as workstations, servers, switches, routers...you name it. For example, a proprietary airport computer system would need specialized versions or extensions. Other systems, those that operate with completely different computer architectures such as those controlled by PLAs, microcontrollers, etc., won't involve nearly as complex of a process for infection; a more direct approach was used to attack those, all via Frëge. There's also the whole series of network attacks, the "carpet bombing" I referred to before and that I'm not going to get into right now. It is, however, a whole other topic deserving of a separate briefing. We'll do that later."

Q-Directorate looked into the front row, and Manmoth indicated his agreement.

"What I *would* like to talk about, however, before I finally get to Frëge, is another way in which Ørsted proliferates. It's a very alarming development."

Q-Directorate was on a roll. He barely paused to take a breath.

"First of all, just like a nuclear explosion, Ørsted is a chain reaction. By this I mean that as soon as a computer becomes infected, it gets the Frëge payload dropped onto it. That involves a specific instruction set, part of which comprises a way to cause Ørsted to spread through botnet activity—the infected computer acts like a zombie and becomes part of the botnet. Ørsted then spreads to other computer systems in a controlled, stealthy fashion, thereby avoiding self-DDoS. Another part of that instruction set, however, involves a much more sinister way of spreading; it significantly moves the needle of what we consider state of the art..."

"Hold on, wait a minute," Corver interrupted, holding up the palm of his hand, his voice elevated. The volume of his voice jarred everyone in the room. He had been thinking about something Q-Directorate had said earlier, still trying to process it.

"Yes, what is it?"

"You said Ørsted is removed from the infected system."

Q-Directorate tilted his head and looked confused.

"You know, before, when you were talking about the removal of all of the infected firmware on a PC."

"Oh, yes…back to that…right. You mean when I said we can completely eradicate Ørsted from a PC."

"Correct. And it just occurred to me, what prevents it from becoming infected again?"

"Ah, excellent question. I actually skipped some slides without covering this, so I'm glad you asked. We've developed a way to more securely lock down the boot process. This involved the development of a new boot security driver that's integral to the boot sequence. It's the first driver initialized when the computer boots up and it prevents any unauthorized or modified drivers from initializing during the boot sequence. A driver must be pre-certified and then electronically signed before the boot security driver will recognize it during startup. Needless to say, the electronic signature will be closely guarded, and vendors will need to be screened and validated before they get access to it. In essence, we've re-designed the BIOS and replaced it with something newer and more secure: the Unified Extensible Firmware Interface, or UEFI. The encryption and authentication embedded in it is state of the art and will make computer systems orders of magnitude more secure. And for systems which cannot operate in accordance with our updated version of the UEFI, more pedestrian measures will have to be relied upon. I can briefly discuss that now if you want. In fact, I was going to start this whole presentation with a summary of the various ways a system could be infected, sort of as a refresher of what we previously discussed way back after the June 6th pre-attacks, but I didn't because I know this is all a lot of information and I'm not always sure how much to include."

Corver held up his hand and said, "That's all right. No need to go down that path right now; you can go over more of it later. Not all of us need to hear it right now."

"Well, actually there are a few interesting ways the mules were recruited…"

"It's okay," Corver insisted. "Go back to what you were just about to explain. I think you were getting into another way that Ørsted spreads."

"Right, sure…"

But then Q-Directorate stopped himself, looked at his watch, and turned to Manmoth in the audience. Manmoth realized what Q-Directorate was thinking. "Yes, I know," he said from the front row. "We've got the briefing with the President. I still want to cover Frëge, though. Jump to that."

"Do you want me to get into acoustic transmission?" said Q-Directorate.

"No," Manmoth responded. "We'll get into that later, in a smaller group. Besides, I want to hear more about it myself before it's presented more broadly. Go straight to Frëge, because I still want there to be enough time left so that we can assign new work streams to each of the sub-teams."

Corver leaned over toward Manmoth and whispered, "Acoustic transmission? What the hell's that all about?"

"There's a theory," Manmoth whispered back, "that acoustic signals at frequencies inaudible to the human ear are being used to contribute to the spread of Ørsted. A malicious message modulated onto one of these signals, for example, would be picked up by a computer's speaker system and open up a backdoor for virus instantiation."

"Damn, is that real?" Corver excitedly responded.

Manmoth said, "I think it's bogus, quite frankly. The frequencies involved wouldn't be able to support the bandwidth needed. They'd also be outside the dynamic range of the equipment."

Corver took a deep breath, exasperated.

"I have to see more from the team," continued Manmoth. "If something like that *is* happening—some sort of air-gap propagation—it's more likely through EM wave propagation."

"Really?"

"We're working on that ourselves."

Corver was about to say something when Manmoth held up his hand. "There'll be more about it later." He turned to Q-Directorate, signaling for him to resume. "Sorry, go ahead. Move to Frëge."

Q-Directorate fumbled momentarily with his PC, collecting his thoughts and getting himself back on track.

"Right. Frëge...the incredible power of Frëge."

"It's the heart of the whole thing, part of Ørsted, yet separate. It supports transport and proliferation, and also serves as the payload comprising the ultimate instruction set for the target. Encrypted during transmission, it can only be unlocked and detonated when certain criteria is met. Ultimately, its operation is in some ways similar to the remote BIOS flashing, with C&Cs playing a crucial role. Only a fragment of Frëge is initially resident in an infected computer, nefariously hidden in firmware using a technique similar to the one just described for the BIOS re-flash.

"Portions of it are buried in firmware outposts, hard to find because it's so fragmented. We couldn't find it for the longest time. It was only after this major attack that we were able to "trap" it. Remember how I previously explained that we had honeypots inserted into certain systems? In essence, we were able to take snapshots of the underlying software...even changes in the operating system itself, and a lot of other aspects of the software, and then compare it with stable, virgin code. In doing so, we were able to see the actual assembly of Frëge in action, and then its eventual implosion. At first we saw the changes in the code but couldn't explain how it all fit together. We couldn't see it.

"But Big Machine did. When it had enough of it, it ran every type of cryptographic algorithm known to man, and automatic permutations beyond that, all based upon randomly generated sporadic vectors. Here's what we found."

Q-Directorate jumped to another slide.

"You may recall that we posulated that Ørsted created an encryption key using a derivative of the SHA-2 cryptographic hash function, something we referred to as SHA-2-xtent. We've found what that modified hash function is. It starts with a one-way hash function generator called a Finite Quotient Subset Sum, or FQSS hashing.

"Technically speaking, this is much different than SHA-2 by virtue of the insertion of the C-sub-r mix function tying two quotients together. In fact, it's so different that we really don't consider it a variant anymore. This simple insertion of the C_r mixing function—which takes as its own input OUI polling information from the target to create the salt—actually adds a huge level of complexity to the overall generation of the encryption key. To be honest, it's quite elegant."

Q-Directorate stared at the figure on the screen for a few extra seconds.

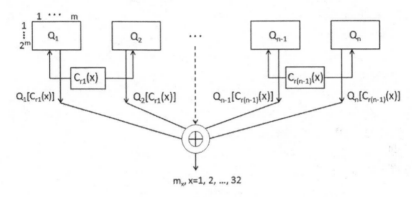

Modified FQSS hash function generator with C_r insertion.

Lieutenant General Harold Manmoth looked at it as well. He anticipated what Q-Directorate was going to describe next and knew it was too much complexity for his colleagues in the front row. He had to move the presentation forward.

"Skip the decryption," Manmoth suddenly interjected. "Go straight to the explanation of what the payload is."

Q-Directorate was surprised by the order but didn't miss a beat. He navigated to the slides that addressed the Frëge payload.

"Alright, let's talk about what Frëge is, and its actual purpose. A major part of Frëge's function is to match instructions sets, detrimental ones, to specific targets that would be responsive to them. Simply put, Frëge contains a mammoth encyclopedia of microprocessors, PLAs, PLCs, FPGAs, GPUs, motherboards, PCI-express devices…you name it. Everything under the sun that was made by man; as long as there was a corresponding data sheet, app note, API instruction set, SDK, etc., it was included in the complete version of Frëge. It's only when the OUI matching is used in decrypting Frëge that a specific instruction set for the attacked device is extracted and written to it. In a sense, this laundry list of targets has a separate, corresponding massive instruction set. Put another way, Frëge contains a giant table, and depending upon what type of system is being attacked, Frëge selects the corresponding action code set. Each table entry has a particular type of target, say a Primecall MicroP, or an AxtelMid PLA, and a corresponding set of APIs, interface data, and debilitating execution code."

Q-Directorate raised both of his palms outward to his sides. "It's what we postulated in the beginning: a brute force list of anything and everything from an electrical control standpoint, and a corresponding set of malicious code to infiltrate and incapacitate the system!"

Q-Directorate continued without pausing for questions. "Think about the amount of work this would require. Page after page of data sheets, some electronic, some not even available anymore, even in paper form, for older generation technology. Think about all of the interface information necessary to enable the malicious code to interact with the legitimate code of a target and make itself look like firmware. There must be an army numbering in the thousands to have done all of this, and it would have taken years—a huge investment in manpower!"

"Something right up the RCA's alley," CIA Director Sam Neles suddenly said, looking at McCoy. McCoy nodded.

Without Q-Directorate able to say anything further, a group discussion commenced among those in the front row. After a while, CIA Director Sam Neles stood, and NSA Director General William Powers followed. They had worked with Q-Directorate and his team beforehand to develop a new set of work streams that would need to get staffed. They were just about to start making the assignments when a hand went up toward the back. Q-Directorate saw it and called on the person.

"Is there any truth," the person began, "to the rumor that the Russians were actually helping us at one point? I mean, there's a rumor going around that Russia is cooperating with us on an operation to get that guy you talked about before...the guy named Strenzke."

Neles bristled at the question and became furious. He turned toward the audience and said, "Alex, you know very well that even if that *were* true, we couldn't talk about it. Let's stay focused on the task at hand, shall we?"

Neles turned to Q-Directorate and said, "You and your team have done excellent work. Your efforts are greatly appreciated, I can assure you. It hasn't gone unnoticed how much your team is burning the midnight oil. Now, switch the presentation to cover the new work streams. We've got to get them assigned so we can get out of here ASAP. We need time to prepare for our meeting with the President."

Q-Directorate began working with his computer to move to the appropriate slide.

At the same time, Neles looked out into the audience and said, "Alex, why don't you come down here. I need to speak with you in private."

32

Turned by but a Blue Note

Falls Church, Virginia
Monday, July 20

A MILITARY ESCORT MET ANGSTROM WHEN HIS PLANE LANDED; they were to take him straight to Inova Fairfax Hospital in an unmarked vehicle. Davis had been flown there by medical helicopter because of the severity of her injuries.

It was 1 A.M. He hadn't slept, yet he was wide awake. He had been told in Finland what happened to Davis.

None of the military personnel dared speak to him as they drove in the car—they knew what had had happened to the woman he was going to see. They watched, nervously, as the man sat stoic, a blank expression on his face, as if he were in a trance, vacuously staring out of the window in a state of trepidation.

The doctor who met Angstrom at the hospital saw an ashen man, fragile, such that he wondered whether Angstrom himself might be in need of medical attention. He began to provide Davis' status as they made their way through the hospital. Angstrom struggled to concentrate, to comprehend what was being said. The debilitating news continued as they took the elevator.

"She has multiple contusions to her body, a fracture of the right femur," the doctor said. "There must have been a severe twisting of her lower body because she had a herniated disc, which caused nucleus pulposus fluid to leak from her spinal disc into the epidural space. This caused nerve damage to other nearby discs."

Angstrom said nothing, listening intently. When he didn't ask any questions about the spinal injury, the doctor continued, "We don't think there will be permanent spinal damage, but because of the TNF-α present in the fluid, we're administering an inhibitor."

The doctor continued, indicating all of the bones that had been broken in her body and the resultant surgeries required; after a point the words barely registered with Angstrom anymore. Finally there was a pause, and then the doctor delivered the direst news.

"She also suffered a severe trauma to the head, resulting in bleeding in her brain. She was put into a medically induced coma to reduce the swelling."

When Angstrom heard that, he couldn't look at the doctor anymore. He closed his eyes and his head fell forward in sorrow. The doctor again wondered whether he should ask Angstrom if he was alright. He decided against it and continued. But Angstrom wasn't listening anymore; the words were for no one.

"...brain activity charted over a period of...

"...EKG indicated no abnormal pattern...

"...and..."

In the middle of the doctor's report, Angstrom looked up at him and struggled to say something. "Is she..."

The doctor paused.

Angstrom took a deep breath and said, "Is she still...in a coma?"

The voice was weak. Angstrom could barely utter the words.

It was the doctor's turn to take a deep breath. "No. We took her out of it after twenty-four hours, and the swelling has subsided."

Angstrom kept looking at him, waiting.

The doctor spoke slowly and clearly, making sure to look directly into the eyes of Angstrom: "Early indications are that there's no brain damage...but she hasn't spoken yet; she's been highly sedated and unconscious the whole time. Mr. Angstrom, her condition is critical."

He held the elevator door for Angstrom when they reached the appropriate floor. The hallway was narrow and the lights were dimmed at that hour. The doctor stayed behind, giving Angstrom his space; it was clear which room was Davis' by virtue of the several soldiers that stood guard outside of her door. Angstrom remained stationary for a moment, reluctant to move, paralyzed. He fought the urge to vomit.

The soldiers in the hallway all turned to look at him; he began a slow walk toward them. There had been no visitors to the room. Instructions were that no one was allowed, except for John Angstrom. The guards looked past him and saw the doctor, who signaled his permission.

Angstrom gave no acknowledgement to the other men as he neared the room. He stopped at the door and stood there for a moment, gaining his courage, bracing himself; he took a deep breath and exhaled. He was afraid—terrified at what he was about to see. It was the first time he felt such fear in a long time. There was a reluctance to enter the room.

When he finally did, he found it completely dark, save for a small light over Davis' bed.

He stood and watched her from across the room.

The combination of the white linen on her bed, the overhead light shining over her, and his slightly disoriented state made it seem like she was bathed in a mystic whiteness. He felt a sudden pain in his stomach, as if he was experiencing an ulcer, and he became dizzy, on the verge of fainting. A strong, powerful man was rendered feeble at the sight of her. The thought of losing her crushed him, almost bringing him to his knees. Moisture formed in his eyes. A small step forward, but then no more.

Fear. He couldn't go closer. He held her in reverence.

"Anne," he whispered. He could barely evoke a sound.

His own utterance slightly revived him, hearing her name spoken out loud, quiet as it was. It caused him to become sufficiently alert to notice that someone else was in the room; another man sat in a chair at Davis' side. The man rose, and Angstrom recognized him. It was her watcher, Magdos.

He slowly approached Angstrom, who himself was engulfed in the darkness of the room. When Magdos reached him, he took Angstrom's hand. While still holding it, he put his other on Angstrom's elbow, carefully, gently, and urged him to Davis' side.

Angstrom grew almost terrified as he came closer, reluctant to look at her with the injuries so evident, this woman that was everything to him lying there helpless, injured...beautiful. He was there now, looking down at her. He had entered her sphere of light.

There was a firm squeeze of his hand, and he turned to look at Magdos. Each looked at the other; no words were spoken. None were necessary. A nod of the head, and Magdos was gone.

Angstrom was alone with her.

There was no sound, no movement; just a stillness; a vacuum devoid of the world.

He pulled the chair closer and sat next to her. Her right leg was in a large cast and held in traction. There was a formed cast around her skull, and part of her face was wrapped in bandages. Her whole left arm was also in a cast, with a metal plate extending under her broken fingers, holding them in place.

Her cheeks were exposed where the facial bandages ended, the skin heavily bruised and fragile. He wanted to touch some part of her, to connect with her, but he was afraid to because she looked so delicate—so completely vulnerable and helpless. He raised his arm, and with the back of his fingers, touched the skin of her neck. It was all he could bear. He pulled back. His head slumped into both of his hands.

Then he rose, and slowly, ever-so-carefully, he stood and leaned over her. His face came close to hers. He was so close that he could sense the very life in her skin and the faint air from her breathing. He looked at her closed eyelids through the openings in the bandages; how delicate the skin seemed. She was unadorned, only her innate beauty brought to bear.

Then he sat again, leaned back in the chair, and fell into deep thought.

How could he have left her? How could he have let this happen? He would never leave her again. He would always be with her, protecting her, watching over her, for the rest of his life. His work, his job, it all seemed insignificant. Everything in the world was meaningless without her.

His mind raced, going in directions it hadn't gone in years. What did he have to show for it all anyway, the traveling around the world, the plotting...the killing? What could he point to and say, "There—that is what I have accomplished. That is what made it all matter, the sacrifice, the danger"?

He became conflicted and confused, for of course he knew the answer to that question. It was his country—the safety and well-being of its people. He was almost ashamed to think of it, but it was also for himself. It was his life. It was his passion for so many years. It was in his veins.

For over two hours he undertook such reflection. He mulled it over again and again, playing one notion against another, balancing regret against accomplishment, joy against sorrow, and considered what ultimately was most important to him—now, and in the time to come.

He had had such ruminations before—all people do at various points in their lives—but this was different. This time what was most vital, what was foremost in his mind, was obvious to him. He was looking right at her, lying there in front of him, pained, frail, and vulnerable, dependent upon him.

Then he allowed his eyes to close so as to remove everything from his mind, to purge his thoughts and enter a state of blankness. It was thus he remained for a long time, in deep meditation. On short occasion, when his anxiety returned, he would open his eyes and look at her, even say a prayer for her, and then, a return to the vacuum, until finally, sleep.

When he eventually awoke, he wasn't sure what time it was, or even what part of the day; there were no windows in the room. All was quiet. Davis was still unconscious. He looked at the medical instrumentation around her, the dials, the lights, the signals, bags holding fluid. He turned away from it.

Then he noticed something—a small piece of paper resting on the table near him, close to where Magdos had sat. He hadn't noticed it before. It seemed to be beckoning him and he reached for it. A handwritten note:

This was provided to the authorities by Nik Shulman, the owner of the music store. He said Anne had told him that it was one of her favorites. –M

Angstrom was confused. It looked like it was written by Magdos. What did it mean? He stared at it, then turned to look at Davis.

Nothing. He was at a loss.

On the table where the note was, there was a portable CD player. He looked at it curiously. It didn't seem like something that belonged in the room. Someone must have left it there. He reached and pressed the "EJECT" button, causing a lid to open. A CD was inside; no words on it, no label. For a moment it made him remember something; a different CD, or rather, a DVD, one from a while ago that had a file with her digital image stored in it; his first introduction to her, but before he knew who she was. The memory caused him to become even more confused. Was he still asleep, dreaming? He looked back at Davis and wondered whether he dared play it; a break in the silence could shock her. Perhaps he could turn the sound down. It felt ridiculous for him to be thinking about it, but there must have been a purpose in it.

The desire to play the CD grew. "Her favorite," the message indicated.

The thought of her now, and the times they had together listening to music, to jazz, talking about it...her questions...it made him smile.

Her favorite.

Coltrane? Adderly? Maybe Corea. No, it must be Miles Davis, he figured. How could it not be? Which one of his songs, though? Which did she like the most? There were so many, and they had had such long discussions about them.

After pressing the "POWER" button, he quickly turned the volume down, and his finger hit "PLAY."

He couldn't go back to that world anymore, he thought to himself. He had served his duty. There were other things he could do for a living—different places they could go. He was thinking about his situation, and Anne. These thoughts continued to flood his mind.

The sound came. He turned the volume down even further. There was clapping—an audience. Someone must have entered the stage. It was a recording of a live performance. Maybe Gillepsie—the live recording he used to play for her? But it didn't sound like that. Next, cheers from the audience.

When the music came, it surprised him at first, but then it created joy in his heart, so divine was the sound, the sound of a cello. It was Dvorak's *Waldesruhe*. The orchestra joined, but the cello remained prominent. He was unfamiliar with the piece and could not recall having ever heard it before.

This was no jazz...it was *her* music...it was her: she was speaking to him. All this time, he took such great pleasure in sharing his music with her, his jazz. Now, for the first time, she was sharing her music with him, right there as she lay unconscious next to him. He felt almost ashamed at not allowing this disclosure, this giving of herself, to have occurred before. Only now, in the precarious condition that she was in, did he become aware of her love for this music. Tears fell from his eyes he was so moved, so happy at hearing it. The more it played, the more beautiful it became, as if it were coming from her very soul. He looked at her as the music played. He could see her face through the bandages. He closed his eyes as he listened and saw her image.

I love you, Anne.

And he was liberated.

"A Message to Our Readers"

[Front page special notice, July 23 print edition, New York Daily Tribune]

If you're reading this message that means you've been able to obtain a copy of our first publication of the New York Daily Tribune since the massive cyber attack that started on July 13. It is only due to the hard work of countless individuals that we were able to get some of our editing and printing systems back on line. A special acknowledgement goes to the Federal Government which, through the contractors it engaged, was instrumental in helping us get our systems working. To its credit, the government felt it was imperative that news distribution entities be reestablished as quickly as possible so that citizens may become informed.

It is somewhat ironic that in this day and age, what with the explosion of internet news services, the only news we can make available to you is in the printed form. We are printing at thirty-percent capacity. As you can imagine, at this time we have very limited distribution resources.

We will continue to work around the clock to get the New York Daily Tribune delivered to as many people as possible. We consider it our civic duty, for we understand how disconcerting it is to not know what is going on in our country—and all over the world—during this strange and unusual period in our history. In the few pages comprising this edition you will read about the countless tragedies that have occurred across the United States and in Eastern Europe. It is certainly one of the most devastating accounts this paper has ever provided.

After you are finished with this copy of the newspaper, we ask that you pass it on to someone else, a friend or a neighbor. Share the news. Help each other. Together we will help our country recover from this terrible situation.

33

New Composition

ANGSTROM SPENT EVERY MOMENT HE COULD WITH DAVIS in the hospital. No obligations from his organization were impressed upon him, no requests made of his time. A post-op report on the mission in Russia would have to come from Gordon and the team, because Angstrom wasn't going to provide one. He was on temporary leave of absence. The hope within CIA administration was that "temporary" would not become "permanent," though they knew there was a chance that it might. They were treating the situation delicately, giving him as much space as he needed. It was their goal to do anything they reasonably could to appease him, to make him want to stay. The successful completion of his responsibility in Operation Cyberknife, utilizing a brand new team handpicked by himself no less, reaffirmed that Angstrom was the man they needed to build their special team in the CIA.

Sitting in the corner of the hospital room was a small vase filled with flowers. The card simply read "F.B.," which was enough to inform Angstrom that it was from Banks. The gesture was appreciated. No one from Angstrom's team was able to pay a visit to Davis' hospital room. It wasn't because they didn't want to; they couldn't afford being seen with her. And for security purposes, even Nikolas Shulman was not told where Davis was (though the authorities assured him that she was being cared for).

Angstrom never left Davis' bedside; he never left her room. A change of clothes was brought to him daily by currier. He slept in the room on a cot furnished by the hospital; his feet extended off of the end of it he was so tall. He ate hospital food brought to him on trays.

The nursing staff was intrigued by this mysterious man who was so admirably dedicated to the woman that lay before him. They had no idea how physically magnificent Davis truly was; her beauty was unapparent because of the casts on her body and the bruises and bandages that covered her head and face. He was polite to the nurses when spoken to. Otherwise, he was mainly quiet, constantly keeping vigil at Davis' side as she remained unconscious. Only when the doctor entered the room did Angstrom become more animated, always hopeful, always with questions.

Two guards stood watch outside at all times. Even then Angstrom was concerned it was not enough. On those rare occasions when he did need to leave the room, he did so with great reluctance.

After several days of this, Angstrom found himself alone with her again on one particular evening. The overhead light above her head was turned off. The room was completely dark, save for the faint trace of light that came from the indicators on the medical instrumentation. He liked it that way. It made him feel spiritually connected to her. As he sat at her side he held the tips of the fingers of her right hand. He was waiting for her, waiting for a sign that she would be alright.

He held a rosary in his other hand; the beads moved through his fingers as he silently prayed. The rosary had come with the last delivery of clothes earlier in the day. When he first saw it, nestled within the bundle of clothes as it was, he stared at it in wonder. So long had it been since he last held a rosary and used it to guide him in prayer. It was ages ago, a different life. There was no indication as to who was responsible for providing it. There didn't need to be. He knew.

As he prayed, he focused on the words. With his eyes pressed tightly shut and his head bowed forward, his prayers were filled with emotion and earnestness. He beseeched the Creator, prayed to Mary for intervention. He was transported to a different place, a different plane of existence. Nothing around him in the room was there. Alone in the darkness with such intense concentration, he felt like he had no physical body, no presence on the earth— only a spirit, a soul, floating in space, supplicating, connecting.

His final prayer of the rosary, one that he had not said since he was a young man, was somehow recalled without effort, retrieved deep from within his subconscious:

> Remember, O most gracious Virgin Mary, that never was it known that anyone who fled to thy protection, implored thy help, or sought thine intercession was left unaided.
>
> Inspired by this confidence, I fly unto thee, O Virgin of virgins, my mother; to thee do I come, before thee I stand, sinful and sorrowful. O Mother of the Word Incarnate, despise not my petitions, but in thy mercy hear and answer me.

When he was done, he kissed the beads and placed them into his pocket. Then he cleared his throat; tears had formed in his eyes.

It was then that he thought he heard it. Was it real or did he imagine it? Was his mind playing tricks on him? In the stillness, the blackness of the room, a single word, an answer.

Faint, soft, weak: *John.*

* * *

They were moved to a military base near Washington, D.C. When they first arrived it was summer. By now it was mid-fall.

A large grass field extended in front of the barracks that contained the small apartment at which they stayed. The leaves on all of the trees surrounding the field had turned to their glorious fall colors; red, yellow, and orange abounded. Davis liked to be taken outside in her wheelchair to watch the soldiers conduct their marching exercises on the field, as well as the flag ceremonies. Mostly she just liked to be out in the fresh air.

Angstrom sat next to her on a wooden bench, the sun gently impressing its rays upon them like a rejuvenating, healing energy. Although a cast remained on her right leg, the one on her left arm had been removed, as was the one around the top of her head. The bandages were gone as well. The bruising had healed, her beauty again evident for all to see, her rich, black hair blowing in the gentle breeze, though not nearly as long and flowing as it was before.

As they watched the marching drills, Angstrom spoke.

"Anne, we should talk about what we're going to do next. We need to make plans."

She didn't turn to look at him at first. Although she knew the day would come when they would need to have this conversation, she dreaded it. The time spent together with Angstrom during this period of recuperation was magical, like being in another world. It didn't even matter where they were. The carefree, slow-paced living, left to enjoy the little things of everyday life, she didn't want it to end. A conversation like the one now being introduced marked a return to reality.

"Anne, did you hear me?"

"Yes, yes, I'm listening," she responded without turning to him.

"I've made a decision," Angstrom said. "I'm not going back. That's it. It's over."

She turned to look at him.

He said, "I'm not going to do it anymore. It's a life that is behind me. You...our time together, that's my future...our future."

She couldn't believe it. She was stunned.

"Have you already told them?"

"No. Not yet. I haven't spoken to them about anything. They've left us alone."

"Then don't do it. Don't make any rash decisions. It was your life, John, and you loved it."

"You're right; it *was* my life, but not anymore. *You're* my life now. Without you there's nothing."

She breathed the fresh air and turned back to the marching exercises. Angstrom thought he detected a slight smile on her face, as if a weight had been lifted from her shoulders.

"What will you do?" she said without looking at him. "What will *we* do? Where will we go?"

"I've been thinking about that. We can go into what's called an A-Track Program. New identities, new location, I'll get set up with a new job."

"Doing what?"

"I don't know yet. Usually there's a choice among a few different things."

She turned to look at him again, their eyes met, and then she turned back to the field, a stiffness evident in her neck. Nothing was said for a while as she contemplated what Angstrom had told her. Angstrom got the feeling that she seemed dissatisfied, almost disappointed in what he said.

"And where would we live?" she finally said.

"That will have to be determined. Again, there's usually a choice among a number of places."

"Here in the United States?"

"Yes. Somewhere in the continental United States."

A long pause. Angstrom could tell she was thinking about something, wrestling with it in her mind. Maybe she was trying to decide where she might want to live. He sat and patiently waited. There was no rush. What they were discussing was significant; their life together was going to change forever.

"John, I'd like to share something with you, if I may. A secret. Something very important that I never wanted to talk about unless I knew that I absolutely had to."

"Of course. Please, go ahead."

He watched her as she continued to look off into the distance. He became nervous, concerned about what he was about to hear.

"As you know, my father was a professor at university."

"Yes, a brilliant scientist. I wish I could have met him," said Angstrom.

"He was a professor at his university for a long time, highly respected by his peers. He was admired by everyone and had many friends. One of those friends, a fellow professor at the university, had a son. A young boy...um—how does one say it?— a stepson. My father used to talk about him, how he watched him grow for many years—from boy, to young man, to..."

Davis paused for a moment. She was getting a little emotional. She always did when she spoke of her parents.

"When he was young, the boy was always around his stepfather at the university, in his office at seemingly all hours. My father liked the boy, thought he was smart, incredibly talented. Through the years, the boy would often come by my father's office as well, and they had taken a liking to each other. They spent a lot of time together. The boy became fascinated with computers. My father, being the scientist he was, was happy about this and taught the boy a great deal about programming. This boy's name was Sergei Strenzke.

"I still remember how my father used to talk about him at the dinner table when I was young; by that time Sergei was already a young man. My father marveled at how fast Sergei learned, how much he could accomplish with his programming.

"At some point, something happened. My father stopped talking about him. It was strange how it happened so suddenly. In fact, I eventually asked him about it one day while we were at the dinner table, because I used to like it when my father talked about him. Whenever he did he would become happy and animated. I liked to see him that way. So when he stopped talking about Sergei, I asked him why, and he became very sad. He told me never to bring Sergei up again.

"Of course I never did. Not long ago, however, shortly after my father planned our defection, he spoke of Sergei once again. He told me how Sergei had turned to a life of crime and had become a bad man. I could hear the sadness in my father's voice as he told me this. Anyway, because of what was going on in my father's life, in our lives, my father was desperate, and he got into contact with Sergei. Sergei was apparently the head of a very powerful hacking organization. My father asked him for help—he asked Sergei for money. Not for me or my father to use just then; it was for the future, in preparation for what my father was planning. Sergei was overjoyed that my father had reached out to him. In a way, my father was his mentor, and he immediately agreed to give my father whatever money he needed.

"My father later told me how guilty he felt in asking Sergei for this money, but there was no other choice. To make himself feel better about it, he insisted that Sergei obtain this money only by using his hacking skills to steal from the accounts of certain government officials in Russia. Sergei was surprised by this request, reluctant, but ultimately he was so happy to see my father—he loved him—that he agreed."

Davis stopped telling her story for a moment and turned to Angstrom. She was surprised by the look on his face, almost like he couldn't believe what he was hearing.

"John, it was a lot of money. A *lot* of money."

Angstrom could barely summon the words to speak. "Are we talking…"

"Around eight million dollars...eight million U.S. dollars, given the exchange rate at the time," she said. "All in a Swiss account. This is one of the reasons those men were after me."

Angstrom watched her, stunned.

* * *

When the phone rang in their apartment, Angstrom and Davis were surprised and looked at each other. Unless it was a random, unsolicited call, only a select few people knew where they were. At first Angstrom didn't want to answer. When he finally picked up the receiver, he heard the telltale sign—a very faint, temporary tone resulting from the call being routed through the telephone's switching network so it couldn't be traced. When that was done, there was a clicking sound, and then the audio changed. A female voice followed.

"Hello. Is this John?"

"Yes."

"Please enter cipher mode."

Angstrom disconnected the telephone cord from the receiver and plugged it into a small electronic box that sat next to the phone, and then from there he plugged another cord back into the receiver. Davis watched in puzzlement.

"Done. Can you hear me?"

"Yes. Thank you. John, Fred would like to see you."

Angstrom didn't respond.

"Hello? Are you still there?"

"Yes, I'm here. I heard you. I'm not leaving here."

"Yes, I was told you would say that. Fred is willing to come there. Would that be acceptable?"

"Are you sure? Fred really said that?"

"Yes. Would that be acceptable?"

"Yes...of course."

When the knock came at the apartment door, Angstrom opened it just enough to verify that it was Banks, and then opened it slightly more so that he could go outside without fully opening the door.

"Hello, John. It's good to see you."

"Hello, Fred. Likewise."

Two guards were called to the door, and then without any ceremony, Angstrom started to lead Banks down the hallway to another room in the building.

"John," Banks said without moving.

"Yes, what is it?" Angstrom stopped and said.

"Can I say hello to her?"

"What? Oh, sure. Sorry, I didn't know you wanted to, or I would have invited you in."

Banks said, "I'd like to personally meet the woman who has so captured your heart." He smiled, and Angstrom did as well.

"Let's go," Angstrom said, leading Banks inside.

When they entered, they found Davis sitting in her wheelchair by the window, one that overlooked the field and all of the colorful trees. She turned to look as she heard them enter.

"Anne, I'd like you to meet someone; a friend of mine. You can call him Robert."

Banks approached her and gently took her hand as she remained seated in the wheelchair.

"Anne, it's a pleasure to meet you," Banks said.

"Thank you. And you as well."

Banks had to be careful about what he said. No real names, no reference to what his true position was in the organization.

"I hope your accommodations are acceptable and you're being well cared for."

"Oh yes. I love this place. I'm so grateful to be able to live here. Thank you."

After seeing her up close and hearing her voice in person, Banks was immediately arrested by her beauty.

"How are you feeling physically?" Banks said. "Is the doctor pleased with your level of recovery?"

"Yes, he is. He thinks it's a miracle how much better I've gotten already. I should even have this cast off in another week or so," she said, tapping the cast on her extended right leg.

"Good, good, I'm glad to hear that."

Davis suspected that Banks was part of the CIA, or at least some important person in the government, but she didn't ask. She respected the cautious approach this man took, and his reserved manner of conversation.

There was period of silence between them as they studied each other. Banks looked deeply into her eyes as if he were fathoming her soul. Her eyes were captivating. He couldn't get over them.

"Well," Banks finally said. "Do you mind if I borrow your significant other for a while. I was hoping we could have a talk."

"Of course not," she responded. "I'll go into the other room and close the door."

"That's okay, Anne," Angstrom quickly offered. "We're going to another place in the building. Two armed guards will remain right outside the door the whole time I'm gone."

"Oh, okay."

Banks was still observing her, transfixed by her beauty. Finally, he said, "It was a pleasure to meet you, Anne. You seem like a remarkable person. I can see why John would never want to leave your side."

"Thank you. The pleasure was mine as well."

They shook hands. Banks was reluctant to squeeze too firmly because he knew of all of the injuries she had sustained.

And then Angstrom and Banks left. They went to a room down the hall.

"She's incredible, John. I saw some of the pictures and video footage of her before, but to see her in person, she's simply stunning."

"She's beautiful on the inside as well."

"No doubt. I could tell that already—could see it in her eyes." Banks paused and then said, "And how are *you* holding up?"

"I'm good, Fred. I'm good. Thanks for asking."

"How about from the mission? No after effects? Congratulations, by the way, on the success of it. Obviously we haven't had a chance to talk about it yet at great length."

"Thanks. I'm good. To be honest, I haven't even given it a second thought since I've been back."

"Hmm," was all Fred said in response. That wasn't the answer he was hoping for. They both studied each other for a moment.

"Fred, I'm not coming back. I'm sorry, but I'm done."

Fred didn't immediately respond. Eventually he said, "I know. I suspected as much before I got here. After I met Anne just now, I knew it for sure." He rubbed his chin and said, "And there's no way we can talk you out of it? We've got big plans for you."

"I can't, Fred. I appreciate it. I appreciate your confidence in me, but I can't. That life is behind me now. It would be impossible for me to go back—impossible for a lot of reasons, some of them having nothing to do with Anne."

Banks rubbed his eyes. Then he bowed his head and ran his hand through his thin gray hair. After a good while, he finally said, "So, we'll put you in A-Track."

"It's not necessary," was all Angstrom said.

Fred looked puzzled.

"All we need is new identities. We'll take care of the rest."

Banks could've asked a lot of questions to that, but he didn't. He didn't even ask where they would go. For that part he didn't need to; the organization would be able to track them through the furnished identities. Angstrom of course knew this but didn't care. He didn't actually plan on using the identities. He'd already obtained new ones for Davis and himself through his own means. They planned to be anonymous to everyone—to the world.

"We kind of anticipated this might happen," Banks said. "We're going to elevate Gordon. What do you think about that?"

"I don't think anything about it. I told you…"

Angstrom stopped himself. He was getting aggravated at being sucked back into that world, and he wanted to avoid it. He

412

did, however, still hold a great deal of respect for Banks and for his former organization, so he caught himself.

"I think Gordon's an excellent choice. You couldn't do better."

Banks was pleased with the response. "So how much longer are you going to be here?" he said.

"Like you heard from Anne, the cast should come off in a couple of weeks. She's going to go through physical therapy after that." Angstrom next spoke almost as if to himself when he said, "She'll probably have some level of stiffness in certain parts of her body for the rest of her life."

Banks said nothing.

"How's Gordon doing?" Angstrom asked.

"He's good. The whole team is good. You picked a fine group, John. Every one of them. They fit together like a puzzle."

"Good. Listen, I'd like to say goodbye to Gordon. Do you think you can have him come by?"

"Certainly. He's been asking about you. In fact, he's already been here once."

Angstrom turned and looked at Banks with a smile. "Damn him. I should've figured."

Banks laughed as he stood up. Then a serious look came over him.

"Good luck, John. The CIA was lucky to have you. The whole administration appreciates your dedication and service. The President himself extends his gratitude."

34

Overlord

"YOUR TWO O'CLOCK IS HERE."

"Powers?"

"Yes, sir."

"Is Manmoth with him?"

"Yes."

"Okay, send them in."

The President stood behind his desk and waited for them.

"Gentlemen, thank you for coming. Please, have a seat."

"Sir, we could have prepared something more formal for this discussion…"

"It's okay. I need it now, the short form. No slides, no data, no budgets. I just want the information—the answer to my questions—in clear, basic, unadorned fashion. Can we do that?"

"Yes, Mr. President, certainly," said General Powers. He observed the President closely as they sat across from him at his desk. It seemed to Powers that the President looked like he had aged ten years over the last week: he looked exhausted, the signs of stress evident on his face. His shirt collar was unbuttoned, his necktie lying on the desk; the white cotton shirt was wrinkled from having been worn for so long. The situation across the United States and the concern over what was happening in Eastern Europe was taking its toll on him. What the country was facing was unprecedented, and whether it was his fault or not, he was the sitting President when the cyber calamity occurred. What his administration did after the fact—how it responded and helped bring the country back to its feet—would be his legacy. So far he was performing admirably. He was tireless in his approach, eating on the run when the opportunity presented itself, paying attention to all the details; he wasn't afraid to roll up his sleeves and get into the weeds. His leadership was inspiring, and no matter how bad a particular situation was, he remained composed.

"So," the President said as he leaned back in his chair, "Ørsted, Frëge, Gauss, Stuxnet, Shamoon, Snake, Flame…and whatever the hell comes next: what's the solution? Are we forever doomed to be subject to these types of attacks?"

"They're likely to continue at increasing frequency," General Powers began. "Domestic costs alone associated with Ørsted and Frëge will run into the…"

"Don't even try to put a number on it," the President interrupted, holding up his hand.

General Powers nodded in comprehension. Then he turned and signaled to Lieutenant General Manmoth.

Manmoth took the cue and said, "Going forward, the human capital involved in IT prevention, detection, and remediation, not to mention the physical defenses involved, is going to be formidable. As you know, Operation Foil alone is going to involve the deployment of over 10,000 soldiers at strategic oil refinement facilities and energy generation installations. In the end, the costs and resources associated with Ørsted-Frëge will easily skew the data. Bottom line, we all know it's a cost curve that can't continue; staying on the course of this new type of arms race would dwarf the costs associated with the cold war—the military expenditure, personnel deployment, everything."

The President waited, somewhat impatiently, for the answers to his questions.

General Powers noticed the President's agitation—he could tell the President was already getting fidgety—and suddenly interjected, "But we're not going to follow that cost trajectory." He turned and urged Manmoth to continue, the message clearly communicated that he needed to get to the point.

Manmoth said, "Right. We're moving in a completely different direction. In conjunction with DARPA, we've been conducting two programs that will drastically change how we look at cyber security and cyber attacks.

"The first one is termed the 'Clean-slate Design of Resilient, Adaptive, Secure Hosts'—or CRASH."

"Interesting acronym," the President interjected, "a lot of connotations, I'm sure." He shook his head quickly, as if to cut off his own digression. "Sorry, keep going."

Manmoth continued, "Yes, sir. Basically, all of the vulnerabilities exploited by cyber attackers can be categorized into three main areas: one—the failure by current computer systems to enforce memory safety; two—distinctions between code and data; and three—constraints on information flow and access. We're looking at this whole problem from a 'clean slate' perspective. We're designing new methods and systems with virtually no concern for backward compatibility. New architectures and designs for hardware, system software, programming languages, design environments...everything. And it's not just that it's 'new' that makes CRASH significant; it's the radical inspiration for the new design approach: the human immune system."

The President's right eyebrow involuntarily arched upward. "Go ahead, I'm listening."

"You see, the human body is constantly battling assaults to its immune system. These assaults can be thought to fall into two different types: first—traditional invasives, and second—new agents.

" 'Traditional invasives' are just what the name implies: the immune system has seen it before, knows the defense, and institutes it, and if damage is done, a known remedy is activated. This happens, of course, down to the cellular level. CRASH will duplicate this from the ground up, with analogous implementation down to most basic aspects of hardware and software; we're talking at the gate level.

"The 'new agents' portion will be even more complex, relying heavily on our knowledge of artificial intelligence. Micro-sensors will constantly monitor and assess new threats. Structural remedies will be learned and computed, and then repair at the appropriate level will be invoked. It will be adaptive. Slow, but adaptive. However, in combination with the 'traditional invasives' portion, rapid responses can be developed for newer threats that become repeat offenses. More importantly, the adaptive nature will result in the computer systems themselves becoming somewhat unique in nature. One will not be exactly the same as the other, thus viruses and attacks will become more localized, thereby avoiding pandemic-type concerns."

The President sat in silence for a moment, processing what he had heard. "That's quite impressive. Is it real, or are we just talking science fiction?"

"Mr. President, CRASH is real," Manmoth responded. "The research was actually started four years ago, and they've made significant progress. Prototypes of CRASH implementations are being tested in military systems as we speak."

"Is this envisioned for civilian use as well?"

"Perhaps eventually," responded Manmoth. "As you can imagine, a system that has no regard for backward compatibility has limited immediate potential. Specialized rollout is contemplated: banks, transportation hubs, power generation. But that's some time off; this is highly valuable technology, providing a significant military advantage. We want to be extremely careful with commercial deployment."

The President drew a deep breath and exhaled. "Okay, got it. So you mentioned there were two programs. What do I need to know about the other one?"

Manmoth resumed, "Sir, the other significant program is called 'Programming Computation on Encrypted Data' — or PROCEED."

"Another great acronym. I love those guys at DARPA," the President said with a sarcastic smile. Even under pressure he still retained his sense of humor, a hallmark that helped him get elected in the first place.

"Yes, well, although PROCEED is contemplated to work in conjunction with CRASH, it's a totally separate initiative. Quite literally, we're creating systems that will operate on encrypted data only, without the need to decrypt it. It will be extremely difficult to write viruses in such an environment. Think of the analogy of a normal conversation in English; it's processed and acted upon. But for those without authority who nonetheless overhear the conversation, the information can be exploited. To avoid this, we envision a computer system that only functions in an encrypted mode."

"*Envision*," the President said, sitting forward and upright in his chair.

Manmoth and Powers shot a confused glance at each other.

Manmoth responded, "I'm sorry, sir, what did you say?"

"You said '*envision*'...'we *envision* a computer system.' "

Powers and Manmoth again turned and looked at each other, still confused.

"Look, gentlemen, these programs sound fascinating, and I'm sure we're on the right path with them. But this is pie-in-the-sky stuff. It's not going to be in our hands for a long time. Please tell me we have something more — something to deal with the present. We're at war here, and you're telling me, in essence, to be patient, the weapons...these cyber defenses...are coming."

Manmoth was about to respond, but Powers quickly put a hand on his arm to stop him. Then Powers said, "Mr. President, we understand what you're saying. As Lieutenant General Manmoth said, CRASH is beginning to be implemented in our military systems as we speak, and PROCEED is being implemented as well, but you're right, that's limited deployment."

Powers paused. His admissions had their intended effect. The President had somewhat calmed. He could see it in his body language.

Powers Continued, "Over the shorter term, we're already working with anti-virus and cyber security companies to address the immediate need to more effectively defend our nation's IT infrastructure from cyber attacks." Powers turned to Manmoth again and signaled for him to continue.

Manmoth said, "We're doing this with a new approach we call 'Trap and Contain.' It's basically an acknowledgement that with our current computer and IT infrastructure, it's impossible to patch all security vulnerabilities and prevent all attacks. Therefore, instead we are inserting certain vulnerabilities on purpose, in essence creating ever more sophisticated cyber traps, or what we call honeypots. This even includes fictitious data that would be attractive to the attackers: passwords, banking info, etc. When an attacker penetrates, the system recognizes it and contains it. It might even deliver some of the fictitious data to appease the attacker, but once in, the attack is contained. Little to no damage would result. It's that, plus a lot of other defensive protocols and mechanisms—point-to-point encryption, tokenization standards, etc.—all of which I'm sure you don't want to hear about right now."

Manmoth stopped. Both Powers and he waited to see what the President thought. They knew he probably wasn't satisfied.

They were right. The President wasn't greatly impressed, but he didn't' tell them that. "Good," he said as he looked at General Powers. "As always, I'm glad I called you. We've got a lot on our hands right now—things are a mess. Sometimes I just need someone to tell me things straight, in plain English. I know I can always count on you for that, so thank you."

"You're welcome, Mr. President," Powers answered. But it was just as Powers thought: the President really *wasn't* pleased with what he heard. He seemed underwhelmed—maybe even frustrated. Powers turned to momentarily look at Manmoth, who in response nodded his head in a way that signaled back to

Powers that they should continue with the discussion, and that Powers should now take the lead.

The President noticed this and said, "What is it, General Powers, something else on your mind?"

"Mr. President, if I may, there's one more thing you should be aware of in this regard," Powers said.

"Hmm, yes? What is it? I'm all ears."

"Thank you. Well, you see, a strong military capability involves both the ability to defend and the ability to attack. This is true for traditional kinetic warfare, as well as in the cyber world. So far, we've presented to you two far-reaching projects that will help us *defend* in the cyber world."

Powers paused. A serious look appeared on his face as he held the gaze of the President.

"But now we want to talk to you about something else. Something that isn't in the research phases—something we have now. It's a new and powerful ability to *strike*. It took DARPA the last five years to develop it, but it's basically finished, ready to deploy. All you essentially have to do is press the proverbial red button, so to speak. We've been eager to discuss it with you."

The President was intrigued. He sat up in his chair.

Powers turned to Manmoth, who took his cue.

"Mr. President," Manmoth said, "I'd like to tell you a little something about what we call *Overlord*."

35

A Ride in the Wind

THE RED CONVERTIBLE RACED ALONG THE NARROW ROAD, a cliff on one side, a wall of solid rock on the other. The top was down, and the wind blew freely against the two passengers.

Angstrom's hair flew wildly, his face unshaven with stubble; there was no concern for it. Davis wore a pink babushka, a stark contrast to her jet-black hair. With the sun setting, sunglasses wouldn't be needed much longer.

The car carried them forward on the winding road's gradual ascent toward the top of Mt. Maunxë. The blue ocean extended to the left of them, just beyond the steep cliff. A wicker picnic basket sat on the car's floor behind their seats, an empty bottle of Viognier wine sticking out of it. On Davis' lap sat a paperback copy of Tolstoy's *Anna Karenina*, a white paper napkin serving as a bookmark. For Angstrom, it was an old, hard-covered copy of Conrad's *The Secret Agent*. The cover's blue cloth was worn thin, signs of heavy use; a small number was scribbled in pencil on the upper right-hand corner of the first page, the price paid at the local bookstore. It lay on the floor behind his seat.

Davis pulled a new CD out of her purse, having purchased it earlier that day in the local market. Angstrom watched as she inserted it into the car's player. He looked at her for a moment and then returned his attention back to the road, wondering what it would be. He liked her choosing the music now. He liked the surprises, being exposed to something he was unfamiliar with, being introduced to something he couldn't believe he had missed all his life.

It was an opera he'd never heard before: Catalini's *La Wally*. Renata Tebaldi began with *Ebben? Ne andrò lontana*. He was instantly transfixed. He didn't look at Davis, nor she him—they listened to the music and allowed the breathtaking beauty of the countryside envelope them. When the chorus began, Angstrom's eyes grew moist, so moved was he by the music and the happiness he was experiencing. He steered the car calmly, almost in a serene state. There was no need for firmness anymore, distanced and detached from the world as he was. There was no hurry to get anywhere, because there was nowhere they were going.

They rode in silence as the music played; the world convolved around them. Memories were forgotten, data erased. All calls to him went unanswered, for there was no place for them to go.

The clear expanse of an orange sky towered above them, a glow so powerful and magnificent it should've burned them like fire, radiant. Perhaps it did: the spiritual transformation of the soul.

When they reached the end of the road they found themselves on a small mesa covered with a carpet of green grass. It looked mowed, maintained, but how could that be so high up where they were? It was just as the local villager had insisted.

When the engine was turned off and the music stopped, there was silence; so high were they in the sky, away from everything, looking out to the horizon, the world was before them, the curvature of the earth evident.

He got out of the car and stood for a moment, looking at the vastness. He was fully released from the existential vacuum that he had been in since his mental collapse those several years ago. The struggle in his soul was over, the purge complete.

There was only themselves to contemplate. He took the blanket out of the car, set it on the ground, and held her hand as she sat down. He sat next to her. She was like a goddess, and he treated her so.

It was some time later when he leaned over and kissed the skin of her bare shoulder, and he smelled her sweet, womanly scent. It was turning dark outside. She turned to look at him with a smile, and their lips met.

Then they sat in silent meditation, observing the existence around them as it evaporated. It was Angstrom that put his head down first. Anne's eyes stayed open much longer, even to the stars. What did the future hold? What paths lie ahead? The very nature of the question held the promise of their future. When Angstrom curled over onto his side, she reached and caressed his cheek.

And then she lay down next to him, and they slept.

Author's Note

When I first started this novel, Russia's invasion of Crimea had not yet occurred. When it did, at first I became nervous, wondering if I'd have to switch directions in the story out of fear that readers would think I just ripped material from the headlines. Instead, I stayed the course. This is because as I continued to research the cyber aspects of the novel, I'd found that there were many parallels with what happened in the past (i.e. Russia's cyber and kinetic invasion of the country Georgia), the present (the continuing conflict in the Ukraine), and the future (cyber warfare is just at its infancy, and Russia's sociopolitical ambitions remain ambiguous to say the least). In the end, I'm very happy with the result; I hope you are as well. If you *really* enjoyed the story, please take the time to write a positive review (anonymous or otherwise) on Amazon's website for books—us unknown authors thrive on reviews. Suggesting the book to others is also greatly appreciated.

As to the theme of jazz lurking in the background of the novel, I must admit that there were several inspirations behind it, all of which I won't get into here. I will say, though, that one of them is the movie *Bullitt* directed by Peter Yates.   Is John Angstrom modeled after Steve McQueen's portrayal of Detective Frank Bullitt in the movie? No, not really. But from the music playing in the background during the opening credits, Meridian West's jam session during the nightclub scene at the Coffee Cantata, to the sad, melodic flute playing *Just Coffee*, the whole soundtrack of the movie and how it supports the story is a masterpiece! While I could only dream of obtaining a similarly stellar result in the form of the written word, it nonetheless served as a profound motivation.

For the music itself associated with *Cool Jazz Spy*, perhaps you'd be interested in exploring it further. Here's a recap of some of the artists and music mentioned in *Cool Jazz Spy*:

Miles Davis

In my opinion, the seminal Cool Jazz album is *Kind of Blue*. No jazz collection should be without it. The song *It Never Entered My Mind* was mentioned in the novel. How can one describe it? Sad? Uplifting, full of promise? Answer: Beauty, in its simplest form. For a different period of his career, try one of his collaborations with arranger Gil Evans, most notably *Miles Ahead*—pure heaven. An album mentioned more than once in *Cool Jazz Spy* is Davis' *Bitches Brew*. This was recorded later in Miles Davis' career when he experimented in what some call Fusion Jazz. It's not for the beginner and takes patience to appreciate.

John Coltrane

Coltrane plays a special part in the lives of John Angstrom and Anne Davis. The masterpiece *A Love Supreme* was the first jazz album they listened to together (see my first novel, *Source*Forged Armor*). As a point of reference, Coltrane played the tenor saxophone in Miles Davis' *Kind of Blue*, but without question he established his own legacy. I never get tired of listening to the version of *In a Sentimental Mood* he did with Duke Ellington; it's haunting.

Thelonious Monk

Clint Eastwood did an excellent documentary on him. I've never heard anything by Monk I didn't like. When I first played a song of his to my mother (now close to 90 at this first printing of *Cool Jazz Spy*), she thought it was a child playing (listen, e.g., to *Sweet and Lovely*). Don't let his style with the piano fool you. Anyone who listens to *Ruby, My Dear* or *Crepuscule with Nellie* and isn't blown away should just step aside.

Chic Corea

Like Miles Davis, he had many phases in his career, including

Fusion Jazz (he played electric piano on Miles Davis' *Bitches Brew*). Chic Corea's *Windows* (song) was mentioned in Cool Jazz Spy, as was the album *Return to Forever*. By the way, if you're ever down and need a lift, give a listen to *What Game Shall We Play Today* from the album. Flora Purim nailed the vocals.

Other Artists or Performances Mentioned:
Oliver Nelson's *Stolen Moments*. (song).

Dizzy Gillepsie's *Kush*. (song—try the 1967 version from *Swing Low, Sweet Cadillac*). If this doesn't knock your socks off, I don't know what will.

Julian "Cannonball" Adderly—Lord have *Mercy, Mercy, Mercy*, and be careful of the *Country Preacher* or he'll sneak up on you. For something to get you going, but gradually, try the song *Jump for Joy*. If you have to play a swingin' song on a date, try *Dis Here*, recorded live at the Salle Pleyel, Paris.

-Paul

(2015)

427

ACKNOWLEDGMENTS

Many thanks go to my beta readers, including Judy Ortiz, Kristin Kruska (especially for her "high level" input), Deborah Pardini (incredibly thorough and rigorous), Michael Brizic (thanks for reminding me where Mexico is), and of course Alison (even as busy as you are you took the time to read). Thank you all for your careful reading and for providing such insightful comments. Special thanks go to my good friend John Ortiz for his incredibly thorough analysis and suggestions, as well as his thoughtful comments and feedback concerning the more technical subject matter in the novel (and for trying to push me "further" in terms of the relationship between Angstrom and Davis). It's quite fascinating how each person focused on different aspects and issues in the story—after all the vigilant reading, I'd like to believe we caught all the typos. If not, I hope readers will overlook any minor ones still remaining.

REFERENCES

While this novel is entirely fictitious, the underlying science and technology is not. The following is a list of source of information and other materials used as research for this novel.

JOURNAL ARTICLES

[1] Dudorov, D., Stupples, D., Newby, M., "Probability Analysis of Cyber Attack Paths," *2013 European Intelligence and Security Informatics Conference*, Uppsala, Sweden, pp. 38-44 (2013).

[2] Nguyen, H.D., Cheng, Q., "An Efficient Feature Selection Method For Distributed Cyber Attack Detection and Classification," *2011 45th Annual Conference on Information Sciences and Systems*, Baltimore, MD, pp. 1-6 (2011).

[3] Gifty P Jeya, M Ravichandran and C S Ravichandran, "Efficient Classifier for R2L and U2R Attacks," *International Journal of Computer Applications*, Vol. 45, No. 21, pp. 29-32 (2012).

[4] Kotenko, I., Chechulin, A., "A Cyber Attack Modeling and Impact Assessment Framework," *5th International Conference on Cyber Conflict* (2013).

[5] Ye, Nong, Farley, Toni, "A Scientific Approach to Cyberattack Detection," *Computer Magazine*, Vol. 31, No. 11, pp. 55-61, IEEE Computer Society (2013).

[6] Irwin, Barry, "A Baseline Study of Potentially Malicious Activity Across Five Network Telescopes," *5th International Conference on Cyber Conflict* (2013).

[7] Jones, Willie D., "Declarations of Cyberwar: What the revelations about the U.S. –Israeli origin of Stuxnet mean for warfare," *IEEE Spectrum* (August, 2012).

[8] Dehlawi, Zakariya, Abokhodair, Norah, "Saudi Arabia's Response to Cyber Conflict: A case study of the Shamoon malware incident," *2013 IEEE International Conference on Intelligence and Security Informatics*, pp. 73-75 (2013).

[9] Raymond, D., Conti, G., Cross, T., Fanelli, R., "A Control Measure

References

Framework to Limit Collateral Damage and Propagation of Cyber Weapons," *5th International Conference on Cyber Conflict* (2013).

[10] Hashimoto, H., Hayakawa, T., "Distributed Cyber Attack Detection for Power Network Systems," *50th IEEE Conference on Decision and Control and European Control Conference* (2011).

[11] Xu Li, Xiaohui Liang, Rongxing Lu, Xuemin Shen, et al., "Securing Smart Grid: Cyber Attacks, Countermeasures, and Challenges," *Communication Magazine*, IEEE, vol. 50, no. 8 (2012).

[12] Brossard, Jonathan, "Hardware backdooring is practical," *Blackhat Briefings and Defcon Conferences*, Las Vegas, (2012).

NEWS ARTICLES

[13] Jacob Bunge, Bradley Hope, and Leslie Josephs, "Technical Glitch Hits Trading at CME," *The Wall Street Journal* (April 9, 2014).

[14] Reckard, E. Scott, "Hackers withdraw big sums at ATMS", *Chicago Tribune*, (April 4, 2014).

[15] Ahmari, Sohrab, "Waking Up to the Russian Threat," *The Wall Street Journal* (April 12, 2014).

[16] Shishkin, Phillip, Marson, James, "Kiev Sees Unrest as Work of Kremlin Agents," *The Wall Street Journal* (April 21, 2014).

INTERNET SOURCES & MISCELLANEOUS

[17] http://www.nsa.gov. (Accessed March, 2014).

[18] http://en.wikipedia.org/wiki/National_Security_Agency (Accessed March, 2014)

[19] "Rogers Tabbed as Next Cyber Command Chief",
http://www.defense.gov/news/newsarticle.aspx?id=121584. (Accessed January, 2014).

[20] http://www.dni.gov/index.php/about/leadership/director-of-national-intelligence. (Accessed March 2014).

[21] Green, Matthew, "A Few Thoughts on Cryptographic Engineering,"August 15, 2012. http://blog.cryptographyengineering.com/2012/08/on-gauss.html. (Accessed March 2014).

[22] Raywood, Dan, "Gauss: The latest example of malware using identity-based encryption,"*SC Magazine*, August 15, 2012,
http://www.scmagazineuk.com/gauss-the-latest-example-of-malware-using-identity-based-encryption/article/254697/.
(Accessed March 2014).

[23] GReAT, "The Mystery of the Encrypted Gauss Payload,"
http://www.securelist.com/en/blog/208193781/The_Mystery_of_the_Encrypt

ed_Gauss_Payload. (Accessed March 2014).

[24] Program: "Clean-slate design of Resilient, Adaptive, Secure Hosts (CRASH)", http://www.darpa.mil/Our_Work/I2O/Programs/Clean-slate_design_of_Resilient_Adaptive_Secure_Hosts_%28CRASH%29.aspx.

[25] DARPA, Information Innovation Office, Program site for: PROgramming Computation on EncryptEd Data (PROCEED). (Accessed April, 2014).

[26] Korns, S. W., Kastenberg, J. E. "Georgia's Cyber Left Hook," http://www.army.mil/article/19351/Georgia___039_s_Cyber_Left_Hook/ (April 7, 2009).

[27] Constantin, Lucian, "Proprietary firmware poses a security threat, Ubuntu founder says," PCWorld. (March 18, 2014). http://www.pcworld.com/article/2109267/proprietary-firmware-poses-a-security-threat-ubuntu-founder-says.html

[28] http://www.federalreserve.gov/newsevents/testimony/tarullo20140206a.htm (Accessed February 6, 2014).

[29] IDG Reporter, "Proof-of-concept malware infects BIOS, network cards," computer news middle east. (July 30, 2012). http://www.cnmeonline.com/news/researcher-creates-proof-of-concept-malware-that-infects-bios-network-cards/ (Accessed October, 2014).

[30] U.S. Pat. No. 5,608,801

[31] Goodin, Dan, "Meet "badBIOS," the mysterious Mac and PC malware that jumps airgaps," Ars Technica. (October 31, 2013).

[32] Cobb, Michael "Utilize Windows 8 ELAM to secure the boot process, detect rootkits," http://searchsecurity.techtarget.com/answer/Utilize-Windows-8-ELAM-to-secure-the-boot-process-detect-rootkits (Accessed November 2, 2014).

[33] http://www.usbr.gov/pn/grandcoulee/index.html (Accessed December 24, 2014).

[34] Hypponen, Mikko, "Fighting viruses, defending the net," Edinburgh, Scotland, https://www.youtube.com/watch?v=cf3zxHuSM2Y (uploaded on YouTube July, 2011)

ABOUT THE AUTHOR

Paul J. Bartusiak obtained his BSEE from Tennessee Technological University, his MSEE from the University of Texas at Arlington, and his Juris Doctor from Chicago-Kent College of Law. Over the past 25 years he has worked at Fortune 500 companies, first as an Electrical Engineer, and then as a Corporate Attorney. He lives with his family in Lake Forest, IL.

Made in the USA
Middletown, DE
11 July 2015